Giddy Midnight

Levity Brown

This novel is entirely a work of fiction.

The names, characters and incidents portrayed are the work of the author's imagination. Any resemblance to actual persons, living or dead, is purely coincidental.

Giddy Midnight

ISBN: 978-1-0682391-6-8

Copyright © Levity Brown 2011

Editorial support and publication assistance from Creative Words Ltd www.creativewords.cc

www.levitybrown.co.uk

Some deaths are so dramatic and shocking
they remain in the memory forever.

1

Nightfall brought its own lullaby hum on Waterloo Bridge. Tyres rolled wet across tarmac, shoes quickened their pace, grousing heads dodged menacing umbrellas and someone else, making no sound save for his breathing, the blade tucked up his sleeve nice and sharp.

At a strategic bend in the river, he had seen something in the grey curtain of rain. The shape was vague, a ghostly smudge emerging and dematerialising on the far horizon. False alarms were not uncommon. He buttoned his leather trench coat, flipped the collar around his ears and waited. Dark hair, which hung soaked about his strong-featured face, gave to his dark blue eyes an unearthly look. Startling as his aspect was, he operated on the right side of justice, living by his wits in the shadow of a curse. His name was Lukas Giddy, keeping vigilant with his thoughts until another sight drew his eyes.

The *Abracadabra*, which had made her way through the approaches and turned west on the snaking River Thames, came into view, her powerful twin shafts churning a quiet wake. Above her stern flew the British Standard, its silk plume billowing damp from a gilded post. In the rarefied world of super-yachts, neither charged nor engaged by a crew, this one shaped the future.

As she drew her bows under the bridge, with what looked like a death-defying casualness, Lukas made the hundred-foot leap, his arms outstretched to manoeuvre his landing, as sweet as a nut. He wanted to dry off in his suite of rooms, say hello to his pet and get some serious sleep. But as he pushed through the boldness of opulence, the exacting standards of doors with polished chrome portholes, and carpeted treads that wound to unexpected levels, a degree of irritation changed his direction. Within seconds, he was taking the steps to the captain's quarters which preached a lordship's comfort.

His cousin's head snapped up behind a paper-filled desk, the whiskered face shaded by a braided cap. Thomas had every reason to worry the encounter would be met by steaming silence. He had not only broken the cardinal rule but something worse had come on board. Watching Lukas dry himself off, he admitted his first sin. 'I picked up a couple of clients.'

'Tell me something I don't know.'

'Aw, Luke, let's not get all stroppy. A deal's been sorted with a banker and his daughter.'

'We don't take passengers, not under any circumstances.'

'Woo's a passenger.'

'Woo's your wife.'

'And what a good wife she is.' A cream cake was shoved under the nose. 'Look, she made your favourite.'

Lukas cast his eyes down at the chocolate éclair, a tempting bribe but not tempting enough. 'I'm not hungry.'

'Okay, okay, it's for two nights, that's all, but not discounting tonight.'

'Now we have three nights.'

'Look, Mr. Grumpy, three nights is nothing, cruising up and down, protecting fair maiden in distress.'

'I'm distressed.'

'A hundred grand distressed?'

Lukas coolly whistled. A hundred grand for three nights? The client needed his head examining. He took a bite of his much-loved food but could see something or other deeply moved Thomas and knew by observation this was where he had buried his worried thoughts over the last twenty-four hours. A bottle of whisky stood half empty on the desk, elsewhere unwashed mugs and the door wide open to a pretty bedroom that lacked a pretty Japanese wife. He licked his fingers and shrugged out of his blood-flecked coat. The bright green jumper he wore had a slogan *Die Another Day,* which just about summed up his mood.

'Where's Woo?'

'Now that's a very good question.'

'Do you intend to answer it?'

At the grumbling percolator, Thomas removed his braided cap to his premature greying hair, cut very short, close shorn, with lighter blue eyes, and an expression of countenance which allowed no one for a moment to think he was weak in character, or a fool. So, it was to some surprise when he said, 'Oh man, she wants a baby for Christ's sake. I mean, we can't have kids swarming the decks, it's unprofessional.'

Predictably, Lukas smiled. In a flash, the whole scenario of motive and charm seemed to evaporate, and something else was in its place. 'You have a greater chance of winning the lottery than having a kid like me.'

'But the odds grow less when she decides to have another, and then another.'

'So have one and be happy. Throw them off.'

'Two days, Luke. That's not a lot to ask.'

'We don't take passengers.'

'Her father is ostensibly worried.'

'That's a long word.'

Thomas shook his head like a man who had been transported to some strange country. 'All you have to do is mull around in another direction, read some books, look at the stars, watch films, have a swim, keep out of sight.'

'Now why should I keep out of sight?'

He gulped to his second sin. 'Hodge came on board.'

'Excuse me?'

'I swear, Luke, I never knew they would bring him along, scout's honour, my man.'

'Let me get this straight,' he said, a low threatening resonance building deep in his throat. 'You left me to have a bath on Waterloo Bridge while you picked up a nasty piece of shit and expect me to keep out of sight while you figure it all out?'

Thomas looked suitably guilty. 'I'm just doing the business here, while you go trotting off to shoot villains. Frisk is prepared to pay a hundred grand for two days. Two days, Luke, that's all. Two days to babysit and get the truth out of his daughter.'

'I don't care if she's a pathological liar, we never take passengers and we never take babysitting cases. Christ, you put this vessel at risk, Tom, and you put our operations at risk. What the hell is Hodge doing here?'

'That's what I intend to find out.' Thomas picked up his feet and donned his braided cap, anxious to steer clear of further confrontation. 'We can talk about this later. I need to see our clients.'

Lukas held him back. There were other ways to vent anger. 'Perhaps I should join you.'

'I can handle Hodge.'

'Like you handle Woo?'

'That was uncalled for.'

'Gee, now I feel really bad.'

'Okay, okay, just try to be diplomatic.' Asking Lukas to be diplomatic was like asking ice cream to melt in a freezer.

Without further word, their thoughts travelled to different matters; their steady pace carried them toward a sweeping stateroom that was now playing to the great metropolitan city of London. Once inside, they sneaked a preview of two smart suits through gaps of a broad leaf banana plant whose cool green colours reflected off the mirrored bar. Woo, with a rather wistful expression, her skirts dripping over bare feet, went to join Hodge, who seemed very much at ease in the presence of a dignified, well-groomed, powerful banker.

Thomas lowered his voice. 'Do you think she's putting on weight?'

Alone, Lukas would agree. 'So, where's his daughter?'

'No idea.'

'Did they say why they brought Hodge along?'

'Gave Woo the impression she and him were an item.'

'Well ring a ding, ding. Hodge in her pants and rich daddy wants him gone, case closed. They can bugger off tomorrow.' A tap on his shoulder and he turned to look down at narrowing brown eyes, and peaches and cream complexion, ready to upset the roots of his order.

'Mr. Giddy, your deductive reasoning amazes me. Why, it seems you have solved the case without so much as a blink.' Daphne Frisk, wearing a kaftan with feet pushed into Bugs Bunny slippers, switched her attention to Thomas, inflicting further embarrassment. 'Your cousin is a living monument to ineptitude.'

'But we can all live in hope.'

'Hope is an indulgence I don't have time for.'

It was all Lukas could do to keep his thoughts to himself. 'Why did you bring Hodge along?'

'To carry my bags.'

'Expensive porter.'

'Unlike you, he comes free.'

Keeping the expletives to himself, his 6ft 3in frame, topped by the trademark of his unsavoury profession, towered menacingly above her. 'That man would slit your throat as soon as look at you!'

'Well, since you have the jumper,' she said pushing by, 'what else do you need but to die another day?'

If distinction remained between victory and defeat, Lukas was hard pressed to weigh it. Lost for a moment in her consummate performance, he roused himself and watched the complaining brunette move to measures of spirit. Her tangled departure was not unlike the way she managed her pile of tangled hair, in which was threaded a chopstick for no apparent reason.

As captain of industry, Thomas said, 'That went down well, I thought.'

As captain of fate, Lukas replied, 'She started it!'

'Christ, you're like a little kid. I told you to be diplomatic and what did you do? Upset the client.'

'That's no damn client; that's a threat to mankind.'

'Yes, she is rather attractive…hey up, here comes her father. Now leave the talking to me.'

So doing just that, Lukas went to the bar and poured himself a pink gin over crushed ice. The liquid trickled cool at the back of his throat. On his mind a single thought - how to get rid of Hodge.

Hodge had played a foolhardy game on a moonless night, the prey Lukas Giddy leaping walls and banks of prickly hedges in desperate flight. To catch Lukas would bring its own reward, eliminate the opposition and open the opportunistic floodgates. Rivalry could so easily degenerate to open hostility. In resorting to gunplay, an innocent bystander caught the force of a bullet. For Lukas, scarce able to breath with the fury of his disappointment, was gone. For Hodge, scarce able to believe his charmed life, was also gone.

'Well, looksee here.' Hodge seized the moment with his plastic grin, appearing like he wanted to provoke something, even if it cost him some blood. 'That was a poor do in Rome, Giddy. I hope you compensated the victim.'

'And what part did you play in that endeavour?'

'If I remember, it was your finger on the trigger.' The colourful Hodge with a beak for a nose grabbed the shoulder, blessed him with another plastic grin, then walked through the porthole doors and disappeared.

Lukas was not a man to dwell on the psychological warfare his enemies generated. No, he would snatch back his dignity, wait for the cover of darkness, and make the kill sweet.

'You like roll?'

To the dusky silk mane of Woo, whose English was not quite up to par, he gave her a long look. Her unspoken worry had obviously been that if Thomas discovered she was pregnant, he would ask her to abort. 'What do you make of all this?'

'Tum is, um, how say…oh how you-'

'Bonkers?'

'Ah, tha' it, bonkers, entertain tha' silly woman. Is there plan to get rid of the plick?'

'You should have married me.'

Woo gave a throaty giggle, as she always gave a throaty giggle in the complex geometry of their lives, and proffered a plate of miniature sausage rolls. 'I made them special for you.'

Garnished with black pepper, he popped one in his mouth and panted earnestly to cool his tongue. The only real practical justification to keep her sweet, he rather enjoyed her king prawn balls. There was however another side to the familial coin. She, wife of Thomas and far from her homeland, was a woman to be sheltered from reality, not someone to look to for help or advice.

'How pally is her father with Hodge?'

'Flisk no like him, no like him at all… make big scene when boarding… she say, he my choice. Better watch back.'

The thought barely troubled him. 'When are you going to tell Tom?' There was confirmation in her eyes as she threw him an awkward glance. 'Come on, Woo. Already he's noticed the change in your body.'

'Wait until too late.'

'Dog's bollocks, Tom wouldn't ask that. Sure, he's going to be a bit pissed off but trust me… he'll come round after I pick him up from the floor.'

She almost smiled at his grin, touched and even moved by his optimism. 'How job go?'

'Do you want the gruesome details?'

'Leave out part where man beg for life.'

'He never went easy.'

'You say every time.'

'That's because they never do. They think themselves invincible, fearless, yup?'

'In my country, to conquer fear you must be fear.'

'So, if I want to conquer fat, I have to be fat?'

'I no say you fat.'

'I will be if you keep stuffing me with pastries.' It always led him to consider what a glorious engine the stomach was, with a brain of its own as reckless as him. 'How do you feel about cooking roast beef and Yorkshire pudding?'

'Wha' wrong with Koon Po Chicken?'

'Hot and spicy.'

'Like your girlfriend.'

'Angel is not my girlfriend.'

'Wha' she is?'

'A prawn cracker.'

In the midst of their laughter, a hand came into view with the plate of miniature sausage rolls. This was going to be interesting. They were silent as they watched Daphne sink her perfect white teeth into flaky pastry without resorting to a fire extinguisher. Making her cast at Lukas, her mouth filled up with quietness while the pools of her brown eyes travelled over his appearance, searching for something derogatory to say, or perhaps waiting for an apology. He would not provide it.

'Tell me,' she said after swallowing, 'do you always drink on the job?'

'If needs must.'

'My father is not paying you to prop up bars.'

'Your father is paying for my brains.'

'Oooh, brains. I quite forgot you had any.'

The arc of his brow rose. It would be his pleasure and her agony. 'And where does Hodge fit into all this?'

'He's here at my request.'

'Then I suggest you go look for his.' Lukas showed her his back, returning his warmth to Woo. 'You were saying?'

'Mm, hem, bleakfast flied at eight.' Woo said the only answer she could muster until the Kaftan was out of earshot. 'Naughty boy, that no way to treat lady.'

'A moment ago, she was a silly woman.' Lukas glanced back and saw the brunette take up conversation with Thomas, who wore his polished brass buttons with majestic pride. He shook his head and quietly laughed. 'What made Tom think he could handle Hodge? Look at him. He's a candidate for the Liberal Party.'

'I like man in uniform.'

'I could wear a uniform.'

'Wha' wrong with jumper?' She plucked a loose thread from the breast pocket. 'Tha' need sewing.'

Now gazing at the sausage rolls, he popped another in his mouth. If Daphne could eat one without breathing fire, so could he. Puffing and smiling while heat came out of his ears, he then broke into a sneeze and a sweat.

'You no like pepper.'

'I no like pepper,' he rasped, calling for a slurp on his drink. 'What happened when Miss Frisky boarded?'

'Tum give double cabin but father say no, put Hodge next to you, then she ask for tour. Tum never ask right question because he angry about money.'

'Money?'

'He say this ship not run on cocoa beans. He say you take job with no money. I say he just as bad, want buy plenty, plenty toys. And see me? No money to buy nice dress for today.'

'What's so special about today?'

She waggled her wedding-ring finger with nothing else to add about her marriage to Thomas. 'Oh, must tell, Midnight in top drawer with socks, move vests and pants to drawer below, no room left for jumpers, so put in wardrobe.'

'Thank God my furniture is fixed.' He finished his drink. 'Make sure Tum Tum keeps them busy.'

She giggled and he left through the porthole doors to a deck below, where three cabins spilled along a corridor. Stopping at the first, he poked his head inside and gained the impression it was the banker's. Into the adjacent one, little eddies of sweet perfume assailed him, together with a strong scent that he associated with Nivea cream. Snooping into the recesses of her wardrobe, Daphne shuffled in deep pockets. From frilly knickers and bras, a black silk dress with plunging neckline, matching satin shoes, and daisy white pyjamas folded neatly on the bed, all the clothes looked new, exquisite and expensive. Then he noticed a gold band on the bedside cabinet and wondered why she would keep her marriage a secret. Perhaps Hodge was her husband, which begged the question, was Frisk invited to the wedding? No matter, soon he would be attending a funeral.

Leaving her cabin, he decided to take a back-door entrance into the third, where Hodge would be found. He went to the end of the corridor and swung into his suite of rooms. It took a matter of seconds to swoop into wet air and vault the rails onto another cantilevered deck. At the glass door, he surveyed the menace pacing the floor, the look of a man who would shoot first and ask questions later. Smiling to himself, Lukas stood back in the gleaming shadows and worked his mind. Death had to appear unplanned, a tragic accident brought down by the vicissitudes of fate. It should be subtle enough to fool the police, not a scratch, not a wound. Yet to push him overboard, there was no certainty of death. And certain death was something irresistibly pleasing.

Emerging from the outside in double-quick time, Lukas grabbed the startled collar and suddenly the murky water of the River Thames was visible again. 'Take a good look at your grave, Hodge, and give me one good reason why I should postpone your death?'

'Don't be stupid, Giddy, we can do a deal!'

Without warning, a fist knocked Hodge out cold, the crack of a bone came next. 'Try swimming with one arm,' Lukas said and cantilevered the unctuous turd over the side, studied the receding head making its journey with the tide. Not a sight for the squeamish or sane.

Now, leaning against the rail, he plucked out a reefer and stuck it between his lips, cupped his hands round a flame and suddenly a shudder of ecstasy closed his eyes. Born very far away between the bedlams of human sounds, he attempted to steal an image of the body beneath the Kaftan having sex with Hodge. The scenario never quite fitted.

'I take it you're a bit happier.' Thomas had joined him.

'Do you know what today is?'

'Is this a catch question?'

'Let me give you a clue. Eleven letters, begins with A.'

Thomas, a keen crossword fanatic, rallied his thoughts in their foxholes. 'Give me another clue?'

'The reader's got more brains than you.'

'I can hardly ask them.'

Lukas gave a roll of the eyes. After a long and patient contemplation in the passing buildings with numerous tokens of their trade, he stole a look at Thomas. 'What info did you get on Frisk?'

'Stanton recommended us. George Stanton? You remember him, lost his daughter to drugs.'

'So he never came through the usual route?'

Ah, the usual route. Employed by an undisclosed Government Department where justice obliged the injustices served up in the British law courts, operatives like Lukas, hired to kill their targets, had an automatic get-out-of-jail-card. Secrecy being of the utmost importance, contact was made via a secure line to a distorted voice. Other than that, little else was known about Exit, how it originated and how far its fingers extended, but once a member, always a member. Those who believed otherwise translated themselves six feet under. Paradoxically, there was no exit from Exit.

'Frisk wasn't asking for a termination, just a babysitting job. Okay, Hodge was a turn-up for the books. Did he give anything away before you dumped him over the side?'

'He gave the wrong answer.' Given his train of thought, it was not surprising his next sentence was a train of enquiry. 'Hodge is a low-life in a flashy suit, and would sooner chance his luck with a sumo wrestler than meet me in the dark, so why was he here?'

'How about we blame it on Woo?'

Lukas cuffed him on the head, dislodging the braided cap, and went inside to rummage through Hodge's limp carryall. Among the usual overnight kit, there was a bundle of readies and a small book, its gilded covers decorated in a monochrome cobalt-blue. Either Hodge was a collector of antiquity, hardly likely, or it belonged to someone else. He opened to the inside cover and read the words *The Lady Threads a Needle in the diary of Elizabeth Whittle*.

'So,' Thomas said, shoving the wad of notes inside his uniformed pocket. 'Fancy your chances with Daphne?'

'I lusted after her.'

'For how long?'

'Zero point six seconds. Give the money to Woo.'

'Reason?'

'Need you ask? Tell her to cosy up to Flisk over breakfast.'

'Are you taking the piss out of my wife?'

'Actually, her English improves every day, which makes me wonder how you two ever communicated on your first date.'

'You're a sad bastard, do you know that?'

Lukas considered the question rhetorical and slipped into his own luxury suite of rooms, reconciling his dangerous days that came to a six-year-old boy in baggy short trousers with socks slipping down to his ankles. He had witnessed the death of his father, sentenced by his uncle whose library walls scribed the tales of Boudicca's revolt in AD61, and of the legacy that cursed the Giddy family; a tale that could melt the heart of a stone statue.

Now, at thirty, with his Smith and Wesson snub-nose .38 lodged in the ankle holster, a lovely little gun that packed a wallop like a brick through a plate glass window, any romantic sense of heroism had been fully tempered by the reality of his fate and circumstance. He could bear the sight of sudden death, sometimes a clean and quiet termination and sometimes a screaming horror.

2

In quarters that smelt of leather and smoke, Lukas walked across the lounge and into his bedroom to collect his pet and pyjamas when discomfort came at him suddenly. The sick blood roared through his veins, sending a stark warning that change was on the horizon. He looked at his watch and considered henceforth every hour was precious, every hour saw him one year older until he could age no more, the fatal pinnacle to tip him near to death. It was part of his genetic soup that he could do nothing about, and however well he concealed his fears, it was always unwanted. A seducer, a rebel, a warrior on the side of good, a man whose lonely nights were sometimes shared with a whore, ageing was unacceptable.

He had recovered the pre-emptive sickness by the time he returned to Hodge's cabin and donned a pair of silk pyjamas, exposing the throat of his bodily hair. But something was missing. He clicked his fingers and returned to his suite of rooms, collected his pet, length 6cm long, weighing in at 15g, this female Hazel Dormouse now sat sleepily on his hand.

Picking his way back to Hodge's cabin, he drew the curtains and slipped into a single bed that offered no comfort or joy. His attention now drawn to the diary, he flipped through the pages to discover the words were undecipherable. Of all the languages he could speak, Latin had never been on his curriculum.

'Midnight, wake up.'

'*No, I'm still dreaming.*'

'Have you missed me?'

'*Recognition is not a prerequisite of the job.*'

'So you did.'

'*Action speaks louder than words.*'

'It was too dangerous to take you. Have a grape.'

'*If I say thank you, that shall imply I am grapeful.*'

'For a dormouse, you sure have bad jokes.' He held the diary to the overhead light. 'What do you think?'

'Now you want my opinion.'

'Okay, what's your beef?'

'Woo shut me in the drawer.'

'She's having a hard time of it, so cut her some slack.'

'I peed on your socks.'

'I don't care.'

'Um,' she said, poking her wide black eyes at the diary, not that her instincts were always correct. *'It's older than you, better looking and written by a seamstress who speaks Latin.'*

'I could have said as much. What can you smell and cut out the chemicals, just give it straight?'

'Talcum powder,' she sniffed indignantly, *'Tobacco, fish oil, almond body moisturiser and a roll in the hay.'*

Perhaps Daphne Frisk and Hodge were an item; nevertheless, Lukas was on a mission. If his hunch was correct, there would be a certain someone unable to suffer their curious mind for much longer. So he placed the diary under his pillow next to his gun and switched off the overhead light in the offing.

The darkness never lasted for long. The door moved by some unseen measure, briefly flooding the cabin with shadows. The scent unmistakable, the intention yet to be determined as Daphne surreptitiously tiptoed across the spongy carpet, feeding her nose wherever it would turn. The curtains slowly parted to afford some light from London's glitzy city, where he could now make out a pair of daisy white pyjamas shapelessly humped around the body, the hair extravagantly wild and long, the hands and head working over and under the surfaces of white-oak furniture.

'Can I help?'

Daphne stumbled in fright, knocked over a fruit bowl, crashed into a chair and terminated at the foot of his bed. A tangled mess popped into view. 'I was sleepwalking.'

'A feeble excuse.'

'No, I don't think so.'

'Yes, I do think so.'

'It's really late.'

'Why, can you read the time?' He switched on the overhead light. Rarely had he seen it before, but it was her eyes he found so mesmerising; they were simply irresistible. 'Would you care to tell me why you're here?'

'Err, um, well, it was like this,' she said, adjusting herself. 'I couldn't sleep so…so…so I left my cabin and went um, err, for a stroll, then I returned a little disoriented and walked into your cabin by mistake.'

Lukas folded his arms. 'Shall we try again?'

'How about, I left my cabin for a chat?'

'Perhaps I should have a chat with your father.'

'It was a mistake, alright? I apologise. It was a silly thing to do.' She approached, blinking comically at Midnight. 'Is that a Hazel Dormouse on your shoulder?'

'No, it's my hairbrush.'

Taking up a position on the bed, he could see it in her face that she was about to change the subject. 'Did you know they are unique among rodents in that they lack a cecum, a part of the gut used in other species to ferment vegetable matter…their dental formula is similar to that of squirrels, although they often lack premolars.'

'Was Hodge just as fascinating as my pet?'

'Certainly not.'

'Then why are you in his cabin?'

'Huh?'

'Now who has the brains?'

'Alright!' She barked, defeat her position. 'I stumbled upon a mystery, like it or not, and was placed in a precarious position that required unprecedented action.'

'The only mystery I read is Hodge.'

'He claims to have a handle on the case.'

Lukas gave a contemptuous laugh. 'The only handle he grabs is attached to the emergency door.' He twisted round and foraged under a duck-filled pillow. 'Is this what you were looking for when placed in your precarious position that required unprecedented action?'

'That's mine!'

'Mine now, I think.'

'Well really, call yourself a gentleman!'

'I call myself tired.' He switched off the light.

She switched it back on. 'I found it first.'

'I found it last.'

'I'm not leaving until you give it back.'

'What an interesting proposal.' This oblique, but unmistakable reference to sex enraged her so much that she broke into the National Anthem, annoyingly so. 'Do you want me to shut you up?'

'You can shut me up by giving me what is mine!'

With that, he swung into action and threw her over his shoulder, the titan against a lightweight challenger, screaming her mouth off. Nothing could demonstrate more graphically the length to which he would go to reinforce his view. Her kicks and protestations carried all the way to the pool house, noisy and crude, taking exception to her flight in the water. There was some hint of concealed pain where a word might have put her at ease but he had none to give. She would bring nothing but trouble, and he was best keeping right out of her way.

3

Hauled back to earth by a furry tail tickling his nose, Lukas woke warm and lazy, squeezing a pillow to his chest. Clearly absent of a female's arms, he bathed in the dream of holding someone close against him, her bottom snuggled into the basin of his pelvis, his arms wrapped tight round a sleeping beauty that smelt of refuge and comfort. Dreams, they were only ever dreams craving permission to become real. For the likes of Lukas Giddy, there were no tomorrows' wishes.

At the mirror hung over the washbasin, he smiled to a small shining ball perched on his head, the toes of her feet grasping his mutinous mop of black hair. 'You know,' he said in the midst of a shave, 'things have improved. I got to feel her bum.'

'Tragic. When it shines kinder skies, you want even more.'

'Kinder skies do not encompass all, Midnight. I suspect she will have a lot to say for herself when she discovers her knight in rusty armour is missing. Now we must ask two questions. Is she married? If so, was it to Hodge? And does the diary hold something more, other than its intrinsic value?'

'That's three questions.'

'Here's another; what did you find?'

'There was nothing in her handbag, no mobile or even a lipstick. What woman carries an empty handbag?'

'Perhaps you looked in the wrong one.'

'Perhaps you slept in the wrong bed.'

The confirmation or otherwise of telepathic creatures might seem to be more a matter of waggish speculation than the proven reality of a Hazel Dormouse. Bound together by a greater force that offered no explanation whatsoever, brought compensations. Where Midnight had the ability to forage in places unseen, his alternative talents were immensely powerful, infinitely more powerful than any man who dare take him on.

At Daphne's cabin, he rapped softly on the door, waited a beat before poking his head inside. She was not there. Perhaps she was searching for Hodge, in which case her search would be futile. Moving on with an upward glance, Midnight secured in his tatty breast jumper pocket, the noise of London sounded in his ears to the next level up, the sweeping stateroom doors in sight.

Thomas, filling his mouth like a pelican, was seated next to Woo when Lukas swung in and passed over the diary. 'As suspected, she came into the cabin looking for it. Gave no explanation, just made herself a bloody nuisance. Woo, did you get any info?'

'No seen her,' she said, fondling the antiquity. 'Tha' is beautiful, pretty blue and gold like Ben's watch. Must be worth many, many dollars.'

'Sweetheart, tell Luke what Frisk said.'

'Ah, Flisk say he heard ruckus last night. He say job in London, daughter have habit of picking up strays.'

'Fancy that.' Thomas enlightened Woo with one of his jokes. 'Luke got thrown out of McDonald's. The girl serving him was an absolute stunner and she told him she could make it large for 30p. He replied that she already had but could she finish him off for a £1.'

Woo looked blank for a moment, then her face lost its confusion. 'Haaaa, finish him off pretty cheap.' Her English was very much work in progress, but the implied meaning was there with a quick change of expression. 'Lukas pay top dollar now.'

Thomas murmured his censure. 'Plenty top dollar.'

'Hoy!' Lukas recoiled in defence. 'I contribute to their stable economy!'

'Look, pal, you contribute to their reputation. Has it ever occurred to you that sex is free if you find a nice woman?'

'My legacy would scare them off.'

'You don't know unless you try.'

'And where am I supposed to try?'

'For certain, you won't find one in a brothel. What's wrong with Miss Frisky?'

'The wedding ring on her bedside cabinet infers she married Hodge.'

'Nah, unlikely…she was poking around the lower decks looking for him….Hodge, she called, damn it, Hodge, stop doing this to me. If she was married to that git, would she call him Hodge?'

'Then she married a spineless idiot. Either way, it appears her father has more influence over her than anyone else. Where is he?'

Thomas went mute and motioned with his head. Lukas looked round. Wearing figure-hugging jeans and a pink matching twin set, Daphne gave a brief nod of acknowledgement from afar, helped herself to a bowl of cornflakes, and then sat on a barstool, burying her woeful face behind a newspaper. Even from this distance, Lukas could see her extreme sense of isolation existing in a cloudy atmosphere, the notion that a curved course rather than a straight one was his shortest route to get into her mind.

'Lukas,' Woo whispered across the table. 'Tell how loverly she look.'

'I don't do loverly.'

'Go on, my man, calm some waters…see what you can wring out of her.'

Having learned from his earlier experience, Lukas padded over and considered he was about to enter a tempest storm. 'About last night, perhaps I was a bit out of line. You must admit you were a problem.'

'Oh look, first you see me,' then she ducked behind the newsprint. 'Now you don't. Amazing how your problem goes away.'

'My job is to deal with problems.'

'Like Mr Hodge, I presume?'

'Unfortunately, I had to let him go.'

'Mr. Giddy, that diary is mine. It will only serve as a hindrance if you keep hold of it. All you have to do is give it back, and I will gladly leave this boat and-'

'Yacht.'

'Are you being deliberately antagonistic?'

'A reflection of yourself.'

'Uh!' She rustled her paper portentously. 'We are so far removed two planets march between us.'

'Does your father know what you get up to?'

'Does yours?'

'He's dead.'

'How sad, did you bore him to death with your arrogance?'

Lukas let out a short burst of hysterical laughter. Midnight had crept into her dishevelled knot of hair, shaking a disbelieving head.

So Daphne let crumble the paper to her lap. 'And what do you find so amusing, Mr. Giddy?'

'Truthfully, I think I walked into a mad house.'

'For someone who brings a dormouse on the job, I hardly think you're in a position to comment. What significance does it hold?'

'What significance does that chopstick hold?'

'You claim to have brains, you tell me.'

Having laid down the gauntlet to his boasting mental acuity, the stillness of all things was only interrupted by the distant echoes of river traffic. He was stretching his mind, tugging at his earlobe, thinking it would be wrong to assume it held up her hair, for that would make her challenge too easy. On the other hand, was it a double bluff?

'Do you give in?'

'I never give in.'

'Perhaps your dormouse does your thinking for you. Would you like time to confer?'

Lukas would give her something to think about. 'Where does your husband fit into this?'

'He doesn't.'

'Okay, let's ask why you cosied up to Hodge?'

'I was legitimately entitled to take back what was mine.'

'That's not what I asked.'

'If you intend to die another day, you should give back that diary. Now, if you will excuse me, I prefer to have my breakfast in peace.'

With Midnight racing to his tatty breast pocket, he strode to the open air and caught a whiff of something old as Big Ben, the yielding of industrial waste to the water's despairing beauty. Faced with her bloody-minded attitude, he submerged his anxieties in a reefer, equally determined to fight it out. Somehow, the diary was now the most important aspect of the case. Appreciating the implications of Hodge's involvement, reading the spirit of her signals, understanding the vital need for speed, Lukas turned to consider Frisk had every right to be concerned.

Midnight's intelligence never helped. '*That chopstick is in two parts.*'

'No doubt to eat her bloody noodles.'

Thomas stepped up and placed a shielding arm across his shoulders. 'You look a little washed out, my man. Are you on the change?'

'Hell, it couldn't have come at a worse time.'

'Don't be a martyr, Luke. I can take care of things.'

Smothering his face with his hands for a moment, Lukas was unsure whether to speak his thoughts, if it was wrong to create more worry. But there again, people's burdens were their business. 'Something isn't right, Tom. I think she created a ruse to hold Hodge's interest so she could get that diary, and Frisk intervened, yup?'

'So that was a good thing.'

'But why would Hodge play along with it?'

'Okay, we have to ask if Hodge knew this is where you lived, eh? Best guess, I'd say no. You're always careful in that respect.'

'I disagree. He faced me like a blunt hammer, no surprise shown.'

'Right, so he expected to see you. With that in mind, maybe he thought his involvement with Daphne gave him some form of immunity. Maybe he fancied her rotten. You have to admit, she's tasty, and rich. Hodge might have thought it was a good bed to lie in.'

Lukas looked at his watch, was always looking at his watch. 'I'm thirty-six and three months.'

'You don't look it.'

'Is that supposed to make me feel better?'

'Aw, come on, Luke, we can work around it.'

'See, this is why we don't take passengers, yup? If they see me age, they're going to be asking questions, and I shall look a prat. Notwithstanding that, the mechanics of this vessel must be kept a secret.'

'No one can access the terminals except you and me.'

'But we have no crew, an instant light bulb.'

Thomas remained quiet, stroking his whiskers while they watched the Tower of London, home to the English Crown Jewels and symbol of one thousand years of Britain's royal history, come into view. They were leaving those patient stones behind in attitude of painful attention.

'What confuses me is this husband lark,' Lukas said. 'She says he doesn't fit into this. Maybe the diary was given to her from him. He found out she was having an affair and threw her out so she had to get it back.'

'Can you see her in bed with Hodge?'

'She may not have fancied him, but she needed to seduce him, yup? Midnight said she could smell sex. Okay, what do we have, a diary written by Elizabeth Whittle in Latin?'

'Do we assume she's a seamstress?'

'She threads a needle, yup? There again, did seamstresses in those days have knowledge of Latin?'

'So she fell on hard times, wrote a sexy story.'

'There's just a slight fault in your observation. What's the point of writing in Latin when sex sold like hot cakes in those days? Unless…unless she wrote about an affair…an affair with a married man, a famous man, yup? Then we ask why rich Daphne wants more riches unless that diary holds sentimental value, the sentiments of a distant relation, yup?'

'Hodge is the only fly in the ointment. If he stole it off her, why didn't she call the police? Instead, she's that pally, she invites him on board to rub shoulders with her father, who hates the sight of him. We need answers, my man. I am going to give Dad a ring, he knows Latin backwards.'

For Lukas, he was forming ideas of his own and moved back into the stateroom to seek out Frisk who was sat at the bar, blinking so tight under his salt and pepper hair that both his cheeks lifted up as if they were trying to meet his eyebrows. Garbed in a fully bespoke Savile Row suit, minimum cost three thousand grand, the yellow silk monogrammed handkerchief spilled over the breast pocket as if to point to the highly polished bespoke shoes.

'We need to talk.'

'Indeed we do, Giddy or do I call you Lukas?'

'Sure, Giddy, Lukas or shit. I get called many names.'

A companionable silence fell between them as Frisk poured two shots of early morning whisky, passed one over and rolled his own glass between his palms. Lukas knew something dramatic was going to pop out of his mouth.

'Let me tell you where I'm at, Giddy. My daughter refuses to talk to me, not because we are separated by age or animosity, but because she takes on the role of mother since my wife died…a rare commodity nowadays, having a loving daughter. A month ago, I popped in to see her on the off chance and what did I find? Her surgery ransacked and a black eye to boot. Rather than make a meal of it, I contacted a private eye to watch over her.'

'Hodge turned up.'

Frisk used his glass as a pointer. 'You catch on quickly. I did my research on the abhorrent creature, into all sorts. He had his filthy hands on my daughter and I want him punished.'

'It may not be Hodge.'

'Who else could it be?'

Indeed, who else. 'Does the name Elizabeth Whittle ring a bell?'

Frisk went blank for a while then his expression changed to one of comprehension. 'Strange you should ask. Hodge mentioned that name, something to do with a diary. Does it play an important role in this investigation?'

'He had it on him. I think your daughter invented a ruse to get it back, then you stepped in.'

'Too right, I stepped in. Stanton said you were the man to get the job done. Where is Hodge?'

'How frank do you wish me to be?'

'Frank pays your fee.'

'I got rid of him. The good news, I have the diary…the bad news, that's all. What else did Hodge say?'

'He began by asking if there was a seamstress called Elizabeth Whittle in my history closet. When I told him no, he had the effrontery to call me a liar. Look here, my man followed Hodge to a flat in Hackney. We might find some answers there.'

'Not we but me.'

'You forget who pays your fee.'

The music of Frisk's response was not lost on Lukas, and he sacrificed a stuffy response. 'Tell me what was she like as a child?'

'When she was eight, she made one hell of a mess in the kitchen baking fairy cakes, lots of fairy cakes, convinced we had starving fairies in the garden. It never stopped there. Soon she had her entire class baking fairy cakes. Then she wanted to save the animals, became a jolly good vet. Mother, my wife, helped her convert one of the stables. Then she died, hit us very badly.'

'How long ago was that?'

'Six years, lost to cancer. I found it difficult to stay among the memories so my daughter suggested I get a place abroad.'

Lukas finished his drink and leaned back, lacing his hands behind his head and considered it was time to be frank. 'I saw a wedding ring on her bedside cabinet, claims her husband isn't involved.'

'Are you suggesting my daughter is married?'

'Is there another reason not to wear a wedding ring?'

Frisk was silent a moment, probably back to not knowing what to say. 'I had her watched and there was no man other than Hodge.'

'You never remarried?'

'When a woman takes your heart, she takes your life. This ring I wear on my finger is the promise I gave to my wife. No other woman could ever replace her.'

'And your wife's wedding ring?'

Frisk undid a third button down to his shirt and revealed a wedding band fed through a chain hung round his white collared neck. 'My daughter's idea.'

'And now she's remote.'

Frisk sighed, his eyes falling into his drink. 'Pride, Giddy, that's her trouble, takes after her mother, has this independent streak as long as the M1. Still, you never stop caring. And you?'

'Me? Mother died in childbirth, father died when I was six. I have so many hang-ups it's hard to close the wardrobe door.' It may not have seemed so to Frisk, but that was a difficult confession to make. Overshadowed by his curse, not knowing his mother, the deep silence was an unconscious rebuke to his father, the impact of a traumatic event. He looked at his watch again. He figured by six he would be forty-five, grey at the temples, a little slack around the cheek with no explanation to give. 'I need to get a few things. Meet you on deck.'

In his palatial surrounds, which catered to his every need, including a forty-inch screen and the entire collection of James Bond films, he picked up his gun and twizzled the five-round chamber. It was full. He lodged it in his ankle holster then slipped on his blood flecked coat, the blade up his sleeve nice and sharp.

'Bad idea to bring Frisk along.'

'The man pays the fee. Are you good to go?'

'Have you ever met a fairy?'

'Midnight, you will never guess how many there are.'

Thomas walked in unannounced. 'Luke, I gave Dad a bell. He said under no circumstances must we lose that diary, end of explanation until we see him. Where are you going?'

'To case Hodge's joint with Frisk.'

'Keep your line open so I can hear what's going on.'

'And you make sure Miss Frisky behaves, even if you have to lock her up.' At the door, he forestalled his journey and glanced back. 'If Ben is coming, then this is personal.'

'Not necessarily.'

'Tom, you should know better than to doubt my senses.'

_4_

Beneath the face of London's East End, it was a megawatt funnel of enticement to greed that burned twenty-four hours a day. Strip joints and corner street rats frequented the pavements with bold promises of drugs and sex. Kids never knew how to spell, but they knew how to carry a knife, if only for a second, just to get an idea what was out there.

The taxi drew into Leytonstone High Street and stopped outside a launderette. Lukas passed over a fifty-pound note and told the driver to wait.

Frisk remained quiet until his feet hit ground. 'This is a Godforsaken place.'

'It's where the dross live.' Lukas walked on in the grey light of clouds, his eyes searching, pushing through a wave of human traffic. Among the derelict and abandoned structures, they slipped through a passageway which broke open to a block of flats. It was the kind of place Hodge might seek short-term rest or shelter. Few others with money would care to visit. 'Chances are someone else lives there.'

'Why do you say that?'

'Look about you. Hodge wears Armani suits.' He smiled. 'Or I should say, did do. What number?'

'Twenty-four.'

Green paint peeled off the door, which went unanswered, so Lukas picked the lock. He rarely went anywhere without the tricks of his profession. In seconds, they were in, but someone worse had visited. Years in the business heightened the senses, alerted the nerves, a sound, a smell, a taste in the air.

The body was decaying into the surrounding mess strewn on the lounge floor. Her head had split to the impact of an iron that lay close by, the dyed-blond hair clotted with blood, obvious she had died for Hodge, on account of Hodge.

'My guess, I'd say last night or in the early hours of this morning, so that lets Hodge off the hook.' Lukas turned to the monogrammed handkerchief clutched to the mouth. 'If you're going to be sick, do it in the toilet, leave no trace of yourself, yup?'

'I am okay, Giddy, just a little sensitive to this poor creature's plight. Do you think someone was looking for the diary?'

'It certainly points that way. Time is short. Look around and see if you can find anything interesting. I'll do the bedrooms.'

Bedrooms were his favourite places, places where people hid their secrets, between the mattress and base, under the rug, on top of the wardrobe, and behind the bath panel. It was there that Midnight found a stash of money, forged passports, stolen driving licences and credit cards. No doubt about Hodge's game. No doubt the killer was only interested in one thing. Gathering the bounty in a pillow case, Lukas went into the living room where Frisk had his head bent low.

'Found anything?'

'My daughter's photograph.' Frisk turned it over. 'There is a number on the back, not hers, mind you.'

Lukas knew it well. He took a last look round the place that had told him far less than the body, a woman who had taken her secrets to the grave, probably protecting Hodge in the process. 'We need to get out of here.'

In years past, Lukas would have tipped off the police, but things were different now; everything hinged on targets. Easy pickings and databases and also prints taken from people on the sly meant nobody was safe from their scrutiny. Britain had become that kind of place where a terrorist could claim off the dole against a sixty-year-old granny being done for smoking weed. And of course, the money disappeared into the dark to pay for investigations and high-tech equipment.

Lukas told the driver to take them to Charnel's Modelling Agency, Charing Cross Road, and be quick.

'Look, guv, I can't go any faster.'

'Just do your best.' He sat back, modulating his voice. 'Frisk, you should leave this to me.'

'What has she got herself into?'

'I deal with this shit most days. It's no different wherever you go, Paris, Venice, you name it, people act no differently, some worse than others.'

'Are you saying my daughter is corrupt?'

'Look, she got involved with Hodge, yup? She hides her marriage, yup? She told you nothing about the diary, where she found it or its importance that led to a flat occupied by a dead woman who just happened to have her photograph.'

'My daughter may be obstinate, even to the point of my exclusion but she is far too intelligent to get mixed up with rotten eggs.'

'I'm just telling it like it is. After all, Frank pays my fee.'

The conversation might have stopped there. Frisk looked away like the answer would be found in the street, then looked back as if he had just picked it up. 'Why do you do it? Both of you, Tom especially…his good wife was telling me that vessel of yours runs by itself, what? Quantum computers; negates a crew. He has a good technological brain; both of you could reap great benefit from that yacht.'

It was Lukas who now looked away from the predictable outcome of curiosity for the *Abracadabra*. That she was magnificent and sleek, above all, to be operated by quantum computers made her the most desirable piece of equipment was beyond imagination. Aware of his dangerous professional situation, intuitively defining it with inspired public relations, he looked back at Frisk and said, 'And who's going to protect the likes of your daughter, or Hodge's woman, certainly not the police? Take Stanton. He lost his daughter to a drug pusher. No, Madam Justice wears her blindfold. I blame it on the liberal parasites who have this absurd notion pieces of shit should be recycled back into society.'

'Stanton speaks very highly of your endeavours. I am not a do-gooder, Giddy. All my life I have worked for my family…families are what matter. I felt so damn guilty after the banking crisis, but what was there to be guilty about? I had no hand in subprime or speculative markets. Yes, I live in a nice apartment, have a nice view, have a nice car, my carbon emission is probably high, so my daughter keeps reminding me, but if you step off the escalator, you step into poverty.'

'Most people do live on far less than the cost of a fancy motor. I expect most people live on the cost of your wheels.'

'We're here,' the driver said, the meter running.

'Go back, give Tom the gear.'

Without further word, Lukas jumped from the taxi and into the glass building occupied by high-class hookers. He pressed a red button by the lift shaft and spoke his name into the grill. At the sound of a buzzer, the lift doors opened, he stepped inside and travelled one flight up, thinking his way round the situation. Normally, he was not one to miss such an opportunity.

Among voluptuous prostitutes lounging in their suspenders, he said, 'Sorry ladies, not today,' and continued in his stride. Everywhere was encompassed by velvet that crushed against walls, shutting off natural light. If it was good for the man below, up here it was beyond their wildest imaginings.

Ahead, the matriarch lounged like a prostitute waiting to become a nun, holding court behind a desk. 'Why, Luke, back so soon?'

He planted the photograph on her desk. 'Let's ask why your number was found in a dead woman's flat?'

Charnel looked surprised, he could see that, but this was his way, marking his territory, reducing villains to panic. She looked up. 'Is she a classy hooker?'

'I'm the one asking the questions.'

'You're the one who plays cards with Angel.'

'Yes, well, err…we'll skip my moments of relapse.'

She smiled to her feet. 'Drink?'

'Go for it.' Softening under this soothing process, he sat down and pushed Midnight's nosey-nose back into his breast pocket. 'I think the dead woman is a poor tart who latched onto Hodge. Know the name?'

'That would be breaking a confidence.'

'Then break it and feel better about it.'

'Between you and me, okay.' She spun on her four-inch heels, allocated the drink and lit a pink Sobranie, her mind glancing off to the immediate subject of their conversation. 'Yes, Hodge is good for a passport, and my girls are all legit. I never met his girlfriend. He kept strictly to business.'

'So, he never had any of the girls?'

'Uh, uh,' she said, shaking her head. 'Never even enquired after those he got documents for, but he sometimes introduced clients.'

'Any he was particularly pally with?'

'Not really. You think Hodge got on someone's bad side?'

Lukas was thoughtful, sat considering a little before he answered. 'Whoever killed his woman was certainly leaving a strong message. Your number was there to be found so I ask myself why. A message for me, perhaps. Any weirdoes he introduced, say a bloke out of the ordinary?'

'Come to think about it, there was this one guy, about two months ago, maybe less, gave Hodge as a reference. Oh my, was he something, had the looks. He asked for Angel. That was odd because Hodge never knew Angel.'

'Name?'

'Marcus Metal…Metit…something like that, about your height, wavy black hair, dark skin, very suave, lit his cigars with a fifty-pound note.'

'Do you have his number?'

'You know damn well they only leave a name.'

Lukas picked up a pen and wrote down his own. 'If this Marcus bloke calls again, give me a ring.'

'I don't want any trouble, Luke.'

'Is Angel about?'

'Up top in the Jacuzzi…five minutes, and no more.'

Behind the curtained door and up the stairs where only the privileged go, Angel was basking in her perfumed and watery surrounds, red hair draped around her shoulders, the strawberry-tipped breasts floating. It was enough to stir the loins in any man.

'Marcus' He came straight to the point. 'Do you remember him?'

Without any brains, all she had was her tits and fishing-pole legs, painted toenails teasing his crotch. 'Coming in?'

'I've only got a minute.'

'So?'

Something below was unravelling in a hurry. He switched off his watch, cutting communication with Thomas, dumped his clothes on the floor and waded into the Jacuzzi. Always ready for sex, she locked her hands around his neck and opened up to him, her mood as pliant as her wet and willing body. Though it was clear their relationship, which occupied no dimension other than the physical, had no life outside this particular time and space, it was all muscle and sinew throbbing with the paid heat of hers. What he did not expect was to see an image of Daphne Frisk zooming into his head. In a flush and glow, with the haste he had made, and the pleasure of being inside, he withdrew limp and grabbed a towel, all over in three minutes flat.

Then it was back to business. 'So tell me, this Marcus, yup?'

Closing her eyes, Angel sketched a mental picture, subdued in the gravity of her whorish existence. 'Bastard, dirty rotten bastard took my arse, held me down, everywhere, arms like a fucking octopus.' She withdrew from the Jacuzzi, realizing much too late she had misjudged her client. 'The bastard laughed, threw the money in my face, said it was worth a grand. It put me right out of action for three days.' Then she added worriedly. 'Don't tell Charnel. I told her I only got two hundred.'

He could not condemn her for that, would not judge such conduct when surrounded by insanity. 'Charnel never mentioned he was a pervert.'

'Well, she wouldn't, would she, sweetie, because I never told her. I went up to Mum's, took her to the seaside, rained all the bloody time…met a nice bloke. He took us for lunch. Shall we make it twenty-five?'

'He put you out of action for three days and you took your mum to the seaside.' He studied her, unsure what she was getting at. 'I don't get it.'

It was something she was reluctant to delve into; he could see that and watched as she grabbed a packet of cigarettes off the shelf, clicking the lighter a few times. 'I don't want you to think me crazy,' she said between pursed lips and then brushed the smoke away. 'I asked him the usual, anything special. He says he wants to be in control, no touchy feely, take time to strip and lay on the bed, stomach down. I says I don't do arse and he says it's okay, so I switch on some music, takes my time while he's in the chair sucking on a cigar, big smile on his face, smarmy bastard. Then he says Okay, get on the bed, he drops his pants and climbs on top. But I can't move...like I'm in some kind of time warp and I can't shout because he's got his hand over my mouth, bastard. Then he does the business, rolls off laughing and flings a grand in my face, says Thanks for being an angel. And I'm left wondering what the fuck just happened, yeah?'

A layer of sweat broke across his forehead. Was it possible she encountered the man who could possibly be his counterpart?

'Do you believe me, sweetie?'

He nodded and picked up his trench coat, gave double the amount she was asking and walked out.

Rather than return to the *Abracadabra*, he strolled the broken pavements working his mind, going back years. The dynamics of his legacy, truly complex, was infinitely more so when he was told two are born to share the curse, one is good, one is bad. At fifteen, what did he know? '*My Lukas,*' his uncle had told him, '*there are always opposites in all things. Like black, there is white, like good, there is evil, and to be certain, your counterpart is evil. Do not seek that which is beyond redemption, live your life, be true to your heart and be a brave warrior on the side of liberty and justice.*'

And he honoured Benjamin's sincere words, took up the gun and thought no more about the man that in all probability was this Marcus.

'*I don't wish to be a party pooper, but shouldn't we be making our way home?*'

'I'm thinking, Midnight.' He stopped outside a jewellery store and pressed his nose against the cold glass. 'There are too many coincidences to ignore, Hodge's involvement, the diary which now holds Ben's interest, the lead to Charnel's and Angel. Yes, why Angel, why pick her?'

'*Does that need an answer?*'

'Sarcasm is the lowest form of wit.'

'*I have a question. You paid fifty quid for three minutes in water, how much do you pay for three minutes in bed?*'

'You should be paying attention to the problem.'

'*So, what was the problem again?*'

'He could have picked anyone, but no, he requested Angel because he knows she's my favourite. Ergo, I'm in the middle of this. Why?'

'The book seems to be in the middle; you're probably on page thirty-fourr.'

Lukas smiled and hailed a taxi. Weighed against the facts, by instinct, he knew he was about to enter that turbulent world which Benjamin often portrayed.

5

Bound for the lower levels from which sprung the heart of easy living, Thomas was emerging from a doorway to the galley. 'I got some info.'

'Has she behaved?'

'Not really. She went snooping in my quarters then threatened to jump ship so I locked her in the brig, said it was your idea.'

Lukas grinned and promptly took the bacon roll off his cousin. 'When do we expect to see Ben?'

'That's his supper you're eating.'

'The gear?'

'Ah, yes, good forgeries. There was a hundred grand in fifty pounds notes, ta very much. The woman was Silvia O'Hara, had a police record for shop lifting and one for driving without a licence. She rented the flat, was on benefits, possibility she never knew Hodge stored the gear, more than likely he was using her place as a safe house.'

'I go along with that. Any luck on the diary?'

'Now that is the right question, my man. Dad has the link pinned down to Joshua Giddy. Yes, I thought that might please you, cocky sod. I won't take all his fun away. But listen to this. Among Hodge's papers was an auction house address in Hammersmith. So, I checked them out and the guy running the show said two people came in. The first was Daphne Frisk. She hands it in for auction, then she comes back the next day and changes her mind, meanwhile they've already plastered the entry on the internet. Then sometime later a guy fitting Hodge's description walks in with it…wants to get a rough idea of its value. Between her and Hodge, their offices are broken into, nothing stolen. So, I figure Hodge broke in and got her details, makes contact with her and she gives him the diary.'

'Did you confront her about it?'

35

Thomas raised his brows. 'Are you kidding? The mood she's in, you're likely to get your ears tuned.'

'Okay, here's what we do. Get everyone in the stateroom and turn on the coms links so when I talk to Miss Frisky everyone can hear, yup?'

'We can't keep her locked up.'

'Why not?'

'Dammit, Luke, she deserves some respect. Frisk won't pay if we treat her like a prisoner. How about letting her loose. I'll keep an eye on her until bedtime and you take over the watch.'

'And do what?'

'Keep an eye on her door. Make sure she doesn't go a wandering. She's just up the corridor from you then I'll take over when she wakes, no hassle, you stay in your quarters, they leave, we get paid, Bob's your uncle, can't say fairer than that.'

'Okay, and Tom, cast off, we don't want any nasties boarding.'

'Hell, is it that bad?'

'Wait till you hear what she has to say.'

Daphne Frisk took a jaundiced view of virtually everything Lukas had done after boarding the *Abracadabra*. And what with his storming in, holding her back from escape to close the steel door behind him, it held no surprise to be greeted with animosity.

'This is tantamount to abduction! I demand to be set free this instant!'

'No can do.'

'Why?'

'You might try to rape me again.'

'Eeuuw! The moment you stepped on board-'

'I know-'

'Are you so in love with your voice you find it hard to listen?' She waited a beat, tapping her foot to the ground, folding her arms before continuing in a more moderate tone. 'The moment you stepped on board you deliberately went out of your way to insult me. You have the brains of an imbecile, running around like a headless chicken making my life intolerable. It was my Father who hired you to watch over me, not drown me in the pool or lock me in here. Do I have to talk more slowly in order for you to catch up?'

'Your father hired me to find out what trouble you were in, not babysit to your juvenile needs.'

'My need was for you to give me back my property.'

'Listen to me!' And she jumped with the severity of his voice. 'You got hold of that diary, how and when is left for speculation yet you had it in mind to do whatever it was you thought you were doing, and guess what, let's put it up for auction, see where that goes, let the whole damn world know. It triggered a response from a man that not even the silliest of women would wish to encounter. But meet Hodge you did. Correct me if I'm wrong or do I have to talk more slowly in order for you to catch up?'

The anguish in his voice had provided the perfect soundtrack for self-pity. 'No,' she said bleakly, and sat on the edge of a hard-pressed mattress, her hands falling to her lap. The little stratagems she had devised to try him, came back as vividly as if something infinitely worse intervened. 'He threatened to strangle Billy.'

'Who's Billy?'

'Jed's ram. I told him not to put Billy on wet grass, not any of his sheep, it rots their feet.'

'He left with the diary, yup?'

'No. He just upped and left when Clive came in with Daisy. But I said to him, it's no good complaining about it now. In the end he agreed it was best that I should have it.'

'What, the diary?'

'No, the cub…you see he let Daisy-'

'Christ, you're giving me a headache.' He sighed and sat down beside her, sweeping his fingers through his hair, reason and reasonableness in his voice. 'How did the diary get into Hodge's hands?'

'Now that was a very unfortunate event. He walked into my surgery with a dead spider. I mean, how obtuse can that be. I knew something was up the moment he offered to buy it. I refused, he threatened Billy then Clive walked in with Daisy. That night he broke into my home, at least I'm sure it was him. He never found the diary because I had in bed with me.'

'So, he beat the crap out of you.'

'Don't be ridiculous.'

'Your father said you had a black eye.'

'Billy is temperamental.'

'So what happened next?'

'Well, he came back again and tried to reason with me, upped his offer. But that man just wouldn't leave so I considered it was in my best interests to sell.'

'Do you know a man called Marcus?'

'No. Should I?'

Now it was fitting and for the benefit of his listeners, he said, 'You spread the news about the diary through the auction house and Marcus reads the details. But he can't buy the diary because it's withdrawn from auction so to get its whereabouts, he ransacks the auction house for your details. But rather than announce himself to you, he makes a bargain with Hodge, and Hodge goes to see you. Ah, but Hodge thinks he can turn Marcus over, so that evil piece of shit kills his woman.'

'What! A woman is dead because of me?'

'She's dead because of Hodge holding back on Marcus. What happened next is obvious. You have the bright idea of informing Hodge you know its true value, that it's worth zillions but there's a problem. How do you get him to hand it over? Well, here we go…another brainstorm. Your father, concerned for your safety, offers you a trip on the Thames so what better opportunity to invite Hodge along and ransack his luggage. Of course, when he boarded, he saw me.'

'How was I to know you had history with Hodge?'

'Why oh why did you withhold this information?'

'What an inane question. You, Mr. Clever Dick had already cracked the case, remember?'

'I was angry. Angry that Tom had taken on the job. We have a strict rule. Never take on passengers.'

'Why?'

'Never mind why. What were you hoping to achieve?'

'I would have thought that obvious, to find out more on Elizabeth Whittle. She wrote a wonderful story, you know.'

'So you can read Latin?'

'Is it hard to confront a woman with a brain?' Daphne had placed Lukas back in his box. 'Obviously you have no idea what the tale is about.'

'I'm sure your about to enlighten me.'

'It's about Boudicca and her revolt against the Romans.'

Lukas took a deep breath. He had suddenly felt very weary and stupid. No wonder the diary brought Marcus from out of the woodwork.

Daphne pressed on. 'Tell me more about this poor woman. Where did you find her?'

'Your father had you followed and traced Hodge to a flat in Hackney. There we went to find a photograph of you with Charnel's number on the back.'

'Was that her name, Charnel?'

'No, Charnel run's a brothel in Charring Cross Road. It was through her I managed to fit some of the pieces.'

'Did you stay very long?'

Lukas slowly turned his head and searched the enquiring eyes. Was she there to taunt him or haunt him for the rest of his life? 'Do you have a problem with that?'

'It's your life. Who am I to judge? I mean, you're single and stupid.'

'And you're married and stupid.'

'Don't be ridiculous. I wouldn't marry you if you got down and begged.'

'Excuse me?'

'No, excuse me! You had husband on the brain the moment you came snooping in my cabin, whatever next. Did you tell my Father I was married?'

'Your father is not a stupid man.'

'Fathers are usually over-protective or very naïve. He would have a fit if he knew I let my boyfriends in through my bedroom window.'

'Your father is listening to this conversation.'

Her hands flew to her redden cheeks. 'Oh, my God, what did I say?'

'The truth, perhaps.'

'Dad?' She called out. 'I was only seventeen and love you very much.'

He expected worse to come. 'Others heard too.'

'What!' She stood in a swoop. 'You let me prattle on about my love life in front of your relatives, you, you, you look a little older than you did this morning.'

'That's what women do, they age men.'

'I can see I'm getting no sense from you whatsoever.'

'Gee, likewise. Care to tell me how you got the diary?'

'Gee, care to tell me your involvement with Hodge?'

He buried his head in his hands. She was so bloody obstinate and so bloody clever, hard to believe he had met his match. 'At least tell me how you got Hodge on board with the diary.'

'That was simple. I just told him my father was prepared to pay zillions. May I go now?'

He indicated to the door. 'You are free to come and go under supervision.'

'Why under supervision?'

'Because you're not to be trusted, that's why! You withhold information, go snooping in Tom's quarters and cause worry to your father. And you know how I can tell when you're lying, when your mouth is moving.'

She held two fingers three centimetres apart to his eyes. 'You are that close to oblivion. Try locking me up again and I shall sing Abide with me until the cows come home.'

Indeed, that could be irritating. But underneath his veneer he was smiling, observing the plush of her hour glass figure storming onward with that ridiculous chop stick sprouting from her knot of tangled hair.

On the cantilevered deck of the sweeping stateroom where river-borne breezes caressed the matrix of the *Abracadabra* Lukas embraced his uncle Benjamin, a man with a knowing mind, face as hard as granite, and a voice to match.

'I pray we endure the battles to come.'

'You and Tom play no part in this, none whatsoever. Kate and Woo must be protected, do I make myself understood?'

Benjamin brought out his pipe, filled the contents with tobacco and struck a match on the rail. 'You forget we all serve our purpose, my son. And you are my son in heart and mind, no different from Thomas.'

'Woo is pregnant. She's just into her second trimester.'

'I thought she had gained some weight. Kate sends her love, thanks you for her birthday card but would prefer to see you.'

'I've been busy.'

'That excuse is rapidly becoming an old record. Now speak to me, tell me about Daphne?'

'You heard what she had to say, feisty and complicated that's what she is and ready to obliterate a man's senses.'

'Nevertheless, she is here.'

'I'm not entering into this discussion.'

'Then what do you propose? She has opened a locked door and gained a sneak preview of your life. If she is to stay-'

'Stay? You have to be kidding me.'

'Come on, my Lukas.' He fondly jabbed the stem of his pipe into the chest. 'This is Benjamin you talk to.'

'She hates me.'

'She likes you.'

'Like her strays.'

'Do you believe she would put up with your insolence if she did not need your help, your guidance?'

'Then what do I do? Show her my battle scars?'

'Show her the truth.'

'To become her pet snake, no doubt.'

'*Since you both hiss, she might be one too.*'

Lukas chuckled at Midnight's thoughts and looked at his watch, gathering he was now forty-five. 'How old do I look?'

'Now, now, have we not been through this before many times over? The worse is yet to manifest. I understand from Thomas he will keep an eye on her movements. Do you wish me to take second watch?'

'No, I can handle it.'

'There, problem solved.'

They moved back, pulling softly to the bar. Before them, sat on stools was Woo, Thomas and Frisk, and lounging at further distance was Daphne. The friction between her and her father was evident.

Benjamin performed as spokesman. 'Joshua Giddy, we know the name of our ancestor, a man who spent many years in Egypt as an archaeologist, a seeker of history and artefacts. He returned with his wife and son to England in 1876 and was introduced to a socialite, Elizabeth Whittle at a banquet held by Sir Erasmus Wilson. What do we know? We know in the summer of 1878 his body was found on the steps of St. Paul's. We also know his son and wife were taken in by his cousin, Edward Giddy, who chose to live a quiet and obscured existence. We know that much. What we do not know is why Elizabeth would copy the tale that is written in Latin on the walls of the Giddy home that once belonged to Edward.'

Frisk interjected. 'Who is this Marcus?'

The question was expected, the answer to which the common man was ignorant of such things, so methodical Benjamin replied the only way he knew how. 'Let me tell you a fascinating account taken from the annals of Tacitus, a scripter that lived in the time of a great warrior. I say great because she was a woman, Queen of the Iceni tribe of present day East Anglia, Boudicca or as the Victorians renamed her incorrectly as Boadicea. Tacitus claimed she was possessed of greater intelligence than often belongs to women. From what we know, when the Romans invaded Britain, they came with bounty to buy loyalty from the local tribes yet to the east, they were not to be bought like cattle. There had been conflict in minor parts but nothing as when Prasutagus, King of Iceni died. His wife, Boudicca, expecting her husband's wishes to be honoured by Nero himself, that she would inherit half her husband's estate, was instead flogged and her two daughters raped. So, she gathered her supporters and felled two cities, Colchester and London then marched onward to engage Suetonius and his Roman troops in battle. Tacitus writes of this battle, how 10,000 Roman troops slaughtered 80,000. History tells us of this outcome. But there could have been another. And this is where you must widen your gaze for over there,' and Benjamin pointed to Lukas, 'is living proof.'

Allowing the moment, Benjamin filled a glass with water and took a sip before recommencing. 'Edward, my ancestor who built a very fine house not only scribed the annals of Tacitus on the library walls but also of a lasting message. And it presents itself as the Goddess Andate, called upon for victory by Boudicca, a plea before the final battle took place. In her wisdom, Andate stilled the air and chose two men from opposing sides to settle the account. Unfortunately, from what can be ascertained they chose not to fight. The war played out to its conclusion but not without leaving a human message, carried in the veins of these two opposing sides. Every three or four hundred years two are born. Sometimes they choose to ignore each other, and sometimes their paths cross. Marcus is the opposite number to Lukas.' Benjamin smiled at Daphne who attracted his attention. 'You have the look of a woman who accepts what she sees because she is expecting to wake up.'

'I just find it absolutely incredible.'

'Ironically, that is not far from the truth. My brother, Simon, believed such a legend existed but sadly I did not, not until I saw with my own eyes. Be that as it may, it was your destiny, Daphne Frisk, your destiny to receive Elizabeth's story, your destiny to make it known to Lukas.' Benjamin indicated to Lukas. 'It was his destiny to tread a warrior's path, his destiny to meet you. Would you care to enlighten us how you received it?'

'Well,' she said, after lingering her eyes on Lukas, 'quite simply, I found it in a charity shop. Do I understand correctly that Edward lived like a hermit because he was like Lukas?'

'You have a quick mind, Daphne. You are correct.'

'Then the diary has nothing to do with a curse. I mean, Joshua was an archaeologist and in love with Elizabeth.'

'I am reminded of my father's words regarding Edward, how he longed for love himself. So it makes me wonder who Elizabeth really loved.' Benjamin took from his back pocket the diary and Daphne's eyes lit up. 'From what I can ascertain, her story is identical to that on the library walls as if she herself spent time to copy it, and from what I know of our history, why she would title her work the lady threads a needle for she was no seamstress.'

Thomas spoke. 'There I may be able to help. The street is famous as the site of the Bank of England…the bank itself is often called the old lady of Threadneedle Street and has been at its current location since 1734. It may be possible Joshua left a clue there to perhaps some hidden treasure.'

'Is that so,' Lukas said in amusement. 'The name of the street could also be a euphemism for its possible former name, Gropecunt Lane.'

Daphne harrumphed. 'Why am I not surprised you know that.'

'Why am I not surprised you said that?'

'I was merely stating-'

'No, you were insinuating.'

'Mr. Giddy, let me give you a piece of advice-'

'Never give anything to a man he cannot take to bed.'

To his quick wit and scandalous tongue, they all doubled up, could not speak for laughing, could not laugh without hitting each other. They would find little left of Daphne Frisk. Her tale-tale shape was on the stateroom's deck under a dark glum sky, her hair blowing free to the March winds, the chopstick drumming hard against her thigh.

Soft footed, Lukas joined her. Very quiet in his manner for in the calmness of respectability he might have numbered fifty years as well as thirty. 'I shouldn't have said that.'

'Actually, I thought it rather funny.' She leaned on the rail looking at the lights across the Thames, the buildings losing their top floors to the profound night sky. 'I have never seen London from the river. It really does look lovely, mysterious even. I suppose there's a certain freedom living and working from a yacht, lots of places to visit, no booking hotels, no worries in flight delays…do you ever encounter bad seas?'

'This little beauty eats rough weather thanks to Tom.'

'So when you take on a job, does Tom go with you?'

'Is this the inquisition?'

'I want to know more.'

'Well of course you do. Ben has excited the noodles in your brain.'

'And what excites yours?'

Uncomfortable with that, he pulled at his ear lobe and stuttered a bit. 'Err, um, I prefer to keep my private life out of this discussion.'

'Then may I ask why the Bank of England?'

'Why indeed.'

'So you think it means something else?'

'One can make many meanings from many things. The trick is to find the code in order to decipher the case. Or, perhaps there is no code, the story itself unimportant, just Joshua seeking his little patch of infidelity in the home of Edward.'

'Then why should Marcus be interested?'

'The same way Ben would be interested in anything connected to Boudicca.'

'But the story is widely known and I never read anything about a curse.'

'Yes, that crossed my mind too.'

'So do we dismiss the Bank of England?'

'Your father believes it's worth considering, perhaps a clue to be had on such an edifice.'

'Can I come with you?'

'Tom is going to take care of you until I return.'

'I see.'

'No, you don't see. That's your problem. You put your life in front of a ram.'

She turned to face him, lifting one hand to try and smooth back the windblown tangle of her hair, the tone of her voice full of emotion. 'Remember what Ben said. It was my destiny to receive Elizabeth's story, my destiny to make it known to you. It was your destiny to tread a warrior's path, your destiny to meet me.'

In quiet amazement he shook his head and retreated to the world beyond the *Abracadabra*, the streets of London, low places to creep through, high churches to fall down from. Formally known as Gropecunt Lane was not a very nice spot for late night expeditions and was not that kind of place in which many people were likely to take the air, or to frequent as an agreeable street which housed such a rambling edifice. It looked distinguished and proud but had no story to tell, nothing faintly painted or written on the walls to suggest a possible link with Boudicca.

He travelled on, once more looking at his watch, once more feeling that little bit older and once more thinking of Daphne Frisk. He was unable to explain it but she held a fascination, had so strong a tendency to check the conversation and to disconcert the very fabric of his soul.

Back on board the *Abracadabra,* Benjamin was the only one in the stateroom, but then that was to be expected. He sought to serve on the bench because he cherished the values that decent people shared, values such as the freedom to enjoy life without fear of crime. Frustrated by the erosion of these values which seemed to be under attack by Britain's depraved culture, and by many politicians, he recommended Lukas to Exit.

Taking a draw on his pipe, he looked up when Lukas walked in. 'Was anything to be found?'

Lukas went behind the bar and poured himself a pink gin and lemonade. 'There is nothing except the smell of confusion. Drink?'

'Not for me.'

'You know what I can't get my head around, why you never mentioned Elizabeth Whittle before.'

'What is there to mention, a brief liaison with Joshua, nothing more. However, to say I am unconcerned is an understatement. Marcus is your equivalent. Whatever powers you possess, he too, this I have told many times. You must tread carefully, my Lukas. Evil is not to be trifled and let us not forget we have other considerations. We have taken into our confidence a good father and his daughter. They must be separated from that evil.'

'So what do you suggest? I keep them on board until I wipe the man out?'

'No!' Benjamin was quick to say. 'Have no such thought in your mind. Do not stir the pond of evil. Put the diary up for auction, let him take what he so desires. There is nothing written which is not written on the library walls. I cannot think why Elizabeth would copy the annals of Tacitus unless she was involved with Edward.'

'Then why was Joshua killed?'

Benjamin shrugged. 'Another consideration is to say Elizabeth loved Joshua who had made an important find and in so doing kept Elizabeth from harm by installing her in Edward's home. There she bided her time in perhaps learning Latin.'

'You mentioned Joshua's wife and son was taken in by Edward, yup? So what happened to Elizabeth?'

'It was said she disappeared after Joshua's death, more reason to consider it was he whom she loved.'

'And yet there is no headstone for Edward in the cemetery.'

'We know Edward was a recluse. We know he spent a good portion of his life submerged in his anxieties. It is not unreasonable to assume he later took another name for the sake of Joshua's wife and son.'

'Why not assume Edward and Elizabeth were an item, yup? After Joshua's death, they disappeared into the sunset leaving Joshua's wife and son in the house.'

'Then one must beg the question, why?'

'I can think of one, such as Edward killed Joshua and so forced to take an escape route, two men loving the same woman. That makes more sense, especially if you consider the diary. Perhaps she never wrote it. Instead, it was Edward taking with him the writings he scribed on the walls.'

'My Lukas, you have a fine mind. Mine is ready for sleep. Now relieve my son from watching her door lest we have a mutiny on our hands.'

6

Lukas was patient, anonymous, and never made any demands through the night. He just sat by his door, ajar, keeping an eye on the corridor, keeping an ear to the ground with Midnight for company. Every rocking motion was a bandit, and every puff of wind was a ghost. At six he looked at his watch and crawled to his feet, pulling softly into her cabin. There she was in her daisy white pyjamas curled up like a hedgehog, sound asleep. He pulled the covers over her shoulders and left. Once again, he bent to the way of surveillance.

When Frisk stirred, wrapping his dressing gown round his thickened waist, he gave distant Lukas a nod and went to the galley, later returning with a cup of tea.

'May I ask a personal question?'

'Sure, what's on your mind?'

'Why have you aged so?'

'If I truly knew the answer to this cursed affliction, perhaps I could handle it better.'

'Then what you have must be a curse. I am not without understanding. Your entire family appear a mystery, locked in some kind of vendetta against evil. I wish I could help in some way.'

'You could keep an eye on Daphne…make sure she stays in her cabin until Tom comes on the scene.'

'I do apologise for her misdemeanours. She should not have rummaged through your cousin's drawers. But she wants to be involved as do I.'

'Does she always sing when she gets stroppy?'

'Even I have my crosses to bear.' Frisk crouched to face him. 'She needs a good man, someone to love and protect her.'

Lukas blinked, wondering if that was a smile or just his lips sliding off his teeth. 'If I'm not putting a bullet in someone's head, I'm shagging a prostitute.

49

Here, there, everywhere, this is my home from which to sally forth and strike at the world. Every so often I hide in my quarters to watch James Bond movies, listen to music, or read a book while I'm smoking pot. Does that sound like good husband material?'

'You certainly tell it like it is.'

'You said frank pays my fee.'

'Her head is lodged in the clouds, no idea about commerce, runs an unprofitable surgery for all sorts. If it's not rabbits, it's the damn gypsies. I blame her mother. She was a gypsy, damn lovely one at that, met her on a beach dancing around a bonfire. Yes, lovely woman, miss her lots…' The voice trailed off to silence. Frisk had leapt so suddenly from nostalgia to melancholy there seemed nothing else to say.

Lukas went inside his quarters drained of energy. He swept through the sumptuous lounge, ducked into his bedroom, drew the curtains, removed his clothing and then hopped under the shower smelling the freshness of desalinated sea water. It reminded him of radishes, earthy radishes freshly plucked from the ground. And again, his thoughts returned to Daphne Frisk who, probably in her anxiety to be part of a mystery, was creating a problem in order to get out of a problem. And then there was Frisk, the sadness and worry scorched in his eyes, the deep furrowed lines between the eyebrows. Lukas had told it like it was and yet as he heard himself saying it, there was an ounce of disbelief in his voice as though he still had a little left of dreaming.

To the many unanswered questions, his head hit the sack, no dreams, no thoughts just nothing at all, the eyes shut tight with his gun tucked under his pillow. And it seemed to him that he had slept for a passing moment when movement betrayed a presence.

Quickly, he ducked under the covers. 'Daphne, go back to your cabin!'

'I have an idea.'

'What time is it?'

'Never mind the time. I made you a ham sandwich and tea…oh and a nice cream cake from the fridge, lovely fresh cream oozing out of choux pastry, yummy.'

He considered she was almost as dangerous as Hodge. Even in rivalry there were agendas, subtle undercurrents which could hide lust or hatred, love or revenge. The chocolate éclair decided. 'You promise not to look?'

'Cross my heart and hope to die.'

Slowly, he peered above the sheets. Her silhouetted Kaftan sat with her back to him, a cup of tea in one hand, a plate piled high in the other. He grabbed a pair of rimless spectacles off the bedside and looked at his watch. 'So what's this idea that needs you to invade my privacy?'

'Well,' she said without peeking, 'the story begins in 1872 when a young civil engineer, Waynman Dixon went to Egypt to help build a bridge over the river Nile. Acting on a request by the Astronomer Royal of Scotland to carry out survey work at the pyramids, Dixon went to the Great Pyramid and started investigating one of its large internal rooms, the so-called Queen's Chamber, and discovered a tunnel. Six feet into the tunnel he found three relics. His brother, John Dixon arrived in Cairo a few weeks later and was given the relics. Now we come to the best part.'

'Oh good,' he muffled, unsure where this was heading, eating and drinking with the ferocity of a famished hound.

'Cleopatra's Needle had been presented to Britain in 1819 by the ruler in gratitude for past victories but our Government refused to pay for the transport. So, nearly half a century later Sir Erasmus Wilson, you remember him, the one who held the banquet where your ancestor met Elizabeth Whittle, he put up ten thousand pounds to bring the Needle to London, and John Dixon was given the job of arranging its passage. Thus in 1878, the time Joshua Giddy had been in England for two years, John Dixon had designed and built the monument's pedestal on the embankment.'

'And you think these so-called relics from the Great Pyramid are buried there.'

'Maybe, maybe not…anyway, leading on from there, Dixon put two jars under that Needle, full of present day things, sort of like a time capsule. Now what if Joshua knew what Dixon had buried? What if he left a clue before he got killed? Perhaps Joshua was killed because of it. The lady threads a needle?'

'And you came up with this all by yourself?'

She puffed herself up. 'Yes.'

'I suppose your complicated brain would have thought it too simple to keep whatever it was within reach.'

'Eh?'

'Joshua or Dixon would hardly have buried anything valuable under a 68 foot high obelisk which weighs 180 tons that's placed in a position for visiting tourists. They were in the business of digging up relics, not hiding them.'

'Well really, that's gratitude for you.'

'No, fair dues, your research was faultless.'

'Then how about letting me see you?'

'Nope.'

'Why?'

'Because I say so.'

'You're hiding something.'

'Gee, how did you guess?'

She sighed and said with a despairing voice, 'You know you're being terribly selfish. I go to all this trouble, make you a nice sandwich, pinch Tom's cream cake from the fridge and this is what I get, looking at a painting, a very nice painting as a matter of fact. Is that Boudicca?'

'No, it's the Goddess Andate.'

'Have you met her?'

'Can we move on?'

'It's obvious you have some form of skin complaint. I see it all the time, not that I'm saying you're an animal.'

'If your intention is to cure me then you're under misapprehension.'

'Well, what about quid pro quo. You let me see you and I'll let you into a little secret.'

His interest had been aroused. 'What sort of secret?'

'I promise faithfully you will like it.'

Would it be that bad? After all, he was only sixty-six with all his hair and teeth. Some women preferred the older man, though usually that came with life's experiences, of which he had much with whores.

He put aside his cup and plate, rushed his fingers through his hair and unbuttoned his pyjama top. On second thoughts he buttoned up his pyjama top, his chest not at its prime. 'Okay,' he said and she turned. But her eyes seemed to see and to tell so much, were fixed upon him with an expression that he could not bear, a figure so ancient that she looked away. 'It's alright, I understand.'

'No…no…it's not alright.' She moved abruptly and drew back the curtains with such force it was almost as if she was angry at herself. 'In less than forty-eight hours I have been told of a legend that is just too incredible to believe and then suddenly I see a man who, not so long ago was young with rich black hair, now virtually as old as my father, if not older. How old are you?'

'Old enough to give you a spanking.'

'Does that include the removal of my knickers?'

He burst out laughing. She had taken upon herself to conduct a dangerously bad game, had asserted her will over his and now stood with indifference to his condition.

'Oh, Lukas, let's not be mistrusting of each other. The situation is intolerable. I can't go anywhere on this boat…oh, excuse me, yacht, without being attached to Tom.'

'Quid pro quo, Daphne.'

'The ring,' she said. 'I use it as a toggle when I wear a scarf round my neck.'

The exchange of information was unequal as it was unfair. 'Are you joking?'

'No, I really do wear a scarf round my neck.'

'I don't care if you wear a bloody giraffe round your neck. You faithfully promised I would like it.'

'Oooh, excuse me, Mr. Detective. I just added a jigsaw piece to your immense puzzle. Why are you so grumpy all the while? No, don't tell me, let me guess. You're afraid a woman might get into that head of yours, turn your world upside down…and we can't have that, can we? Who knows, you might find some civility rolling off your tongue.'

He took a deep breath and peeled off his rimless spectacles. 'I am in real terms thirty years old,' he said in hushed tones and measured words. 'There is no other narrative more suitable to describe the condition, no set pattern, it just happens and the older I become the weaker I become, my strength considerably declining every hour. Soon my body will take on the usual ailments associated with old age…and, no doubt, I shall be screaming my nuts off for there is the rub. I reach a point where I can literally feel death at my door before the reverse happens, an immediate effect.'

'An immediate effect?'

'She's deaf as well as nosy.'

Surreptitiously, Lukas pushed Midnight under the covers lest Daphne's interests widen. 'Mostly unconscious when it happens, I wake back to my age.'

'When did it first occur?'

'So, I'm to be dissected by a vet?'

'I'm sorry we got off to a bad start,' she said wistfully and took a spot on the bed. 'But I was angry too. I thought to myself, who is this man that my Father admires, the one who stands aloof and aloft…certainly aloft for I would need a soap-box to be at your level but not in the way of intelligence.'

'So, you have more brains than me?'

'I know I have brains, how much you have is left for conjecture.' She smiled with an air of the very kindest patronage and took his hand like a mother leading a child out of the wilderness. 'You know, I have a very good listening ear and besides I can keep secrets, live by the same code as a family practitioner. What you say is said in confidence.'

'In confidence.'

'Yes, not the confidence in the belief of oneself but the other confidence as in confide to someone.'

'Gee, as if I need a language lesson.'

'Actually, what you need is to loosen up.' She lifted her skirts and hiked over his pillows to get behind and massage his neck. 'I do this for my Father. It helps a lot to relax the tension.'

Oh that felt good, the squeeze of comfort. The strategy worked. 'I was fifteen years old when it first occurred. Christmas morning, we had opened our presents then suddenly a sickness as if I was going to throw up. Ben noticed. He took me into the library and told me about the curse, hours later I got a taste of things to come. Kate almost fainted. Tom blinked a lot, stuttered too. He does that when he's lost for words so I knew he was upset. I don't think Ben could face me, not properly. He disappeared on Boxing Day and returned a different man. We don't know what triggers it off, if anything. There's no set pattern. Sometimes I can go a whole year and sometimes it can happen twice in one month. Ben once said both sides of war are ugly. And I think Andate just reminds me how painful war is.'

'This Marcus, does he suffer the same?'

'There is nothing written about my counterpart.'

'Mrs Granger, her son brought in his pet tortoise. He wanted to know why its shell cracked in places. I hadn't a clue to be honest until I discovered he was shoving it down the slide, bang, wallop, landing on concrete. Poor little devil was too young to comprehend animals have feelings too.'

'There is nobody I can ask.' His gaze switched to the painting on the bulkhead wall. 'She, no doubt comprehends the madness of her curse. Pity she forgot to pass it on.'

'Why do you have a dormouse?'

'Why do boys have pet tortoises? Your father said you had a menagerie at your place.'

'He would consider two rabbits a menagerie. I love him very much. But sometimes he can be overly protective. Ideally, he would like to see me married off but I've never found a man that could meet my shopping list.'

'Do you go shopping a lot?'

'No, can't be bothered, too much heartache.'

'Ah, shopping list as in the qualities of a man…so, err, um, as a matter of interest you understand, what's on your shopping list?'

'Above all he must love me for what I am, be honest in the relationship and kind, especially to animals, naturally, because I love animals too, and brains would certainly go a long way.'

That sounded good. 'Anything else?'

'Oh, the usual, like coming home for supper, putting bread on the table.'

That sounded bad. 'How much bread?'

'It's not so much the bread but the job. For instance, an oil worker is away on the rigs, or someone in the army can be called up for duty, dreadful occupation, on the other hand it can be very appealing to be a crusader for justice, although, sometimes men can be so mind-numbingly sanctimonious, or even boring, a non-stop talker about victories and medals.'

'Am I boring?'

'Gracious, far from it.' To his disappointment she stopped the massage and bounced round to face him. 'You're arrogant and rude, completely off your rocker. What man in their right mind would wear a jumper with the words die another day.'

'The same could be said about you. What woman in their right mind wears a sixties Kaftan, Bugs Bunny slippers and a chopstick in her hair?'

'Well, the Kaftan is very comfortable and I'm very attached to my slippers. They were given to me by a little girl's mother who was so grateful I saved her cat. Do you know what the chopstick is for?'

'Are you offering to tell me?'

'I thought you never gave in?'

'A bit like you then.' He held her gaze, said nothing further, his face calm and patient, almost solemn, but inside his head he was throwing buckets of water onto burning hot coals and considered every easy choice today would create a problem for tomorrow. But so fierce for the want of her, he swallowed hard and the words just popped out of his mouth. 'Is 66 too old for you?'

'What does your heart say?'

'I don't know. It's beating too loud.'

Closeted in his quarters, hidden from general view, she dropped her reserve and let fall her Kaftan, confirming she hid her light under a bushel. She held out her arms for him to drink in his fill of the sight of her, those virgin breasts that came long after school.

Sex deserved its pageant while Midnight skittered across the luxuriant carpet. Against his advanced years, her breasts were firm and responsive, greedy for the pleasures he was bringing. This was a first. In a whore's arms he would avoid the reinforcements of tenderness, leaving the mind to conjure up an extravaganza of images, rampaging vividly down. Their lips and tongues coupled, moaning, moving slow, moving fast, and shifting, laughing in their tangles, exploring in their needs. He would reduce her to a quivering shake, would stand like Hercules and watch the liberation explode upon her face. It was raw. It was passion. It was simply uncontainable.

As the sound of Big Ben echoed across the waters, he left her to laze in the afterglow of contentment, the close of his bedroom door felt deceitful. Lodging a reefer between his lips, he lit up and moved on with a fragmented loop of unease. Like a delicate flame, he had burned brightly long enough to be engulfed by a woman who had left an indelible mark upon his soul. And that frightened him.

A cold wind pushed suddenly down the deck, his grey hair lifted up as more clouds scuffed in from the south, swelling and darkening. He leaned against the rail and considered how his choices were mapped that day. One year upon another he had pursued garbage, snatched tit-bits for self-gratification, drew curtains and squeezed back pain. What unmerciful hard reflections those moments were.

'Tell me your thoughts.'

Lukas turned to face Benjamin, a distinct figure that radiated strength even in age. 'Do you know his full name?'

'Marcus Metellus.'

'And you thought not to tell me?'

'What to tell in a name when greater things occupy your mind, such as Daphne.'

'She knows more than she's telling.'

'Perhaps words are a better seducer.'

'I need no lectures on women, their predictable habits.' He returned his gaze to the darkening sky, the wind lifting the water from the river and flinging it against the side of the *Abracadabra*. 'A man knows where he stands with a prostitute.'

'So whores are your answer, a transaction which conspires to harden your heart?'

'You forget they embrace their position as do I. We're comfortable in that thought. Sure, their remuneration is money. Mine is sexual gratification. No better arrangement.' Who was he kidding? With these idle words passing through his lips, the mobile had trembled in his pocket. Glancing now at the screen through his rimless spectacles, he answered leisurely to Charnel.

The reply came swift. 'I think it's time we met, old boy.'

It took a second to register the caller. 'Couldn't agree more.'

'On the steps of St. Paul's in one hour.'

The tinged of apprehension increased a thousand fold. He faltered, muttered something inaudible then said to Benjamin without due care and attention, 'I promised to meet an old friend. Best I see Tom to keep an eye on Daphne.'

'Woo has turned his world upside down.'

'Has she told him?'

'Alas, you kept your line open when you informed me. I think he worries about his toys.'

'His toys have saved my life on many occasions.'

'Then tell him so, offer a kindred mind.'

Uncertainty nagged in the steps of Lukas, limping on like a wet piece of linen hung out to dry. At the entrance to the galley door, he watched Thomas poke around as though on a secret mission, tight-lipped as a gunboat commander.

'Tom, I respected her wishes.'

'Well bully for you. In less than a minute you filled the gap between rhetoric and reality.' Sharp in his shoes, one hand to his whiskers and the pan beating time with the other, Thomas continued. 'We never keep secrets from each other, never, and I find you plotting behind my back. I'm her husband for Christ sake. I should have been the first to know she was pregnant. Even at home you had a knack for getting yourself in the shit. Personally, I ought to wring your sodding neck.'

'Well unless you pretended to understand Japanese, she told it straight before you married her.'

'But not now, not now, Luke…now is not a good time.'

'It will never be a good time if you continue to think like that. Have you told her to get an abortion?' In the short silence that followed, Lukas noticed the eyes had become as bleak as blue marbles. 'Tom, for God's sake, you're putting your marriage at risk. Woo never planned the pregnancy, it just happened.'

'She was on the pill, never missed a day. I know I sound like a bigot and all that but-'

'But, but, but… I hate buts.' Lukas embraced him long and hard, felt a return of the familiar, protective love that he had always had for his cousin. 'You came into Ben's library and said we make a good team, yup? Gave me reasons not to blow out my brains, built this vessel which gave us purpose, and look how well our purpose has served. Now I'm begging the same, for your baby's sake, for Woo, for your marriage, give the life you both created a chance, like you gave me.'

7

Nearing a building that rose from the ashes of 1666, Lukas was on the hunt, his ears tuned, his eyes searching, his sixth sense reaching ahead as the rain came down in drizzles. The real prize was there, Marcus Metellus, a dark skinned man that looked beyond reproach in a white robe and turban, something that suited him dangerously well, waiting under the canopied steps of Wren's masterpiece. Close by, couples kissing hungrily for love.

In spite of his piteous condition and near prospect of death, Lukas confronted his opposite number. In the game of uncivil relations, he refused to take the proffered hand.

'We can stand here all night and make small talk,' Marcus obliged in an educated accent, 'or we can agree to a truce.'

'How can a man make a truce with a stranger?'

'I am not your enemy.'

'Neither are you friend.'

'You know, I was like you…angry, bitter, cut off my hand for that is what it amounted. It was my choice to make, not anyone else's. I am not complaining, you understand. Shall we walk? I so dislike skulking in the shadows.' Marcus moved on in the sodden misery of downpour. To his side was Lukas, the knife tucked up his sleeve nice and sharp. 'Now where were we? Ah, yes, skulking. I did that a lot in the early years, thanks to a fool of a father who tried to convince me life was not so bad. If only he could see me now, flowing into the mist of fullness to find the joy in my life.'

'And your mother?'

'My dear chap, you really are without a clue. She died in childbirth. They all do, a trade off or rather a gift for Andate, and they all cohort with weak men who just want to get rid of their sons. My own conspired with Benjamin to cage me like an animal, worse than an animal, no sunlight, not even the sound of rain, all of which had nearly driven me to suicide and then where would we be…you dead, me dead, the curse caries on. Only now am I able to think calmly of that terrible incident…though I am never wanting of blessed relief.'

'Perhaps I can oblige?'

Marcus halted their progress, turned to face Lukas and smiled as if he anticipated such a reply, opening his arms to accommodate. At this hour, in this situation, the offer was hard to refuse. The blade sliced through cloth but the chest did not peel open and Lukas stood confused, an event he had not foreseen. Nothing had prepared him for that. Perhaps he homed in on the wrong chap. Perhaps he should've gone to Specsavers.

The hedonist had become unsmiling. 'Now it is my turn.'

For the moment, Lukas would keep alive and stepped back into a doorway. 'Which is versed in cunning ways?'

'Look at yourself, old man. What are you, seventy? I should know and remember what I was doing forty hours ago. Your body turns to corruption after I kill. Every time I kill, you receive the impact. We are linked, bound by the same rules.'

'What rules when I stand before a younger man?'

'You know nothing what was written by the will of Andate. Benjamin will not tell you. Why should he? Thomas is the son he protects, the last of the Giddy to continue the line. Did he say we cannot destroy each other? Did he say if one dies the other dies too? Yes, false promises and hopes coming from your silence. Andate punishes me far more severely, a lesson in humility, ah!' With that he spat his contempt at the pavement. 'She provokes me beyond endurance. The people you kill are no different from the scum I obliterate. Hodge was a piece of scum. We had a bargain, thought he could hold me to ransom so it suited my purpose to send him a message. As it so happened it sent a message to you.' Marcus went quiet, folded his arms and leaned against the return wall in the doorway. 'I know much of your history. I made it my business to know. When that diary came to my attention, I asked one question. How did she get it?'

'She found it in a charity shop. Why did you want it?'

'As I told you, I make it my business to know. I am not denying my interest, less so Daphne Frisk, a nice woman to leave in her shallow accomplishments.

But listen, old boy. It's brought us together, not a bad thing. You take great risk with your life at my expense. Will I wake to live another day, not if you continue to take chances. I can do without the worry, selfish, I know, but I want the love of a woman, have children. I am the last of my line, thirty years old, sick of slaughter. Which is the worse for their curse, you or me?'

'So let me get this straight. You kill at my expense yet when I kill it has nil effect on you. Methinks I am the worse for their curse.'

'I kill to remain sane for a short blessed relief, the only way to get Andate out of my head.' Marcus showed a round blue mark on his right palm, the dark side of a full moon. 'I was given her sickly stain which runs in my veins like a demonic virus. You were given a pet to stroke. I say again which is the worse for their curse? Unless you submit to the truth, you will be forever in doubt. I bore my chest now bear me a measure of good faith. Besides, I will be kinder to a weak old man. Extend your arm instead of your heart, the blade will not hurt.'

The words were hypnotic, plucked at his vanity, played on his fears. There was reason for Lukas to retreat, reason for him to stay. He stepped forward with some hesitation, and instead of his arm bore his covered chest, closing his eyes in trepidation, a prayer heavenward maybe answered and he might just live to die another day. He felt the impact, the thud of the blade's hilt ending its journey. The only pain was the expansion of his lungs, holding his breath in anticipation of death. Another second, a further minute, it was a matter of necessity as truth rendered judgement beneath swollen clouds.

'You see. We are one split in two.'

'An ancient curse is the sum of many parts.'

'Together we can explore them, find a way to end this without wishing each other dead.'

'You believe Joshua Giddy found the answer?'

'A fool, like our fathers who believed he could break the curse by submitting himself to Andate on the steps of another deity.'

'It makes no sense. Joshua was not like me.'

'Another detail, another omission…best you enquire further. Until then, I am soaked.'

Lukas was left drenched and redundant, spitting a loose tooth to the ground. His mood was as dark as the sky. His glum despondency matched the leaden drops streaming across the pavement. He considered what had been said and sensed some truth while making his wearily way back to the *Abracadabra* moored alongside Cleopatra's Needle. And though it was hard to eradicate the bloody taste in his mouth, he boarded respectfully silent, unsure in which direction to take. His heartbeat was returning to normal, though it would never slow down completely, not while his mind was a jumbled affair.

'Lukas.' Woo advanced in a state of flutter. 'Everyone gone…Daffannee gone, Flisk gone, he say goodbye, took Tum and Ben for dinner.'

Lukas moved on, his saturated clothes clinging with a damp embrace about his limbs. 'Did they give a reason for leaving?'

'Tum say case solved.'

'Now wouldn't that be something.' Sweeping into his quarters, trying to catch his breath, he removed his sodden clothes.

'Ben say you go meet Marcus.'

'Ben celebrates my death too soon.'

Woo threw him a towel as well as a glance of piercing, anxious encouragement as she side-stepped in front of him. 'Tell?'

'I shall probably die any moment, my life expendable and why not. Who am I to carry on the Giddy line?' And it all welled up as he sat despairingly on the leather sofa in his underpants, the smell of Daphne lingering on, and a further reminder of lost dreams. 'What's the point of living? I don't live anyway. If I'm not killing, I'm either playing cards with whores or closing my eyes in pretence of a woman loving me for what I am. And if I'm not talking to Midnight, I'm talking to myself.'

Woo knelt in front of him, drooped beneath those dispiriting words. 'Wha' happen to make you sad?'

'Ben lied to me…he damn well lied to me. If Marcus dies, I die too. We are interwoven like two ships roped together in a storm.'

'No, Ben would no lie.'

'I saw the truth, Woo. I thrust my knife into the man's chest as he stood with a smirk on his face.'

'He trick you.'

'No trick. I felt the blade go deep. I couldn't believe it, no, I just couldn't believe it. But I had to know, I had to know so I let him do the same. I thought, this is it, the end is nigh. But here I am. I got a hole in my favourite jumper to prove it. I'm an aging commodity…just an old man, my strength diminishing, out there, in the rain acting like a bloody fool. Marcus knew everything about me and I knew nothing about him, absolutely nothing, diddlysquat.'

'Think wha' you say. Ben save you…kill his brother to save you. Oh, he be hurt bad you feel tha' way.'

No one could condemn him as severely as he condemned himself. 'It's my fault. I should have gone into things more deeply, took up Latin, read the walls for myself and looked for Marcus, instead of accepting my lot, the fearless defender. No, Ben wouldn't put forward his son for Exit, too damn risky but he certainly had his eye on me. Who was I kidding? I'm nothing more than a paid assassin. It makes me worse than him.'

'Blame is an inconsequential factor.'

Lukas turned his sight to Midnight, nosing her way through the humps and bumps of his dishevelled pile on the floor. Only now had he realized his furry heartbeat was near to death herself. He picked her up. 'I'm sorry, Midnight. I was so absorbed, I never considered you in my breast pocket.'

'While you live, I live.'

'Then indeed, three are interwoven.' He returned his gaze at Woo, the very picture of feminine health, a perfectly beautiful nose, expressed her preference for Thomas. 'There you were,' he said, sweeping back her shiny dark fringe, 'Sydney Harbour lost in transition. You looked very pretty in that spotted dress. Your eyes were glued to Tom and he wasn't paying an ounce of attention, tripped over a women's basket and fell head long into your lap.'

She laughed. 'He never ask me. I follow him to tha' ice-cleam stand.'

'Ah, but what you didn't know is that he'd already seen you the day before. Luke, he said, see that Japanese girl, that's for me. I told him to go for it. Then he did his stuttering bit. Wwwhat if she snubs me.' He made her laugh again. 'I told him best you don on your braided cap and impress her with your brass buttons.'

'If you had tha' chance, would you change his mind?'

'He's just scared, that's all, Woo. Sometimes men are like little kids, they say things they don't really mean. He's scared the baby will turn out like me, scared of losing you, scared it will change everything.'

'Babies do change everything. I never plan for tha' to happen but I want baby. I want baby to have best chance ever.'

'If you think roses around a cottage door in a provincial town will give that best possible chance then you're very much mistaken.' He lifted her chin. 'That's the rub, isn't it, Woo? What if Mr. Scary comes out to play?'

'I worry wha' happen to Tum.'

'If you make him leave this vessel, you're condemning your marriage. He made it perfectly clear and you understood this vessel was his life. This is a wonderful experience for children, see the world and meet different people. Sometimes I wish for my own place, walk around naked or plant some bulbs but it comes at a greater price. There's no freedom anymore if you set your roots down in one spot. Anyway, what difference does it make?' Lukas gave a sigh, and for reasons obvious placed his hand on her belly, felt the beating heart inside her womb. There was no curse here, no threat of her life being taken.

'I say 9th September.'

'Best guess?'

'Good guess.'

The farce of nursing a broken heart, pulling his life back together was all too familiar. He patted Woo fondly on the head and rose slowly to his feet with a shiver. 'I'm going to take a shower.'

The water raced hot, scolding his skin as if by doing so he could rid himself of every vestige of old age. Approaching seventy-four, hair loss was another sign, coming away in droves, the inevitability of the unacceptability. And suddenly, the crying he was holding into his throat came away into his hands, his body racked with sobs, all the grief and misery refusing to be suppressed, refusing to go unacknowledged.

Fighting the almost irrepressible inclination to look at his mirrored reflection, he donned on a jumper. This one had the words *licence to kill*. It was acknowledged that he had a weird sense of humour, that he likened himself to James Bond, the adventurer turned rebel, going head to head with one or many adversaries. Though, at this point in time, he certainly never looked the part. His height had diminished by three inches, his vision impaired and importing moreover a near bald wrinkled facsimile peppered with aging spots.

In the stateroom behind the mirrored bar, there he sat, taking his wine, and taking a good deal of it, trapped in memories of a time long ago before his world was turned upside down. Benjamin's tales of Boudicca had him in awe, her bravery and feats of endurance. His younger years grew to become the thrill of walking a perilous route separated from the enemy only by the wit of his mind. If he drowned himself, then the lake spat him out and if he jumped off a roof, the tree broke his fall. He reasoned, quite rightly, that his uncle's anger would be swallowed up by his larger anxiety on finding him again near to death.

Then his eyes lifted when Thomas and Benjamin emerged, cheerful and quick with ruddy complexions, shaking off rain.

'He paid us a hundred grand, Luke.' Thomas waved the cheque under the nose, a profound lack of interest showed. 'Come on, my man, give us a smile. No more passengers, got rid of Hodge, case solved, huh?'

To Benjamin, nothing but death would achieve such a look, bereft of substance, white and blood drained with angry dark eyes. 'You met Marcus.'

'We had an interesting dance in the rain. I tried to kill him on my wobbling feet, he tried to kill me on his strong ones, of course, we wouldn't be having this inane conversation if he was dead because I would be dead too.'

Benjamin scarcely knew what to say. He drew on his pipe and let the smoke drift from his nostrils, keeping his stare fixed upon Lukas who could hear the pounding of his heart. It would pound even louder yet.

'Dad, what's going on?'

'Son, we need to be alone.'

'No,' Lukas gruffed, 'Tom stays.'

With a weighted and worried look on his granite face, Benjamin opened up. 'I wept that Christmas, unsure what to do, unsure of many things, turning to the one man who could possibly help. But his son was beyond redemption.'

'You conspired to cage him like an animal.'

'No, never, neither conspired. He was kept from self-harm, and safe from those to whom he would harm. I soon understood the parallel between you and him. He had chosen his way of life, triggering your affliction, rendering your choices invalid. Remember what I once told you? There are always opposite sides in war, both are ugly. Had he been decent, he would have curbed his inner lust, sought for help and your life would have been blessed, a life without whores.'

'Are you telling me he started it first?'

'That is the way.'

'Andate's way, her to provoke a young man in the fullness of youth…what does she want, that we should work together to resolve these differences?'

'He kills without remorse.'

'He kills because she has poisoned his blood with her mark and he in turn poisons me.'

'It will be him to convert you if you think that way.'

'What way shall I think? He wants out, believes there's an answer to end our curse.'

'Do you honestly think he seeks a settlement, a resolution when he has the world at his fingertips? The diary has exposed your position, has roused his appetite for a solution to his dilemma.'

'The curse is both our dilemma. If I get killed, so does he!'

'He is the master of illusion as he is the master of deception. If you allow him, it will be your loss and his gain, advantage to do as he pleases, as he continues to do as he pleases. Do not be tempted to consider otherwise.'

'No! He could have done as he pleased this very night. I could hardly throw a 12lb bowling ball in the air let alone take on a fifteen stone bloke.'

'And that is exactly what he intended you to think. You have been beyond his reach, now another threat is at hand. He does not want the curse to end.'

'I'm not sitting hear listening to this crap!'

Benjamin banged his fist on the bar. 'Your anger should not be directed at me but at your enemy! If you let him, he will lull you into false security. Already I see this happening. A successful parasite never drains his host!'

Chinking glass summoned their attention at Thomas. 'You two have got to calm down. Everything was hunky-dory until the diary popped up. That has to tell us something. First, there is nothing in there to indicate a solution to end the curse. Secondly, and more relevant, Joshua was not cursed. We all know the history of Joshua and his family. This has to be about something else.'

Lukas let his gaze return to Benjamin who was puffing out smoke rings, a habit he inherited from his days as a judge. 'Why withhold this information? Why offer my name to Exit?'

'I wanted you to live, not hide as Edward had done. He spent his life scribing the walls of his affliction.'

'Did he scribe the loss of women who gave birth to cursed bastards like me? Another detail you failed to mention.'

That alerted Thomas. 'Forgive me if I take Luke's side, but that piece of information would have been handy to know before my wife fell pregnant!'

'It has never been known for two pairs born in the same era.'

'There's always a fffffff...' A struggle was underway, subsided as quickly as it had started. 'First! I am more disposed to anger than I can tell you, Dad.'

'What happened with Daphne?' Lukas asked. The question was directed to any or all but eyes fell away. 'Tom?'

'Sorry to see her go?'

'I was just surprised, that's all.'

'They paid for two days and two days they got, mystery solved, case closed.'

Lukas slugged back his drink. 'I'm going to bed.'

The empty spaces swallowed him up. He dropped into her cabin, his eyes dark pools of worry. There had to be something he was missing. No matter which thread of thought he plucked at, they all seemed to lead back to Daphne Frisk. He stooped to pick up her forgotten pyjamas and buried his face in the smell of her. The imprint of Daphne was here, the effects of her spirit everywhere. He wanted to feel her arms about him, he wanted to hear her voice but most of all he wanted resolution.

Faint, exhausted, worn out, almost dead, in the end he realized his quarters was the best place, a bed to lie on like a dog unconscious of earthly things, a spot to hide and smother his cries so that waking would be a moment of gratitude, deliverance miraculously gained.

Nonetheless, between this sleeping and waking, Lukas had a re-occurring delusion, faded and diminished hourly, stark images stealing their way over the brown ground like threads of silver. And a voice laced in French spoke his name.

'Lukas Giddy, my surroundings have grown quietly older and older together. Dead you would think me, know the truth of Benjamin and my cursed son.'

In these hallucinations he looked through windows and saw dry walls, the black trees bending in the wind, of witch-doomed warriors at certain landmarks about a valley that was certainly older than Christendom.

And again, the same words haunted him. 'Lukas Giddy, my surroundings have grown quietly older and older together. Dead you would think me, know the truth of Benjamin and my cursed son.'

8

Lukas stared as if hypnotized. He was not concerned that Benjamin felt a need to return home. That seemed acceptable and measured no more than two points on his worry scale. It was the pyjamas Daphne left behind that puzzled him. So what? She had money to burn. Frisk had his daughter back. Hodge was dead. Marcus had no interest in her. The answer had to lie elsewhere.

Then it all crystallized when he considered the diary, and the extent to which she would go in order to obtain it. Abruptly, he turned on his heels and swung out of the port-holed doors and with him his thoughts, all small details now twice sharp. The way Benjamin had said only what was necessary, and how Thomas clumsily eluded his questions in an unsettled interlude.

The captain of industry had his head buried in the navigational screen when Lukas charged into the bridge house. 'She stole the diary and made a quick escape!'

'We don't need it, Luke.'

'I damn well knew it! I want it.'

'*You want a grin and tonic.*'

'No, what I want is the diary.'

'*The opportunities of the past do not come to the future.*'

'I refuse to believe that.'

'Well believe this.' Thomas broke the bubble of Midnight's thoughts. 'There is nothing in that diary that's not on the library walls so stop getting you're knickers in a twist.'

'And that makes it alright? What do you think she's going to do? Return it to her knitting basket and forget it exists?'

Thomas went to the percolator and poured two coffees, his calm exterior wounding the angry air. 'It's all under control.'

'Like you control Woo?'

'Come on, Luke. That was below the belt. If there was one small benefit, it was that she made up with her father. Besides, you were hardly in a fit state to absorb anything, pissed as a newt.'

Lukas exhaled slowly, recognizing it was not really the diary he wanted but a reason to see Daphne again. 'Okay, take us to Agde.'

'Huh?'

'I'm going to see Marcus's father.'

'He's alive?'

'Apparently so.'

Thomas stepped up to the chart table and picked up a pair of dividers. 'And this information, how did you come by it?'

'In dreams, over and over again, the same one, and I'm not in the mood to defend these dreams only to seek out the truth. On a much lighter subject, is Daphne's intention to auction the diary?'

'Dad said it was the most sensible thing to do.'

'Now it's my turn to say you plot behind my back.'

Thomas turned to face him. 'Luke, you should watch your mouth and get your head in gear. Not that I agree with Dad holding back info, his reasons were solid, not deceitful. He was pretty upset and so were we all, Marcus popping up like that is not something to cherish.'

'Marcus was convinced Joshua was afflicted.'

'So he got his story wrong…maybe Dad got his story wrong…you know how stories can be embellished over time. But we have some facts, Luke. Facts are what we go on. I checked. Joshua Giddy was found dead on the steps of St. Paul's.'

'And Edward Giddy?'

'Nothing, unable to get a handle on him…it's not inconceivable these two men swapped places. Maybe it was Edward who fell in love with Elizabeth. Maybe Joshua was after her too. Maybe Joshua's son deliberately passed on false information…lots of maybes.'

Lukas glanced beyond the glass of the bridge where the rain came down in drizzles, feeling compelled to agree. 'Yes, lots of maybes. So what makes Marcus think there's a way to end this curse?'

Thomas shrugged. 'You know Dad's feeling on that.'

While Lukas bit his fingernails working the windmills of his mind, Thomas cheerfully entered the new co-ordinates into his magnificent creation. 'What if,' Lukas finally spoke, 'there's a way to break the curse. I mean, when does it stop? Does it stop when there are no more of us?'

'Why do you think I didn't want kids? Inside Woo is my child, a child who will continue the bloodline. What does that make me?'

Lukas lowered his eyes, now in full possession of his senses. 'It affected you badly, didn't it?'

'It affected everyone, Luke. Mum was beside herself. She couldn't stop crying. And Dad was never the same. I won't be the same if Woo dies.'

'Woo is not going to die. Now stop being a prick.'

'I like being a prick.' Thomas smiled, but the worry was still defined in his eyes. 'Do you remember what happened that night?'

If Lukas was truthful, he remembered it all. 'My bag was packed in a hurry that I do remember…I wanted to bring my teddy. Strange, the things one remembers, I really loved that teddy.'

'You did bring your teddy. You threw it in the river the next day.'

'Did I?' Lukas shrugged and took a pew in the captain's seat, cupping his hands round a warm mug. 'He wouldn't say where we were going, not that it would've made a difference. Kate smelt of roses and tucked me in bed with hot chocolate. I can't remember how long after when he woke me. God I was cold, the stingy nettles got me and he kept pulling me along, shouting, telling me not to cry…so what, when you're six years old you can't help it…the water was freezing and then the lights of the house behind Ben giving him a holy appearance, I thought he was an angel…and did I feel relief when Kate dragged me into her arms.'

'Do you feel any loss?'

'Not really. I never knew my mother and to be honest I can't remember much of him.'

'That night, it was your cries Mum heard. Dad held no reservations in stopping him. His aim was slightly off, intended to maim rather than kill. I was looking from my bedroom window, couldn't see much at first. Mum got you out of the river and Dad was bending over Simon sobbing his heart out. But something else happened that night. Look, this may sound a bit crazy but I swear that moon shone brighter than I'd ever seen it before and it looked one hell of a lot closer.'

'It was Andate. She sent me Midnight. I woke up in the morning and there she was, right on my nose. I shall never forget it. She asked me to get her a grape.'

'We thought it was your imagination.'

'You must have known something was different. For a start she lived beyond her time.'

'See, that's the funny part. Dad said you kept finding new dormice and we all accepted it. Hell, what did I know? Just because I was five years older doesn't make me the expert.'

'I see. So you sort of pretended until I turned into an old man at fifteen, yup?'

'Couldn't have put it better myself.'

'Does Ben ever talk about Simon?'

'Never has, not since that night. Mum did say he was mad, not right in the head because he honestly believed you were cursed. As it so happened he was right.' Thomas turned to his chart table. 'Anyway, you have a decent family, one more on the way.'

Since the conversation came to an automatic pause, Lukas crossed his legs in the perfect stillness and tried to think of something unrelated. 'I don't buy the Needle.'

Thomas turned about again, leaned against the chart table and folded his arms. 'Daphne made a very good case.'

'No man with any sense would bury anything of great import under that obelisk. It has to mean something else. The Lady Threads a Needle in the diary of Elizabeth Whittle. Do we assume the lady is Elizabeth? So what is she threading other than a needle?'

'Why not assume Elizabeth was actually a seamstress before she became a socialite?'

'Nope, don't buy that. Do you?'

'Not really.'

'Did you find out how Joshua died?'

'Someone stabbed him in the gut, took off with his wallet. The report said it was a robbery.'

'But you have to ask why he was there.'

'That's simple. He was a Christian. If he wasn't taken by surprise, he would have probably put up a good fight. Apparently, he was an excellent swordsman.' Thomas picked up a long rule in playful camaraderie. 'The troglodyte gets there first. I counter-strike, flanking his side with impact.'

Lukas responded in similar fashion. Enjoying their roles, forgetting other considerations to fill both time and mind, they engaged in mock sword play on the bridge as the *Abracadabra* traced its bow through the English Channel.

'Am I not the finest warrior?'

'Methinks you're under delusion.' Lukas performed the run-in. 'No life for you!'

'Ugh!' Thomas accepted his lot, fell to his knees and rolled away into instant surrender. A kinder face looked down. 'Sweetheart, what's that I smell?'

'Pickles and peaches.'

'Yuk? How can you eat them together?'

'Baby like pickles, me like peaches. Do tell Lukas wha' Ben say?'

'We know everything there is not to know without really knowing anything. To quote Ben,' and Lukas mimicked the deep and serious tone of his uncle, 'That is what we know.'

Woo giggled and Thomas picked up. 'What I'd like to know, who gave the book to the charity shop. I mean, surely you could see it was worth more than a few bob.'

'Much to know when offer to Flisk.'

Lukas gave Thomas a long, hard stare, taking in those frank and intelligent eyes. 'Care to tell me why?'

'Oh man I gave my word.'

'Tell me or I shall hit you with my sword.'

'What sword?'

The rule bounced off his head. 'This one.'

'Okay! Okay! He overheard the conversation between you and Dad, especially the bit about comparing her to the whores. He tried to make him see you had a soft spot for Daphne and then Daphne walked in and all hell broke loose. The problem is, Luke, you should have told her you go with whores.'

'To play game!' It just popped out of Woo's mouth like a champagne cork. 'Oops,' she said and Lukas buried his head in shame.

Thomas swiped the rule. 'You tell my wife secrets!' Thwack on the head! 'I should've been the first to know she was pregnant!' Again, thwack! 'You have seriously gone down in my estimation, pal. Now give me the run down. Is this some kind of kinky transition?'

'No! Sometimes I lose the will to have sex.'

'Oh man, that's terrible, just terrible. You could've paid Woo to play cards.'

'Wha' is wong wif you!'

'Sorry, sweetheart. I just thought-'

'Tha' your ploblem, you no think. Daffannee have more brain than you. She like Lukas, take him bleakfast in bed. Wha' you gonna do about it?' Her eyes glittered with anger, her glance sweeping him so scathingly that Thomas felt stripped to the bone.

'I tried, sweetheart. I tried my best. But she just wouldn't listen. What else can I do?'

'Ring Daffannee, tell her he play cards.'

'But not all the time.'

'You ring Daffanee,' she told Lukas.

'And what am I supposed to say? Oh, by the way, Daphne, I play cards sometimes with whores?'

'I sometimes cook beetles.'

Lukas and Thomas looked at each other with amused forbearance as she promptly disappeared below deck. Then the Daphne subject came back in on the equation.

'Give her a ring, Luke. Make a date, nice music, soft lights, gets them every time.'

Till that moment, the reality was beginning to impose itself heavily, the implications at least he could acknowledge that her world was so different from his, precious, proper and glitteringly upmarket. It was up to him, with a flash of insight to bring an air of truth into this matter since he considered himself as in an even worse state, especially for a man who had never been able to pencil appointments beyond tomorrow.

'I don't know what my future holds. I don't even know if I want to get involved with a woman who has the capacity to crack my nuts.'

'That's what women do, my man.'

'When is the diary being put up for auction?'

Thomas punched a few keys into his magical computer and declared it was next Friday at Diss. 'Dad recommended a local auction house due to the nature of Boudicca coming from East Anglia.'

'Then I shall be there.'

'Why, to irritate Marcus?'

'No, to irritate Miss Frisky…nobody ever thought to ask me who seduced who. There she was offering it to me on a platter and I get to be the bad boy.'

'You could have refused.'

Lukas rolled his eyes, speechless.

9

For two days the Abracadabra beat the waves on the ocean road. From Portugal, the straits of Gibraltar, Spain and west coast of France, it was altogether a splendidly varied coastline of rock outcrops and long surf beaches, notwithstanding grumpy Lukas. In his dreams he kissed her lips a thousand times, refused a sheet change and studied the stars searching for some peace of mind.

On the third day he huffed and puffed unrealistically to Thomas. 'Put us to fifty knots.'

'Go and watch a James Bond film,' he barked, cramped behind his pretentious desk, head bent low as if he sniffed the crossword puzzle as he read the clues. 'Or make yourself useful by changing your sheets. Woo said they stink.'

Disgruntled Lukas walked off. To have a sheet change would take away her smells. Though he did have her pyjamas.

'If you make up with hair brain she might introduce me to a better mate.'

'What's wrong with Charlie?'

'He's dead.' Midnight would say no more after that.

Tucked between the newly formed French resorts was the lesser well known fishing town of Adge, one of the oldest settlements in France and steeped in tradition. There, the *Abracadabra* wended her way through deep-water and moored alongside the riverbank while the resident French gawked from their windows and doors at her size and composition.

Thomas left the bridge and shouted to Lukas under a star-peppered sky. 'You're on!'

Wearing leathers, Lukas gathered his helmet and moved fast to his chosen redoubt, gracefully treading a tightrope as the portside extended a platform from which sprung a yellow Ducati and its black rider. His destination was in the verdant hills of Lamalou, some 30 kilometres inland. As beautiful as it was remote, some came for romance, some came for adventure, and some came for miraculous cures.

For all of his world-wide travels, this was an area new to Lukas, himself melting into the landscape as he drew fast distance from the coast allowing his senses to feed his directions. In places the gradient was steep, a road which took him over a high causeway and into the heart of health spas and up-market casinos. Then he continued for another mile, the winding road taking him to the gateway of a sprawling country seat nestled among flourishing greenery.

His noisy arrival drew its occupant to the front door. With grey hair, wizard's beard and handlebar moustache, it was a bizarre departure from the image he had created for Philippe Metellus.

'Mon nom est Lukas Giddy. Savez-vous de moi?'

The hand anxiously waved him in. 'Come, I can speak your language.'

Led by a blue smoking jacket, Lukas walked into a formidable treasure house of fine French furniture from the eighteenth and nineteenth centuries, including a piece made for Marie Antoinette shortly after her wedding. He stopped to admire it. 'There is one very similar at Scone Palace.'

'Oui, I have been there. Scottish kings were crowned on the Stone of Destiny for 400 years before it was removed to Westminster Abbey. Such is destiny. Wine, I think. Sit, do sit.'

'You're not as I imagined you to be.'

'Ah, but you are, Lukas Giddy. Benjamin always argued you would dominate a room with your physical presence.' The Frenchman passed over a glass and raised his own. 'To destiny,' he said then swallowed it whole, pouring himself another. 'How does Benjamin keep?'

'Oh, I would say his usual all-knowing pompous and obstinate self.' Lukas lowered his glass and smiled. 'He still thinks I'm six years old.'

'Imagine his guilt and loss, taking from you a father, his brother in fear of your life. How does a good man balance such things? Still, we cannot look back in hindsight, blame lack of foresight when insight was there.'

'That's a good analogy.'

'It followed the same pattern, the death of my wife, although she was never my wife, not on paper. Marcus consumed my time and worries, always into mischief, demanding attention.' The hand extended, palm up. 'Here, right here an image appeared at six years old when your father was shot.'

'So, Ben started it off?'

The Frenchman waved that thought away. 'Andate was sending her message, the sign of things to come. This should not concern you. What should concern you is my son.'

'I met him.'

'Oui, it was expected.' The Frenchman sat back and stroked the long white tresses of his beard, clearly judging that Lukas was lost. 'You wish to know about Benjamin, what happened. I shall tell you…nothing but sorrow. My wicked son, I locked in the basement that Christmas Day, best place for an animal. He had taken from me my true wife, Maria. And so, in taking her he declared war. I regret telling Benjamin the link between you and Marcus for it caused him great concern. How does a good man balance such things? How does a father balance his own affairs when another seeks an equally robust response? Throw away the key?'

'Then what, he escaped? He must have because I had another fit six months later.'

'Marcus cried many nights and days. Would not eat, such pity welled inside. My son, my flesh and blood, mon dieu, I could bear it no longer.'

'Ah, Benjamin came here to gain a clearer view of basic truths, yup? Marcus is locked in a basement and you both agree to keep him there. Out of pity you release him six months later and he decides to forgive you. I don't buy it.'

'The truth comes in many disguises, mon ami. He came, he saw, he conquered and you sit with stupid hope for his salvation.' A finger tapped the side of his nose. 'I have what you most desire.' The Frenchman was on his feet and brought down a book from a shelf gathering dust. He blew upon its cover choking the air with age and sat it on the vacant lap. 'Knowledge, mon ami…knowledge is what you seek in peace and war. Andate stilled the battlefield and chose two men from opposing armies. Ah but it was, how you say, the subtle of human nature she found most elusive. My ancestor had no love of war only the spoils of war. Giddy also had no love of war only love of freedom. Paradoxically, they had something in common, neither wanted to fight. Each to their own the silly fellows…one carried his spoils, the other carried his freedom to Scotland.'

'Ben never mentioned Scotland.'

'Alors, Scotland, Ireland, where no war exists, the tale is told the same.'

'And this means what?'

'The inquisitive lady, mon ami, does bring Marcus from out of his woodwork, the little worm poking his head in the breeze of change. Now he needs to meet the real Lukas Giddy, the man who remains elusive, disappears in the shadows of that invincible yacht which keeps his little pet safe.'

'Ah, so he wants Midnight?'

'Why, when he can find one himself.'

'Is it the book he wants?'

'What point when he already knows the story?'

'Not this one, the other one written by Elizabeth Whittle.'

'You have her diary?'

'No, should I get it back?'

'Only if you like happy endings.'

Lukas shifted uneasily. 'You twist my thoughts, Philippe Metellus. I have endured more than is reasonable for any man. I have taken upon myself the burdens and hopes of others. Now you tease me with knowledge that is no knowledge at all. Can the curse be broken?'

'Oui, the curse can be broken. It is meant to be broken for Andate herself made this possible. She is Dark of the Moon as well as Cutter of Threads, love and hate, justice and injustice, these things meet in conflict such as the horns on the same goat.'

'Benjamin is convinced Marcus does not want the curse to be broken yet I have my doubts. The man claims that Andate taunts him, his reason to kill for sake of mental relief.'

'He kills for lust of slaughter. You kill for lust of justice.'

'Then why does Andate make me suffer?'

'It is you who allows your own suffering. Her message is clear. Two may walk away and live a good life. Like two countries, they do not encroach upon each other's territory. The Romans wanted to conquer, like Marcus, he wanted to conquer and so set the seeds of your future when he made his first kill. It is for you, like Boudicca, to make a stand. You make a stand, enough is enough. How do you think Joshua died and Edward lived?'

'Excuse me?'

'Listen, mon ami, your brain cells are clogged. Poor Joshua paid a price to render Edward weak, but for what? He did not do his homework, did not care to look. Marcus would kill an innocent to render the same injustice, would keep you restricted to make his point. Think of your losses if not your life before finding this way. You put at risk those you love and put at risk your life. Walk away or be certain of victory.'

'Not so simple.'

'Alas, simplicity is not her way. Like love, it provokes many symptoms, pounding heart, fear of loss, memories on paper for others to mourn. Edward sought his protection by running away to live with the woman he loved…poof, gone, but not his pain and so ended his pride.' The Frenchman cocked an ear and lifted his finger as though to warn of a sound. 'Take a moment's contemplation in war and peace.'

Lukas looked down at the dusty volume Philippe had laid upon his lap and turned the pages over, secretly, silently, one by one, beautiful words, beautifully written on parchment. 'Night and day is no longer unequal,' he muttered softly, 'a last chance to kiss the memory, to traverse the bloodied ground and find release…'

As his tongue loosened on the grip of translation, there came a swift and sweet onset of scenery change. Gone was Philippe Metellus along with his home filled with beautiful things, fizzled away like a drop of cold water falling into a hot pan. Now he was stood in front of a burnt out ruin under a star-peppered sky in sheer amazement. It needed no explanation.

Fumbling for his mobile he considered whatever else took place this night, Benjamin needed to know some things. 'I never blamed you,' he told him.

'You did what you did at your own expense to give me hope.' Lukas paused for a response, the delay too long. 'Ben? Are you still there?'

'Have you spoken to Philippe?'

'Yes. I'm outside his home, what's left of it. Marcus did this, didn't he? He burnt his father's home with him in it, six months after his first kill, yup? His first kill was Philippe's wife, Maria, when I was fifteen years old.'

'This may be difficult for you to understand. Philippe wanted his suffering to end. Marcus had taken the life of the women he loved, the child she was carrying. When I looked through the barred door at Marcus, I felt nothing but contempt. Philippe did what any father might do in his position, he let Marcus go and in return found his own release. And yes, it affected you the second time round when Philippe chose to leave this world, easy to comprehend the pattern.'

'But you said nothing. In fact, if I remember correctly, you went away again, twice you left at the point of my changes.'

'After his funeral I went there, probably stood where you stand now believing my earlier intervention had caused such terrible tragedy. You are privileged, my Lukas. He never came to me as he has come to you. This is a good sign. Has he indicated your next step?'

'He said the curse can be broken, not how it can be broken…spoke in riddles mostly.'

'No, my Lukas, he speaks wisely. Take what he says into your heart and break this curse.'

'And lose Tom? Woo? Edward's counterpart killed Joshua, lesson learnt, far better to walk away and play safe.'

'You cannot live at another man's determination.'

'Not so long ago you were telling me to steer clear.'

'I did not know the curse could be broken. Now there is hope, my Lukas. Grasp it with both hands.'

'This is not up for discussion.'

10

Thomas, Gaze & Son based in Diss mainly catered for the local farmers and land owners ridding their old machinery and furniture yet, under cover within its brick walls there was junk rubbing with decent stuff. From jewellery cased in glass cabinets to market-trader finds, people crowded the scene for the regular Friday auction.

Lukas came out of curiosity, not for the diary, so sure was he that Daphne Frisk would be there. Garbed in his customary pullover with the words, *the spy who loved me*, he lazed back against a pillar with his crash helmet in his hand, his eyes stopping on every woman, of whom there were many.

Then Daphne emerged in a navy trouser suit, and that damn chopstick stuck in a complicated hair style. Lovely. She walked right past him as if he was a ghost, wended her way to the glass cabinets and set her sight on the diary then looked around as if expecting to meet someone, or perhaps hoping to see Lukas. But before Lukas could respond, a tall man wearing a lone ranger hat had cornered her.

'Marcus!' Lukas said under his breath.

'*This is going to be interesting.*'

'Yes, very interesting.'

'*Well don't just stand here, get on your horse and rescue the damsel in distress.*'

'She doesn't look that distressed to me.'

Laughing, she looked at the ground then looked at the diary, looked back at Marcus, gesturing with her hands. There were faces appearing around them, people had hovered observing Marcus. There was no doubt he commanded attention, enjoying the role he played.

Suddenly the auction room was on a high state of alert. Dozens of people milled about, or grabbed seats, or chatted with their eyes darting around. The auctioneer made an announcement and business commenced. From a long list, the diary stood as lot 116.

Lukas glanced across the room at Marcus, their eyes met, and each offered a polite nod. The miracle of the auction was that the two men treated each other with a modest dose of civility. His next cast was made at Daphne who responded in a likewise manner. No attempt was made to come in contact and that irritated him further.

So, each stuck fast to the floor with the auctioneer piling through the items, banging his gavel and hardly stopping for breath, the diary finally came under the hammer.

'Lot 116, the Lady Threads a Needle in the diary of Elizabeth Whittle, a nice example of mid-nineteenth century workmanship, its gilded covers decorated in a monochrome cobalt-blue. I have several bids on the table, so we shall start at two hundred pounds.'

Someone in the room offered 220, and then another at 240, it was rolling along like a marble without Marcus entering into a bid. It reached 475 out of the room then it went to telephone bids when surprise, surprise, Marcus came into the equation at an astounding bid of four thousand. The room gasped, even the auctioneer blinked twice.

'Four thousand I'm bid,' he announced and referred to the assistant hanging on a line. She nodded and the auctioneer referred back to Marcus. 'Four thousand, one hundred, do I hear four thousand, two hundred.'

Marcus nodded.

Now it was going back and forth, word reached outside and the floor was packed in amazement. Marcus was loud and daring, loving every second of the attention, almost disappointed when the telephone bid dropped out at six grand. But then, just when he thought he had his purchase sewn up, Lukas put the cat among the pigeons at six thousand, five hundred.

'Seven,' Marcus volleyed.

'Eight,' Lukas returned the serve.

'Nine.'

'Ten.'

'Eleven.'

'Twelve.'

Marcus let his gaze fall on Lukas and smiled, unlucky for some, thirteen, so he said, 'Fourteen.'

Quietness blanketed the scene. The auctioneer, responding to Lukas's shake of the head was about to bring down the hammer when the telephone bid reignited interest. What had been conveyed made him wipe his rubicund face. 'I have a bid of twenty thousand, do I hear more?' The room went silent. 'Going once, going twice,' down came the hammer, 'sold at twenty thousand pounds!'

Lukas could hardly believe it. He stood transfixed as Daphne made her way to the desk to collect her winnings while Marcus rolled up to his side.

'What do you make of that, old boy?'

'You got me.'

'That's the problem I haven't got you, not yet.' Marcus moved off with a smirk on his face, seemed unconcerned leaving without the diary.

'What the hell just happened, Midnight? Who in their right mind would pay twenty grand for a diary?'

'Let me think now, someone who gets their money back.'

Indeed, someone who gets their money back. He picked up his feet and met Daphne at the counter waiting for her cheque. 'What the hell do you think you're doing?'

'Waiting for my cheque.'

'Exactly, and no doubt the diary.'

She squeezed her eyes at him. 'You astound me with your mathematics.'

'And what's that supposed to mean?'

'That you're not in my equation.' She turned to the woman in brown behind the counter, picked up her cheque and stuffed it in her bag. 'If you don't mind, I have better things to do than listen to your crap.'

'Dap, speak to me.'

'Do not call me Dap. My name is Daphne.'

'Well how do you spell it?'

'Correctly.' She walked off.

'*Diplomacy has never been your finer attributes.*'

'Maybe it was my jumper.'

'*If she's the spy, I wouldn't get your hopes up.*'

Lukas always felt Daphne was in the centre of something, now he had further reason to believe the diary was in there too. Leaning his elbow on the counter, he said, 'Midnight, find who purchased the diary, I'll wait here.'

Her nose poked over his breast pocket. '*Ohh, it's cold out there.*'

'Do you want me to put you in that jug?'

'*No crunchy nut cornflakes,*' she moaned scrambling down his arm, '*what sort of establishment is this.*'

She made her way across the counter in fits and starts, dropping behind a computer, and then her tail disappeared in a vase. The vase was taken into the office and no more could be seen of her.

Fifteen minutes later, Lukas began to worry. Out of earshot, out of sight, his fingers drummed hard on the counter. Twice he was moved along for obstructing the course of business, and twice he played it dumb.

And now he was attacked for the third time. 'Can you please stand over there, you're holding up the customers.'

He turned to the woman in brown. 'I'm waiting to be served.'

'Where is your ticket?'

'I haven't got one.'

'What did you buy?'

'I bid on the blue monochrome diary.'

'Are you Mr. O'Lentilk?'

'That's me, the one and only.'

'I saw you bid for the diary.'

'I just said that.'

She peered suspiciously at him, no doubt asking herself who was bidding on the telephone. Then her eyes flickered to the jumper, not a very good sign. 'Wait there a moment.'

He watched the woman in brown go into the back office, obviously to conduct a quiet and careful investigation which rather put him on the spot. 'Midnight,' he cursed, 'where the hell are you?'

'*Ants, lovely ants.*'

He looked down and breathed a sigh of relief. 'Leave the ants alone. We need to get out of here.'

They had completely left the urban sprawl of Diss and the sporadic patches of neighbourhoods when Lukas drummed on his brakes for a confab with Midnight.

'What did you get?'

'*Cecil O'Lentilk.*'

'I could have told you as much.'

'*Then you stick your head in a vase.*'

'What else did you get?'

'*I got waylaid.*'

'Ah, see, it's the ants, they're no good for you.' He kicked up the stand and looked back for traffic before moving off. What did it matter? He made a balls-up and Daphne was out of his life. And even though the purpose was to get rid of the diary to Marcus, it seemed he was not prepared to go the distance, confirming once again it was not the diary Marcus was after but Lukas Giddy.

Keep your head down, he said to himself as he drove on the highway to Felixstowe. Keep your head down, keep safe, keep everyone safe and chase my own ghosts.

11

Silhouetted briefly against the flare of a match, Lukas was waiting for his target. In the distance, a party bellowed in celebration. But here under an olive tree there was no cheer, save for his shallow breathing.

'Arrivederci mio dolce.'

The voice belonged to a snazzy dresser in open neck shirt leaving the merrymaking of Italians at a wedding. His name was Marconi, a shitty piece of work allied to the local mafia. He took an unhurried route to his red Ferrari, twirling the car key round his finger. The kill had to send a gruesome message.

Stepping forward, his gun already drawn, Lukas spoke in the native tongue. 'Let's take a walk in the olive groves.'

It followed the usual pattern, the opening line we can do a deal and then the pitiful excuses. Scum never asked why he was there, guilt always followed a pattern.

'Do you know who I am?'

'Sure, you're a shitty piece of macaroni.'

There was a hysterical tinge to the voice now, a useless attempt to threaten and when that failed, the Italian made a bolt for cover. Not one to miss an opportunity, Lukas immobilized his target, such was the power he had. The Italian could not move, could not even turn his head or scratch a festering itch. It was conceivable he forecast his own death, whatever his musing, Lukas had other concerns.

'I have a message from the bereaved husband. You remember him. Georgiou? He told you very nicely to leave his premises and wife alone.' Lukas patted his back pockets. 'Midnight, remind me. I left it behind.'

'I will not kill you quickly. I will break your little legs then I will break your little arms and then I will take your little peewee and shove it in your mouth.'

'Is that so?' There was humour in his seriousness. 'What part didn't you understand?'

GIDDY MIDNIGHT

'The bit where you said you left it behind.'

Lukas peered into the frozen eyes. 'I will not kill you quickly. I will break your little legs then I will break your little arms and then I will take your little dick and shove it in your mouth.'

'I think he just pooped in his pants.'

He was a small and wretched gangster comprehending the horrors of his plight. Had he surrendered with dignity, he might have won concessions. There was none. Lukas cut him open with a single deft stroke, left him alive long enough to watch his own intestines spill out. In the background the party played on while Marconi dropped to his knees, drowned in his own blood and shits. His exploits were now at an end.

'Tom,' Lukas spoke into his watch, 'Inform the client done deal. I'm on my way back.'

'I took her around Rizzuto and moored at Crotone.'

'Why?'

'Speak to you later.'

'Dammit, he's done it again!'

On the slopes he picked out the lights of Crotone, a coastal resort romantically perched on the heel of Italy. Maybe Thomas was right. The bike stole a shorter route to the *Abracadabra* where she was moored at the end of a boardwalk. In the gap of her starboard side, Thomas was there to greet him.

'We have a passenger.'

'I knew it!' Lukas wheeled the bike round. 'We don't take passengers, not under any circumstance.'

'Woo is a passenger.'

'Woo is your wife.'

'And what a lovely wife she is.'

'Haven't we had this conversation before?'

'Ah, the difference, he's not staying.' He patted Lukas on the back, and they fell into step. 'We'll cast off when he leaves.'

'Do we have a name?'

'Oban, first and last.'

'Carrying?'

'A pair of Ray-Bans, Omega watch and a Glock 17.'

Lukas stopped in his tracks. 'A 9mil semi and you let him board. Are you out of your tiny mind or what?'

'Look, he's not out to kill you. He's out to see you.'

'And how do you know that?'

'Because he said so.'

Lukas rolled his eyes in the gait of Thomas who removed his braided cap before opening the door to his quarters.

And there sat Oban with a misshapen nose, heavy lids, and fingers like sausages, eight to a lb. He stood in his tailored light-weight suit and greeted Lukas with two words. 'Marcus Metellus.'

No smiles. As Thomas took a seat behind his desk, Lukas poured himself a drink. 'What about him?'

'Good looking, likes to dress up, has a magical tree which grows money faster than the rate of inflation, and here's the best part, he's just like you.'

Lukas played dumb and said nothing.

'We know what you are, Giddy, and what you can do, have done since the day you joined Exit.'

'And how do I know who you are?'

'I'm about to tell you.' Oban sat down and overlapped his legs. 'I sort out problems, a cross between a delegate and a land mine. Some while back we were approached by a client to get rid of their headache. Guess what, in getting rid of their headache we get rid of the best operative we have. Are we on the same page?'

'I do believe we read the same words.' Lukas sensed the anticipation behind the deadpan of this seasoned, hardened, tough as nails negotiator. 'You bid for the diary.'

'Bingo!'

Lukas shook his head. 'Yes, nice touch, the anagram.'

'What anagram?' Thomas asked.

'Cecil O'Lentilk, one for the reader to work out, yup?'

'Giddy, you can kill two birds with one stone.'

'The last one who tried fell flat on his face, in the process cost Joshua his life. Have you got the answer? Tell me because I would love to know.'

'Have you ever stopped to ask why he failed?'

Lukas stood over him, topping up his glass. 'You have not been doing your homework, Oban. He failed because the likes of Marcus can age the likes of me. In spite of that major hiccup, I have no bloody idea how to invalidate the link to make it possible to wipe him off the face of this earth without me going too.'

Thomas addressed Lukas. 'The answer might be under Cleopatra's Needle.'

'Ah, the informant speaks.'

'Aw, Luke, I had to give Oban the run down.'

'Then you missed out the part where there's nothing under there! How many times do I have to keep telling you? Andate is the Cutter of Threads, she who threads a needle not Cleopatra. Do you think I enjoy being curbed by that bastard? If he ever found out I was attempting to take him on he would hold my family to ransom. I hope you're taking notes, Oban.'

Oban did not argue. He leaned forward and sunk his heavy lids into the glass. 'I could sit here all night and cross the globe on the horror he begets or I could tell you the client isn't fussy who kills him.'

'Are you threatening me?'

'Just giving the facts.'

'Oh Jesus,' he whispered, realizing he had exchanged one set of complications for another. But he was a professional. He served Exit as well as Exit would allow, and he never failed do what Exit instructed him to do because Exit paid well and was on the side of justice.

Thomas stepped into the breach, again. 'Luke, we're behind you every step of the way. Dad, Mum, even Woo agrees you cannot live with this hanging over your head. Since Philippe, you've hardly said a word, take more risks on your targets, mope about in your quarters smoking pot, look bloody scruffy and smell like a fish. Now it's come to a head. You've got to fight off this apathy. Philippe indicated the curse can be broken. So, let's find out how.'

Lukas took a seat opposite Oban with such a trembling hand that the ice in his glass tinkled like a little bell. 'Who is the client?'

'A young man, not much older than you, is briskly walking to a nice little castle in a nice little spot with a Chinese takeaway. The girl he intends to marry is pouring the wine, laying the table, dishes warming in the oven. A couple of minutes away from his door a black flashy motor rides the pavement and squashes his brains. Then the driver gets out, empties the pockets, and makes himself at home with the girlfriend six days later. What marks there were on her body, suggested he put one hand around her neck and pulled her down to her knees with her mouth to his crotch. For his next trick, he pushed her to the bed face down, stuffed her nickers in her mouth, spread the legs and forced his penis up her anus. For his third trick he goes to the kitchen while keeping her pinned to the bed, picks up a frying pan and bashed her head in. One year on, two murder files have made their way to the bottom of the pile. Two families, Giddy, two families raising the stakes in search of justice.'

If this was meant to touch his heart, then Oban had certainly achieved it. He sat quiet with the talent for seeing patterns, reasons where most others perceived only blanks. His voice was a little thicker when he broke the silence. 'But for the fact she had no other contusions put you on the trail of a man that had something in common with me, yup?'

'Giddy, the man operates like a phantom. He puts nothing in his name, I mean nothing. We traced the motor to a hire company and drew a blank. He used an intermediary that turned up at a mortuary. We never had a face to go on.'

'But now you do.'

'Minus our fee, you get half a mil.'

'Half a mil!' Thomas exclaimed.

'Not much pressure then.'

'Aw come on, Luke. That was uncalled for. Tell you what, if you don't make it, your half can go to charity.'

'Gee, that makes me feel so much better.'

Oban finally cracked his face. 'It might interest you to know Marcus will be attending a banquet next week held at The Savoy.'

'I don't do banquets.'

'Exit has invested heavily, a lot of man hours into setting your stage. You need to keep him amused while you go traipsing for your answer.'

'And how do I do that?'

'Perhaps the banker and his daughter can help.'

'Excuse me?'

Oban finished his drink. 'I left a file on the desk and my number. Anything you want, let me know.'

When Oban moved off escorted by Thomas, Lukas grabbed the file. He had to know what part Frisk and Daphne played in all this. And it began with the diary, put to a London auction house, flagging up interest from two parties, Exit and Marcus. But she withdrew it for some unknown reason which caused her father to come in on the equation and so take matters into his own hands. They were nothing more than a couple of pawns that were now going to unwittingly play on an elaborate stage held at The Savoy set up by Exit.

'Well,' Thomas said as he walked back in. 'That's a turn up for the books.'

Lukas looked up. 'It says here she fits the profile. Rich, intelligent and in the public eye, Marcus wouldn't dare lay a finger on her. How damn convenient for Exit when she found that diary…or did she?'

'Dad never knew the diary existed.'

'*Philippe Metellus?*' Midnight suggested.

Now it was falling into place. 'There you have it, Philippe Metellus, the wizard playing a wily game. He sees Exit on the trail of his son, yup? But they can't get a fix on him. So, he sends the diary to Daphne and there's Exit rubbing their hands together in thanks of a miracle. But why did she withdraw it from auction? Remind me to ask her, Midnight, when I see her. Next is bloody obvious what happened, due to Ben's intervention, she finally puts it to auction and hey presto they have a fix on Marcus so even if I disappear on an island, they have their mark.'

'Luke, we can do this. Even Philippe is behind you.'

'Philippe plays on a different stage, tells me the curse can be broken yet refuses to tell me how.'

'Well maybe there are other things to learn, like how to dance and be diplomatic.'

'Excuse me?'

Thomas stepped forward. 'This is what you do. Go up to her, smile, say nothing, bring her nicely to her feet, take her waist and place her hand close to your chest, like this. Don't look at me, keep your eyes fixed ahead, be a gentleman, don't suffocate her, move easy until you feel her surrender, and make every word count. Of course, before all this you have to contact her father.'

'Why?'

'Because you screwed his daughter, numb-nuts.'

'She screwed me!'

'Yeah, you just thought of England. Besides, you need him to buy the diary off Cecil vis-à-vis Oban.'

'Why do I need to do that?'

'Asking Frisk to get it makes him feel he's doing something constructive and so opens a door to get Daphne on your side and on board.'

Lukas smiled. 'So, I get to screw Daphne?'

'And God help us all.'

12

Thomas held out his hand. 'Come on, give daddy your toy. It's a banquet not a bull fight.'

'I keep the knife.'

'No, I don't think so.'

'That wasn't a question.' Lukas turned to his mirrored reflection, refined, full of hidden strength couched in a black tuxedo. From his breast pocket, Midnight popped into view. 'No leaving your station.'

'*Ohh.*'

Moored just beyond Waterloo Bridge, Lukas picked his way to a British icon, The Savoy with an enviable location near the River Thames. He was consciously rebuilding a dignified presence in the five minute walk. He would make his gestures caressive yet instinctive with power, slow in manner, a proper gentleman. Already the sweat was running down his back when he swung into stunning Art Deco. It sparkled with timeless elegance and glamour the world had ever seen. Each liveried employee had their station, knew their steadfast place among a rich and colourful scope of billionaires. There were the gold and scarlet of sheikhs, the black tuxedos of commerce and the cream cummerbund of the British Ambassador. Around them, ladies parading in satin and silk, bound up and bedecked in diamonds, greeting, preening, jostling and flaunting.

Midnight summed it all up. '*I need my sunglasses.*'

A hand came upon his shoulder. Even Frisk had been seized by the privilege of wealth, wearing proudly the Order of the British Empire. 'Do not be intimidated, Giddy. This is all show to dress the wheels of commerce.' He took Lukas to a quiet corner, concern written on his features. 'Marcus Metellus, the man introduced himself as a naval officer, had the audacity to challenge me in front of the British Ambassador, whatever next. What chance of decommissioning the fellow?'

'You're a very bad man, Frisk.'

'Due to the company I keep.' Frisk clicked his fingers and a silver tray came to his side, champagne at the ready. 'This is damn good stuff,' he said, passing a glass of bubbly to Lukas. 'There was a beggar in the street. He made me start by muttering as if he were an echo of the future. Some of the bods here lost a fortune, thought they would make it up quickly…never dreamt the Government taking their pound of flesh in this economic climate.'

'Did you get the diary?'

Frisk looked round, the capricious amateur sneakily passing it over. 'No sooner said than done. You owe me thirty thousand.'

'He bought it for twenty.'

'The man was a hard negotiator.'

Lukas dug deep into his inside jacket pocket knowing full well Oban sold it to Frisk for twenty-five. He was a banker all right. 'I owe you five less deductions for your daughters keep.'

'She eats very little.'

'She gives me a headache.'

'Then take some pills. So where are we at, Giddy?'

'Daphne will be under my wing from tonight onwards. I need you to close up her surgery, find someone to look after her pets. Does she have many?'

'Enough. Jed, next door will help. If she gets under your feet, send her to me. I shall be staying at the Claris in Southern France.'

'Stay with Ben and Kate.'

'I'm too set in my ways, Giddy. Like my own bed and strawberries for breakfast.'

'You have your own bed in the Claris?'

'Anyone can have their own bed if they pay for it.'

Before Lukas could respond he caught sight of Daphne, and somewhere behind his rib cage, something fluttered and jerked in recognition. Beautiful were her motions in a lemon gown, her hair tied back in a French pleat, her eyes brighter than stars and her hand to the cut of her bosom as she approached.

'Do you know I had this indiscernible feeling you might be here.' Daphne glanced at her father. 'Hang your head in shame why don't you. This is your doing.'

'Now, Daphne, the man is here at my request.'

'Well of course he is. Why do you think Marcus is here, to eat caviar?' She caught Lukas grinning. 'Have I got to suffer your intolerable ego all night?'

'I hope so.'

She flapped her arms and walked off. He followed because he had no choice, he was already committed.

War was so much simpler than love, Marcus mused. He studied the receding form of Lukas Giddy with a mixture of admiration and enmity. It was remarkable how he dodged those bullets, even more remarkable missing his shot, butchering an innocent in Rome and fleeing the scene. Aimless prick. A glass cabinet in front of him held a treasure of glittering items from The Savoy's good old days, which rather brought him to consider Daphne Frisk, her meddling into matters that did not concern her, scratching at clues and scratching at Hodge. Why, it was Giddy who got rid of Hodge, an imbecile who played a dangerous game. So what game was Giddy playing? He could deal well enough with whores. He could deal well enough with rivals. Could he deal well enough with the likes of Daphne Frisk? Tape up your letter box for Marcus has arrived.

Daphne, to whom each painful mile seemed longer than the last, toiled wearily along while Lukas lingered not far behind. Now he was at a sumptuous banqueting table, richly laid and boasting of splendiferous food despite the fact Midnight kept him confused.

'*That one, no, not that one, the other one.*'

'That's not a nut.'

'*Then give me a drumstick.*'

'Don't be ridiculous.' He tore a piece of darker meat off the bone and slyly shoved it in his breast pocket.

'Did you get caught in the speculative market?'

A woman as prying as she was fat attached herself to his side. Diplomacy was not an option. 'Rather,' he said in a posh accent. 'I had to withdraw my bid for Buckingham Palace.'

Daphne burst into quiet titters, handed him a plate and a monogramed napkin, and then helped herself to a piece of chicken and some salad. 'Mr. Giddy, why don't you tell the Ambassador's wife about your time with the French attaché, Charnel I believe her name?'

Lukas, for all his display of optimism, had his doubts of what had really been achieved in the past two hours. She had flitted from one spot to another, trotted off twice to the Powder Room, and with an original sense of timing broke into a form of freak intelligence which he felt bound to honour. But not this time, he considered.

'I'm sure the Ambassador's wife would find your own story with the Russian attaché far more interesting, Hodge I believe his name.' If he thought that had her cornered, he was wrong.

'There I was on the precipice of danger,' and the fat lady's eyes grew wide, his wider still. 'My unspoken worry had obviously been that if the tapes contained any vital information, they would land in the wrong hands, thereby alienating his Embassy and ending my own career. It was a make or break point in the investigation. Hodge was a gnomish man whose whole life revolved around armaments, though as a Russian attaché he carried the diplomatic bag. The case was looking more and more like a slam dunk. The only hitch was getting the tapes, achievable through Admiral Thomas who ordered his disguised submarine to surface in Russian waters. Hodge boarded, the case was snatched and the rest is highly confidential.' She was, after all, high spirited.

'My dear,' the Ambassador's wife said, grasping a neck full of diamonds, 'how intriguing. Are you both in British Intelligence?'

'Oh look!' Daphne waved. 'There's Lady Gallery.'

A quick glance of his eye towards the spot where she was walking with the Ambassador's wife, showed him whom she meant. But beyond that, he was quite lost. This was an opportunity to escape outside for a smoke on the veranda, craving for solitude as if he was unable to hold himself together except in silence.

Save for the dull creaking of the open doors and the light fragments of voices like the ticking of the death-watch beetle only made the stillness he invaded deeper and more apparent. Then he heard a cautious footstep. It stopped, advanced again then seemed to go quiet around it.

'Quite a departure from your usual haunts.'

'Could the same be said about you, I wonder.' Lukas turned to face the uniform of a high ranking naval officer, the details were impeccably correct. 'How vast is your theatrical wardrobe?'

Without so much as a twitch of a single nerve on his face, Marcus lit his cigar with a fifty pound note and stood gazing at the river and the bridges. 'There are limits, old bean. For instance, I refrain from wearing poodle knit jumpers.'

'And there was me thinking you might copy my style.'

At these words, Marcus smiled. The silence between them seemed to stretch to infinity until he said, 'I told myself I wasn't going to be paranoid though I can't help but wonder why you disappeared for three moons and now chance your luck with the banker's daughter.'

'Funny you should ask that. Didn't I once hear you say you had no interest in that direction?'

'So why did you come, to take her off my hands?'

'I never realized she was in them.' Lukas lingered awhile. His focus was on subtle persuasion, convincing his opposite number reasons and method. 'I knew nothing about you then I knew as much as I wanted to know about you, and somewhere in between there was only one choice to make. I have lived at your determination for fifteen years, so why should I risk any more than I have before.'

'You risk my life at the expense of yours.'

'Is that what really bothers you, Metellus? Methinks not. So let me tell you why. Before you stands a man, like it or not, who got to the diary first. Does that make you incompetent? I should say so. You hired a wanker who turned you over and then expected me to fall for the crap coming out of your mouth.

If you had taken your brains out of your wardrobe you would have discovered there is no easy fix between us. The diary is a reminder of that. For certain, I want to live without the aggravation, find my own happiness no matter how short a duration.' The diary was waved under his nose. 'Do you know how I got this?'

'From a prat called Cecil.'

'Then we're on the same wavelength.' He slapped it against the chest. 'It's yours, call it a parting gift, find your true love, have kids and keep on your side of the territory.' Now it was the turn of Marcus to encounter the smatterings of arrogance. His whole motivation was as a unit commando, a conqueror bent on winning. Lukas was the very opposite, unable to appreciate that being right was never the route to success.

In the Edwardian Hall where the lights were low, soft music played and Lukas searched for Daphne. She was lingering quietly in a corner, alone in a cloudy bubble, just like before, that morning at breakfast on the *Abracadabra*. He would do as Thomas advised him to do. He went up to her, smiled, said nothing, brought her to her feet, took her waist and placed her hand close to his chest, kept his eyes fixed ahead, moved easy until he felt her surrender to the music. He would make every word count.

'Ben once told me long, long ago, we make but a bad job at managing our affairs. I think we both handled each other badly, so why don't we start again?'

'And do what? Add another notch to your gun?'

'Ouch! Can you drive the wedge any deeper?'

'I should never have boarded the *Abracadabra*.'

'But so glad you did.' He nuzzled her neck, smelt and kissed her skin. 'I see you have relinquished your chopstick.'

'Is that by observation?'

'Well unless it's tucked up your knickers, what else is there to observe?'

'Marcus?'

'He's not as interesting as you.'

They continued to dance in the lull in their conversation. With a lighter heart and step, and eyes the brighter for the tear that dimmed her for a moment, Daphne resumed the dialogue. 'You have the diary, so what else do you want?'

'I need your brains.'

'What do you wish to know?'

'Woo serves up a terrific bleakfast.' He felt her chuckles vibrate against his chest and let slide his hand to the small of her back, pulling her closer still. 'She recognises I'm rude, arrogant and take the Mickey out of her accent.'

'How have you been?'

'A little lost.' Then his gaze fell on Marcus observing them. She likewise turned her eyes in the same direction and surveyed the man as if he had the plague. 'And you, how have you been?'

'A little lost too.'

'Shall we get lost together?'

In the street, pausing to cross the road, Lukas shrugged out of his stifling jacket and slung it over his shoulder leaving Midnight squashed in his pocket. 'We go this way.' There was hardly a sound in the road, how easily they walked together.

'Ask her where she got the diary?'

'So, you received the diary from an unknown benefactor not out of a charity shop?'

'Would you have believed me?'

'Probably not.'

'I found it in my shopping bag with a note to put it up for auction and give the money to charity.'

'Why did you disobey the benefactor's request?'

'I was curious, is that so hard to understand? Do you know who sent it?'

'I do.'

'Will you tell me?'

'His name is Philippe Metellus.'

'Any relation to Marcus?'

Some things he would hold back. 'The story is a little convoluted but in effect his father chose you for your beauty and brains not that you had any when you decided to rush off and leave without saying goodbye.'

'Why should I say goodbye to an idiot.'

'Not such an idiot to unravel the mystery.' He watched her feet as they sprung between the paving slabs, enjoying the bounce of it, her ruffling skirts picking up dirt. 'You should be working for me.'

'I prefer my independence.'

'Before tonight, was Marcus in contact with you?'

'He's very handsome, quite a charmer. He asked me out on a date at the auction.'

'Did you go?'

'Do you think me stupid?'

'How did you manage to persuade Hodge?'

'I never slept with him.'

'You have this canny knack of reading my mind, Daphne Frisk or should I call you Clever Clogs?'

'What happened to him?'

'Use your imagination.'

'Is that what you do, kill people?'

'I prefer to use the word punish.'

'So, who made you judge and jury?'

'Is this going to be a lecture?'

'Suit yourself. Have you made any progress?'

'It was Edward who loved Elizabeth, Edward who supposedly tried to find a way to break the curse and somewhere in between Joshua was killed, leaving a stark message.'

'Wow.'

'Yes, wow.' He stopped at the water's edge and looked down into her face. She was at the heart of all his cheerful hopes. 'I'm going to take Marcus on.'

'Have you told him?'

'Why would I tell him?'

'He might fancy himself as your second in command.' She laughed, nudging his shoulder with her head. 'I'm kidding, only kidding. So how are you going to take him on?'

'Not a clue.'

'Then you mustn't take him on.'

'I have to take him on.'

'You cannot take him on until you know what to do.'

'I have no intention of taking him on until I know what to do.'

'Are you being antagonistic again?'

He nudged her with his elbow. 'Kidding, just kidding. Shall we board?'

She gathered the folds of her dress and moved up the ramp. 'How fortuitous I left my pyjamas behind. Or did you dump them?'

No, he slept with them. 'If I never knew better you planned it just right for your trip.'

'Trip?'

'To East Anglia.'

'Ah, where Boudicca lived.'

'Now you're getting the drift. You go on ahead. I shall join you later with info.'

Lukas dropped down to the ship's hold, picked up a pair of night vision binoculars and eased back up the stairway onto the side of the deck, keeping his presence circumspect. For long moments he scanned the shadows across the embankment and finally picked out Marcus. That man haunted every scene.

'Do we make sail?' Thomas whispered.

'Go for it.'

Loosening his top button, Lukas moved on and began to think idly of the hours to come in her company, hopefully her arms, the struggle to absorb everything, feeling as though he had just stepped off a fairground ride, dizzy and exhilarated.

As it so happened she was flat-out on the bed in a spare cabin with bubbles of sleep migrating from her lips. He removed her shoes, covered her over with the counterpane and caught sight of that chopstick on the bedside cabinet. So, she did have it up her skirts after all. Not wishing to miss an opportunity, he picked it up and fumbled the two halves apart. A loaded dart shot out, stabbed him in the arm and suddenly the world went black.

13

Consciousness returned, arrived with a cold impact of a wet flannel to his face. He groaned, aware that he stilled lived and opened his heavy lids from a chemically induced sleep. A figure dressed in a white shirt stood over him, the hair short and brown, premature grey came into focus.

'Curiosity, my man, remember? You stabbed your arm with a sleep-inducing drug, strong enough to knock out a rhino…here, drink this to clear out your system.'

Not that his smouldering dissatisfaction was visible, Lukas shifted his weight on the bed, slipping his socked feet to the floor and said nothing.

'Midnight alerted Daphne, she alerted me but there was nothing we could do other than put you in your quarters and let you sleep it off. Some weapon, eh, Luke? She had a Chinese guy make it up, damn clever sods. I thought you could use something similar, say a pen. James Bond used a pen on Fatima Blush.'

'Do I look as though I need a pen?'

'Luke, it was an accident. Now clean yourself up and go see her in the stateroom, have some crunchy nut cornflakes.'

'Yes, yes, crunchy nut cornflakes.'

Lukas looked thoughtfully at Midnight. His furry heartbeat, the pet of his watch, though fond of stirring up trouble, preferred to haunt his bed. 'Traitor.'

'Cheats never prosper.'

'Ah, I thought as much! You knew and never told me. No crunches for you.'

'I should have left you on the floor.'

Still woozy, he went into the bathroom and splashed cold water on his face, telling himself this was not something out of the ordinary, this was something that happens, not an unbearable disaster but a thing to be bravely soldiered through. At his wardrobe, he chose to wear jeans and a T-shirt befitting his mood, the words *live and let die* seemed appropriate. Midnight stowed in the breast pocket, old affections persisted.

The morning weather promised a glorious start for July and gulls were screeching in their flight over Lowestoft. Water was the most active thing in East Anglia where rivers trod their echoing shapes. The *Abracadabra* had taken her place in the old fish dock. Here she would stay in calm water with a burning wish to be at liberty.

When he swung through the portholed doors, Daphne looked up from her yellow gown. 'If you had the decency not to cheat,' she said unapologetically, 'it would never have happened.'

'No mention was made of terms and conditions.'

'It was a given you would use your brains. But then I forgot, they only work part-time.'

'Around you, I'm surprised they work at all.'

That brought a smile to her face. 'After encountering Hodge, knowing I was to encounter him again, I had to make provision to protect myself. Had I known you were licenced to kill, the circumstance would have been different.' Her next cast was made at his T-shirt. 'Who is to live and let die today?'

Nobody quite relished the last say as Lukas Giddy. Pouring milk over his crunchy nut cornflakes, he asked, 'Can you guess my favourite title?'

'What are the terms?'

Confident she would be unable to rise to the challenge, he said, 'One guess and one guess only, no looking in my wardrobe, and no prompting from my family.' He swiped the chopstick from her hair. 'Guess right and you get to keep it.' But the thought that she should actually guess correctly seemed to him something worse than being sucked down the eternal drain so he added a time limit. 'Take as long as you like, answer before close of day.'

'Oooh, that's unfair.'

'Do you give in?'

'I never give in.'

Touché. Easing himself on a stool, he took in the sight of her. As lovely as she was presentable to the cuddly mistress residing at Giddy Lodge, he was hard pressed to imagine her riding pillion in an evening gown. 'Have you ever been on a motor bike?'

'Tom said we take the motor launch through the lock to your home on Oulton Broad.'

'I prefer my independence.' He watched her turn a length of her hair in her finger, probably too proud to admit she was petrified of the idea or probably wondering what to wear. 'You can borrow one of my jumpers.'

'You promise not to go too fast?'

'It depends on your definition of fast.'

'Do you exceed the speed limit?'

'Me? Law abiding citizen exceed the speed limit.'

Her eyes veered to Midnight who was balancing precariously on the rim of his bowl. 'She's very special, isn't she?'

'*Ask her now.*'

Though it was seldom discussed, and never with strangers, the facts of Midnight were familiar to the family, common consent buried the thing down deep. So it was to some degree Lukas only said what was necessary. 'She wants a mate. He must be a Hazel Dormouse, keeps himself clean, plenty of oomph and more importantly a lot younger. Charlie, the last one was too smelly and dropped down dead.'

'Dropped down dead?'

'I gave him a decent burial.'

'Her species is classified as endangered which means nobody is allowed to kill or capture. That said, I think I know the very place we can look…okay, bike ride it is. Now tell me about Philippe Metellus?'

And so, Lukas began to tell of his tale with the Frenchman who looked like a wizard and that the miracle of his ghostly survival was made conventional by the durability of his love for a woman to whom Marcus had destroyed.

Soon after that, preparations were rapid. With a sea wind and a herring smell coming straight off the old fish dock, the *Abracadabra* parted company with its motor launch where Thomas and Woo would journey by river to Giddy Lodge. For Lukas, he launched the Ducati with Daphne riding pillion. She scrunched up her dress, tucked it between her legs and donned on a crash helmet. It was quite enchanting.

Despite the regular twists and turns, back roads and side roads in a built-up area, Daphne accepted her doom without complaint, her body clutched taut against the rider who bent close to the machine. But the journey built to a dramatic crescendo when nearing the backwaters of Oulton Broad. He called out, 'hang on tight!' to which she responded by a hue and cry as the bike sped up an incline, its roaring grumble outstripping a noiseless environment. Then suddenly it took flight over a low boundary hedge, landed with a speedy thump, coming to a sudden halt at a pair of wide concrete steps. Daphne sagged off the seat like blob of jelly, her helmet went rolling away.

'Dap! Are you alright?'

She scrambled to her feet. 'Excuse me while I change my knickers!'

In a sleepy landscaped spot seemingly composed of brushstrokes by Norfolk artists, there stood a stone-walled house with chimney pots reaching for the sky. The tall and short windows stirred in priceless history and offered a view to the river and Anglican Church. For him it was the end of the line, time to stretch the legs and taste a plate of home-cooked beef.

Now Kate was Benjamin's wife, a doctor by profession though it had been a number of years since last she practiced. She loved her home. She loved her family. And she loved to knit jumpers for Lukas. Always a smile in her slippers, she greeted his flushed and healthy face in the same degree as it was for him in pleasure.

'Oh, Lukas, she's lovely.'

'Don't get too excited. We're still in working progress.'

'I made up a bed in the room next to yours and laid out some of my clothes although I think she's two sizes smaller than me.'

'Does the door still creak?'

'Tut, tut,' came her noblest indignation and waltzed off to the lounge under the smell of fresh paint. 'Would you be a dear and help me move the sideboard?'

'I see Ben has been busy.'

'Lord knows what goes through that man's head.'

Kate had not exaggerated his position. In a myriad of rooms to eat, sit or hide, the refineries of furniture had been stacked in corners or moved to thwart and confuse the occupiers. With a hefty push, the sideboard went clonk and the leg snapped in half.

As if on cue, Benjamin walked in with a shaking head of disbelief. 'Did I not inform that would happen?'

'Benjamin Giddy, you certainly did not! You told me that leg was fixed.' Kate turned to the old grandfather clock whirring sickly behind a chaise-lounge. 'And I suppose that's fixed as well!'

Bong, bong, they all stood to listen, bong, bong and a relapsing twang! Benjamin offered a weaker smile. 'I can explain.'

'Might I suggest,' Daphne interjected tying the corners of Kate's blouse to her waist, 'that we all pull together and get this house organized?'

'There!' Kate announced, pointing her finger, 'there is the voice of sense and reason.' Her words seemed to make Thomas appear. 'Oh, Tom, you're just in time to help us move the furniture.'

'Yes, nice to see you too, Mum.'

'Never mind that, dear, we can have cuddles later. Woo can put on the kettle.'

In no time at all, Kate, a natural mother who coloured her hair with Henna bossed everyone into submission. She vacuumed over their toes, served tea, ran about with a duster, aside the occasional tête-à-tête between Daphne and Woo who was now touching into her third trimester.

'Baby due 9th September.'

Daphne nodded and went down on one knee to lend an ear to Woo's swollen belly. 'Boy or girl?'

Woo shuffled her handkerchief from one hand to the other, looked at the ground, the wall, the ceiling and finally at Daphne. 'Tum want girl.'

'We can't be choosey.'

'Kate say tha'…she buy two booties, pink and blue. Tum say better to buy pink for both feet.'

Daphne understood. To surround anything, however ridiculous, with an air of mystery is to invest it with a secret charm of attraction which, to Thomas, was irresistible.

The day was almost over and they had used it, returned to the kitchen, to its smoky comfort among twisting walls and old stained cupboards. Thomas and Woo, Lukas and Daphne sat opposite each other leaving Kate to carve the beef at one end of the table and Benjamin to pour the wine at the other.

'Daphne,' asked Benjamin. 'Would you like red? I made this from plums grown in our garden. Your comments would be appreciated.'

'Very well, though rarely do I drink alcohol. It tends to go to my head pretty quickly.'

Lukas took note. 'Is that why you collapsed on the bed last night?'

'A classic example.' She took a sip before giving her verdict. 'Actually, it's very sweet as red wines go. Do you add sugar?'

'Honey, pure honey at its final stage, a recipe handed down from my father and his father before him.'

'When did Edward build this house?'

Thomas answered. 'To be exact, it was completed in 1863 when he was twenty-four.'

'Gosh, that would have made him thirty-nine when he died…or did he die? No, got that wrong, it was Joshua who died so his son would be your great, great, great grandfather?'

'Add another great. Edward and Joshua were cousins, a bit like Luke and me. We don't know when Edward died because his grave is not in the cemetery.'

'Is that where all the Giddy line is buried?'

'From Joshua onward,' answered Lukas. 'His son added the east wing and called it the Giddy Lodge, although it looks more like a patchwork quilt.'

'Oh, I don't know. I think it looks full of character and charm.' Her gaze returned to Benjamin. 'I wonder if I may be so bold as to ask if I can enter your domain, read the library walls.'

'How good is your Latin?'

'I have a degree.'

Not to be outdone, Thomas told her, 'Luke has a degree in five languages, including English.'

'But not in Latin,' Kate reminded. 'I required him to learn against my husband's wishes. We would not be in this position had Lukas been taught Latin.'

Benjamin came to his own defence. 'To teach one and not the other is-'

Kate waved it away. 'Benjamin Giddy, the only language our son understands is fore and aft, port and starboard. Now, Daphne dear, before you were so rudely interrupted, you were saying?'

'I was thinking…I tend to do that a lot sometimes. But it occurred two pairs of eyes are better than one. There may be a clue, a suggestion or a misinterpretation. One word can easily be misconstrued if you're not looking at it from the right angle. I mean, there has to be something that triggers a reversal in order for two men to draw blood. It could be a designated spot, or a designated time.'

As Lukas looked beyond her, out through the window his eyes blinked in the golden light of the setting sun and knew in that moment she might be on to something. He glanced back at Midnight, watched as she whizzed round his plate, choosing whatever she preferred to eat. She had told him her name, knew her name as though born to it. 'Ben, would you know if Edward mentioned a time on the wall?'

'Not to my knowledge.' Benjamin referred to Daphne. 'Let me explain, young lady. Prior to the advent of that diary, there was mixed confusion. We had assumed Joshua fell in love with Elizabeth. We now believe Edward loved Elizabeth and wanted to share a good life with her yet his condition made that impossible. He went out of his way to break his cursed affliction we think, which resulted in the death of his cousin, Joshua. Not only did Edward fail to achieve his desired goal, he left behind a wake of misery. Joshua's wife never remarried, his son was without his father and Elizabeth, we assume, made her escape with Edward. My Lukas was of the opinion to let sleeping dogs lie, to keep this family safe.'

'Now threatened because of me?'

'No, no, you must not think that. Philippe sent the diary to you for good reason and we must not question the wisdom of a saintly spirit. A man cannot live at another's determination. Lukas may not be our son but he is our family, even Kate's nincompoop brother and his wife. Fortunately, they are distanced apart living in California. Now you are part of our family by process of that diary, you have shelter and protection until the issue is resolved.'

'It has to be resolved pretty sharpish. I have a practice to run and animals to feed.'

'As we speak, your father has arranged for the closure of your surgery, the animals tended on your neighbour's farm and he himself settled in the South of France.'

'South of France,' she repeated with assumed confusion. Now turning her displeasured attention to Lukas, she said, 'You planned the whole thing, you and my Father?'

'I told the position before you boarded.'

'You did nothing of the sort.'

'So, your understanding was what? That you board for a joy ride until you got bored?'

'Oh, stop being so damn condescending. You said you needed my brains.'

'It seems they are a little vacant.'

She narrowed her eyes at him, used her fork as a pointer. 'You are a wily man, Lukas Giddy. Just you watch your step in future. I shall challenge every word you say.' The table was still waiting for her final rendition. 'What if I had refused to come?'

'The question is immaterial.'

Daphne laid her utensils aside, patted her lips with a serviette and nicely rose to her feet with a rhythm of a lady. 'Then I shall make it material in your immaterial world. Please to show me the library?'

There was certainly no visible anger and if he felt such emotions his heart and mind were well armoured to contain them. He drew back his chair in the dumb silence and took her down a hall barely wide enough for them to go abreast.

'Why the interest in Latin?'

'Mum spoke it fluently.'

'I thought she was a gypsy.'

'Even gypsies are entitled to have brains.'

He descended the stone steps that lead to Benjamin's private library, only just able to think calmly of the effect she had upon him. Closing the door softly behind them, he remained anonymous, patient, moved behind Benjamin's desk and picked up a book not really reading but rather trying to occupy his time where so great a silence reigned. For upon these library walls that had stood for two hundred years or more there also scribed a legend reserved for the cursed souls born to wear a mantle of doom. Whatever the case, the tale gave no indication of any soft passages. Indeed, many settled their accounts in early death.

'Obsura luna et talea,' she uttered at the wall, 'dark of the moon, cutter of threads…why dark of the moon?'

'She has two sides to her nature, bright and merciful, dark and vengeful.'

'The light of her moon, yes? Say, a clear sky at night under the light of a full merciful moon. There are thirteen full moons in a year. Do we assume it can be any full moon or must another ingredient be added, say the place of Boudicca's final battle.'

'Nobody knows where the final battle took place, only speculation by amateur historians.'

'Edward could have known. Perhaps that's why he felt certain he could face his enemy but his enemy outwitted him. How can you get over that problem?'

'Three problems,' Lukas said, holding up four fingers. 'First, discover the formula. Second, I need to keep Marcus in the dark, metaphorically speaking. Third, I have to set the trap, not an easy task.'

She went to him, her gold earrings framing her lovely eyes. 'You showed four digits?'

'How do I obtain your forgiveness?'

'Oh, it's not a question of forgiveness. We had sex and that was that, no ties, no promises. However, I did expect some decency, such as your involvement with prostitutes.'

'Charnel always has her girls tested.' He bit his tongue, watched as she covered her face with her hands, fearing, as it seemed, to look towards him. 'What do you wish me to say?'

'Nothing, absolutely nothing! I was the servant of love. You were the servant of shame.'

The silence was heavy. It was like a thick impenetrable wall between them. Lukas felt misery settle inside him like a lump of lead. 'Okay,' he said, his mouth twisted a little as he looked at her. 'I play cards for most of the time.'

'Oooh, do you ever believe the crap coming out of your mouth?'

'Not until I'm finished talking.'

'Alright,' she said, composing herself. 'I shall be understanding and very mature in the process. You are, after all different from other men and in light of your circumstance probably feel like James Bond. Are you licenced to kill?'

'Let's just say I have a get-out-jail card.'

'Do you have the gadgets to go with it?'

'Tom is still working on the exploding alarm clock which guarantees the user will never wake up.'

Smiling, she walked round to where he was sat and hoisted herself up on the desk. 'You have a very strong affinity with Tom.'

'He gave me reason to live. On the first change, I was more in shock and awe, conflicting elements to my new life. Six months later, when it happened again, reality dawned so I took Ben's gun from this very drawer, held it to my head and pulled the trigger. Amazing, I forgot to check if it had any bullets. And over there, by the door was Tom who saw everything. He grabbed my arm, took me to his boat yard, showed me plans for the *Abracadabra*, and suddenly a whole new world opened up.'

'It's an amazing vessel. I have never in all my life come across a vessel that has no crew. Do you know we literally glided in the fish dock then, as if she knew the spot, sort of wiggled her way in and shut down engines? And there was Tom busily doing a crossword.'

'Consider it like a program. Once she has gone through the motions, the computer has registered the act and then knows what to do.'

'I think she has feelings.'

'Tom would agree with you.'

'And Ben? He seems very protective.'

'Ben was my mentor. He was a judge, had heavy connections and there I was, a Giddy warrior fighting for truth and justice. I don't consider what I do illegal, though in truth it is. I feel it my duty, born to protect the weak, those everyday people which have been forgotten by the judiciary system. You once asked who made me judge and jury. Well, that's your answer on those walls. Andate made me what I am.'

'I don't suppose there's any chance of getting in touch with her?'

'In my desperate hours, many a time do I try. Ah, well, nobody answers, not even God. Perhaps Andate existed two thousand years ago and now she's gone with only her curse remaining. Who really knows of these things?'

'Do you dream? Do you dream of nice things or are they always nightmares?'

'Nightmares are the brothers of my sleep.' He pointed to a scar on his chin. 'This was my first encounter with a piece of shit. I had a stupid notion I could talk him round, get some psychiatric help. I was the dreamer, he was the victim. So, after he responded with a broken neck of a beer bottle, I cracked his jaw and put him in hospital for three weeks. What I should have done was to follow my client's instructions. Instead, the police left a note to pop into the station and on the way from the hospital he raped another woman.'

Daphne stared at him for a long moment then let her gaze fall behind him. She slipped off the desk and bent to the wall. 'The first I see,' she read aloud, 'is the last I see before I see all over again.' She looked back, a crease formed between her brows. 'Who wrote this?'

'Edward.'

'Strange thing to do.'

'Well Edward was strange. He covered these entire walls with his obsession.'

'He covered these entire walls in Latin and yet here he scribes in English.'

Lukas stared at the majestic clock, centrally positioned on a polished mahogany bookcase. He had no real answer, probably no answer at all. 'Let's say he got fed up with Latin.'

'Or let's say he never wrote it. The two people we have overlooked are Joshua's son and his wife. Surely, they must have known what was going on. Since Edward left them this house, why not the son writing that piece. So now we ask, what does it mean?'

He crouched beside her. 'What do I see?'

'You see a stone.'

'Right, I see a stone so the stone is the last to see…no, no, that makes no sense.' He traced the mortar joints and considered the discolouration was not consistent. 'I see a stone, I remove the stone and see the last thing to hide behind the stone and then I see the stone all over again.'

'Oh, well done!'

'Get Tom, tell him to bring a lump hammer and chisel.'

From the shed came the rattle of implements and scrambling feet while Lukas moved back the desk and rolled up the carpet. These walls were four feet thick, could hide valuables, spoils of war, a multitude of secrets.

Thomas bore his muscles with the first whack as the family looked on, blood up and bent necks. Whack, whack, the steel head of the chisel grew flatter. This was not binding, for the men fancied themselves as Builders, so they took it in turns to whack, whack at the mortar joints while the ladies discussed bath oils and babies.

Eventually the stone gave fraction. Lukas worked his fingers deep into the crack and pulled. The stone came away, rested heavy in his grasp. Placing it down on the floor, Midnight disappeared to probe a deep cavity, was gone for several seconds.

'Midnight,' Lukas hollered, 'is anything there?'

'Ants, lovely ants.'

'Leave the ants alone.' Lukas glanced back at his grinning audience. 'One has to make allowances.'

'Ohh, this is interesting.'

'What is?'

'Do you know the meaning of incompetence?'

Then emerging through the void, kicking up dust was Midnight, her sharp incisors dragging a postcard. It was a bleak irony that portrayed a picture of Cleopatra's Needle!

'I'm not going to say, I told you so,' Daphne said, 'but I will.'

A finger went to her face. 'You have two hours left to guess my favourite title!'

'I don't need another two hours.' She turned her back on him and walked off. 'Die another day, why don't you.'

Family rarely went far, they merely lingered, adding to the atmosphere. 'Not a word,' he told them severely and strode to the kitchen mumbling expletives under his breath.

Thomas joined him. 'You have to admit, she did figure it out from word go.'

'Christ, if I never knew better, she's Andate herself.' At the sink he poked his eye down the neck of an empty wine bottle and decided to make hot chocolate, so mixed was his feelings. 'What prat would hide something under the Needle? It makes no sense.'

'Sure it does. There's no guarantee this house would still be in the Giddy hands. But under the Needle, two hundred or more years, there is.'

'Like what?'

'Well obviously something important.'

'He could have hidden it behind that stone.'

'I thought we covered that?'

'Christ, my mind is like spaghetti junction. Just when I had it sussed, this happens. Philippe was right, simplicity is not her way.'

'Look, you said Philippe told you Edward did not do his homework, did not care to look.' Thomas pulled out a chair and sat down heavy, his hands clasped and resting on the table. 'It's doable, Luke. I checked it out. There's an old Victorian culvert approximately a hundred yards from the Needle, gets partly submerged when the river rises with the tide. It runs under the Needle and terminates just beyond before it bends to the North into a chamber that was filled with debris after Hitler dropped his bomb. I figure it like this. We go under cover of darkness, just right for low tide, locate the prime position, blow the ceiling, and the load drops right into our laps.'

'How long will it take?'

'With the right equipment, a couple of hours, no more I reckon. Of course, there is one slight drawback and that's Marcus. If he's figured it out, you need to keep him busy to make him think you haven't.'

'How can I keep him busy when I'm with you?'

'I'll take Dad.'

'Ben is needed here, to protect the girls.'

'Then I'll go alone.'

'And who's going to watch your back?'

Their attention was drawn to a polite cough. Leaned against the door-jam with her arms folded was Daphne. 'I don't understand why you make things so complicated. You have the *Abracadabra* to protect us all.'

'That is exactly what I'm talking about. We have the *Abracadabra* to protect you all.' Lukas wiped his face with his hands, it being chaos in this time of uncertainty then poked his head round the kitchen door. As suspected, there stood three others listening in. 'I suppose there's no point in asking if you want to come?' They shook their heads vigorously, no point at all. 'I must be out of my head. Tom, you're in charge of equipment. Ben, you're in charge of planning. Kate and Woo are in charge of food. Daphne, you're in charge of research. I'm in charge of sleep. Goodnight.'

There could be no greater symbol of impending calamity, conspiracy overtook events. He climbed the stairs as though his entire world was decomposing, shut himself in his bedroom and flopped on the bed. The ceiling was a better view than a picture of the *Abracadabra* turned into a passenger liner.

Of course Midnight wanted her pound of flesh. *'When do I get my mate Marmite?'*

'Your wedding is postponed.'

'Ohh...not even an engagement ring?'

'Not even I come close to that. How the hell did she guess my favourite slogan?'

'I never said anything.'

Lukas smiled and rolled on his side. He tried to take his mind off Daphne, more convinced every minute he had at last discovered the secret of human happiness, which was backed by no authority save his own courage in the long struggle to admit he was actually falling in love. He roused himself with an effort from this dismal state, switched on the bedside light and recalled with a sigh how he left her that afternoon in bed, guiltily closing the door behind him and telling Benjamin with a troubled face why he preferred whores. Already he could feel the wave of human stupidity strike fiercely throughout his body.

In the exhaustive catalogue of his misfortunes, he tip-toed to her room, hoping to find some germ of comfort and very carefully opened the door to a squeak. The main light went on and almost blinded him.

'Ever heard of knocking?'

'I thought you might be asleep.'

'And then what?'

'A cuddle?'

She turned a deaf ear to the request, pushed him back into the hall and shut the door in his face, nicely.

'What were you doing in the dark?'

'Waiting to throw you out.'

Elsewhere, Benjamin smiled on his pillow. 'She is perfect for our Lukas.'

Instinctively, Kate's hand curved protectively around his middle, soft, squishy belly from years of happy life. 'But is he perfect for her?'

'They are like two peas in a pod, good hearts with painful scars.'

And Benjamin knew about painful scars, the occurrence with his brother being one of them. Cold as that night was, the perspiration stood in beads upon his face, his every limb trembled, the power of articulation was quite gone, and there he knelt with a smoking gun under a bright frozen moon, gazing upon his brother's lifeless form. It was in this emergency that Benjamin displayed strength of mind which rendered him the admiration of his wife and son. They had the least notion of what his thoughts were and they ventured not to ask. But he had got by this time into such a complication of knots that it was perfectly clear to him his brother had to die.

14

Rising in splendour from spacious surrounds, the Castle Museum in Norwich was as magnificent and awe-inspiring as it must have appeared to those who saw it built as a Norman keep, the finest in England.

Certainly no respecter of law when it came to off street parking, Lukas steered through the iron gates and parked under the lift's bay.

'You can't park here,' said Daphne.

'I just have.' Lukas pressed a button on his key ring, and suddenly the bike took shape, locking grippers and folding seats transformed the Ducati into a thief-proof vehicle where not even a wheel-clamp could take possession. 'Now you know why Tom is my best mate.'

The lift doors opened. They stepped in. Please select your floor came the sexy voice from a speaker but there was only one button to press.

'What idiot designed this?'

'The Council owns and runs the museum.'

'Ah, that explains it.'

Following the wave of human traffic, they paid their entrance fee, dropped off their helmets and walked into the rotunda, going directly to the area devoted entirely to Boudicca.

'The name comes from bouda, meaning victory,' Lukas informed.

'But she never won.'

'I was demonstrating the extent of my Latin.'

Inside this hub of knowledge and artefacts, Lukas went to a revelatory footnote to the first uprising by the Iceni tribe which took place twelve years prior to Boudicca's rebellion.

Ostorius Scapula, the roman governor of Britain, decided to forcibly remove the personal weapons of the men of Southern Britain. Although the Iceni were allies of Rome they were included in this repressive measure. Their weapons were of great significance to them and they were outraged. The Iceni were a proud and independent people and became the first to rise up in open revolt against Rome.

The Iceni led an alliance by neighbouring tribes against the imperial armies. The roman historian, Tacitus tells us that the Iceni chose a battlefield at a stronghold, defended by earth banks. The roman army stormed the embankments from all sides. The Iceni were imprisoned by their own defences and were overwhelmed. Tacitus says that the Iceni fought for their lives with great courage. The Iceni were humiliated by their defeat and the roman armies marched west and left behind the Iceni tribe ruled by a king named Prasutagus who was husband of Boudicca.

Daphne came to his side. 'I discovered most of the military fittings were found at the roman forts at Saham Toney and Swanton Morley. Several came from Caister St. Edmund.'

'Do we assume Edward discovered where the last battle took place? Let's say he did. Let's say he found the place, went there at midnight, and even though he was encumbered by age, he still had to go because another element dictated the timing. Look here, Dap. When the Romans came over, they presented large sums to prominent Britons and tribal leaders. The Iceni took it as a gift. But when the Romans tried to recall these loans, the Iceni were shocked and offended.'

'That's the year when Boudicca revolted.'

'The south of the Thames, tribal leaders had already given up their land to the Romans, but not the Iceni or Trinovante to the east. The Romans left them alone. Why? Because they were a fierce and proud race and the Romans preferred to steer away from conflict. It's obvious, when her husband died and his wishes ignored she had every defence to initiate war.'

'Do you think the Romans were the instigators of the small print in contracts?'

'Is your father a Roman?'

'Probably. Do you know what Boudicca looked like?'

'In stature she was very tall and her voice harsh, the glance of her eye most fierce.'

'Sounds like a man.'

'Oh no, Dap. She had hair just like yours, except it was much longer, brilliant red, falling to her hips, and around her neck was a large golden necklace. She also wore a tunic over which a thick mantle was fastened with a brooch.'

'You talk as if you admire her greatly.'

'What's not to admire. She risked everything in the name of justice…my greatest wish, to turn back the clock and be by her side, fight the good fight. Have a poke around and see if you can find a description about her weapon.'

Lukas moved to study the locations of the two known battles. First was Colchester, a Roman stronghold left to be guarded by civilians and old soldiers. Boudicca had toppled the statues of their Gods, her army cut clean through spines and chests, women hung high on stakes, leaving corpses to moulder in the afterlife, flies hatching in their shits. She then marked south. London destroyed, razed to the ground. Further notes claimed she turned north, twenty miles away (St Albans), pushing forward, treading down corpses, oblivious to anything but her reward. After which she marched north again. But to where?

As he further looked around, he considered there was no harm in asking for help, and there, on the galleried landing was a young man wearing rimmed glasses, had a beard which was not quite a beard but gone beyond designer stubble, his head sometimes poked in a box of dead bones.

'Do you know much about Boudicca?'

'Try me.'

'Tacitus records Suetonius and his army arrived in London from the Isle of Mona, specifically to face Boudicca, yup? Yet here we have her turning north, destroying St. Albans then marching north again and meeting up Suetonius before he arrived in London.'

'You cannot rely solely on the annals of Tacitus. Archaeology also plays an important role.'

'What's your name?'

'Laurence, Laurence Holbeck.'

'So, Laurence Holbeck, has anyone dug up 80,000 skeletons near St. Albans?'

A warm smile played on the lips. 'There is a difference between intelligence and knowledge. Consider a mixed population of vast numbers, including farm animals all needing water. Either you follow the river north, crush St. Albans and carry on, or you take the A11 and return to Thetford.'

Right away Lukas liked him. They talked for several more minutes covering likely scenarios, compelling arguments for and against two armies seeking a head-on clash in a forest that no longer existed.

'Let me show you something.' Laurence took Lukas to a slim-line cabinet, glassed both sides, housing many small artefacts made by the metal workers of that era. Pointing to a particularly delicate stone that looked like a cartoon representation of Boudicca, he said, 'This is called a Millefiori, Italian, meaning a thousand flowers. Imagine the process using different coloured glass, like making a stick of rock then slicing pieces off. If we go round the back, we can see the same picture. The metal worker would no doubt encase the edges in gold and silver. We can speculate that it was designed for a ring. Take a look at that one with a raised profile. What do you think it is?'

'It looks deadly.'

'That's a roman key. The man would make a fist and insert the square profile into the lock. When we look at these things, we begin to appreciate the knowledge they had.'

'I don't see any coins with the head of Andate.'

'Andate?'

'The Goddess Andate to whom Boudicca paid homage, known probably by another name but specifically referred to as dark of the moon for she was generous as she was venomous with her light.'

'Childish revenge for a perceived injustice,' Daphne said. 'Learn anything new?'

'This is Laurence. Laurence has never heard of Andate.'

'That's because he's smart.' Her features bunched together and sparkled. 'Shall we have coffee? I'm told they do lovely chocolate cake. Laurence, care to join us?'

Professionally, Laurence declined and with this decision went back to his dead bones.

It seemed that Lukas was no further forward. 'Are we barking up the wrong tree?'

'If Andate is a tree then you lie in her shade.' She picked up a tray. 'Two coffees and two slices of chocolate cake, please. You have to remember only one thing. The curse can be broken. How, where and when is mere formality, like getting to know your next door neighbour.'

'£8.90,' said the girl at the till.

Lukas dug deep for some change. 'Why do I have this feeling you know something.'

'That's because I do.' Daphne walked off with the tray.

'Christ,' Lukas mumbled. 'She can be so bloody irritating.'

'You're the servant of shame and not its love.'

'Say another word and I'll eat you instead.' At the table he grabbed a chair, swung it round and sat down, leaning his folded arms on the backrest. 'Okay, hit me with it.'

'Why sit like that?'

'I like looking at my watch.'

'Luke,' she said quietly, keeping her voiced trimmed. 'If Marcus was to kill every night, what state would you be?'

'Tom has it covered.'

'Can you be more explicit?'

'End of me, end of Marcus.' After that, Daphne went silent, did not touch her chocolate cake or look at him. It gave him food for thought. 'Dap, would you miss me?'

'You know sometimes I think I know you and other times not. On the one hand you take a life without even a blink, and next you're prepared to sacrifice yours.'

'You wouldn't keep an animal alive if it was in pain.'

'But there are drugs, Luke.'

'Nope, don't go a bundle on drugs.'

'And what, may I ask do you smoke if it's not a drug?'

'It's a natural weed to numb my brain from questions like that.' He grinned. It had not endeared him.

'I have seen what pain does to man and beast, both lose the will to live so do not dare lecture me from a pedestal of self-sacrifice. I want you to be strong, confront him and bring him down, get a life, a better life with someone to love.'

'With my reputation, who would have me?'

'I would.'

His eyes flickered. 'You would?'

'I would.'

'Yesterday you were cracking my nuts.'

'And today I am inclined to stroke them…a little…only a little on the basis of your behaviour. Do you think you can meet my shopping list?'

Midnight reminded. '*The come home for supper and put bread on the table cannot be met.*'

'Ah yes, bread on the table.'

'What is wrong with you? Anyone can put bread on the table. I can put bread on the table. Even the tramp in the street can put bread on the table.'

'But it was on your list.'

'I know it was on my list.' She waved it away like she was emotionally imploding. 'Look, just forget it and eat your chocolate cake.'

'*Ohh, no nice Daffannee to cuddle.*'

'Dap, I-'

'My name is Daphne. If you have to use a term of endearment, please try something else, like Daphne.'

'Ohh, the last nail in your coffin.'

'Excuse me for one moment.' He strode out of the cafeteria, across the rotunda and into the men's cloakroom. 'Do you want me to flush you down the toilet?'

'Oh, please not the toilet.'

'If you have to give your opinion, make it noteworthy. I need to get her on my side.'

'I thought you needed to get her in bed.'

He shook his head and returned to the cafeteria, temporarily caught between two female minds. 'So,' he said, in the hope of reviving her interest. 'Tell me your thoughts?'

'Well,' she replied, licking her chocolaty fingers, 'the tribes to the east were wonderful metal workers.' And he sighed to this disappointing reply. 'From knowledge passed down by the Beakers who came to Britain three, four hundred years prior to Boudicca, they fashioned metal into wonderful objects, including axes, spearheads and swords. Now, interestingly enough, most of these objects were considered not as wealth but as status pieces so when they died these status pieces would be buried with them.'

'Boudicca's body was never found. Tacitus confirms this. Historians confirm this.'

'I'm not disputing that. Yes, we could say she was lost among the many, those who were slaughtered by the Romans or we could say her body was taken to a burial ground, along with her spear or sword, or whatever. If we skip a century or there about when the first affected Giddy was born, would it not be reasonable to assume that he had a fair idea of his condition. So what would his next step be? Ask around, talk to the tribe, and find out where Boudicca was buried.'

'I see. So, you're suggesting he raided something important, say her spearhead. Tacitus wrote she held a spear when addressing her army.'

'Christianity came late to Britons. He probably still prayed to Andate. Further, I am suggesting he not only took her spearhead or sword, he was also a metal worker, a possible descendant of the Beakers. They came from the Alps, you know. Anyway, this man, your ancestor Mr. Giddy Beaker says to himself, I have the spearhead of Boudicca, the greatest warrior ever lived. So, what would a metal worker do with such knowledge?'

'Depends what other knowledge he gained.'

Leaning to wipe the chocolate off his nose, she said so matter of fact, 'I would be inclined to re-use the metal.'

'Why.'

'Because Mr. Giddy Beaker was a metal worker, that's why. He reused the metal to make something far more interesting, something that could be used in defence against his counterpart.'

'He lost the battle, Daphne. The curse is still around to prove it. Every time a Giddy felt the need to confront his enemy he was thwarted, probably by old age…the exact same scenario that happened to Edward.'

'You don't know that. It's all guess work. Maybe he lost the battle because he wasn't a very good swordsman.'

'Can it be that simple?'

'But it's not simple, is it Luke?' She gave him a long look. For a baffling moment he had the impression of sadness, and when she spoke her voice was soft. 'Here we are trying to put pieces of a puzzle together without any pieces save for what Philippe told you. Is there anything…anything at all you might have missed, or misconstrued, anything, no matter how small?'

As this was said in the tone of one who cared and asked the question as a thing of course, Lukas went into his own internal distance and recalled the moment.

'Alas, simplicity is not her way. Like love, it provokes many symptoms, pounding heart, fear of loss, memories on paper for others to mourn. Edward sought his protection by running away to live with the woman he loved…poof, gone, but not his pain and so ended his pride.'

Only now did he fully comprehend. 'What an idiot. Philippe was not telling how Edward sought his protection. He was conveying Edward's thoughts and actions.' Lukas spoke into his watch. 'Tom, are you ready for this?'

'Excuse me!' Daphne protested. 'Why didn't you tell me that watch was a whatever?'

'Is there something to hide?'

She opened her mouth to speak then closed it, trapped in her own argument.

'Good, I shall continue. Edward, the recluse, meets Elizabeth Whittle, probably introduced by Joshua, the excavator, the sniffer dog. He found something important, so important he buried it under the Needle. Then it goes pear-shaped. Joshua gets killed, that weakens Edward. So what does Edward do? He leaves England and takes Elizabeth with him to wherever, another country. And in this other country he writes in the diary, wrapping the memories on paper for others to mourn…not to mourn in the sense of bereavement but for others to take note of the hidden clue, the lady threads a needle…Andate being the cutter of threads, the Needle being the same Needle erected on the Thames. And Joshua's son fashions a message in the library, leaving the same clue behind that stone. Tom, you were right, they were leaving the same clue in two places just in case the diary got lost or the house got sold.'

'What about astounding me further?' Thomas asked. 'Tell me what's under the Needle.'

'I have no bloody idea. One thing I'm certain. Edward's counterpart knew. He knew Joshua had found something important and killed him but it was too late because Joshua had already buried it and nobody knew where except Edward and Elizabeth so they decide to get lost.'

'Joshua's son must have known.'

'Yes, much later after Edward had established a new identity. You must remember, Joshua's son was very young at the time, confused probably as to what it was all about, thus his story handed down was vague. All he did was to follow Edward's wishes and hide the postcard behind that stone.'

Daphne spoke. 'Is there any chance of telling me why Philippe would send the diary to me?'

'You speak Latin,' Tom said.

'There,' Lukas agreed, 'you speak Latin.'

'Lots of people speak Latin.'

'True,' they voiced together.

'I can see the brains have stopped working.' She gathered her bag. 'We should make our way back…any chance of converting the bike into a car?'

'Do you really want me to answer that?'

Without further word they walked through the rotunda, picked up their crash helmets and advanced toward the entrance. As Lukas opened the heavy glass door he glanced back and caught a glimpse of a cassock scurrying up one flight of stairs. Trusting and troubled, he moved on in the semi-light and swung his focus on a gleaming hood parked nearby the gated overpass. Were the priest and the motor an item? The aggressive front end of the black Porsche was a typical choice for a man like Marcus.

Upon returning to the Giddy Lodge, the smell of new paint as evident now as it was when they first arrived. Daphne switched on the kettle while Lukas stuck his head in the fridge for a beer.

Thomas emerged in the rough, his whiskered face covered in grease. 'Mum popped next door to see Mrs Jones. Woo tagged along with Dad.' Thomas homed in close to Lukas so that he was almost whispering in his ear. 'Are you alright, my man?'

Lukas did not answer. Setback required planning. He looked straight ahead, beyond his cousin and watched Daphne lay the table. What he would do to be with her. If he could just get through this, if he could surmount the impossible hurdle, find another way then she was there for the taking, his little piece of happiness.

Again Thomas tried. 'Luke, what's on your mind?'

Lukas indicated with his head and went to the back door, Thomas close behind. As they met the air across the threshold, he said, 'Marcus was at the museum.'

'Do you think he figured things out?'

'Good question, ergo, do I take that chance or put the animal in captivity.'

'An animal with crocodile teeth and a tongue as smooth as a snake…the hand that feeds such an animal would be hard pressed to avoid their conscience.'

'He lived off me for fifteen years.'

'And that gives you the right to be his jailor?'

'It gives me the right to live by my own determination.'

'Okay, where do you suggest we put him, in the brig, because that's the only place we got, Luke?'

'Just for a bit until I find somewhere else.'

Thomas blotted his forehead against his sleeve. 'Look, I know things look hopeless, a setback, yeah? Hell, even I felt sick about him hovering close by but think of what you're saying. You're going to cage a man and above his stink you're going to try and live an existence with Daphne. Will you expect her to feed him when you're away killing a rodent? If so, then he's got you by the balls either way.'

'Then what do I do? The client wants a kill. You might as well put a gun to my head.'

'We get what's under that Needle.'

'He was there, at the museum or did that slip your mind?'

'That's good, Luke. Well bad really, but we have to look at it positively. We have the girls under our wing, right?' Thomas cocked his ear. 'I hear Dad's motor.'

'You go ahead. I need to think.'

Lukas squeezed his eyes shut, trying to quieten the pounding in his head then walked on with his beer, taking in the summer fragrances. Seating himself under a spreading honeysuckle close by the river, and stretching his legs over green grass, he took from his pocket a reefer and began to smoke. It was a lovely late afternoon of that gentle kind. He looked at his watch, content to linger his eyes on the time wishing this moment to stand still forever. Midnight scampered out of his breast T-shirt pocket and settled on his leg. *I have a headache too.*

'Since meeting Daphne, the world isn't the same, Midnight. She takes all the rough edges away, smells like a bunch of flowers and looks like a garden of Eden.'

'*And you want to be her Adam.*'

'But I am Lukas Giddy, so far removed from the everyday things two lovers take for granted that I don't even know where to begin.'

'*You begin by telling her the truth.*'

'Which part did you not understand?'

'*I was never in love with Charlie. He just happened to be in Woo's picnic basket and I thought a little sex could go a long way.*'

'I wondered how you got him on board.'

'A word if I may.'

Lukas looked up. 'Sure.'

Daphne came down on her haunches cupping her hands together, something hidden, something delicate she was holding. 'I found him in the rough by the church.'

They interchanged one brief glance as Midnight came to inspect, her nose running free as unchecked as her feet. She sniffed him, bit him, licked him and chased him across the lawn, procuring the happiness she deserved between the Holy and the Ivy.

'Daphne, we need to talk.'

'We most certainly do,' she said, taking a patch beside him. 'I saw him too.'

'No, I want to talk about us. Not specifically us but the general view of us.'

'Can you meet my shopping list?'

'Not at this point in time.'

'Then there can be no us with that attitude.'

'It's not my attitude, rather the circumstance of my position.' He paused to let his smoke curl slowly away, and to sniff her grateful perfume. 'Most of my clients come via an organization that has people like me on their books, yup?

Tom gets a call, he susses the job and if it meets my parameters he takes it on. The money is good. It pays for his toys. It pays for our keep. And it supplements the poorer clients I take on.'

'A very noble cause. Is it Government backed?'

'I'm not at liberty to say.'

'James Bond doesn't have a problem. He tells his readers he works for MI6.'

'Nobody knows who's who and the guy running the show might well be a block of ice for all I care. What I'm trying to say is that Marcus-'

'It's alright, Luke. I understand perfectly.'

'I don't think you do.'

'You sit there looking at me as though you're the worst possible bet I could take on.' She shrugged her shoulders. 'You are the worst possible bet I could take on. But you can beat him, Luke, and be as happy as you were that Christmas day, before the change.'

'Does this give me licence to take you to bed?'

'Your application is presently under review.'

A part of him yearned to cry on her shoulder, a qualified sob about his predicament, the greater part worked against it. He reached for her hand and pressed his lips to her fingers, the best that could be achieved. 'Tell me how you guessed my favourite slogan.'

'Well,' she said, resting herself against him, 'the jumper you wore when first we met was frayed around the breast pocket. After meeting Midnight, and comparing the jumpers in your wardrobe when you left me in your cabin, it seemed logical that had to be your favourite.'

'So you already snooped in my wardrobes?'

'You never asked me if I had, only asked me not to.'

There were birds to watch, ants, worms, dormice as they darted across the grass, and other living things on the water to have interest in, and yet his entire concentration was on Daphne, the smell of her hair haemorrhaging over his shoulder and the feel of her bosom pressed soft against his side. Even in the throes of uncertainty, she could inspire awe.

15

'Best scenario, he'll contact me for a meet. Worst scenario, he's looking for a window of opportunity to snatch one of the girls. If that's the case then we can be sure he knows what we're up to.' Such were the thoughts of Lukas.

Planning took time. It stretched the patience and exhausted the nerves. Marcus had dogged him for four days, and now the Giddy men revolved around the desk in the same cool library reporting their progress.

Thomas went next, pin pointing a spot on the map. 'We moor here. Daphne leaves to survey the area. When she gives the all clear, I go in with Dad. She then goes to the Needle and stands here. Her beacon will locate the position where we blow. We need half an hour to drill and plant the Semtex. We then wait for Daphne to give the signal. We mustn't blow until the road sweeper vehicle passes over this spot. We then have fifteen minutes to gather the loot, duck out of the culvert, lock the gates and we're on our way home. Luke, did you contact Oban?'

'He said the stuff is in the old boat house lodge in the barrel marked tar.'

'Great. Dad, over to you?'

'As chief planner I am entitled to sit behind my desk.' With Lukas directed to stand, Benjamin focused on his son. 'You drive like a tortoise. Do you know what the accelerator is for?'

'I was keeping to the speed limit.'

'There are no limits in what we have to do. As we speak, the enemy is parked outside The Wherry. We must assume he is going to make his move tonight, so we shall turn it to our advantage. We shall take the tunnel to the cemetery. Lukas, you will secure the stone and return here, ensuring you keep Marcus busy for the duration of our task. We shall call upon the vicar for the use of his car.' Benjamin looked at his watched. 'We have approximately ten hours in which to board the *Abracadabra*, advance to London, make a raid on the Needle and evacuate the area before the river police patrol the area. Are you up for this?'

'Count me in,' they said in unison

'Thomas, tell the girls to ready themselves.' Benjamin held Lukas back. 'Do not do anything foolish, my Lukas. If our endeavours fail to bring results we shall talk of caging the lion.'

That lifted his spirits. 'Thanks, Ben.'

'You look a little peaky. Are you on the change?'

'Truth? I'm sexually frustrated.'

'Kate opened to me six months from the time I dined her on chocolates and roses.'

'Hell, I could be dead tomorrow.'

'Have you told her of your predicament with Exit?'

Lukas shook his head. 'I was about to then I thought of the repercussions, moreover she might look at me as a lost cause.'

'That is good. Not for pity sake but for decency. You cannot look upon her as you would a whore. You need to earn her respect.'

'That's all very well in the days of yore but she had boyfriends climbing in her bedroom window.'

'She was a young girl seeking affection at a vulnerable stage in her life, when her mother was diagnosed of cancer. Yesteryears or now, the days of yore are still applicable. A woman requires a man to respect her wishes, to know he can be trusted, for therein lay the foundation of love.' He patted the arm. 'Enough sermonizing, we must proceed.'

And so, the plan was taking place. Lukas, working hard to quell his anxiety went to the kitchen and opened the hatch lodged behind a secret panel. It was Edward who had created this escape route, linked to the relative sanctuary of the church and used many times by Lukas in his younger days when the world seemed so exciting. The wind whistled through the tunnel then died off, seeming to pass round the kitchen, the ghosts of dead people unable to sleep easy in their graves.

Daphne came into view. She peered in a dark and dank space. 'Wow, I bet that's full of cobwebs.'

He brought from his top pocket Midnight and Marmite, put them in a paper bag and gave them to her. She burst into laughter and passed her arm around his neck, a brief moment of intimacy.

'No heroics, Dap. Keep to the plan, yup?'

'I promise.'

Lukas took the lead with a torch. At the end of the tunnel, he climbed the short rungs of an iron ladder flaked with rust, pulled the bolt and slipped it out of its clamp with little resistance, the trapdoor flew down and above that he proceeded through a vacant coffin. With his shoulder he put strength into the effort of dislodging a gravestone riveted down by overgrowth.

There would be no loitering. Wordlessly, they climbed the short rungs, all slipping away silently in the hushed surrounds of an eerie cemetery. Then Lukas shouldered the gravestone back into position, bolted the trapdoor and flew down the tunnel. At the point of dusting himself down, his mobile trembled in his back pocket. No two guesses the caller.

'Coming out to play?'

'Where?'

Expecting Marcus to say The Wherry, instead he was told to leave via the front door. He walked on the path, the brown body of earth, his eyes glancing to left and right. There was a mild wind in the evening air, a sudden satisfaction Marcus was waiting, casually leaning against his motor and looking like a jewellery shop.

'So, what brings you to my neck of the woods?'

'I thought we could have a drink.'

'Is there something to celebrate?'

Marcus plucked a blade of grass from the T-shirt. 'Been doing a spot of gardening?'

'I buried the cat.'

'You don't have a cat.'

'That's why I buried it.' Lukas could see frustration on the face, the mental agony of neediness. They remained staring at each other in mutual contempt, until he broke the silence. 'How's your love life? Found anyone yet?'

'Since we share the same fate, I thought we could share the same woman.' Marcus leaned forward, his heavy gold necklaces framing his crazed eyes. 'Do you think she'd be up for some arse?'

That hit a nerve. The blow to Marcus came swift, was returned in equal measure and strength. From a skirmish, they went at each other like hammer and tong, anything to cause injury, anything to draw blood. Perhaps it was best this way, the only way to keep Marcus busy.

They fought for a good half hour, ducking, weaving, pounding, and goading, forgetting in the intensity the outcome was predictable. It was written by the will of Andate, the inevitability of what was true of one was true of another. Two people linked by a curse that made them invulnerable to each other, not even a scratch or a small bruise. And suddenly somewhere in the parting clouds the moon shone her light on their foolishness, a reminder of their useless endeavours. When all said and done, they sank back, exhausted.

Marcus rolled to one side and brought from his back pocket a gold flask, took a swig then proffered it to Lukas. 'I never understood why she made your side worse for their curse. What's the point? My kind just buggers off and your kind hides in a rabbit hole. Ironic, don't you think?'

Lukas had himself suffered from these torments, forced to agree. 'I fear Andate has forgotten us. She leaves us to our fate as she leaves her mark on both of us.' The whisky trickled hot down his throat. 'What made you do it? Your first kill?'

'No mystery. The old man wanted to give his entire fortune to the unborn brat…couldn't let that happen.'

'Why not contest it?'

'And be judged by the same men who steel lollipops from kids. Wake up, old bean, and take a look around you. Show me a place on the map where humans don't defecate. I do this planet a favour.'

'And me no favour at all.'

'Interesting you brought up that subject. I have a proposal to make. Reconsider your position and join forces with me.'

Lukas threw back his head and laughed. The irony was palpable. Here he was, sat on the grass entwined to his target in the middle of nowhere, a target he could not kill and offering a deal that would ensure both their deaths. He had done nothing but reconsider his position.

'Do you know how I make my money?' Marcus never paused for an answer. 'Out there are thousands of rich widows, gone past their sell-by-date. Some treat me like a son, some like a cuddle, some like a bit more, and some just want to show off. But they pay for it, Giddy. Their husbands build up a fortune, die of old age or die of a heart attack and I get it all.'

'Hell, you must pay a lot of taxes.'

'Try not to undermine your level of intelligence in front of me, Giddy. You know damn well I have nothing in my name that's why I never get caught. And I can show you how to do it.'

'I am what I am. You are what you are. The hand of Andate balancing our lives, our punishments merely deferred.'

'Wake up, Giddy. You'll find no sweet scented luxury from the likes of Daphne Frisk, but with me, I can show you something more appetising.' Marcus jumped to his feet and dusted himself down. He was a lone man waving boldly in the corrupt sands of human conflict.

Considering there was no choice, Lukas glanced at his watch and reasoned quite rightly the *Abracadabra* was now on its way, lambasting the North Sea waves at forty knots. It would be the darkest of times.

16

Above the unending voice of water, the women were drowsily gossiping and taking no notice of Benjamin who had fallen half-asleep across the stateroom table.

'Oh, he was so handsome,' said Kate folding her knitting in half. 'That black hair sweeping back from his proud forehead and then of course those extraordinary lashes no man has a right to. He claimed his hair turned grey because of Lukas. Poor Lukas, he was such a handful. He painted Nitwit's tail, though to be honest that's what cats do. They eat rodents. We never bothered with another after that episode, which put our son's nose completely out of joint. Daphne dear, Lukas was telling me you collect animals like picking daisies off a field.'

'Only unwanted pets, and yes, unfortunately there are many. But where I can, I find them good homes. What about you, Woo? Do you like animals?'

'I married one.'

Their laughter brought Benjamin out of his doze. He sat upright, wiped his face with his hands and then regarded them all, exchanging complicit smiles. 'Thomas takes after me.'

Kate rolled her eyes. 'Benjamin, you are a pussy cat in comparison to our son. It took you six months to show me the colour of your underwear.'

'Good things come to those who wait.'

'Now you understand why Lukas is so arrogant,' Kate told Daphne. 'Still, underneath their bravado, good hearts beat.'

'How did you two meet?'

'We bumped into each other on a ski slope…the nature of his betrayal was entirely sexual for the very first thing he said when his eyes wandered over my breasts, is that padding.'

Benjamin coloured. 'I was referring to your ski suit.'

'Yes, dear, of course you were.' With that, Kate packed her knitting away and kissed the top of his head. 'Wake me when it's done. Woo, you should get some rest.'

Having brought their conversation to an end, they parted company. Woo and Kate to their respective beds, Benjamin to the hold of the vessel, and Daphne to pursue her interest in the gadgets on the bridge, where sat Thomas, hunched over a cryptic crossword with his fist supporting his chin.

'Are we there yet?'

Thomas looked up. 'What's a point in time for two to meet? Eight letters, third letter U, maybe.'

She peered over his shoulder. 'Coupling?'

'Damn, you're good.' Thomas scribbled it in. 'We're not far off. Where's the gang?'

'Your mother went to bed after destroying your father's ego… Woo followed, the instigator of said destruction and somewhere in the hold lurks a man stowing his pride.' Daphne glanced about, at the shiny screens and blinking lights, and said, 'So, this is where the hub of your exciting invention happens?'

'They don't talk.' Thomas smiled in the turn of his head. 'I enter the co-ordinates and docking procedures from here, right? The sensors fore and aft project distance from oncoming vessels, automatically steering to avoid calamity, a bit like the sensors on your father's motor except I don't need to be at the wheel.'

'And that screen, why is there a dot blinking on a street map?'

'Ah, that's Luke keeping Marcus busy. You see lodged under his skin at the base of his neck is a small device which transmits his location.'

'I thought his watch transmitted his location.'

'It could do but it's no good if it's lost or stolen. I need to know where he is in case of trouble.'

Unexpectedly but expectedly, she peered closer at the screen. 'Charring Cross Road? Isn't that-'

'Over here,' said Thomas quickly to avert her attention, 'we have a secondary back up system should the cooling system fail on the main drive. And here, you will really like this…we can seal her up tight and dive under water.' But he could tell from her expression she was trying hard to figure it out. More avoidance tactics were needed. 'We are coming up to Waterloo Bridge.'

But she was not happy, any more than was Thomas. He gathered his overalls and went directly to the hold where stood Benjamin garbed in his own bent over a power drill like bending over a pile of weeds. 'Dad, Lukas is at Charnel's.'

'No doubt keeping Marcus occupied.' Benjamin straightened, unperturbed. 'I cannot find the bolt cutters.'

'Under the bench behind the tool box…Marcus doesn't go there to play cards.'

'Look upon this as his duty.'

'I doubt Daphne would see it that way.'

'There is no other way but to give him the benefit of the doubt.' Benjamin's eyes wandered ahead. 'Ah, we have our third conspirator.'

'The first thing men do is look at breasts.' Daphne unzipped her cardigan. The men blinked. She had taken it upon herself to wear Lukas's T-shirt. *For your eyes only* spread across her bumps.

'Well,' said Thomas scratching his head, 'If Lukas was here, he would definitely appreciate the gesture.'

'My son, even I appreciate the gesture.'

Daphne, with a sort of beholden gasp zipped up her cardigan and said, 'So, chaps…are we there yet?'

'Nearly,' replied Thomas. 'Let's quickly run over our duties. Daphne, you first.'

'I parachute from the stern, duck under cover, scout the area, give the all clear, take a hike to the Needle, wait for the road sweeper, inform HQ, return pretty sharpish and aid in the haul.'

'No! No aid in the haul. We can handle the jars.'

'The jars will come crashing down. You need me there to help pick up the pieces.'

Thomas made no further appeal, his blue eyes levelled steadily at his father. 'Do you ever get the feeling this might go disastrously wrong?'

'My son, what could possibly go wrong? You have instructed your mother to teach Woo how to make English tea and I still cannot find the bolt cutters.'

Interdependent upon each other and refusing to seek the more ominous picture of failure, Thomas shuffled under the bench and passed over the bolt cutters then brought from his pocket a watch for Daphne. Surgery or raid, her eager persona was the same. She strapped it to her wrist, platted her hair, gave him a salute and disappeared topside.

'She will make him a wonderful wife,' said Benjamin.

'Not if he keeps shagging whores.'

'My son, James Bond would do no differently.'

'True,' said Thomas nodding in agreement.

Halfway between Waterloo Bridge and Golden Jubilee Bridge, the white presence of the Needle hung immense above its base. The *Abracadabra* made a sweeping turn to point her bow east, slowed upon the approach and held fast alongside the embankment one hundred yards distance from the Needle. For here was the disused culvert, which once allowed water to pass underneath the road, and one of many subterranean rivers built during the growth of the Metropolis of London.

After Daphne disembarked and gave the all clear, Thomas punched the bright red button. In slow motion, the starboard doors slid back revealing the gated culvert just above the current waterline. Benjamin used the bolt cutters and snapped the padlock. Men and equipment leapt into the breach. They would go unnoticed, would not be challenged by any authority save for a higher divinity.

Bounded by slime-deck walls and the light of their torches, they moved on to trace the prepared course. Its generous conduit gave rise to a number of discarded pieces that once floated freely on the Thames. Avoiding old kegs and squashing by foot twenty-first century paper waste, they finally halted and surveyed the scene, torches arching over walls built with precision, brick by brick laid in soft mortar joints. It could not get any better than this.

Then Daphne's voice came over the wire. 'Roger, roger, all quiet on the street, road traffic minimal.'

'Are you in position?'

'X marks the spot, over and out.'

All was going to plan. Not minding that they trod on each other's toes like chicks in a nest, they worked fast to hack fissures in the brickwork above, filled in turn with plastic explosives.

'It's possible,' said Thomas, his voice not sounding too reassuring, 'that the whole thing might collapse around us.'

'I have every confidence in you.'

'Thanks, Dad.' Thomas spoke into his watch. 'Daphne, confirm your position and situation?'

Over shadowed by history with the dawn clawing pink across the sky, she was crossing her fingers as well as her legs, watching the road sweepers' sweep on their feet, not in their noisy chariot as forecast by Thomas. If ever there was need for improvisation, it was now. 'The sweeper is sweeping most energetically.'

'We detonate in ten seconds, over and out.'

Giving time to make her escape, they crouched in their watery grave ten feet away in pitch darkness and dead silence. It had taken only a small amount of Semtex to blow the ceiling, unravel the fuse wire and hit the button. With an eruption of sound and dust, the ceiling collapsed and with it came a pile of rubble. Then quietness blanketed the scene. Shining his torch into a haze of dust, Thomas was the first to venture forward, seemed to be content to stand around under the flat base of the Needle, scratching his head.

Benjamin looked up. 'Perhaps the base was thicker than you calculated.'

'I was certain of my calculations.'

'My son, nobody can be certain of anything.'

Daphne had joined them and reconciled all anomalies. She picked up a lump hammer and gave the base a thwack. With a splintering crack, Thomas shouted 'move!' and suddenly the base split open, bursting upon its seams, bringing with it two clay jars, showering them in the wreckage. Certainty had certainly provided inevitability.

In coughs and splutters, shaking the debris out of their hair, off their shoulders, suffocating themselves with laughing, there was not a moment to lose. By the light of their torches they gathered their bounty, even the fragments of broken pottery, stuffed their sacks, collected the equipment and made haste to the exit point. They were a fine team, had worked well together. Everything was as it should be. Yet someone had climbed on board, unnoticed.

Thomas, the last to scramble into the open side of the *Abracadabra*, reversed to shut the gated culvert entrance and replaced the padlock. It did not matter their blackened faces or the odd bump on the head. All that mattered was to empty their sacks and sort out their load on the floor.

And what a load it was. From photographs of the best looking English women of the day, there was also a box of hairpins, a box of cigars, several tobacco pipes, a set of imperial weights, a baby's bottle, some children's toys, a shilling razor, a hydraulic jack, a complete set of English coins, a rupee, a portrait of queen Victoria, a 3inch bronze mould of the monument, plans on vellum, a translation of the inscription, copies of the bible in several languages, a copy of Whitaker's Almanac, a Bradshaw railway guide, a map of London, ten copies of daily newspapers. And a steel tube, length seventeen inches, diameter six inches, the rusty screw cap constricting access.

'Nope,' Thomas puffed, 'it's not budging an inch.'

'Give it to me.' With a whack from a spanner, Benjamin unscrewed the cap and withdrew three sheets of badly stained parchment upon which Latin dictated the language. 'My God!' he astounded and squeezed his eyes shut for a moment to focus more clearly. Written in the pen of Tacitus, it was known two of his annals were lost, now one had been found. He gasped again. 'Boudicca!'

While they grouped themselves around their find, in the shadows not fifteen feet away, Lukas laid his head flat against the bulkhead wall. God knows what magic that name had for his ears. He breathed out his condition of guilt for not so long ago he was bereft of hope. It pursued him through his time with Marcus and the relapse into his former self. And suddenly the face of Angel had become the face of a gutter grotesque. There he remained, for a good space, silent, penitent and resigned.

There being now a great relief, talking over each other, the sound of their voices and footsteps caused Lukas to back off and quietly pad to his quarters. Here he ducked under the shower to rid the smell of Angel's perfume, his face, chest and private locations were scoured like a chalk board.

Wiping the fog off the mirror with a hand towel, he saw a face that was not his face, not the face he wanted to see, a face of innocent survival, not of guilty looks. He took a deep breath and ran his fingers through his wet hair. Sleep had hardly been thought of all night and his expression was so aggravated by want of rest that Thomas coming into his quarters would have supposed some mortal pest or plague.

'Had a nice time?'

'You can look at me with those judgemental and incriminating eyes all you want. I did what I had to do.' Lukas pushed by, wrapping a towel round his waist. 'Did Daphne know where I was?'

'I'd like to say no. Still, the good news, we found-'

'Get some sleep, Tom.' This was not the time at which he wanted to enter on the state of his mind.

17

With the sun brightening on the waters of the Thames, Lukas was in his silk pyjamas striding down the main deck, the wind blowing free in his hair. What Thomas had told him, and what he had supposed to be a delusion of his, now came into sight. Great numbers of people were out, even the tourists clicking away at their cameras, and round the leaning Needle of Cleopatra people stood with gaping mouths, apart from one another, not venturing to guess the cause.

Thomas turned in his towelling dressing gown. 'I heard this almighty crack,' he explained, 'made little or no thought until Woo pushed me out of bed.'

'Would you mind telling me why we're still at the scene of the crime?'

'Ah, that is the right question, my man. I remembered after talking to you that Dad left my bolt cutters in the tunnel.'

Lukas fell back and gazed at him while he poured out these words. But anger and fear soon got the mastery of him. 'What the hell is wrong with you!' He pointed to the Needle which was slowly increasing its angle of descent. 'Not only will that catastrophe hit the Thames and alert Marcus, you left evidence behind! Well don't just stand there, get us out of here!'

Thomas was speedily gone.

Lukas was anxious for their safe return, and yet, though his own wellbeing hung upon it, felt a relief when the *Abracadabra* made distance. He returned to his quarters and switched on the goggle-box, his eyes glued to the news.

'…this is not the first time Cleopatra's Needle posed a mystery,' the TV reporter said. 'When the British defeated Napoleon in the early 19th century, the Viceroy of Egypt commemorated the victory with a gift of ancient mason. Unfortunately, the Needle's tremendous weight delayed its journey back to London by several decades. When the shipment finally got underway in 1877, tragedy struck. A raging storm hit halfway round the Bay of Biscay and a rescue crew dispatched from the steamship were dragged to the bottom of the sea. Another ship was sent to tow the boat home, and it finally arrived in January 1878 where John Dixon was given the job of designing and building the monument's pedestal. We are now going over to Julian Chubby.'

'Thank you, Angela.' A well-fed bloke with a fruity voice and floppy hair conveyed the news on site. 'Yes, as you can see the area is now cordoned off by the Port of London Authority. At approximately nine-thirty this morning, an American tourist alerted the police when he observed the Needle was tilted toward the river. Prior to that a maintenance contractor, George Shelly claimed he heard a loud thud and the ground trembled beneath his feet. With me now is George Shelly.' The camera went on to the road sweeper clinging fast to the handle of his broom and just as he was about to be interviewed the Needle had finally submitted its weight to the Thames.

Lukas dropped his head into his hands and whispered, 'Oh Jesus, how worse can it get.'

'Look on the bright side, nobody died.'

'What do you think Marcus is going to do when he figures this out?' He crooked his head round at Thomas as if he was still searching for that answer. 'Are the others up?'

'Mum and Woo are making scrambled eggs. I'm real sorry about this, Luke. The only thing I can work out is that Dixon made short-cuts in his design.'

They looked at the screen. The police got involved, of course, ambushed old ladies and tourists, but discovered nothing. Their enquiries were met by stares, though they kept within the area to the accompaniment of the Mayor of London.

Suddenly, Daphne, wearing her daisy white pyjamas burst in. 'Is it true?' she asked, wiping the sleep from her eyes. 'Has the Needle fallen into the Thames?'

'You told me the sweeper was sweeping,' said Thomas.

'Oh fiddlesticks, I had to make a board room decision, either that or Lukas spends another night with whores.' She looked from him to Lukas and said in a gentler tone, 'Did you want that?'

'Not really.'

'There.' Then she turned her attention to the news, viewing the Mayor of London. 'Oh my goodness would you look at that. Surely he can afford a decent barber.'

As Thomas left the room, carefully and without noise, Lukas remained in his seat, with his gaze intently fixed upon Daphne. 'Well,' he said with a deep sigh, 'where do we stand?'

For a moment she withdrew her eyes from the screen and looked at him with wonder. 'You did what you had to do just like I did what I had to do. I think I shall catch up on some sleep.'

Her words had an effect. It humbled Lukas and made him uncertain. Hard words he could have returned, violence he would have repaid with interest, but this cool, content reply made him feel indistinct than the most elaborate arguments. He wanted her to be upset, angry even, for that would have shown the depths of her feelings toward him. Or had he actually broken the camel's back?

He switched off the goggle-box and fell asleep on the sofa, a chequered sleep with starts and moans, and sometimes with a muttered word or two. His dreaming was so strong that it was full of vague terror with someone calling in a strange voice, and the voice becoming louder, so loud he woke with a start.

Just as he looked at his watch, four in the afternoon, and about to give his legs a stretch, Benjamin waltzed in with a tray that sizzled with the smells of bacon and eggs, to be washed down by a full mug of tea.

'Did you have a good sleep, my Lukas?'

'I heard a harsh voice or was I dreaming?'

'No, you heard right. We were boarded by a very brisk Harbour Master.'

'Are we in Lowestoft?'

'That we are. Thomas and Woo were inclined to return the vicar's car and bring back your motor bike and motor launch then we plan to take a trip to France.'

'Why?'

'Due to current enlightenment, you need to see Philippe. Let me explain.' Benjamin settled opposite, smiled with amuse forbearance. 'Tacitus wrote in the language of the Romans but he, himself was Greek. These two languages were often combined. It had to be Joshua who found one of the missing annals of Tacitus, most likely on a dig in Egypt and came to England to see Edward. Edward, long past hope was encouraged by his cousin to break the curse. Let us say that Joshua took Edward to the banquet held by Sir Erasmus Wilson where many eminent scholars would no doubt be invited. There he meets Elizabeth and falls in love. Edward had half the answer, this I am certain yet he chose not to pursue it further after Joshua died and ran away with Elizabeth. We are half way there, my Lukas. We know the when.'

'We know the when?'

'Yes, indeed, we know the when.'

'Was Daphne of help?'

'Most certainly,' pursued Benjamin, nodding his head and pointing his finger playfully, 'she is of tremendous help in establishing the correct translations of Tacitus. He writes a most avid account of the last day in battle where night and day is no longer unequal, the armies stilled and two men came forth, a last chance to kiss the memory, to traverse the bloodied ground and find release-'

'I saw it, Ben! I read those words in the book Philippe passed over-'

'And nothing further, good reason to see him again. Everything Andate gives is in equal and opposite measure…two are born from opposing sides, linked but divided, and two times a year this division can be joined so blood may be spilled on the ground to find release…the equinox, either of the two occasions on which the Sun crosses the equator, making night and day equal in length. We have missed the March equinox but we have one to come. Thomas has run this through his computer and confirms it will occur on the 23rd September.'

'So, what we have left is the place?'

'What we have left is clues, perhaps in the history of Gaius Suetonius. Little is known of his early life. The earliest record of his career dates from 42AD, during the reign of the Emperor Claudius, when he suppressed a revolt in Mauretania and became the first Roman to cross the Atlas Mountains. He was much later appointed governor of Britain, by which time the area south east of a line between the Wash and the Severn estuary was under Roman domination. Beyond that, the situation was more unstable. Suetonius engaged in war against the Ordovices in Wales and was attacking the Druids in Anglesey. Here he was victorious, but, far to the south east, in the rich, settled region around Colchester, rebellion erupted. The uprising endangered not only the province but also his career. Though outnumbered, the professional efficiency of his men won the day and defeat of Boudicca's army turned into slaughter. What became of him after that is not known…but known to Tacitus who wrote the man's words, how day and night was of equal measure and how the battlefield was stilled, his feet planted on a mound from which trees grew and his men fixed with roving eyes, unable to move. This is why you and Marcus have the gift of keeping men still in their place. All things add up, my Lukas. Some clues have been right in front of us. As we speak, Daphne is cross referencing data with archaeological finds.'

Lukas placed his tray on the side table and stood, upon which Benjamin stood. 'Shall we see how far she's got?'

'You may see. I am still in the throes of translation. She is so very much like you, my Lukas. Once the bit gets between her teeth she never gives up. She is in her cabin with Thomas's laptop.'

'How are the girls?' Lukas asked on his way.

'Kate has near completed your jumper, and Woo made sausage rolls and mince pies. Do you know she can cut oranges into slices as none of us had an idea of?'

At Daphne's door, he rapped lightly and walked in saying, 'Got anything?'

Crashed out on the bed, supported by her elbows, she turned from the laptop screen with a thoughtful face, the two dormice huddle together on her pillow. 'What happened last night?'

'I got my arse kicked. Marcus threw the first punch, a bit touchy on the Daphne subject. He was unable to appreciate it was my magnetic personality that had you in a spin.'

She smiled and returned her eyes to the screen. 'I remember speaking to the real Lukas Giddy when he was sixty-six and not an hour older.'

'All of which has me puzzled as to why you let an old man make love to you.'

'Perhaps I have a daddy fixation.'

'I don't think so.'

'Well how about a sucker for hard luck stories?'

He nodded at the coffee pot as if such grovelling were his due. 'I'm not the best catch in the world, Dap. In fact, I'm probably your broken illusion in consequence of last night. If it helps, I never diverted my thoughts to anyone else except you…wish I could say the same about my body…coffee?'

'No thanks.' She closed down her screen and sat upright. Without a blink or a word, she gazed up, stretched herself and scratched her calf. 'Who suggested Charnel's?'

Taking a spot beside her, sipping his coffee, he wanted to tell her the truth. 'I was quite happy living at his determination but the organization gave me no choice, kill him or someone else will, end of me.'

'Wow, that's a bummer.'

'There's more. The organization discovered you had the diary and let you do your thing to bring Marcus out of the woodwork. He did some terrible things, Dap. Two people in love, he drove over one and later took the girl. They always had your back covered. I was told about the set-up just before the banquet.'

Having relieved his mind, he paused to take questions but it seemed to him Daphne was sufficiently stuck to the bed with tears in her eyes. He put his coffee to one side and took her into his arms. But she wriggled out of his embrace and left the room. Her absence felt like torture.

Then just as abruptly she returned self-composed. 'Sorry about that. I just got all emotional.' Taking her slot beside him again, she took his coffee and returned it to his hand. 'I am here to help and guide you. The most important thing is to crack this curse and send that despicable man to hell.'

'Why do I get the feeling you're treating our relationship on a business footing?'

'I never came on board to make love to you, Luke. It just happened at the worst possible time in my life.'

'It must have been bad if you carried an empty handbag and a potent dart….yes, interesting, why did you carry an empty handbag?'

'I packed in a rush, or whatever…does it matter? Here we are…time limits upon us, the Needle will cause Marcus to be revengeful and you cannot give up.'

'I have no intention of giving up.' He placed his cup to one side again and regarded her eyes, the wavering emotion and the worry defined in her voice. 'If another man was to make love to you, I wouldn't be so magnanimous.'

'My benevolence was out of necessity.'

'I don't think so.'

For a long moment they sat with their mouths very close, breathing the same hot air. They kissed, once only, so soft and cautious like two bees colliding in mid-air.

'Given half the chance, I would spank your bottom and lock you up in the brig.'

'I would welcome every moment.'

Holding her, curved in his arms like a leaf and glowing, smelling her, kissing her, and suddenly he lost himself, all boundaries and all time not existing, bodies and flesh enfolding, as one, a single unit, his pulse jumping from 66 to 106 beats, soft, gentle, protective earthy smells and affection that collided in sync, slow, fast, never had he known such powerless power and just when it was complete he went to heaven and came back alive, on his own but not alone because he was next to the one he loved. It must have been similar for Edward and Elizabeth before kindling the sparks of ambition, before weighing the losses.

This time there was no guilty close of the door, just a preferred state of rest, his eyes closed, holding her, wishing her never to leave and listening to her recent discovery.

'We ask the question, where are the skeletons and if not, where are the tools of their battles…spears, swords, breastplates…yes, few such things have been found but we forgot the most important aspect. It took place two thousand years ago so gone are those things, gone to the elements. But-'

'But, but, but… you either love a conjunction or hate it.'

'There has to be a conjunction until we have solid evidence, and contrary to expectation, Friars Wash is a mound to take seriously. Some while back a Time Team special uncovered a major temple complex, close by Watling Street, an old Roman road leading right to St. Albans. Now of the four temples there was one of significant interest, a circular temple, the oldest, where inside was a middle base, an altar and what you would do in those brutal, pagan days, write on a piece of lead, roll it up and deposit it on the altar…it's called a curser, not anything like the one on a laptop.'

'And you think what?'

'I think this is where Suetonius made his stand.' She sat up and looked into his face with such wide-eyed eagerness, her breasts open to view. 'There was strong dating evidence from early first century onwards…they found a crescent shape broach attributable to the Goddess Diana and the river ran close…water was crucially important. There was found a silver coin, genuinely rare, somewhere about 98AD. Imagine a battle, an important battle that is going to dictate his future in Britain. Friars Wash was not an open field, not then. It was wooded as most parts in England were. I am suggesting this is where Suetonius used the backdrop of trees to protect his rear flank and then divided his army into three legions when Boudicca made her attack. And because it was such a significant battle, the Romans turned the area into a tourist attraction.'

'I would need more than a suggestion, Dap.' He pulled her nakedness back into his arms. 'I get the equinox, yup? But to challenge Marcus on a site which has a 50% chance of being wrong, leaves me open to chance.'

She came up on one elbow again and looked solemnly at him for a moment. 'What are your alternatives?'

Lukas cracked a tight smile and shifted off the bed. It was not something he wished to talk about and began to do up his pyjama top buttons. 'Tom should be back by now.'

'You want to cage him.'

'If needs must.'

'And do what? Feed him breakfast every morning? The client will require a kill not a hypothesis.'

'Since when have you become the expert?'

'Let's simply say it's common sense.'

'No, let's simply say it's our way out.'

Short of making a comment, Daphne grabbed her knickers and started to dress. 'It's no way out,' she finally said. 'You will live a lie, collect an indecent amount for a kill you cannot deliver and expect us to feed a hungry animal that has the capacity to pin us all to the ground.'

'Oh come on, Dap, it was-'

'Do not call me Dap! It makes me sound like a wet nappy.'

'You are a wet nappy. I mean, do you want to be with me or not?'

'Am I not with you now?'

'Oh God,' he said, placing a hand to each side of her face. 'Dap or lovely nappy, you mustn't be impatient for victory because it only guarantees defeat. If I miss this equinox, I have next March but I only have next March if I keep him confined. If he ever got wind of what I was planning he would disappear and keep me aged.'

'And where are you going to confine him?'

'Do you think he won't do the same to me?'

'Oh, you're impossible.' She broke away, leaving the cabin twirling her dishevelled hair into a dishevelled bun, and somewhere between her anxiety and flashes of insight, the chopstick came into view. 'How much are you getting paid?'

'Half a mil.'

'Half a mil!' She stayed in her tracks for a moment, shook her head and continued. There was something more she wanted to say, Lukas knew, but she was taking her time about it. When Woo appeared with a plateful of sausage rolls, she looked relieved and took one. 'Ah, thank you, Woo. They smell sweet.'

'I do mince pie in roll.'

Lukas smiled, taking one himself. 'Is Tom back?'

'He on blidge.'

As Lukas picked his way to the bridge under a blazing sunset, a little ball of dread in his stomach was spreading through his entire body, burning his intestines, squeezing his lungs, and tightening the muscles. He threw up over the side, could hear nothing but his own gasps and the soft sound of water like it was the only thing left in the world.

A solitary hand came upon his back. It was Thomas, now leading the crusade into the bridge house. He sat Lukas down, pushed the head between the knees and poured a glass of water, mumbling some disjointed vocabulary.

'Christ,' Lukas husked, 'this is different.'

'My first thought was, here's more horror coming our way but it could be Woo's sausage rolls.'

With a face the colour of stone, Lukas gulped down the water and back-wiped the sweat from his forehead. 'No, this is the predictable Marcus. Is the bike okay?'

'Ah, you guessed my motives.'

'Not hard when the vicar's car is only worth a few bob.'

Thomas shoved a pen under the nose. 'What do you think?'

'You didn't?'

'I sure did. Look, as soon as you unscrew the cap you set it on standby. Now here's the clever bit. As soon as pressure is put on the nib it releases the gas.'

'Does it write?'

'Oh yes but don't put the cap on the end because that's where the gas is released.'

'So where am I supposed to put it?'

'Give it to Midnight to pee in, who cares. The point being, you don't use the pen to write.'

'So why does it write?'

'It writes because it's a pen-'

'But nowhere to put the cap.'

Thomas snatched it back. 'You're seriously pissing me off. It's supposed to be a disguised weapon, but okay, I can modify it.'

'No.' Lukas snatched it back. 'If it confuses me, it will confuse someone else. Is it loaded?'

'Yes, for one disbursement only, giving your opponent a fuzzy sleep of up to anything between two to four hours.'

'Fatima Blush was struck in the chest.'

'It only works on films, Luke. This is a genuinely practical weapon. You slip the idea into your opponent's head that he needs a pen, right? He takes it from your top pocket as though he's in control where in fact you're in control. Now anyone using someone else's pen never bothers with the cap, they just unscrew it, keep it in one hand or on the desk because it's not their pen and that's why it's set to go off as soon as the nib hits paper. But if you put the cap over the end, the gas will pressurize the vacuum and burst off.'

'It could hit him in the eye, blind him.' Lukas chuckled. 'See, there are always up sides to your inventions.'

Thomas punched numbers into the screen and the *Abracadabra* burst into life. 'Have you seen the latest news?'

'I was busy getting the latest from Daphne.'

'The sweeper who swept with a broom is gaining popularity. He's now claiming he saw a little man wearing an orange dress with the words for your eyes only. Daphne was wearing your gear.'

'I know. I saw her. She looked the part. In fact, if I never knew better, I would say she was made for the job.'

'Yes, she is pretty cool about things. How's it standing between you two?'

'I told her about Marcus being my target. She seemed to take that well, like she seems to take most things well. I think she puts on a brave face but underneath, yup, it's probably eating her alive.'

Their conversation was interrupted when Benjamin walked in, his face beaming like a beacon. 'Ah, Lukas my boy, just the man I need to see. Why are you still in your pyjamas?'

'He's just got out of bed,' said Thomas with a certain condescending roll in his voice.

'Is nothing sacred on this vessel?'

'Not a thing, my man. You should have closed down your watch.' Thomas turned to his father. 'Dad, Luke is on the change.'

'How many times must he kill to suffer Lukas, tell me that? Keep a stiff upper lip, my boy. We are nearly there. Remember how we spoke of linking opposites? Rather like Noah's Ark, things go two by two…the horns on the same goat, as Philippe told you. We have our date, the place is unrelated, and why you may ask. The answer is simple. It bears no weight to Andate, only the when and the how.' Benjamin drew up beside him. 'Let me explain. The when we know, the when affords a time for the splitting of horns, then, and only then do you both stand vulnerable. It will not matter your state of health or aged condition for in this time you both stand equal. As was made so by Andante, she chose two men of equal proportions and strength, like she always chooses the same on new births. She takes their mothers for reason. Mothers give more than paternal love, afford too much protection, and would ransom their needs for the sake of their sons.'

'Would my Mother have gone peacefully?'

'We are all part of an endless cycle, my Lukas. We fade only to appear brighter. Like the pen you hold in your hand, we come from the stars and play our part. With a little faith on the cuff of our sleeves, your mother would have gone peacefully.'

'So we know the when, the equinox, yup? Do we know the how?'

'Philippe will know the how. The book which you spoke of, the book he placed before your eyes. It began with the when and it will show you the how.'

18

In the unsettled certainty of aging, Lukas was like a waning moon as the *Abracadabra* tracked the same course not less than three months previous for the southwest coast of France. Apart from the discomfort, he failed to conceal his mood toward Daphne, whose very presence seemed a silent continuation of their disagreement. It certainly never helped when she kept rushing off in the middle of meal times to throw up over the side. The family had encouraging words for as long as he wished to hear them and reefers when he could no longer bear it.

By the time he was seventy-five the vessel was cruising the Mediterranean shores of Spain, so close and yet so far to the fishing village of Agde. The wind was blowing strong, but which otherwise made a pleasant relief against the summer heat.

'What is it with you two?' Thomas asked when Lukas struck into the bridge. 'She spends time below, you spend time on deck and never the twain shall meet?'

'We have a difference of opinion.'

'Ah, I get it. You told her about caging Marcus.' Thomas reached for his binoculars. 'Damn stupid thing to do. No wonder she can't digest her food…damn if that vessel hasn't been on our tail.' Now there was something else to think about. 'Has she told you she loves you?'

'Well, not in so many words.'

'Have you told her?'

'Well, not in so many words.'

'See, that's your problem, not in so many words. You got to take the bull by the horns and tell her she's the greatest thing since sliced bread and that you're going to get the *how* off Philippe.'

'What if Philippe is not there?'

'Bollocks. Just because he never knocked twice on your door of dreams doesn't mean to say he's not there. Did she cuddle up in bed?'

'Nope, though she came into my bedroom with a cup of tea this morning.' And the thought of it made him grin. He was still young enough to have an erection but too old to see without his glasses. 'Hell, I can't blame her really. Aside the fact of farting, even Midnight ducked for cover.'

'Everyone farts in bed, even Woo. Correction, especially Woo now she's pregnant. Sometimes it's so loud it wakes me up.' There was more laughter at this than had gone on previous. Again, Thomas waited leisurely through his binoculars until the observation had thoroughly penetrated to his brain. 'That's definitely on our tail, Honourable Pursuit, who the hell is he kidding.'

Lukas shrugged his shoulders. It was expected, due, no doubt, to the fiasco on the Victoria embankment. He left the bridge and collided into the bushy brows of Benjamin. 'Marcus is on our tail.'

Benjamin adopted a bold course of action, swung an arm round the aging shoulders and led Lukas back to the bridge. 'What better timing than now to plan a capture.'

'He's not coming on this vessel,' announced Thomas. 'That man can do serious damage, even from the brig. He kept his father pinned while he burnt the house down.'

'My son, your concerns are commendable. If you had used fewer explosives we would be ahead of the game.'

'Err, okay, I'll give you that…it's still a naff idea.'

'Do you have a better one?'

Jokingly, Thomas replied, 'let Marcus capture Luke,' but upon saying it, the concept struck original. 'Hey, that's a plan.'

'Have you lost it completely,' said Lukas with an altered manner and firmer voice. 'What do you expect me to do? Wave a magic wand from behind bars?'

'Oh come on, Luke. You're better than Houdini for getting out of jams. What can he do? He can't kill you. It's in his best interest to keep you alive, then, when the timing is right, do your thing, eh?'

To which Lukas returned no answer, but with a very ominous shake of the head, sat down, stimulated by the very wonder of a preposterous plan. On the basis of coming up trumps with Philippe and working a window of opportunity for Marcus to capture him, it might just work.

'You must see Philippe.' Benjamin took Lukas from his thoughts. 'You must obtain the *how*…be certain of the *how* before rendering yourself to this concept.'

Midnight put her pennies worth in. *'And when you do, remember to bring along the crunchy nut cornflakes.'*

Thomas went to the winding stairwell. 'Let's plan this out properly in my quarters, work on the feasibility.' And in the captain's quarters, he rustled through his drawer and brought out a file, slapping it on his desk. 'Okay,' he said filtering through the pages. 'Exit followed him to a place in Lyme Regis, likely hideout, no questions asked or if he had a mind, he could keep you on his boat.' Then Thomas sent his gaze in the nether regions of his mind. 'There's a thought. How the hell did he get to Lyme Regis, pick up his vessel, and sail the English Channel to catch sight of us leaving Lowestoft? What time did he leave Charnel's, Luke?'

'It could have been just after me, say around five.'

'Then his vessel was moored closer to ours.'

'Gentlemen, we must ask how he precipitated our move.' Benjamin leaned grave against the bulkhead. His passage on board had provoked more than one heated discussion lubricated further by Woo's enthusiasm to serve herbal tea. 'We know he came out of the woodwork when the diary was revealed. We know he does not want the curse to be broken. Do we now assume that all his pretentious actions cover a more devious objective?'

'There's only one way to find out. Tom, do you have your mobile?'

'Sure.'

Punching in a number, Lukas held it to his ear and heard Oban pick up. 'Tell me, when you were setting the scene for the banquet, did Marcus take a trip to Norfolk in his dingy?'

'Yes, he went from Cornwall to a shipyard in Gt. Yarmouth, your area I believe. There he left the vessel and returned to London.'

'I hazard a guess and say he returned in a black shiny Porsche. Question, where did he keep it?'

'I'll look into it.'

As Lukas shut down, fragments of clues shone an image in his mind like a star constellation. 'In all probability, we thought the same thing of each other…his motives obviously different from mine. It seems you were right to be cautious, Ben. I think he does want to capture me. He knows, now that the Needle is in the Thames, I'm trying to find a way to break the curse, so what other alternatives does he have? The same for me, what other alternatives do I have? Do I allow him to capture me or do I capture him, the latter, then where do I put him?'

'On this vessel,' said Benjamin and held up his hand to refrain his son from objecting. 'You have more than one home. It is not unreasonable for Lukas to remain on this vessel with his captive until the equinox. In the meantime, we must plan our endeavours. For myself, I would be happy if Lukas took precautions. By leaving this vessel to seek Philippe in his vulnerable state may well provide Marcus his window of opportunity. Your vision is impaired, my Lukas. Your body is not so lissom.'

'Maybe so, but if Tom takes us up a few knots, it will give me a couple of hours before Marcus docks.'

'Even so, nothing must be left to chance. Thomas, can we make provision for a secondary back-up on his homing beacon?'

'I can give one to Midnight. She needs to keep it up her bum.'

'*Oh, no not up my bum.*'

'Midnight, it's only the size of a pin head.'

'*Then put it up your bum.*'

'Can't she keep it in her mouth, Tom?'

'She might swallow it. She needs to poop it out and hide it in case he scans you both.'

'Have you got that, Midnight?' And because there came no response, he looked into his breast pocket and guiltily met those black round eyes snuggled up against Marmite. 'I could put him up my bum, no problem.'

With that, she quickly rotated and gestured her rear end. It was, after all, no more than a formal salute to the devil that dogged her heels.

Now the summer's day was set in motion. As they rode through its sunny kingdom that stretched in waves like crystal glass, Lukas mooched silently on the stateroom deck, manacled to his thoughts, absent of humour, getting older by the hour. But thoughtfulness begets wrinkles and remembering this when Daphne came into view with two mugs in her hand, he smoothed his eighty year old contracted brow.

'I made you a cup of tea,' she said but never left it at that. 'What are you thinking?'

'I'm thinking of seeing Philippe as soon as we dock.'

'Will you be fit enough to ride a bike?'

'Dap, I still have my faculties.'

'And when do they go?'

'After I take you to supper. There's a nice café on the quayside, or would I embarrass you?'

'Why? Do you slurp in your soup?'

'Something else to keep you amused.'

'Amused? Ya, frequently, I'm in hysterics.'

'Do you love me, Dap?'

'What does your heart say?'

'Funny, you asked me that before. Don't you know the heart is the centre of the blood vessels, which has no more to do with what you say or think than your knees?'

'Forgive me if I say I will not pursue the track which you would have me take.'

As Lukas anticipated, he coldly turned and repaid his view to the open sky. For some secret reason or monstrous fancy, she was resolved to deprive herself of wishful thinking. What was the point, anyway? There were no tomorrow's wishes, not for him, not for her, not until the situation was resolved with Marcus.

'What time is supper?'

'Eight o'clock. I'll meet you there.'

The *Abracadabra* pulled into the mouth of the river Adge at 5.30 with its usual aficionados admiring her lines. She looked less threatening in the light of day and a little more familiar. Although in a different sphere of action now, Lukas disembarked from the portside doors on his yellow Ducati with no mystery surrounding him. His meagre cheeks worn into deep hollows, he cowered down upon the handles peering through the visor of his helmet, once more taking the highway to Lamalou.

The shifting road lassoed his wheels and the long hills slobbered like giant snails, crimson red under a setting sun. And when he neared the pinnacle of panoramic views, he discovered unexpected tricks of sight. He felt fateful, and for the first time, invulnerable to the perils of his plight. For there, at his destination was the wizard, pleasant as ever, the same smile, everything as it had been before in a blue smoking jacket beckoning to enter his majestic home. After that, Lukas just melted away through the door, instantly surrendering to an enchanted vision, where this strange companion, once more, took to his favourite chair asking about Benjamin.

'He's going to be a grandfather,' replied Lukas sitting down. 'Woo is making out she's having a girl, but he's convinced she's carrying a boy. On the whole, we've had quite an eventful journey, unravelling the past. You may or may not know it was Joshua who discovered one of the missing annals of Tacitus, probably somewhere in Egypt.'

'Oui,' the Frenchman agreed.

'We figured it was Joshua who had the foresight to hide it beneath Cleopatra's Needle, which, incidentally, is now in the River Thames. That put Marcus on the alert, hence my condition.'

'Marcus wants what Marcus wants.'

'And what does he want, Philippe?'

'The simplest thing in the world,' he replied, and lazily crossed his legs. 'It lies in a nutshell. He wishes to forge an alliance, like countries merging their territories. As great men are urged on by their whims to abuse their power so Marcus is impelled by the authority of Andate. You have thought of your losses if not your life and are certain of victory?'

'Err, that is not strictly true. My certainty has a small glitch. I know the when but not the how.'

'Alors, you know the when but not the how and ask such a thing? Walk away or be certain of victory.'

Lukas remained quiet, shaken by this and so shadowed by his gaunt face he might have been stone deaf. Then, as if by a miracle, he raised his eyes to the dusty shelves and saw the red spine of that book. 'The answer,' he finally said, 'will be in there.'

The Frenchman heaved a deep sigh as he indulged Lukas, licked his fingers and turned over pages faster than a Formula 1 racing car. 'Ah,' he voiced aloud, 'so it is,' and looked up with a menacing grin without any move to pass over the book or offer further information.

So Lukas asked, 'May I read it?'

'What point if you cannot see? You pay more attention on the visible world than you do on the world in which you were born. Give me reason, Lukas Giddy. Tell me why my abhorrent son offered his hand on your first encounter?'

Lukas gave it some thought, breathing though his nose, polishing it with the cuff of his jacket. 'It is for me to take the proffered hand in pleasure or sacrifice.'

'Bah! Pleasure or sacrifice!' The book was angrily slammed shut. 'How can you see when there is nothing to see except your stupidity? Until you understand war and peace, your enemy will always be one step ahead. Boudicca did not stop to consider pleasure or sacrifice and cared even less of her enemy. Freedom was her purpose. Revenge her excuse, vindication for a war against a jailor who made cunning treaties.'

Finally, Lukas had got there. He could see it all now, the way Marcus introduced himself, the hand of friendship then later an alliance. From the onset, Marcus had been aware how to break the curse. 'He offered his hand in false gesture, a gesture that could have sealed my fate had I shaken it. For in that he would have forged a truce, forfeiting the right to break the curse, yup?'

A single nod confirmed it. 'And the *how*?'

'The *how* is not relevant in its context; in what way, by what means. It is to what extent or degree. We declare war upon each other and keep to the terms of war where battle is done on the equinox.' Then he paused to remember the words Marcus had said when first they met; *I was like you once…angry, bitter, cut off my hand for that is what it amounted. It was my choice to make, not anyone else's.* 'If I should cut off his hand, providing it was offered then he would be void of his power and I would be able to keep mine.'

The Frenchman held his gaze with a smile of far deeper meaning than ordinary, and returning the book to a dusty old shelf, spoke with deeper meaning yet. 'You have come a long way, Lukas Giddy. Knowledge, like truth, arrives in many disguises.' Philippe extended his hand, palm up. 'Here, her mark will make any treaty binding, so be careful in what you wish for. I ask again. You have thought of your losses if not your life and are certain of victory?'

'I shall stand wise in front of my enemy.'

'Then you have planning to do, n'est-ce pas? But you cannot plan while cupid's arrow pierces your heart. She is clearly unable to adjust to a situation where you doubt her good faith.'

'With the best will in the world, twice she has seen me age in less time than two love birds have to get properly acquainted. We differ on the subject of Marcus, we argue on the subject of Marcus and we agree to disagree on the subject of Marcus. I sometimes wonder if I'm not courting Marcus instead.'

'Alors, women are complex creatures at the best of times. My dearest beloved had good intentions to salvage what was left of my relationship with Marcus. It would have been wiser to cast him adrift on an island. I had created a monster, my own flesh and blood.'

'I'm curious, does he ever visit you?'

The Frenchman gave a short snort, and thrusting into his breast, produced a crumpled document, which he laid upon his knee, smoothing out the wrinkles with a flat palm. 'He visits a desolate habitation which he cannot have, angry with himself for yielding to the impulse so soon. What I hold is my will and testament made the day after he slaughtered my wife and my unborn child. This land will never fall into his hands, or hand as the case may be.'

19

Dressed in a little black number with plunging neckline, and exhibiting all her peculiarities of gesture and conduct, Daphne provoked the smile which greeted her attendance at the café on the quay.

'Sorry I'm late, Dap. Have you ordered?'

'Lemon sole with French fries served with buttered green plums. Would you like me to pour you some wine?'

Lukas answering in the affirmative, shrugged out of his leather trench coat to reveal *you only live twice* banded across his T-shirt. 'That's a nice dress, very similar to the one that hung in the wardrobe. It was new, like the rest of your clothes.'

'How did you know that?'

'It still had the price tag.'

'You lie. I cut it out before I came.'

'A good guess, though.'

They smiled and chinked glasses, both in secret possession of each other while the swelling moonlight consumed an ancient town.

'So how did you get on with Philippe?'

'Well, in a nutshell, it went good.' To the meal that tasted very savoury, Lukas spoke earnestly of his time with the Frenchman. He spoke of the how and his changing plans, which, to the clever Daphne, alerted her fears.

'Oh, Luke, you cannot walk into the lion's den.'

'You're against me caging him, now you're against him caging me. What other alternatives do I have? If nothing is done, I will be confined to old age. Now is a good time. Now is the right time. I need to get him pinned on the 23rd September and finish this for good.'

'Okay. How do you intend to do it?'

'I'm still working on that.'

'As I understand it, he has to agree. Do you think he'll open your cell door and say, okay let's have a gun fight? Rest assured that man will make you suffer in your confinement until he gets what he wants, and you know exactly what he wants, don't you? He wants a partnership in crime.'

For some little time they held no conversation, Lukas being unusually silent, sufficiently engaged, keeping alert. There were two men drinking at the bar, whispered very much among themselves, and kept aloof, often looking round as though jealous of their conversation being overheard.

'What's the matter, Luke?'

'See them,' he said uneasily, jerking his thumb to the bar. 'Doubtful they come from around these parts.'

'I have your back covered,' she related between the fish and desert with such a caring look that Lukas felt quite touched by her loyalty. 'Oh, I must show you what I bought, you'll love it.' Rummaging in her shoulder bag, she passed over a chocolate bar. 'They also make lovely sweets wrapped in ribbons. The French are so artistic.'

'Did you go alone?'

'No, Tom stayed on board and I joined the others. Kate wanted to buy some fruit and Woo needed a pair of stretchy shorts. I was tempted to buy you a couple of open-necked shirts but Woo informed it would be a waste of money.'

'I prefer T-shirts.'

'So I gather.'

'How often do you attend those sorts of functions?'

'It's not all fun and games,' she said, faltering under his gaze. 'I mean, some of the guests were sharp-elbowed middle classes who know how to get ahead.'

'Well, that's a relief. I thought most of them were from the British colonies.'

'Sarcasm doesn't suit you.'

'I say it like it is.'

'Then say it another way.'

'Okay, how about this. While glitter may be used in lieu of the job queue, diamonds were a girl's best friend in that place. They shone with such volume I should've brought my deckchair and Midnight her sunglasses. Methinks that ball gown you wore would've paid for a hip operation.'

'Hark at the kettle calling the pot black. And how much is the *Abracadabra* worth, a hospital no doubt, on which you feed your plans for self-destruction.'

'Holey-smokes, I seem to recall it came in handy to get Hodge off your back!' He watched her eyes narrow to dark beads of hurt, making him bound to confession. 'Okay, okay, I had a score to settle. I was doing a job in Rome and Hodge tried to get in on the act, had this bright idea of eliminating the opposition, not that he would be considered by the organization, far too bloody stupid and…anyway, I returned fire, missed him, accidentally killed a bystander.'

'Surely you could have immobilized him?'

'I was trying to get out of the bloke's garden…and no, before you ask, I took a short cut. It's not an easy thing to do when you're on the run.'

'You must have felt terrible.'

'Yup, terrible, disappointed, angry, and the rest…it reflected off Tom as well. I asked him to send my half of the fee to the family, not that it made me feel any better.'

'So, what are you going to do, Luke?' Trust Daphne to remind him again. 'Wait around, dangle yourself as bait?' She reached for his wrinkly hand that was clutched to the stem of his glass. 'Do you think Marcus would stroke your brow and give you pain killers when you're on your last legs?'

'I never take pain killers.'

'Well that's just typical, a martyr to the end.'

'No, Dap, not a martyr. I take the pain from those he slaughters, that's the whole point of it.'

'And who will take your pain? Who will mourn your death? Do you think your reputation carries a debt of gratitude? Most pay from a fat cheque, get rid of their problem, and those you service in kind won't even know where you're buried. The only people who will are those who love you, your family and what they want more than anything else is for you to have a life. In this, there have been complications, admittedly, but I can help if you let me.'

Observing her, and seeing how she held herself, cool, calm inner self cocooned in a beautiful shell, he saw no ruffled exterior, just the equable balance of life. 'Your father gave me the impression you were like your mother, stubborn and that I do agree. But he also told me you baked fairy cakes and need looking after, and that I disagree. It's you now wanting to look after me. What do you have in mind? Dart me with your chopstick?'

'Now you're being ridiculous again. There is nothing wrong in taking a sleeping draft, just to tide you over then you can think clearly when you're thirty again.'

'Okay, what if I captured Marcus? I would stay on the *Abracadabra* with him, yup? You can return home until I figure-'

'He will never give in, and do you know why? Because there is nothing you can do to hurt him.'

'I would offer him freedom if he offered his hand.'

'Am I hearing correctly? You want his hand and not his life?'

Lukas nodded and said nothing, his heart almost up to his throat, for if he killed Marcus he would lose Midnight and that thought was intolerable. His eyes looked away from her intense glare.

'I don't understand you, Luke. You have a chance to break this terrible curse, gain your freedom and peace of mind for Tom.'

'Woo will not die. Her baby is not cursed.'

'You don't know that for fact.'

'It is my right!' His ill-tempered growl made her jump. 'I want to keep my powers, as is my right to keep them. Sure, I want a life, and, err, dare I say a life with you but I have no intention of being your trained poodle. This is me. This is what I do for a living.'

'Which is as easy as cursing,' she wisely added. 'Oh I have no idea why I bother.' She looked at her watch. 'It's late and you look terribly old. I would like to show my independence by paying the bill or is that not allowed in your antediluvian mind?'

He nodded and finished his drink, stood, then with his trench coat thrown over his humped shoulder he tottered off in comparative solitude, which seemed quiet strange and novel. Oh the trials and tribulations of a cursed war. Eventually, she caught up, grabbing his hand in a show of affection as they walked across the river bridge, onward to the *Abracadabra*.

'When you go to Charnel's, do you have a favourite?'

'Did do, past tense.'

'I won't ask again.'

'But you will.'

'Probably, if you're still alive.'

'Well we might as well get this over with. Yes, I did have a favourite. Yes, I sometimes played cards. Yes, I sometimes had sex. Yes, I went with Marcus not just to keep him busy. And yes, Angel served us both.'

'At the same time?'

'He has a perverse nature. Okay, she's a prostitute but she's still a human being.'

'So did he try to be perverse as if it isn't perverse to have a threesome?'

At the point of boarding he stood his ground. 'What do you want from me, Dap? I give you honesty and you throw it in my face. This is me, doing what I can to exist. I have never given thought of a normal life, what is normal anyhow. I am still a man with needs, not that I ever thought my one need could be met so I shoved it aside and then there was you. But I don't know where I stand with you. It seems you're almost afraid to make a commitment.'

Her expression went blank as often was the case when he tried to pin her down. It had taken him some time to realize that when she squinted like that she was involved with mental procrastination.

'Well?'

'I only wanted to know what makes you tick.' She carried on toward the stateroom. 'I mean, you invited my brains so surely I should be entitled to ask questions.'

'And how many men have you slept with?'

She took the gin bottle out of his hand. 'Have a coffee instead.'

'I don't want a coffee.'

'Quite right, you should have a cup of tea.' She popped her head under the bar. 'Woo has some terrific herbal teas.'

'I don't want tea.'

'Yes, you do. You're getting all grumpy. Oh, look, we have lemon, you like lemon tea.'

'Will you stop avoiding my question?'

'It is remarkable,' she mused, dallying lazily with the teaspoon, 'that I am now the subject of your enquiry. Yes, of course I have slept with men.' Pausing to count off the top of her head, she finally said, 'Oh dear, I lost count, was that twenty or thirty?'

'Four if you're lucky.'

'So why ask?'

'Because I want to know what makes you tick.'

'Drink your tea and I shall tell you.'

He picked up the cup and leaned against the bar to drink his tea, and although it nearly scolded his tongue, her eyes were steadfastly upon him. 'Okay,' he said and put his empty cup down with an emphatic smack. 'I drank my tea.'

'You toddle off,' she said. 'I shall be right behind you to stroke your brow. I just need to get something.'

Smiling at the simplicity of her gesture, he picked his way to his quarters, and before he drew the curtains he looked upon the blackening waters which only seemed to anticipate the coming gloom. There were two problems: If he captured Marcus, what other leverage could be employed to draw up a treaty to fight for the spoils of war? And if he allowed himself to be captive, the same scenario would apply. What Lukas needed was a way to control his own situation. In less than a minute he was sat on the bed, scrapping those ideas, and putting together a new plan. It was not an appealing option but if he carried it off, he would be almost there.

At what point he fell asleep, he could not remember but he slept like a bear hibernating in winter, waking refreshed and young. That was new. The world had gone by without any suffering.

'*You snored a lot.*'

With a loud yawn, he raised his body from a heap of covers, and supporting his head upon his hand, appealed to those big black eyes. 'Have a nose in her handbag.'

'*She spiked your drink.*'

'Tell me something I don't know.'

'*She kissed you goodbye.*'

Bollocks! He rolled off the bed and looked at his watch, had slept for most of the morning. The chance to kiss her lips, to salvage something from their odd relationship, was gone. He only had himself to blame. If he had told her his reasons for wanting the hand, if he had confided in her then perhaps she would have stayed. He considered it was something to look upon enjoyment so that it was free and wild. Then every circumstance of his youth came thronging back, the slow and gradual breaking out of that horror in which his darkened plight began, and how, in the midst of all, he had found some hope and comfort in Midnight who now had a mate of her own, further reason to stand steadfast in his thoughts.

Thomas, who had been sunning alone on the forward bow, heaved himself up on his elbows when Lukas emerged, blocking the sun. 'We need to talk, my man.'

Lukas crouched to face him. 'Midnight told me she left.'

'Ah, of course…and, err, how do you feel about it?'

'I thought and hoped she would come to me, and talk about it, whatever. Instead she slips me a Mickey. It bears strongly on the whole drift of her discourse last night. Did she give the info on my meet with Philippe?'

'Yes, she did cover that.' Thomas reached for his shirt and produced his mobile. 'Oban wants you to give him a ring.'

Pressing the redial, Lukas spoke first when Oban picked up. 'What do you have?'

'He's getting sloppy. He parked his motor at a lock-up behind the Cavendish, the bloke who runs it rents out parking spaces, said he paid cash, up front for six months.'

'Who's the bloke?'

'Nobody special, no record, keeps a fish tank.'

'Do we have an address?'

'Yes. Rented a converted barn with outbuildings, some five miles north. Our man looked it over, seems heavy stuff has been going on there. Need anything else, let me know.'

'Cheers.' Lukas closed down and gave Thomas a level stare. 'He rented a space in a garage near the Cavendish, has a place five miles north.'

'Now why would he take pains to keep that concealed?'

'Methinks he has made a nice little bed for me.'

'Daphne said you wanted his hand. What's wrong in breaking the curse?'

'I have my reasons.'

'Care to tell me?'

'Tom, I don't ask much yet what I do ask is for you to believe Woo will not die, your baby is not cursed.'

'And how's it going to stick with Oban?'

'Oban doesn't have to know. Don't give me that look, Tom. I'll work something out, we'll get the fee.'

'So what's our next step?'

'That's something I intend to find out.' Lukas stood. 'Where's his Tonka toy moored?'

'In the quay at Cap d'Agde. Keep your link open.'

Leaving behind the *Abracadabra*, Lukas strode through the old town and then followed his nose like a snail passing over a garden path. Cap d'Agde, though a poor man's St. Tropez, was lively and vivid, and threw out amusements to the blazing masses drawn to its sands. The day now being intensely hot, and the sun striking down its fiercest rays upon those who carried buckets and spades began to grow weary.

He was not too long in reaching the harbour, avoiding the more crowded thoroughfares when he spotted the black and gold lines of a sixty-footer called Honourable Pursuit, and seeming to chill the very sunlight. His first impulse was to clamber on board, burst forth undaunted, but something else far worse was there, a ginger devil with sharpened claws, preening itself topside.

'*Pussy cat!*' shrieked Midnight ducking into the breast pocket. The beast could leave many a hand bleeding before swaggering off to his milk, a cross between Hammer House of Horror and Tales of the Unexpected.

Then Lukas caught sight at perfect symmetry standing under a canopied deck. The dark skinned body in knee-length shorts was pumped like iron, every bulging muscle faultlessly correct like a textbook work out. He greeted Marcus with a bellow. 'Get rid of the fur ball!'

With a nod, the ginger tom went hissing through the air in a ragged spray and disappeared somewhere inside. After Marcus closed the sliding glass doors, Lukas clambered over the starboard side to be under the lengthened shadows of the canopy that threw its carpet of colours on still waters. With no surprise shown, his eyes prowled slowly around a seafood spread laid out on a table for two while his host popped a champagne cork.

'The fish was caught this morning.'

'That's not to say it's edible.' Lukas walked around him, admiring his form. For certain this man never indulged in cream cakes and Yorkshire puddings. 'Own a chain of fitness clubs?'

'I hope to nail victory in Britain's Got Talent.'

'Is your gearstick just as thick?'

Despite the seriousness of the situation, neither Marcus nor Lukas could help smiling. They exchanged glances in a breathless pause then sat down to eat their meal and insult each other further.

'You know, Giddy, a man who makes light of his circumstance is a clown.'

'So you're a philosopher now.'

'Enough to know you dressed up in a monkey suit, hooked the banker's daughter and damn if she never went back to papa. Now why do you think that is?'

'She preferred a younger man?'

'Come now, a small price to prove commitment to my cause.'

'And what is your cause, to become a property developer in Norfolk?'

'As it so happens, I'm looking for a tenant.'

'I can't afford the rent.'

'Care to tell me what was under that Needle?'

'Why don't you ask your old man?'

Marcus remained quiet, holding the glass to his lips, recalling his mistake. His father no more, dying in flames, the moment had passed in ignorance. They were the memories of long ago. 'And you,' he finally said, 'do you ever get to see yours.'

'Considering he tried to drown me, I don't think there'd be much to say.'

'My mark came that night.'

'And you blame him for that?'

'No, I thank him for that. My despondency, not to say despair, was gone in a moment. Six years old, struck me with a half-comical wonder as to what appeared on my hand, and then see him pumping a tart. I never liked him or the whores he brought home so he sent me off to a lunatic asylum, or as good as. It was borstal for young kids with attitude.'

'I suppose that never remained standing.'

'Actually, it stood for a few years. I quite liked it there, being with kids of my own sort, figuratively speaking of course. There was one boy, bright as a button, growled like a double-bass. We were off to the greenhouse to pot seeds when he picked up a stone and smashed a window. I knew enough of the world by thirteen, to have almost lost the capacity of being much surprized by anything…until I encountered his future wife turning the corner of a lane near our house. I should have been perfectly miserable, but for the old books. It was a period of my life, which I can never lose the memory, the recollection of which has often come to haunt me. She walked in happily patting my head like a damn dog, telling me the lump in her belly would not take first consideration to the assets if I could show willing to accept a sibling. Was that supposed to make me feel better? It not only killed my dreams but it killed hers.'

'When is enough, enough? I'm certain you have so much money popping out of your ears, why not take up a vocation, something to suit your personality, say a despot. I hear there's an opening for one in Kaddafi country.'

'Not my scene,' said he lighting a cigar, the smoke wafting gentle in humid air. 'I like to wear the guise of the moment, fit in with the crowd and all that.'

'So your view, take what you want, regardless.'

'Everyone takes what they want, Giddy. Most do it on the sly and the rare breed holding the balance of power, they do it blatantly.'

'And which are you?'

'I do it because I can.' Marcus broke a piece of bread from a platter at his side, folded it into his mouth, and gestured to Lukas to do the same. 'You know your trouble, Giddy. You look bloody stupid in those slogans. What's that supposed to mean, you only live twice? You think you get a second chance at life?'

Wiping his mouth with a serviette, Lukas sat back and folded his arms. 'I could give you a second chance.'

'Do I look as though I need one?'

'Either that or I kill your sorry arse.'

'And kill yourself, how pathetic.'

'Not necessarily.'

In all seriousness, Marcus took to his glass and feet, and leaned against a stanchion, staring away at the blue grass of his garden. 'Am I to understand, you know how to break the curse?'

'You could have saved me the trouble.'

'Did I not offer a hand of friendship?'

'I never shake hands with a desperate man.'

Marcus looked back, his eyes more worried still, missing perhaps some freedom in his dread. 'I had little doubt then, and less doubt now, you will make a bargain.'

'See, that's where you're wrong.' For a split second, he caught the chill flare in the eyes then it quickly subsided to faint suspicion. Having come this far, he would push his luck and the boundaries of Marcus, feed that narcissistic character. 'You and me, we came out of the same nest but not the same egg, yup? So, we can play silly games, each pretending the other is stupid, one cause worthier than the other, who cares a toss. Beyond that, you capture me or I capture you, either way we're both prisoners through willingness or compulsion.' He popped a grape in his mouth and let suggestion roll off his lips. 'Or should we accept our fate, be the soldiers we were born to be?'

'And do what, join the Foreign Legion?'

'We could settle our complaints on the battle field.'

'I have no wish to end the curse.'

'Granted, it goes without saying, one of us could die but I would challenge in contemplation of your left hand and you, no doubt, would do the same for my right. But it would be in the spirit of a war, end this protracted madness, winner takes the spoils.'

'There are no spoils in death, not for me.'

'It seems your confidence matches that of Suetonius. He never wanted to take on Boudicca though the gravity of the moment shadowed his calm.'

A reluctant smile glimmered on the face of Marcus. Beneath his misery was recognition. To be a soldier like Suetonius was to put aside fear and petty sentiment. 'And where would this battle take place?'

'Friars Wash is as good a place as any, an open field, we come alone, say at midnight of this autumn equinox. Until then, you slaughter nothing, not even your cat.'

'At the equinox, we stand equal.'

'Maybe so, but I need to pump some iron.'

'Swords shall be our weapons, nothing else.'

'And when with sword, we are blind to consequence.'

Marcus slid his cold, insidious palm into the proffered hand and clasped it tight, sending a very clear message of unbound strength. 'Agreed.'

For Lukas, it was strange to be absorbed so rapidly into the treaty, stranger still to look upon the mark that broke through his skin. For a moment, he felt his legs give, his stomach convulse in the twilight greyness that suddenly shot ominously across the sky. No doubt Andate sought blood, and on the equinox she would find it.

Without further word, he retreated as the sea-borne breeze coolly kissed the sweat at his chest and neck. It was not fear that gripped him, only restlessness, the heightened sense of things to come, the thought of using a different weapon, a sword that could defend, deflect or cut into flesh by a skilled employer, of which he was not.

Thomas and Benjamin were waiting. They held coffee mugs to their chests, laced with whisky, had been listening on the bridge and had witnessed the sky grow dark, the descending mist which carried the putrid smell of death. They knew Lukas had abandoned one fire in order to enter a furnace.

'Let me see,' asked Benjamin, who took hold of the hand, the palm now stained with the mark of Andante. 'To risk your life is one thing, to risk it at the point of a sword is another? Were you not told he is versed in the art of sword play?'

'He would not commit otherwise.' Helping himself to Thomas's mug, he swallowed the contents whole. 'I need some lessons.'

'You need your head examining.' Thomas put the *Abracadabra* into reverse. 'But we're on top of it my man. Oban recommended a man who can. He trained his entire life to be the greatest swordsman in the history of mankind, or so he claims…a warrior with empty eyes.'

20

From the shores of France, through the Straits of Gibraltar and to part of the Portuguese archipelago, the island of Porto Santo was once home to Christopher Columbus. The island was characterized by two areas; the mountainous northeast with rocky ledges and cliffs, and a superficial plain in the southwest, which included a nine kilometre white sandy beach, something that the nearby island of Madeira had virtually none.

After closing down the engines in the small enclave of a man-made harbour, the *Abracadabra* had finally arrived in an almost not existing little corner of Europe.

'A paradise island,' Thomas told Lukas, who was mounting his bike. 'Untouched sandy beach, relaxing atmosphere, you can even find your own private area, a true luxury nowadays.'

'So what you're saying is this place is boring.'

Thomas nodded with a grin and smacked the red button to open the starboard doors. 'Take care, my man.'

'*Tell him to remember Marmite.*'

'Oh yes, don't forget to feed Marmite. He's in my drawer.'

By easy stages the family were wishing him well, drawn close by this alien country. Kate pressed her lips to his cheek, Woo relinquished a bag of grapes, and Benjamin squeezed the shoulder to disarm what apprehension there might be.

After these fond farewells, the *Abracadabra* left for Italy and Lukas left on his yellow Ducati with a rucksack on his back and Midnight in his breast pocket, now in search of the man with empty eyes.

Mile after rattling mile he went, under the vast blue sky, eyes screwed in the dry salty wind, a sharp difference in every breath. Nature had been generous with this small island, also gracing it with hills that hid Mediterranean style little forests and intriguing shapes in the soft sandstone cliffs of the north side.

It was at the top of the valley that the beauty and simplicity of this land, caught in the secret of such perfection. Deciphering the habitat that surrounded him became a pressing necessity, which required the aid of those who knew best.

Coming to a shuddering halt, 'the Teacher,' he bellowed to a woman who stood by the roadside with a child in her arms. He followed the point of her finger, shuffled and spluttered on a dusty road that was resigned to its loss under a track of high vegetation where eventually he came to a new and more generous vista. Ahead, a low slung building that looked as if it were nodding in sleep, birds chirped in the eaves, the sturdy timbers had decayed like teeth and sprouting creepers strangled the porch. First impressions could be deceptive.

A hairless figure came into view, a short bare foot character wearing little more than a towel wrapped round his pop-belly, his skin richly tanned, his cheeks covered in shaving foam. 'Make the tea, old boy…just have to finish my shave.'

'Where do I put my bike?'

'In there.'

Colliding with dry bunches of spiders Lukas parked his bike in the shed and then went inside to a place that had its areas of dark holes and talking floorboards, together with an infinite range of swords fastened to the timbered walls. Its ceilings were blackened by time, and the only comforting evidence was a worn out sofa on a worn out rug and a stove hissing a kettle to the boil. Lukas let fall his rucksack in private agony. Such circumstance could bring out the politician in any man.

'Do you take sugar?'

'Honey,' the voice called back from behind a curtain. 'You'll find the china in the sink.'

'And where's the sink?'

'Outside.'

In contrast, the garden was beautiful and enchanting. A well-kept lawn, clusters of trees distinguished a path to the cliff-top edge on which shrubs and flowers grew. The sink was a shallow tin bath serving the local wildlife.

'*You got the right house?*' Midnight asked.

'God, I hope not.'

It was between the rinsing of cups and searching for teabags that the Englishman came into view wiping the soap off his face, his oceanic eyes touring the yellow T-shirt Lukas was wearing. 'Do I call you Luke Skywalker or the man with the golden gun?'

Lukas gave him a hard stare. 'Depends what I call you.'

'I am Teacher by the laws of nature and providence.' Smiling from crooked lips, he completed the tea-making routine in the glory of tradition. 'I came out of a British womb, born on this island, taken to England by a fair wind, met and won the best, returning here for a quiet retreat. That entitles me to be called Teacher. Ever handled a sword?'

'Nope, not in combat.'

'An interesting word, combat.'

'The right word.' Looking at him with his little finger outstretched from the handle of the cup, the freshness of the sea-wind was on his face, ruddy traces made as if he had applied himself to the buffeting of rough seas. 'Have you ever killed a man?'

'Have you?'

Lukas was thoughtful, stood considering a little before answering. 'I tell you what. You show me your empty eyes then I'll show you mine.'

The Englishman nodded and went to the wall, took from its cradle an epee. Wielding the blade as though batting flies, swish, swoosh, his demonstration was far from impressive. After glancing at Lukas as a comparatively worthless vessel he inflicted a nick on his chin. Immobility forestalled any further movements.

'You have a gift?'

'A gift denied at the time of combat.' Lukas smeared the blood between thumb and forefinger. Perhaps it carried a vital message. 'You have until mid-September to make me better than you.'

'Swordsmanship is more than a skill. It's the extension of your soul.' The Englishman poked the chest with the point of his sword. 'Your self-esteem is your biggest enemy.'

'So, I lose the T-shirt.'

'You will lose a lot more if you think like James Bond. Let me show you something.'

On a luscious green island, where time and tide moved along at a pace far more suitable to a stress-free life, Lukas was shown a wickerwork basket holding a pair of Portuguese shoes distressed by skirmish and wear.

'I can teach you the moves but I cannot teach you to be comfortable in my shoes.'

'Why would I want to wear them?'

'Earlier you asked to fill them.'

Lukas grinned. 'In time, you might get to like me.'

'In time you might get to like yourself.'

Within the first three weeks of training, the Englishman had bestowed a number of cuts upon his pupil as a form of scorn and punishment. It was the lesser danger to disobedience.

'Try again. Do not raise the arm and expose the body to counter-strike.' Another display and another nick, Lukas would soon be a crossword puzzle. 'No, no, present the flank to an opponent instead of the front.'

'I need a sword, not a pin cushion.'

With that, the Englishman went inside and returned with a scimitar, tossed it to Lukas and then hung two lengths of wood from a tree branch. 'Turn two legs for a table. Do that and you can have a sword.'

The exercise was obvious. At a stroke, he could splinter them apart or at a tickle, he could shave them. He looked back for confirmation and saw the receding form of the Englishman disappearing into the shack.

'What table has two legs?'

'What freedom, Midnight.' He raised the sword. 'Aren't you glad you stayed?' The strike was too hard. 'Oops!'

'Ohh, no sword for you.'

And the sun climbed and the summer heat intensified. By night, he would sleep under the stars in the balmy air, his body aching, his sword hand blistered and raw, every sinew impressed themselves upon him, his extremities required to be at peace before a new day began. No longer did he sleep with a gun under his pillow or rise with a blade tucked up his sleeve nice and sharp. Robbed of his dignity, he was in a place where food was served cold and unfulfilling, where his bed was made of straw, where the water-butt and hose pipe coupled up for a shower. He was a victim of his own circumstance, exhibiting all the signs of frustration as the disappointment counteracted the fresh air that wafted good cuisine from a 5star hotel located down below.

So it was to some relief when he was nudged awake with a pleasant invitation. 'Today we go into town.'

Lukas stirred from his straw bed, sauntered to the water-butt and plunged his head deep inside. When satisfied, he ambled back and focused on Teacher soaking up a new day's sun. 'What time is it?'

'Time, time, you worry about time…you moan for a shave, for a bath, your body aches, your feet sweat and your clothes stink.'

'They stink because you don't have a washing machine.'

'Excuses, excuses…now you can swim in the sea, dine at a table with a sun tan and look into the eyes of pretty things before I pulp you to a sausage.'

'Pretty things, by that you mean women.'

'Yes, of course, women, single women, divorced women, tall, short, fat, slim, they exist on this island. Do you have a woman?'

Had, might just be the operative word. Traces of deep-seated anguish appeared in his voice. 'Once I get this over, and God willing I'm still alive with all my bits, I might.'

'I have been in love three times, Luke Skywalker. The first at eighteen until her mother tasted better. The second, I could stay in her arms for the rest of my life but she couldn't stay in mine so it was a wise move to return and fall in love with this island. Rosita, my current girlfriend works in the hotel on the beach.'

'She sleeps at the hotel?'

'She lives in Madeira, comes over on the ferry.'

'I don't blame her, considering the state of your home.'

'Ha! You kid yourself if you believe this is where I live. It's a disused shack to teach men like you who think my fee should pay for luxury.'

'Steak and the occasional roast would-'

'I'm not a cook, besides you need to lose some weight. You're fast but just have to be faster.'

'Have you ever sparred or taught a man called Marcus Metellus?'

'The name doesn't ring a bell. What does he look like?'

'My height, dark hair, dark skinned, lights his cigars with a fifty pound note, likes to dress up.'

'Dress up?'

'Sometimes he's an Arab, sometimes a naval officer. Last time I saw him he looked like Arnold Schwarzenegger.'

'Is he the man you intend to challenge?'

'Yup. Got any advice?'

'Pay my fee before you leave.' Jumping to his feet like a Jack rabbit, the Englishman flung a white linen mantle in his face. 'Wear this and remove your shoes. Come, I have a surprise for you.'

Lest it should be a matter of surprise to Lukas that the Englishman adopted a bold course of transport, throwing his head back and laughing, his strong desire was to ride his Ducati than taste the backside of a donkey.

'It doesn't get any better than this.'

'Hell, I miss my bed.'

GIDDY MIDNIGHT

'Hell, I miss my drawer.'

'Not to worry, Midnight. We can be assured of two things before we travel to Friars Wash. We get three nights on board in luxury and a soapy shower.'

A straw hat was plonked on his head, swallowing Midnight whole. 'You do a lot of talking to your pet.'

'It's my way of keeping sane. Where are the saddles?'

'No saddles, just blankets.' The Englishman kissed the nose and stroked the ears. 'This is Lulu…a very intelligent animal, like that rat you keep in your hair.' Then he went to the next donkey. 'This is Yoyo. She tends to be hyper first thing in the morning. I shall take her.'

'Why are there no mirrors?'

'Have you forgotten what you look like?'

Lukas was a man inside a white cotton robe which smelt better than him, recalling the moments with Daphne in her oversized colourful Kaftan. Apart from Midnight, all conceivable luxuries had been banned, including his watch, something more than a timepiece, something that kept him connected to the family.

With his feet almost scraping the dirt, he jerked the reins and the donkey broke into a saunter. The road stretched out deserted in its layer of dust and not a thing seemed to move. The highway wound down, innocent of motors, away to the next village, which took summer in its stride.

'So, in point scoring, how am I doing?'

'I would give you a score of nine.'

'Gee, that sounds impressive.'

'Out of a hundred.'

Lukas said no more after that.

Then out of the first walls of Porto Santo's capital, everything was normal again. It was pregnant with the noise and influx of workers, the shaded streets playing host to tourists. Easy, relaxed smiles, cotton tops, strapless dresses and sandals, working or playing, Lukas felt he was back into the 21st century.

The Englishman halted alongside and swung himself to the ground, taking both reins. 'The day is yours.'

'How do I get back?'

'You walk.'

Lukas looked down at his feet. 'Is there some point to all this?'

'Yes, buy a pair of Portuguese sandals. Our economy needs boosting.'

If his manner had been merely passively rude, Lukas would have had no greater dislike to his company than he always felt. He glanced towards him, uncertain whether to go forward or return to pick up his things and find someone else more amenable. But teachers were not meant to be liked.

Smelling rank, Lukas padded on warm marble slabs until he reached the beach, then he took curled-up sleeping Midnight from out of his hair and laid her in his straw hat wondering if it would be safe to leave her on the shores while he went in for a swim.

'I shall take her.' Never more so was he pleased to hear a familiar voice. 'How does it go, lad?'

'Why are you back so soon?'

Benjamin tapped the arm, an encouraging gesture to walk on. 'Things are to be said between us, things you need to know, have a right to know before you lend yourself to this battle.'

'Am I going to like this?'

'Remember what I told you all those years ago, that we make but a bad job of handling our affairs? I am absolutely in the horrors at this point in time so be patient with this old man.' A shuddering sigh paused the moment and Benjamin shifted his gaze to the blue horizon, was plainly summoning his thoughts. 'Many, many moons ago, so many I can hardly recall the reason why. Thomas was four, my world was alive and my love for Kate as strong then as it is now. No man could ask for more wonderful blessings. I make no excuses, none whatsoever, I am entirely to blame for the lust of a woman who found me far more attractive than her husband.' Here Benjamin halted, turning his head towards Lukas, but looking at the feet instead of the face to add, 'my brother,' leaving no further enlightenment to understand what was implied.

The confused emotions that had been tormenting Lukas for days suddenly erupted into anger. 'And you chose to tell me now, to burden me when my mind is like a bloody steam train!'

'Do you wish me to leave?'

'No! I wish you to tell me why!'

'She was absent of Simon's love. Sometimes he would disappear for days, and when he was home, he would brood in her arms, arms that longed for children, arms that loved her husband, a husband who would penetrate so far before withdrawing. It was one time, and one time only, my Lukas.'

'And that makes it alright!'

'No, it does not make it alright! How could I look at her face or at Kate without feeling terrible pangs of remorse? I made excuses not to have breakfast, excuses to stay behind the bench, excuses to hide in my library praying not to see him.'

'You all lived at Giddy Lodge?'

'Yes, we all lived as a family. When your mother knew of her pregnancy, she came to me and pleaded not to divulge our union that night, not that I needed much persuasion. Simon was very upset, could not reason the date she fell pregnant. However, we talked it through as a family and he decided it best they had a home of their own. Then he became very distant after she died giving birth to you, convinced you were cursed. Of course, in my ignorance, I believed I knew otherwise but could not say, did not want to say. The night he turned up on the doorstep with you by his side, I could tell by the flare of his eyes he had guessed. Kate took you to bed. I took Simon into the library where we had a terrible argument. I confirmed his suspicions, tried to calm his anger, blamed me for the death of your mother, and this was true…may Andante forgive me, but this was true. I could not reason with him and left for my bed to sleep beside a woman who had shown nothing but love and loyalty, and my guilt increased, fearful I would lose her-'

'And you said nothing?'

'I said nothing, only to be woken later by your cries.'

'Simon was not drowning me because I was cursed. It was because he blamed me for what you had done.'

'Not so, untrue. Never let it be said so. My brother had always been unstable, even as a child. He was consumed with the history of Boudicca, consumed with Andate's curse. It drove our Father to drink, he could not control Simon's fixation and tore at the heartstrings of our Mother. No, never let it be said his mind was on revenge but on his ability to be certain you were cursed.'

'What an opportunity, kill him and your problem goes away, yup? Tell me this was not so?'

Benjamin lowered his guilty eyes and said nothing.

With Midnight left in the hat on the sands, Lukas made for the waters, unwilling to trust his voice, ashamed of the tears beginning to stream warm on his face. He wanted to put his arms about him, to say he understood, to love the man he had come to worship and now despised. But he should thank this old man with the sorrowful face, be grateful for his life. Had he not always been there in times of grief and sorrow? Had he not always favoured him above Thomas? Had he not given him hope when hope was lost? Had he not loved him like a son for he was his son?

While Benjamin dwelt on the sands and his grief, Lukas drowned his own in the blue azure waters of the Atlantic. He had left his beleaguered father to care for Midnight, further reason to keep things in perspective. He thought of Daphne, his betrayal that night with Angel, his reasons for doing what he did and reasons not. Would he be the hypocrite or would he be the man he had come to be, Lukas Giddy dreaming of tomorrow's wishes.

From out of the sea, he rose. His cotton mantle clung wet to his skin. The world became shadowless, insecurities gone on the tide. Benjamin came to the water's edge. Both men flung their arms about each other and brought further warmth on the sands.

'Forgive me, my son.'

'Father,' he husked.

Whatever the rights or wrongs of the case, Lukas had arrived in the world by chance. Some would consider it fate, others would consider it justice. His mother had paid the price of death for her infidelity, and Benjamin had paid a greater one, living with a secret agony for thirty-one years. There were no more reasons to penetrate further into Benjamin's folly. Lukas had examined the images and words of his past, one by one, leafing through his memory almost absent-mindedly and knew he was not going to find anything substantive.

'I have confessed my sin to Kate and Thomas. It lifted my burden to do so, not my heart when I saw the hurt in their eyes. I was made to spend a day in the brig without any food or water and given a cold shoulder that night. The morning was a happier time where I spent it answering their questions as truthfully as I knew how.'

'Let's have coffee.' Lukas picked up Midnight and buried her in Benjamin's dry pocket then returned the hat to his head. 'Why did you feel the need to tell me?'

'I am part of your weapon, my son. Hold me dear to your heart and know your father is with you every step of the way.'

'I kind of get the impression Philippe may have known.'

'Yes, he knew. I confessed my sin when made aware his son received the mark of Andate at six years old. He told me it was a sign of things to come.'

'Philippe mentioned it made no difference to the curse.'

'Even so, I killed to cover up my shame, and Andate gave you Midnight for comfort as she gave Marcus a warning. How is your tutor? I see he has left you wasted and scarred.'

Lukas grabbed a chair, ordered coffee and cakes then replied curtly under a cooling umbrella, 'His shack is like a pigsty, no damn bathing facilities, no mirrors or clocks and I sleep on a straw bed under the moon. Actually, it's quite nice now the midges have tasted my blood.'

'Why do you have no shoes on your feet, no pocket for Midnight?'

'Well, apart from ripping me to shreds in the first week all I had left was underpants and jeans. Okay, I can see his logic. He was trying to get me out the habit of using my gift, but short of starving me to death, I'm not doing so well.'

'Persevere, my Lukas. Wish that I had the talent to command a sword.'

'Epee,' Lukas corrected.

'No sword?'

'He feels I might slice him to death.'

In course of time the coffee and cakes were served, and in course of time the family had joined their table at Benjamin's gesture. They had been waiting in the wings under the cover of greenery, did nothing more than was necessary to give Benjamin his due. Now they all talked over each other with a buzzing in the breeze as though the world were made that morning. Then Kate asked Lukas if he was keeping his beard.

'Not sure. Do you think it will improve my good looks?'

Woo giggled. She giggled so hard, she suddenly clutched her belly and gave a life-threatening shriek. 'Tha' baby come!'

Lukas shot to his feet. 'We need a doctor!'

Thomas waved him down. 'She means the baby is kicking. Her time isn't due yet.'

'Phew! I almost aged in one second.'

'So what's with the get up?'

'Damned if I know. Mind you, it's very comfortable in this heat. I'm of the opinion I could never survive without current technology.'

'I've been thinking, Luke, and Dad agrees, we should get you kitted out with some armour, light stuff and-'

'Nope, no armour, no fancy swirls. I need to be light on my feet, fast and accurate.' He put forth his sword arm and they gasped at his cuts. 'I kept using my power so he punished me. But that was good because it got me out of the habit of relying on something I won't have on the day. And it also reminds me this is the hand Marcus will go for. The last nick I had was two days ago, so I'm getting faster, will get a lot faster, I hope. I mean a score of nine out of a hundred is better than no score at all.'

Woo started to cry, babbled incomprehensively through her tears like a roundabout getting up steam.

Again Thomas explained. 'It's being pregnant. It makes her vulnerable to the worries.' Then Thomas bent close to his ear. 'If you killed him, break the curse, what happens to Midnight?'

'Nothing!' Lukas snapped but this lie underscored the truth, something he was ill-prepared to admit, not even to himself for the thought was unthinkable. 'Of course, at this rate there is a probability I will die, in which case she goes too.'

'*And you never thought to mention it?*' She leapt from his plate into Woo's lap and gave him the glowering eye. '*I'm going back to the Abracadabra.*'

'Don't be silly, Midnight. You know damn well we go together, you said as much.'

'*Your scoring is not very convincing. I may as well spend my last days with Marmite.*'

21

'How does it feel?'

Under a moonlit sky, Lukas brandished a long sword offered for the battle to come. 'It feels heavy.'

'Your arm is weak.'

'Even a strong arm becomes tired in battle.'

As the Englishman disappeared inside, Lukas withdrew his eyes and looked at the dark patches of the moon to the stain upon his palm as if he was comparing the two when a new weapon caught his wandering attention.

'This is lighter, compensated by the carbon fibre hilt. It was made by a chap who worked on-' In a whistling murmur a shot found its mark, pierced the brain, ending movement, cutting off his words. Empty eyes then slumped heavy to the ground.

In those seconds Lukas had gauged the trajectory and reacted fast, going in pursuit of the assassin. Even in the eerie dimness of a moonlit night, he could see a figure scrambling down a steep bank, the desire for escape obvious in every exertion. With a running leap he went airborne, landed himself on top of the sniper, sending them hurtling down a steep ravine, the rifle descending and deflecting off a boulder, disappearing altogether in the gloomy abyss. By the second, extinction was graduating from possibility to probability.

Lukas was balancing on the precipice of death, the razor touch of the sandstone rocks hard against his skin. Below, the sniper was merely hanging by the tips of his fingers, his howling entreaties unlikely to provoke interest, his pleading voice then diminished in the free-fall of his flight. For Lukas, he could see shapes, the shadows of blackened roots and reached up for this life-line, swinging himself to safer ground. It was either that or perish in front of Andate's moon.

Now, in this garden where he had slept and worked among nature and sea breezes, where he had dreamt of Daphne and victory, tutor and pupil were reunited, death and life side by side. Unless the Englishman had made an enemy, Lukas considered he did not stand that wise in front of Marcus. And the night faded to a pink dawn clawing its way across the sky. Not even Midnight was there to greet it. But someone else was. He came to lean peacefully against the water butt, his ankles crossed, his hand stroking a long white beard that sat against a blue smoking jacket, and against all of this the new day sun had found flesh and blood.

'Is your intention to sit there all day cuddling a corpse?'

Lukas slowly turned to view a miracle. The old expression came into his face, his heart jumping like a seismograph. 'Am I dreaming or are you for real?'

The Frenchman pointed a finger upwards. 'Andate gave me leave in your plight.'

'I did not stand wise in front of Marcus.'

'Alors, fate has not conspired to snatch victory away but to aid victory. I shall be your tutor, n'est-ce pas?'

'You taught Marcus?'

'Oui, for my sins it was a foolish mistake, a ridiculous notion to channel his energy. But we must not dwell on mistakes. Wine, I think.'

'There is no wine,' Lukas said in the Frenchman's steps. 'In fact, there is only tea.'

'This man lives like a pig. Where is your little friend?'

A lid to a teapot was lifted and the Frenchman poked his nose inside. For Midnight there was slumber in the midst of chaos and magic, indicative of her nature and loyalty toward Lukas.

'She's not that happy.'

'She looks happy to me.' From this amusement, Lukas made tea in the bone china cups while the Frenchman toured the swords displayed on the walls. 'He has a fine collection of replicas.'

'Replicas?'

'Of course, there is the epee, plain and simple and this nineteenth century rapier, but others are reproductions, would not last one round.'

'He tried to sell me that sword.'

'Oui, it is the nature of some men.' He took the proffered cup. 'This shall be my first taste since my last taste of life.' Taking a sip, his face wrinkled in disdain. 'Bah! This is undrinkable! We need to do some shopping. But first we must bury the bodies.'

That brought no satisfaction to Lukas's thoughts and turned his eyes into the room with strong interest, curiosity attracting him to a spot. 'Why would he sleep on an old sofa when he had money to burn? Why would he display replica swords when surely, he must have one of his own, somewhere?' Placing his cup aside, he ventured to hazard a guess to this mystery and turned the sofa upside down.

And to all the strange circumstances, they were now looking at a private collection. One in particular held Lukas in awe. From hilt to tip, this double-edge sword shone brighter than steel, but was light and comfortable in its grip. It was for a moment an inexpressible relief to hold something substantive and beautiful.

'Know your enemy.' Philippe turned the blade. 'Know your sword. This indeed was made by a master of metal. We have found someone more deserving to talk about.'

'He advertised himself as the greatest swordsman in the history of mankind, never knew his name, just advertised as the man with empty eyes.'

'Then he took falsely the merits of the man who made this sword. His name was Joshua Giddy.'

'Holy smokes! I thought he was an archaeologist.'

'His fame rode across the desert sands of Egypt where small bands of fanatics wielded their curved steel to rid thieves raiding their ancestors' tombs. Make no mistake he was a desecrater of graves and met his fate on the steps of St. Pauls.'

'So how did his sword come to be here?'

'You ask me of a time before my birth?'

'For someone who died and haunted a house then came back to give me lessons, who else to ask?'

'You should be asking where to bury the bodies, where to shop for good wine and where to find a comfortable bed in the coming weeks ahead.'

'We don't bury the bodies, yup? We dust off our fingerprints, take my gear and the swords, go down the road on my bike and hop on board the *Abracadabra*.'

'A good plan.'

'Contact Tom.' From his rucksack, Lukas passed over his watch. 'Speak into that. I need to get some info.'

Then Lukas took to a rocky route where the sandstone met a small forest. The sniper had plunged five hundred feet, the fall breaking every bone in his body, his eyes staring fixed from a face mired in blood and grime. Not three feet away was the rifle, buckled and forgotten. He must have scaled the northern face during the night and made good his position. In his trouser pockets, Lukas uncovered a wad of British notes, a return air ticket to Heathrow and a crumbled photograph of the man who claimed himself empty eyes. More faintly imaged was a number, which Lukas had come to know so well. He took the photograph and left everything else, retraced his steps, glancing back once. His robe was dank and wet with sweat, his beard unshaven, his body unwashed, and he panted in the flush and glow of a mid-day sun. All that was left to him was the power of his mind, the strength of his resolve and a Frenchman who had come back to life.

Beyond the strange occurrences which had passed, he lifted his eyes to movement in the garden and stood to watch in awe as the Frenchman juggled and spun a sword in virtuoso display. There was no doubt this man was skilled in the art of swordplay. Lukas would have gazed much longer had his presence gone undetected.

'Ah, mon ami, did things go well?'

'I'm out of condition,' he admitted to the Frenchman who now regarded him with some dismay.

'A bath would accomplish many things.' A sword was tossed to him. 'Show me what the imbecile has taught.'

'I need to rest.'

'Do you think your enemy will rest?'

With reluctance Lukas parried, blocked the incoming and failed to see the fist that sent him sprawling into the tin bath. The sword was at his throat.

'The first rule of engagement, to fall is to die.' The Frenchman proffered his hand and pulled him upward. 'You have two weapons. Where one carries a sword, find employment for your other. Again.'

From this experience and scarcely better than his previous moves, a foot pummelled his knee, sent him reeling in agony to the ground. Again the sword was at his throat.

'Expect what is unexpected.'

'It's not my life he wants.' Lukas retrieved his weapon.

'No, mon ami, it is a foretaste of things to come. While the more serious spectacle of falling gives to your opponent opporture to take your hand, Andate will not save it. You have much to learn.'

'And hardly time in which to learn.'

'Listen, can you smell that?'

Lukas promptly looked round then smiled, shaking his head. The smell of defeat still lingered. 'Did you speak to Tom?'

'Oui, and to Benjamin. I am so looking forward to seeing my very good friend. You do the dusting. I shall catch up on current events.'

Though so far removed from the scenes of his past life, and with so little hope of ever revisiting them, the Frenchman seemed to have a strange desire to know what happened in the busy world. Any old newspaper, he caught at with avidity. 'Ah, I see women have a strange propensity to show off their wares.'

'They also take the initiative in sex.'

'Mon Dieu! Is nothing sacred?'

Lukas picked up his rucksack and took a last look round before taking to his bike. He had changed back into his careworn jeans, a T-shirt cut from the midriff down and sockless feet into squelchy sneakers. 'Midnight,' he hollowed, 'time to leave.'

She came scuttling from the bushes, scrambled up his leg and disappeared in the rucksack. At which the Frenchman climbed on board, two good swords in their sheaths slung to his back. In this overloaded state, they put their talk aside and took to the open road leading to Porto Santo's capital, wheels a lot faster than donkey legs. At the cross road, the yellow Ducati turned left and ventured to the quay where the *Abracadabra* floated in the crimson light of a lowering sun.

For Lukas, the moment he parked his bike in the hold was gone, destined for soapy hot smelling water. The relief was so great, and the fatiguing occurrences of earlier so completely overpowered him, that he went down on his haunches, and would doubtless be there all night but for the curious case of Oban's dented number on the photograph.

Skipping a shave, he towel-dried off and grabbed his mobile from the drawer. When Oban picked up, Lukas said, 'Care to tell me why you sent a sniper to Porto Santo?'

'Your teacher was a wanker.'

'You recommended him.'

'Did you find a nice shiny sword?'

'Where do you get off playing me like a bloody chess piece? I have better things to do than hop from one square to another!'

'Listen, Giddy, and listen well.' The words were cold, held hostile down the line. 'You took on a job to eliminate Marcus not bring home a bloody souvenir. Now when you get on your magical mound remember how you intend to leave it!'

Lukas sat motionless, staring at his mobile. A light flickered in his memory. Other than the people on board, Daphne Frisk was the only other person who knew his intentions. Against all reason, perhaps this woman was not whom she portrayed herself to be. In respect of dress, she sometimes looked ridiculous but in respect of brains, beyond dispute. Add to the fact she eagerly seduced him, he was better at reading a whistle from a bullet than get into the mind of Daphne Frisk.

'Why did she come on board with an empty handbag? I shall tell you why, because she wanted to avoid her true identity.'

'*Ohh, Daffannee is in deep poopeedoo.*'

'She's no more a Daphne than I'm James Bond!' Throwing his mobile aside, he grabbed a white cotton T-shirt with the words, *living daylights* banded across the front. 'She should be given an Oscar for her bloody performance!'

'*If she no Daffannee, who is Frisk?*'

'Ah! Good question, Midnight.' He pushed through a pair of shorts and set off for the sweeping stateroom. 'Remind me what I found so bloody attractive about her!'

'*Will this have repercussions if I do?*'

'There's me feeling guilty about Angel, and there's her pretending to be Miss Congeniality. I said, didn't I say, every time she opened her mouth out came a lie.'

'Luke, hold up!'

He swung round and met Thomas half way. 'How many tears did she shed when she left?' Once his cousin, now his half-brother looked blank. 'Miss Frisky, how many woeful sobs did she give before leaving…plenty, yup?'

Thomas scratched his head. 'Sorry you lost me.'

'Oban sent the sniper. Oban knew about Joshua's Sword. Now unless I'm mistaken, who else could have told him my intention to leave Marcus alive, or where the battle takes place?'

'What about Philippe? He might have given Oban a dream?'

'Rubbish!' They moved forward, Lukas counting on his fingers as they swept into the stateroom. 'She knew just enough about me before she boarded. Her performance earned Hodge's death and that suited her fine. All the clothes she brought on board were new, and her handbag was empty of personal things, keep her true identity a secret, so the chopstick made an ideal tool. She left her pyjamas because she knew she would return, ergo, more proof she's in league with Oban. From the very off she was in league with Oban, like Frisk, another one of his sidekicks, no doubt. And, yes, let's not forget Frisk wringing an extra five grand out of us, bloody cheek. Damn banker indeed. They're all in it together. The whole lot of them set me up…Miss Frisky with her chopstick. Well, I have a pen.'

'And a gun.'

'But prefer to use a knife.'

'Does this mean the engagement is off?'

Lukas opened his mouth to speak but nothing came out. He was, after all, linked by love. When his stare broke away from confusion and anguish, he found himself looking at a seated family, their mouths partly open to this new revelation. 'It's nothing I can't handle,' he told them and took a chair.

They all nodded in agreement and sprang to life, helping themselves to the food on the table. It was a substantial meal. For over and above the spread of vegetables, the table creaked beneath the weight of beef, pork, towers of Yorkshire puddings and jugs of peppered-thick gravy ornamenting bottles of red wine.

'You knew, mon ami,' said the Frenchman between mouthfuls. 'Your eyes glowed in mistrust. But what is there to be mistrusting when her endeavours have contributed to your quest.'

'Why did you send her the diary?'

'I shall tell what I know. I am here,' and the Frenchman moved the salt pot toward his right. 'She is here,' and he moved the pepper pot toward his left. 'I see her. She does not see me.' He moved the pots slowly together. 'We cross paths at which point I drop the diary in her shopping basket.'

'I don't buy it.'

'Listen, mon ami, and remember we all have our ghosts. You hunt your way. I hunt mine.'

'Did she know about the sword?' Kate asked.

'Oban knew about the sword,' Lukas muffled then swallowed. 'We knew Joshua was a good swordsman, right Tom?'

'All Oban had to do was pick up on the newspaper that reported Joshua's death. It was there in black and white, his reputation. How he traced his sword to what's his face was a piece of good investigation. I mean, how did he know what sword to look for?'

'That is easy, mon ami. A man who steals another's reputation must also have the sword upon which the reputation is built. Joshua would not have abandoned his sword but rather passed it to someone, perhaps not his son, and that someone sold it to someone else and with it carries provenance, n'est-ce pas?'

The subject closed for a while, the much loved food took precedence, heartedly appreciated by Lukas who felt he had been near starved to death by a popinjay. His stomach had shrunk considerably so in those weeks of near starvation that he finally placed his utensils aside and admitted he had no more room.

'Woo and Kate, that was a splendid meal wish I could eat another Yorkshire pudding.' Now picking up where he last left off, he said to Benjamin, 'Who's your contact in Exit?'

'Names are not to be banded like confetti.'

'So give me your thoughts on Daphne.'

'What do we know,' Benjamin replied in his customary fashion, placing a match to the bowl of his pipe. 'We know she is intelligent. We know she is quick with her tongue, stubborn but kind, yes, I would say kind, and most certainly energetic.'

'I go along with that,' Thomas interjected.

'Then I would say it is likely she has been planted by Exit to keep you in check, not a bad thing but a good thing.'

'A good thing our relationship was built on a lie?'

'And this relationship, what did it consist of?'

'Well, I err, hum-'

'Luke,' Thomas interjected again. 'It's clear Exit set the whole thing up, eh? She had the diary and the reason why she withdrew it from auction was to provoke a response from Marcus. Had the auction gone through, there was less guarantee of him being there, might have got someone else to do his bidding.'

'And Frisk? Is he her father? They sure acted the part substantially well.'

'Forget Frisk, a cog in the wheel or her father,' Benjamin roused. 'You have made the decision to take the hand and therein lay your problem. Exit is aware of your intention and will place its interests first. You must change your location or they will change your outcome.'

Philippe sat back, fondling the white tresses of his beard, gauging Lukas who was gnawing at the prickly growth below his bottom lip. 'Those left standing, defeated, they became prisoners of Rome, put into slavery. By taking the hand, you take responsibility for your prisoner. Yes, you keep your power, but you have not broken the curse. If you do not watch over my son, should his life be taken, yours will go too. That is the price you pay. There is always a price to pay in war.'

Unquestionably, Lukas had his thinking cap on with Thomas deciding the thought. 'Luke, you have to kill him and end this curse.'

'And do what? Lose Midnight?'

'Oh take the hand! Take the hand!'

'It's alright, Midnight, I'm not going to lose you.' The room went deathly quiet as he cherished Midnight. 'It was never really about my power. So what if it gives me brownie points, does that make me a better man? I break this curse I forfeit far more. She's been with me for twenty-four years, my furry companion through thick and thin. We talk, we tease, and lots of things where I'm often reminded how lonely life can be without her. We are bound together by similar rules, and though it may seem stupid and sentimental, I can't imagine my life without her.'

Of course, Woo let out a howl of unimaginable proportions and even Kate was crying into her napkin. It was just unbearable. It was impossible to talk.

So Lukas withdrew to the stateroom's deck and looked upward at the spangled sky, could see nothing there but the reflection of his own stupidity. He stuck a reefer in his mouth and lit it, waited for that shudder of ecstasy to take him far away but the only place he went to visit was a nightmare. There was nothing left but to hold Midnight in a cheerless disposition.

And it was for this Thomas came to place a shielding arm about him. Together they watched the silent wonders of a starlit night but there were no signs in the stars for their reading.

'Luke.' Thomas spoke after pondering for a long time and said with an uneasy shifting of his attitude. 'You take his hand, okay. Bring him on board and he can be our deck hand, yeah?'

'Oh, Thomas, I love Thomas.'

'I appreciate the gesture, Tom, I really do but I shall be a hunted man, no money to keep the *Abracadabra* afloat and personally, I wouldn't let Marcus anywhere near the family.'

'What about asking Philippe to look after him?'

'This so gets better.'

'Philippe is borrowed. After this is over, he goes to meet his Maria, yup.'

'Ohh, find some brains, why don't you?'

'Tom, do you have a contact number for Daphne?'

'Got one for Frisk.' He passed over his mobile. 'It's under Frisk.'

'Gee, I would never have guessed.'

Leaving him to his own devices, Thomas went inside and met glum faces. 'Luke's contacting some brains.' He kissed Woo on the head and poured himself a brandy. 'I am sorry to say this but Andate really sticks in my throat. She gave Marcus a cushy number at my brother's expense. He deserves to die but to take away Midnight is frickin' cruel.'

Kate threw down her napkin and got to her feet. 'I shall blame you, Philippe Metellus. If this had come to light when Lukas had turned, he could have challenged your son. Instead, you let loose your monster and got yourself dead. And all the people he has made to suffer, innocent people, why you should be ashamed of yourself.'

'Sit down, woman and stop puffing like a kettle,' Benjamin told her. 'Circumstance dictated the order of events. I have always believed in my heart things happen for a reason. We are not the only family to have suffered. Philippe has suffered, beyond all justification he has suffered. Would I cage my son? Would I not feel compassion for my own blood? For every evil Marcus has bestowed, so Lukas has counteracted.'

'I go to bed,' said Woo rising, holding her belly. 'Not good for baby to hear sadness.'

'I shall do the same. Benjamin, you can wash up.' Kate, whose gentle heart was touched, went outside to say goodnight to Lukas. 'Did you get in touch with brains, dear?'

He shook his head. 'The number doesn't exist and Oban refuses to give me hers.'

'I know you will sleep restless tonight, but try not to lose hope, dear. The bond of love, I always say, is greater than any manufacturer's glue.'

'I shall bear that in mind.'

'Also, bear in mind it applies to Midnight as well.'

22

'Once more, mon ami.'

Lukas went to retrieve his sword struck from his grasp by the Frenchman. Then a foot to the small of his back propelled him headlong into the pool. With a groan, he hauled himself out of the water, resembling not so much a fearless defender but a drowned rat.

'Keep your eyes always on the enemy. Do not think he will serve tea while you retrieve your weapon.' With another fancy move, the sword was held at the throat. 'See how easily he could take your head instead of your hand. Only his power is lost, not his life, not his lifestyle, not his lust to kill again. He has no little pet only a little irritation. We shall take a break and resume in one hour.'

Each day it was becoming clear that victory could pivot on a single action, the outcome hinging on the weight of a thought to cancel the bond he had with Marcus.

In his cabin, drying off, his mobile whirled on the bed. The number withheld, he answered, 'Giddy here.'

'It's me, your wet nappy.'

There were many stored recriminations for such an occasion, but they floated away on the tide of her voice, a voice that sounded strange, as though she was talking behind a closed door. 'I should be angry.'

'Oban said you were desperate for my brains. Well, here I am so fire away.'

'Midnight will die if I eliminate Marcus. And if I take the hand, the link remains between us, a minor hiccup which eluded me at the time.'

'Did you know about Midnight when last we spoke?'

'Perhaps I should have said. I didn't want to worry her, not that she's any better for it now. It all came out the other night when Philippe put a spoke in the wheel.'

'Am I to understand Philippe is with you?'

'He turned into flesh and blood to tutor me, courtesy of Andate…did you figure it out?'

'Truthfully, it never occurred. But then if you break a curse, all the magic has to go. As for that abominable Marcus, that stood out a mile. While he's still breathing, the link will always be there.'

'I wish you had said.'

'It was like talking to a brick wall, Luke. You wanted to keep your magical charms, be the cape crusader, not my trained poodle…still, let's not dwell on history, let's concentrate on the problem.'

'The problem is solved if we do a deal.'

'What sort of deal?'

'I'm willing to give you my share of the fee, yup? Two hundred and fifty-thousand to make out the target has been eliminated. I get to keep my job, you get a promotion, the client is happy, Tom is happy, Oban is happy, and Marcus is happily plonked on an island where he can't escape. Everyone is happy.'

'I cannot be happy living the lie.'

'Hell, you lie all the time, what's one more? Think of the money, Dap. You can buy a whole new wardrobe of pretty gowns, be one of those sharp-elbowed middle classes who knows how to get ahead.' Had he done enough to convince her?

Apparently not. 'Have you lost the plot completely? What if Marcus escapes? What if he dies of a tropical disease or frostbite, whatever or wherever, the repercussions are too numerous to consider. Where is this island?'

'It's on a need to know basis, and only I need to know.'

'You never cease to amaze me. Your arrogance has an elastic band. If you want me to be co-conspirator, I do need to know.'

'Then I need to know who you really are.'

'You're not putting him on an island, are you? You're going to keep him on the *Abracadabra* as a one-handed deck mate.'

A wave of heat washed through him, instantly lapped by a cold sweat. Pleading was a last resort. 'Come on, Dap. I am on bended knee here. Do this for me. Do it for Midnight. I know you feel something in that heart other than pumping blood round your arteries.'

She was silent for a moment and then said, 'I'll call you back.'

His cool limbs never moved, his mind pondered on the human face that could change in many ways but the eyes always remained the same. Yes, those eyes, rich and wild like her hair, full of mysteries, and perilous as quick sand. The times he tried to take his mind off her hard, not to think about moving slow across that anvil of creation, binding her body with his, caught in the rooted trees of love.

'She's taking her time to think.'

'I took my time to think.' He pulled vest and pants from the drawer and began dressing. 'She's probably covering the angles. After all, if the client finds out we could both be in deep shit.'

'I feel like an old croc waiting to fall off a twig. Is there a plan B?'

'She is plan B.'

'What was plan A?'

'The same as plan B. Look, Midnight, as much as I've tried, the whole thing rests with her.' And just when he slipped on his jeans, the mobile trembled on the bed.

'Question,' she said and he sat down. 'How do you explain away the disappearance of his body?'

'I don't. That's your job.'

'My job?'

'Deny you work for Exit?'

'Had you thought I may be the client?'

'Don't pussy foot with me, Dap. You and your father, partner, colleague or whatever had the finger on the pulse from day one playing me like a damn minnow. Look, all you have to do is inform Oban that I reconsidered my position and that you're going to be there to confirm the kill, that I took the body to the incinerator lest he suddenly pops up again. Use your brains for two hundred and fifty grand.'

'Okay, here's the deal. You get to keep Midnight in return I want half a mil.'

'Excuse me!'

'No, excuse me! You wouldn't have asked for my help if I wasn't your last resort. I'm the one taking the risk so I should have the fee. That is using my brains.'

'That is blackmail.'

'Take it or leave it.'

He might once have respected her had not issues of lies and deceit intervened. 'Let me call you back.'

'You cannot call me back because you do not have my number.'

'Well give me your number.'

'So you can find me, haunt me, pester me?'

'That sounds about right.'

'How long do you want?'

'Ten minutes.' He logged off, scrolled through his numbers and found George Stanton. 'Maybe there is a plan C, Midnight.'

'What was plan A? I've forgotten.'

The line picked up. 'Hello?'

'George, it's me, Lukas, Lukas Giddy.'

'Hold for a moment.' In the background Lukas could hear ruffling of papers and a word said to his secretary. Then he came back on the line. 'What do I owe this pleasure?'

'Way back in March or thereabouts, Tom gave you a bell to confirm your acquaintance with a man who called himself Frisk, a banker and his daughter Daphne, yup?'

'Yes, I remember. Why, is there a problem?'

'You could say that. I have lost their number. Can you oblige?'

'This is very embarrassing,' Stanton puffed down the line. 'I don't have his number or contact details. I met him at my club, told me he had a spot of trouble with his daughter. He seemed a genuinely nice fellow. We had lunch a couple of times.'

'Did he pay for lunch? If so, was it cash?'

'Let me think now. He did pay for lunch the first time round but was it cash. No, I think he used a credit card if memory serves. Yes, he did use a credit card and I tipped Pearson.'

'So, you had lunch at your club?'

'Yes.'

'Any chance of finding out what name he used?'

'Frisk of course. Pearson would have alerted me if it had been otherwise.'

'How about the bank he claimed to run?'

'Ah yes, what was it now, Bank Societal of something, somewhere in London, Leadenhall Street, I think. But there is something that might help. He wore a tie pin with a very unusual motif. I asked him about it, said it was the logo of a sailing club on the Norfolk Broads. I even remember the name, Andate.'

Lukas buried his head in one hand. 'Thanks, George. How are things?'

'Plodding along, business is brisk. Judy divorced me. She couldn't cope. My eldest daughter came into the firm, and my boy got married to one hell of scatterbrain.' He chuckled. 'We should get together, have lunch at my club, what do you say?'

'Yes, I would like that. I'll get back to you, okay?'

'Okay.'

'Ah well,' he sighed to Midnight, 'back to plan B.'

Midnight quitted her spot on his head and went to the drawer joining her mate Marmite. She felt the need to say something, but there were no words to match the enormity of the moment.

Lukas started to rise to his feet when the mobile trembled in his hand. 'Was there ever a tempting moment to leak some remorse between your theatrical curtains?'

'I suppose you could never forgive me?'

He would quote her words, drive home his point. 'It's not a question of forgiveness. We had sex and that was that, no ties, no promises. However, I did expect some decency, such as your involvement with Exit. You must be pretty high up with so much influence.'

'It wasn't easy to stay, so much harder to leave. The sorry mess I made of my life is beyond parody.'

'Well then, half a mil should clear it up. Where shall I send the money?'

'I shall let you know if you're still alive.'

Even with comprehension dawning, it was too late to respond. She had cut the line of communication with a choking in the air. It seemed her patience was strained in similar measure. But he remained where he was, his expression as closed as that of any who served Exit.

But his expression changed quickly when he felt the give of speed beneath his feet. The *Abracadabra* had increased her tempo, her bows careering murderously toward nearest land. There were shouts and frantic tenacity dedicated to a single purpose, because Woo had gone into labour.

He picked his way to the captain's quarters where the drama of her painful journey was unfolding behind a prohibited door. It was little else than a matter of form.

'Come, mon ami.' The Frenchman tapped the arm. 'We shall take our pleasure elsewhere and leave good people to help Woo in her transition to motherhood.'

In the sweeping stateroom, Lukas poured himself a pink gin and lemonade over crushed ice then followed the Frenchman who was making his way to the elevated deck.

'Can you imagine what it is to cross an ocean, to see nothing but a blue horizon, pure, naked, fragile hope?' The Frenchman shaded his eyes from the glare of the sun, and for some moments looked at the sea with a frowning brow. 'At first it is no more than a haze on the horizon, so we watch and look for a smudge, a shadow on the water, the stain slowly spreading along the horizon until you let yourself believe, land, life, resurrection coming out into the unknown. Such great spaces make us tall.'

'I'm already tall.'

'Oui, such height positions the head in the clouds.'

'Daphne rang.' And to this confession he drew the Frenchman's attention. 'She agreed to the cover up but she gets the fee.'

'And this makes you sad?'

Lukas stared at him for long seconds, driving back the sickly sentiment which threatened to consume him. 'Are my needs so great that I put them above others?'

'Think of your losses if not your life. This I did ask, not once, not twice but three times.' The Frenchman took hold of the shoulders and squeezed them firm. 'You have entered into contract. Take the hand and suffer my son, or take the life and suffer your loss. In the latter event, remember she will be recycled.'

Lukas gulped. It had such finality.

Now in restless pacing, and constant glances to the east, they consumed a weary hour in soundless state save for the salty breezes patrolling the decks. Then something very faint and distant, not unlike the murmur of seagulls drew their attention. It grew louder, fainter, and died away. It came once more, grew louder and swelled into a bellowing scream. That which seemed to lie in a haze of immeasurable concern, had popped into the world with astonishing yells, mother and child wrapped in the sheets of life.

Thomas, whose face glowed in a strange light of his own, emerged from the bedroom with a babe in his arms. 'I have a son,' he told them. 'A good pair of lungs, eh?'

'We need a name.' Benjamin said, opening a bottle of wine.

'Lukas!' Woo called out. 'Come see.' Captivating little Woo, her hair dishevelled, her whole self a hundred times more beautiful in this heightened aspect than ever she had been before. 'Lukas, you name baby.'

'Why me?'

'Because I love you, Tum love you, we can say Uncle Lukas name you because he love you.'

He brushed away a tear and made a clumsy laugh, now crimsoned with embarrassment. 'Let me see. It should be distinguished, memorable…hard to get my brain in gear. Tell you what. You get some rest and I'll put my thinking cap on, yup?'

Smelling like milk and honey, she slipped into a daze of wonder and closed her eyes. Then Kate emerged in peaceful surrounds, placing baby in the cradle. He drew away from the scene with the sudden realization Woo was right. Babies do change everything. The captain's quarters all at once had become a nursery, filled with squeaky toys, tinkling bells and cuddly bears.

'We need to talk.' Lukas motioned with his head and took Thomas to a quiet corner. There was much to say and too much to contemplate. 'First, congratulations. Second, I'm going for the kill. Third, your son should be called Edward, yup?'

'Can we just rewind, my man. You lost me on the second line, something about going for the kill.'

Lukas grabbed the braided cap off the bookshelf and plonked it on the head. 'You figure it out, captain of industry. Captain of fate needs to get in some practice.'

23

In the motor, parked on Watling Street, Lukas exhaled clutching his sword. Philippe was gone, Midnight left behind to cuddle Marmite, and those who had first accompanied him to the island of Porto Santo were sat with their faces drenched in apprehension.

'Luke,' Thomas said softly. 'I know you don't want to hear this but it must be said. He won't take your life. He'll go for the hand and if he succeeds, find the strength to make a run for it.'

'Thomas is right.' And Lukas turned to look back at Benjamin in the rear seat, lodged between Kate and Woo whose sleeping baby was cradled in her arms. 'Here we shall be to get you home as speedily as possible.'

'And Luke,' Thomas added, 'put your watch on the other wrist.'

If this was meant to inspire confidence it fell well short of that. With his face a mask of resignation and stern resolve, wordlessly Lukas got out of the motor and walked the quarter mile to Friars Wash. The pivot point had been reached, the critical instant for which he had trained. He had done enough, all that he could to work through his fears, work through his frustrations. He had left Oban in no doubt of his commitment and struggled onward in his commitment. Be swift and be brutal, he told himself. It was nothing that faith and iron-will could not conquer. And the moon climbed.

Marcus was already there, a distant figure in blood-dark shadows that stretched across the field of purple clover. There was something more than faintly ridiculous in the uniform he wore, meeting the standards of a military commander. The hand crafted sandals, the gilded greaves and body armour, its internal plates cushioned by the red of his tunic were veiled by a white cloak which enhanced the white plumes rising from his helmet, his eyes peering dispassionately above gilded cheeks. He allowed his stare to drift to the T-shirt. In these gloomy surrounds where the sky wore black, a view to a kill underscored the enemy's stance.

'I see we have a new train of thought, Giddy.'

'Well, you know how it is in this economic climate, not enough room to house prisoners. But there's a great place down below.'

'Still the same Giddy.' Marcus unbuckled his cloak and tossed it aside. 'What epitaph will be written on your grave, I wonder. Better to end alive at my feet than dead.'

'Then you assure me of my survival.'

Here, on open ground where the grass squelched wet from the previous day's rainfall, Marcus drew his long sword, an impressive sight. He had become the mighty threat Lukas had envisaged. But other threats could loom. That was the problem. A shot could come from anywhere or anyone.

Marcus leaned heavy on his sword. 'You're a stupid fool, Giddy. You trusted dear Benjamin, trusted the vagaries of my shitty Father who hangs limp in the dust, like you hang limp to love.'

'We shall see how limp you hang without your head.'

'Tough words from a man whose been taught by an amateur.'

'Oh contraire, your father was most obliging.'

That hit a nerve. Marcus sent his reply by a lightning strike from brow to cheek, the damage to dignity was done. 'See how you bleed, Giddy.'

Lukas swivelled neatly to parry a down-thrust and rammed home his point. 'See how you bleed too.'

Blood drawn from both sides, and Friars Wash instantly leapt into the realms of history, night had become a bloody day. It was a time exposing encampments, lines of tree defences, the rasp and clatter of armour, soldiers and snorting horses mounting their attack against warriors with spears and unsheathed swords, men, women and children, oxen and carts, a ceaseless sound of war cries. The battle was unfolding as it had before, the Britons scrambling up, the Romans scrambling down with two strangers taking centre stage. Targets of opportune were to be engaged.

Lukas blocked with the flick of his wrist and a circling of his blade, discovering the closer he came to death the more he wanted to live. Now, he existed to kill, to strike at the prodding throng of swords pouring into his vacuum. He was not rewarded in a direct sense but here was the underpinning of his lifelong ambition, by no means lacking in courage or decisiveness. His was the responsibility for Boudicca whose chariot pinned a corridor bounded by men shouting to flee for openings. While he bled, the Romans bled worse, such magnificent acts of bravery. His purpose had eluded him completely. All around him, the solid and consuming noise of combat raged. The cries, the shouts, the clash of steel had lost its distinctiveness, melded into a single and terrifying whole.

Chased by a jostling horde, he somersaulted over the dotted lines of howling animals and dived into their shits beneath a cart load of stores. Instead of a one-on-one battle among sweet smelling grass under a moonlit night, he was inhaling the foulness of Boudicca's war in the heat of a mid-day sun.

'You think your enemy rests?'

Lukas was surprised to see the Frenchman rolled beside him, more so Midnight clinging to his beard. Was there chance this man could protect her ill-fated destiny.

'Can you save her, Philippe?'

'Listen, mon ami, there is your war.'

Lukas followed the Frenchman's eyes, watched as Marcus ran a Briton through, cutting off his high-pitched cries. Another came forward, dispatched in the same frenzied way. Beyond that, new threats loomed. A brace of soldiers emerged in V formation, three thousand killing machines, tearing through, dividing, flattening, and driving back. He had seen enough, had done enough for Boudicca and her army. He could not change the course of their history but he could change the course of his future and kissed his hairy heartbeat goodbye.

Leaping obstacles, spotting ground, weaving and ducking, he marked his target and claimed the hand, swift and brutal. Marcus stared at his blood-spurting stump, breathed and absorbed it while those about took to their own excursions into a time long ago. But it was Lukas who glanced to the heavens in despair for his coming loss. Tentatively he raised his sword, reluctant to take the life that would end a life he had come to love for twenty-four years. And as Marcus slumped to his knees begging for his, the sword was already in flight.

Elsewhere, and earlier on, hidden from general view, and through the scope of a rifle, she saw Marcus throw his white mantle aside then swung her focus on the man who had turned her world upside down. She had left loving him, stayed away loving him and returned to alter the outcome loving him still. No one was immune or innocent in war. And suddenly, against her will she remembered the feel of his body inside her, the glorious flush stabbing at her loins, as hot as the anger against herself to master her feelings.

Sat astride on a branch high up in a tree quarter mile distance away, her observation of the combat was entirely contrary. There were no sights and sounds of soldiers and snorting horses mounting their attack against Boudicca's army, just one man in his T-shirt defending and deflecting the striking blows from another in gilded armour, their swords ringing out death throes over Friars Wash.

She tried to steady her nerves, hesitancy and resolution combined as she homed in on her target, a hated pariah before a hostile presence. The squeeze on the trigger finally yielded to the pressure and let loose a bullet.

And in that briefest of pauses a glittering sword took flight, two lethal weapons racing in separate directions with a view to a kill. Everything stretched into the centre of that moment, the non-stop whistle of the bullet and the non-stop whoosh of a glittering blade. In an instant the body of Marcus Metellus slumped forward, his head rolled undignified and Lukas collapsed in a heap on the ground. Under the fainter glimmering of the moon, and the pale light in the sky where the day was coming, her shattered senses collected to that point.

24

Doors opened, feet thumped, voices stained the air and all objects in the room became molten, changed shape, grew monstrous or trailed off into limitless space. Slumber did not come, only a kind of murky absence like a whale echoing through caves of water, submerging into fathoms of dreams, of complex lives and deaths.

Lukas finally woke to the sound of rustling paper and a patchwork of pain. The right shoulder was bound in crisp white bandages and Midnight was gone. The ghostly wizard, who had risen again, was returned to the grave and with him twenty-four years of his furry companion. So much history, so much agonising, so much exhaustive measures, these last few months his most frequent companion had become doubt and near despair.

Thomas set his morning paper aside. 'A couple of days,' he said, pre-empting the obvious question and poured a cup of tea. 'Mum did an excellent job of patching you up. You got shot, remember?'

It was too soon to remember anything and looked at the palm of his right hand. Gone was Andante's mark, his mission complete then something else. It eluded his first efforts to grasp it then suddenly he felt the lift of his spirits in a weak glimmer of hope. 'Philippe was at Friars Wash with Midnight. I asked him to save her.'

Thomas took no more notice of this remark than if he had been deaf and Lukas dumb. 'Are you hungry, my man?'

'Did you say I got shot?'

'Explanations later, you need to get sustenance in you. What do you fancy?'

'Did Oban pay us?'

'Too right he did.'

'Where are we?'

'Lowestoft, the others are at home.'

'Chicken soup.'

'Chicken soup coming up.'

In the exhaustless catalogue of his mercies to mankind, a sense of triumph overrode the agony of his loss as he considered he had deprived Daphne Frisk of the fee, some consolation. He would give it all for the return of Midnight. Closing his eyes, he now recalled the moment it started and the last thing he remembered. It was war, the memory of a great war, associated with terror and grief.

Pulling back the covers, he winced at the searing pain that shot through every muscle and ligament in the right shoulder, confirming he was lucky to be alive. After relieving himself in the toilet bowl, he studied his mirrored reflection, seven neat stitches to the side of his brow. So what, one more scar to serve as a reminder. Then his eyes drifted to his hair, a blob on his head indistinctively seen in the gathering gloom.

'*Do I look pretty?*'

For the love of Andate there was no explanation. Even among the splintered and bloody blistered core of combat, even among the shattering consequences of breaking the curse, Midnight had survived and found her way to him.

'I suppose you're hungry.'

'*Yes, yes, crunchy nut cornflakes.*'

'Have a grape instead.'

'*Why, have we run out?*'

He padded through the remnants of autumn air that invaded his lounge and plucked a grape from the fruit bowl telling her to chew on that while he thought things through, certain Philippe had taken Midnight on the battlefield.

'The way I see it,' he said, climbing back into bed, 'Philippe must have done a swap.'

'*Swap?*' Her head disappeared under her belly. '*Ohh, I have a big willy! Where are my balls? Have you got my balls?*'

Smiling, he lifted her out of his hair and removed a piece of stalk. 'This is not a willy.'

'*See what happens when you leave me behind. Woo kept feeding me bananas. I hate bananas.*'

'Where's Marmite?'

'*He divorced me.*'

Thomas walked in keeping his expression inscrutable, laid the tray on Lukas's lap and said, 'Chicken soup for a great warrior, crunchy nut cornflakes for lovely Midnight and one missing Marmite.'

'*Ohh, my Marmite.*' She met her mate who seemed forgiven enough and dived into the serial bowl. '*I love Thomas.*'

'I was dying to tell you, Luke, but she shook her head so I buttoned up,' Thomas explained. 'She never left your side, my man, squeaked blue murder every time Mum tried to get her off you. Not even bananas could get her to leave your side.'

Picking up his soup spoon, there could not be a happier man in the entire world. Everything else was irrelevant while Thomas disappeared again and re-emerged with a wipe-board and easel. This was going to be interesting.

'Now,' Thomas opened up like a headmaster. 'There are two suspects under review.' With a felt tip pen, he drew two matchstick men in blue. 'You and Marcus are here, okay.'

'Marcus wore white and gold.'

'I can hardly draw white on white, now can I?'

'Carry on.'

'He's on his knees, you're standing up.' Then he scored a straight line, swapped pens and drew a tree in green. 'From what Oban projected, he thinks the sniper is up a branch quarter mile away. We know that from a few broken twigs found on the ground, the rest is technical at this early date.' Then he drew a crude attempt of a bullet travelling the distance. 'It comes along like this, right? This is the first assumption. If you had stayed where you were, it would have got your heart. But you moved. So it travelled through your right shoulder blade, see, like this, as you lift up your sword arm and then buries itself into his head and out the other side. The second assumption is that if you had stayed where you were, it would have buried itself in his head. Reasons for two assumptions, I only had one viewpoint.'

'You were there?'

'We lost contact, Luke, so Dad made a bolt for it. We saw the raw end of it. You took his hand, yeah? He fell to his knees, then you raised your sword so bloody quick, a shot rings out, off with his head and you stood there in a daze before collapsing. We couldn't make it out at first but then-'

'Oh, I hate the conjunction.'

'There's no two ways, Luke. There's an eighty per cent chance that bullet reached first, ergo he died from the impact, not your blade.'

'And I'm alive.'

'And so is Midnight.'

'Philippe saved Midnight. Who took the shot?'

'Oban put hand on heart, said he never ordered it. Why should he? We told him you were going to take the kill. So other than Oban, who knew you were meeting Marcus?'

'A woman who wets her knickers on a motor bike is hardly a likely suspect to take a kill.'

'Then it's someone Marcus employed, yeah? He makes sure if you kill him, you're dead too.'

'That makes no sense. If Marcus is dead, why would the shooter bother?'

'Well maybe he was an honourable shooter. Or maybe he wanted revenge too.'

'I have no enemies, they're all dead.' In the lull, he tore off a piece of roll, dunked it in his soup and said before popping it into his mouth, 'Okay, who's the other suspect.'

'How did you kill Hodge?'

'Knocked him out, broke his arm and chucked him over the side.' Lukas smiled. 'Perhaps I get to kill him again.'

Thomas rubbed the back of his neck and sat on the bed, clearly conscious of the situation. 'His body never turned up at the mortuary, I checked. Aside this, everyone else is back at the house. I thought it best because Oban is coming to see you.'

'Did he say why?'

'Does he ever say why? You know what bothers me the most about him…he has this knack of always being one jump ahead and yet when I told him about the shooter his face drained. He had absolutely no idea.'

'So he came here?'

'Oh yes, he came to see how you were, plus the fact he had to get rid of the body. Makes you wonder how Exit copes with them. I mean do they put them in a meat grinder or what.'

'It never bothered you before.'

'Well it bothers me now. Exit never had a finger on the button, Luke. You could have been wiped out. Are they as good as we think? Are they who they say they are? By rights, Oban should've had Friars Wash locked down.'

'Is this some form of worry over our future?'

'Hell, yes. Dad always said Exit looks after their own. He was pretty upset about it, I can tell you. It was all I could do to separate him from Oban.'

'That's nice to know.' Lukas placed the tray aside. 'If you're right about Hodge, we need to get a trace on him. He deals in stolen passports and credit cards. Go back from the time I threw him over the side, the usual thing.'

When Thomas agreed and disappeared, Lukas went to the wipe board and tried to recall those last moments. Was he here or was he there? He pulled a long sigh and shook his head. Thomas was right. Oban should have swept the area for nasties. Now he contemplated his future bearing in mind his position and Thomas's concerns. But there was no exit from Exit. He had no leverage. He had no other trade. He pulled another long sigh and shook his head again.

'*You could plant some bulbs.*'

'I'm not a gardener.'

'*That's not the dirt I had in mind.*'

'Are you mad? She tried to do me out of the fee.'

'You tried to do Exit out of the fee.'

'Are we on the same wave length or what? That was plan B if you remember.'

'What was plan A?'

'Do you want me to put you in the drawer?'

Midnight gave him a raspberry and scuttled under the covers with Marmite. They curled up like salted snails and went to sleep, two rebellious dormice idling voluptuously in his bed.

Moments later Lukas heard Oban come into his quarters and help himself to a drink. He strapped on his watch, lit a reefer and allowed the weed to filter through his senses before walking into the lounge as if all could be granted at the whim of Oban.

'I want out.'

'No can do.'

'Can't or won't?'

This tough as nails negotiator dismissed the question and passed over a 7.5mil cartridge. 'This is a bloody mess, Giddy. Some bastard takes a pot quarter mile away, can you believe that…bolt action single feed shot and disappears without a trace. No fingerprints, no footprints, no tyre tracks, now what does that suggest to you?'

'He missed.'

Sipping his Bacardi, Oban carried it through to the elevated deck where Lukas fell behind. 'You know, sometimes I wish myself off this carousel. That's what we are on, a merry-go-round. We get on our white horses and pick off the baddies.' He let his gaze fall on Lukas. 'Frisk and his daughter were the clients.'

'Are you serious?'

'Do you see me smiling?'

'I couldn't get a lock on them.'

'Well you wouldn't. I was told to plan it that way. We were dicing with death here, Giddy. I was pissing in my pants every day. If Marcus got cute, he could have wiped the board with us. The only person who could get close was you.'

How could Lukas have got it so wrong? Daphne felt no sympathy for his circumstance, thought him arrogant, rude and a total imbecile. There was some warming to his predicament, but that blew out of the window when he asked for her collaboration in a wild scheme to turn Exit over. He looked at Oban, old doubts and apprehension on the Daphne subject, all the mingled possibilities of seeing her again was at the mercy of this man. 'Can you give me her number?'

After some scraping of his clean-shaven chin with his sausage fingers, there was no mercy. 'I remember when you joined us, green round the ears and thirsty. You're not thirsty for blood any more, Giddy, which makes you surplus to requirements.'

'If that was so you would be talking to a dead man.'

'Okay, hands up. You and Tom make the ideal jam sandwich to pin down the bastards stealing our secrets.'

'Do I get a bigger gun?'

'You also get to pay taxes.' Oban slugged down his drink. 'We'll iron details tonight at The Wherry round about six. I can see myself off.'

Lukas smiled. Fate had provided. He returned to his bedroom and opened wide the wardrobe doors, choice of wear was suspect, nothing would accommodate the position he would hold. He singled out a pair of brown cords, threw them on the bed and then toured the *Abracadabra* searching for Thomas who was on the bridge making up his mind whether to have a heart attack or put an extra braid on his cap.

'I take it you heard.'

'You do realize he's after our toys.'

'Tom, nobody plays with your toys other than 007.'

'No, but-'

'Q, we don't use conjunctions.'

Lukas was not looking for consensus or a majority vote. He knew Thomas too well and left him with a sense of self-importance ballooning under his braided cap. This was an essential instinct and quality that never left Thomas from the day he proudly launched the *Abracadabra* and it generated a great flow of love and affection from Lukas. Cousin or half-brother, it made no difference, they were interwoven - captain of industry and captain of fate.

The mood was cheerful, as might be expected, though Lukas was troubled by the sniper at Friars Wash.

At the sink lathering up, Thomas walked in. 'I laid a shirt and tie on the bed.'

'This is it, Tom. No more Mr. Scary coming out of his closet, no more worry for Woo, we get to search and pin down the bastards from the *Abracadabra*. Magic, yup?'

'I must say it worked out well. Make sure we get enough money for research and development. Hey, do you think we get to meet the top bod?'

'The thought did cross my mind.'

'Luke, why do you think Midnight still lives?'

'What I experienced was a full blown battle, challenging the Romans as if I was actually there, even saw Boudicca then I dived into a pile of shit under a cart. Philippe was there with Midnight and I asked him to save her, so I am reminded what Kate once told me, that the bond of love is greater than any manufacturer's glue. Let's call it my spoils of war.'

'Surely your spoils of war should be his assets.'

'You think Exit would let me have his assets?' He grabbed a towel off the rail. 'Make no mistake. They knew if I got rid of Marcus there were millions to be had.'

'How did he do it? How did Marcus stash his empire without jotting his name to it?'

'No idea. Did you get anywhere?'

'Taking in age and of course discounting women, I'd say we have about twenty thousand men to trawl through.'

'That many?'

'Look, my man, it was approaching the holiday season and besides who's to say he never laid low with a woman, eh? That's his style.' Thomas stepped up and straightened the tie. 'Luke, what do you think Dad is going to say when we tell him about Frisk and Daphne?'

'I never guessed. Did it cross your mind?'

'For a brief moment it did. It makes more sense if she was the sniper. She knew where to go and she knew your intentions. Do we assume Oban passed on your change of heart? Probably not, so she watches the state of play, sees you take the hand, not a good sign and then pulls the trigger. Obviously not a very good shot because she aimed in the wrong direction. But there again, did she? Kill you and he's dead. Kill him and your dead.'

'I can't see it, her up a tree with a M99.'

'Maybe she hired a shooter, rich daddy, remember?'

'Do you want it to be Daphne or Hodge? Make up your mind because you're giving me a headache.'

'I want to know what's going on, my man.'

'I'll tell you what's going on. I made the kill. Philippe saved Midnight.' He showed his palm. 'Look, clear of Andante's mark. So the prat behind the shooter missed. Now can we move on?'

In the course of time the massive chimneys rose upon his view, and with the same cool importance Thomas dropped out of the launch and greeted his mother and wife in the kitchen. Lukas was not far behind, tucking Midnight and Marmite into his trouser pocket.

'Oh, dear, you should be in bed.' Kate looked beyond Lukas. 'Benjamin, you told me you were just picking up Thomas.'

'Is he not here?' He smacked her bottom good-humouredly. 'We shall join you later. I want a word with my sons.'

They descended the stone steps that led to his private sanctuary and closed the door softly behind them. Yes, here was the library that the boldest never entered without permission or invitation, the mystery of its stoned walls, the hallowed ground. For Benjamin, his faith had been well placed, his journey now at an end.

'What do you see,' he asked them.

Lukas spotted it immediately. 'You've written an account of recent events.'

'Yes, on these walls where space was limited…here, my son Lukas who broke the curse…and here, my son Thomas who felled the Needle.' He laughed heartedly, collectively placed an arm about each of them, taking care not to squeeze Lukas too hard. 'I am so proud my heart is near fit to burst.'

'It's a poor heart that never rejoices.'

'How right you are, my Lukas.' Anticipating such an occasion, Benjamin uncorked a cobwebbed bottle and smelt the air of change in utter satisfaction. 'I purchased this port in Spain many, many years ago with one purpose in mind, and this purpose has arrived. Now, my Lukas, how do you feel?'

'A bit sore in places, my shoulder mostly.'

'You were a very lucky man. That bullet could have pierced your heart, let us thank the incompetent Hodge and repay him for his stupidity.' Benjamin swung his focus at Thomas. 'Why the long face?'

'Not long…much happier being home…not that this is my home, well it's your home, our work is on the *Abracadabra* saving the Government's secrets…bugger.'

Lukas rolled his eyes, Thomas clearly wondering what to say about Oban's proposition. 'He's worried the Government is going to pinch his toys.'

Benjamin indicated for them sit in the snug corner of the library. 'I have everything a man could wish for…two healthy sons in transit of great things to come, a beautiful daughter-in-law, a grandson and a wonderful wife. Now tell me, what are your spoils of war, my Lukas?'

He held up three digits. 'First, I got my life back. Secondly, I have a step up the ladder, remuneration and duties yet to be ironed tonight.'

'That is your true spoils of war, my Lukas…a new challenge, a good challenge shared with your brother who has himself worried about Woo and his son. And the third, equally good I trust?'

Indeed, equally good, if not better was Midnight. 'I'm going to wear a braided cap like Tom.' They enjoyed his joke.

'There were times when I thought this day would never come, to see my sons in this free and simple light. The curse has pained us all in different ways. For my Thomas, there has been many a furrowed brow. But we must not dwell on the past. We must look to the future.'

Lukas had an indiscernible feeling Benjamin knew more than he cared to admit, so eyeing him suspiciously he said, 'I would like to dwell on the past such as what part you played in the charade because thinking about it, you had to be involved somewhere along the line.'

Benjamin made a journey to his desk and seized his pipe and tobacco pouch with the same all-knowing smile, the composed and quiet manner, unruffled and powerful. 'In some ways you are correct, somewhere along the line I played my part.' He paused to light his pipe and savour the inhalation before taking his preferred armchair. 'I asked myself, if the client was willing to pay an exorbitant fee for the termination of an abhorrent creature, what do you suppose would happen when Exit discovered it was Marcus Metellus?'

It took a moment for Lukas to realize Benjamin was asking him a question. 'Well,' he said. 'I think, knowing my history, they would have contacted you.'

'You are correct. My contribution was knowledge of your circumstance, and this was given in a good-will gesture without request for feedback. Had Marcus an inkling, he would have disappeared without a trace only to return in his own time to wreak havoc.'

'Did you know how to break the curse?'

'Emphatically, no. Philippe was correct to withhold this information. You alone needed to take a journey of understanding, to seek out the truth, to weigh the consequences. The choice had to be yours, not mine, not his, not anyone else's. And yes, there was certain leverage placed upon your shoulders but I feel no remorse, my Lukas. I would far rather you disown me than stand by your graveside for that is what it amounted. I had no true history of our cursed ancestors, only the words on that wall, their lost journeys and early deaths. It was fate, fate that Philippe intervened, fate both your paths crossed in this way, fate you should take the bull by the horns and rid that blessed curse.'

Thomas spoke. 'I get the diary, I get Daphne and Frisk, I get Philippe, I even get the Needle, but I don't get the sword.'

'I believed it would serve Lukas well in his endeavours, taking that which was once his ancestor's. Yes, I knew of the sword, and I also knew who held it.' Benjamin turned his gaze back to Lukas. 'Let me explain. You remember the night dining with Daphne shortly after seeing Philippe? She came to me, very concerned with your way of thinking. I had given no thought to Midnight, your underlying reason why you wished the curse to continue but I gathered enough to know war had to be declared and I knew Marcus was an excellent swordsman. It stood to reason if you challenged him and he took the bait, he would choose the weapon that suited him well.' Then Benjamin looked back at Thomas. 'My son, I make no apology for the use of your equipment. I contacted Exit in the early hours of Daphne's parting and made my request for the man to give Lukas the sword, to pay him a substantial amount.' Benjamin turned back to Lukas. 'I was extremely perturbed on your state of health and to be told the man had not passed the sword, I again contacted Exit who made the decision to send in one of their operatives, had not bargained for his death, poor man.'

'That's a point,' Thomas threw in. 'If Daphne wanted Luke dead, she could have shot him then.'

Benjamin took note. 'And why would Daphne want Lukas dead?'

'She was the client, her and her father,' and Lukas saw no surprise shown on Benjamin's face. 'You knew.'

'Yes, I knew three days prior to the equinox. It was Philippe who told me for reasons which I shall explain. Remember we spoke of the mark which came on his son's hand when he was six years old, a sign of things to come, a warning Andate gave to Philippe and his brother, Francois who had his own family, a wife and a three year old daughter. A decision was made to cut family ties. Francois made a new life, changed his name and moved to England, no more a Metellus for Marcus to hound. That is why Philippe gave Daphne the diary, at a time when she was ready to understand her background. I can also inform the tale to melt your heart was of another, quite legitimate and not in dispute. Philippe believed, and quite wisely, that it was necessary to withhold this information. If one word was let slip by accident, the clever and most devious Marcus would make them pay dearly. And the reason why Philippe left your side early was so he could spend some time with his brother before going to meet his Maria.'

'If Oban failed to relate my change of mind, it was one of them to take the shot.'

'No, I cannot accept that.'

'See, that's the problem,' said Thomas. 'Frisk or Daphne saw the hand go and thought Lukas had finished where in fact he hadn't so the trigger is pulled to eliminate Marcus or Luke, either way the job is done. Think about it, Dad. They had a score to settle.'

'There was no score to settle. If Lukas had taken the hand so he would have taken Marcus into custody. Yes, it is true Daphne felt aggrieved this might be the case though we must remind ourselves Lukas would still have his power so there was no concern of his escape. A pity really…I had such high hopes for Daphne and Lukas. She would have made a wonderful wife. Tell me, my Lukas, does such knowledge dissuade you from marrying a Metellus?'

'Huh, that's a question and a half. Every time she opened her mouth out popped a lie. She could have trusted me, but no, instead she made me feel like a bastard. I told her about Midnight, she could have said then. Instead, she asked for the entire fee.'

'Aw, come on Luke. You weren't exactly the diplomat.'

An unwilling nod and Lukas stamped the thought from his head, taking stock for a moment before asking Benjamin, 'You okay with Exit? Tom tells me you could have strangled Oban.'

Benjamin fiercely shook his head. 'I would have shot him. There again, who was to know. Perhaps I was a little hard on the man. He was concerned, as were we all. It was not easy to let Midnight go. She had been your companion for many, many years, a lifetime of fondness and affection when the world about you was so bleak.'

'I had no choice.'

'You had a choice. Thomas was willing to aid and abet in your little conspiracy, so too was I but you sacrificed a loyal companion to do what you considered was right. It takes a special man to forfeit his treasured possession in order to give others their justice.' Benjamin turned his gaze upon Midnight who was now sitting on Lukas's knee with her ears tuned. 'Andate spared your life, my little friend, left a little magic for the duration of your life.'

'My life,' Lukas corrected.

'Are you so sure?' Thomas asked.

'Ohh, am I going to die?'

'No Midnight. Tom is being a prick as usual.'

Benjamin stood. 'We shall speak no more of this. The result was good, my Lukas alive and the curse no more. Let us retreat to the kitchen and make Woo a happy wife. It may do you some good, Lukas, to take a rest for a few hours, you look a little peaky.'

'No, I'm fine.'

As to the probabilities, he was far from fine. The power that had once threaded through his body seemed to be rapidly returning, leaving him to work out why. Was this his true spoils of war? Or was there something to worry about? Rather than join the others, he stood gazing at that wall and smiled resignedly. With so much at stake, there were no rules and nothing but heartache. Daphne too must have felt similarly, her need equally great. Would it have made a difference had he known who she was? He turned away and considered it would have been fatal. Everyone, it seemed, was engaged in subterfuge.

25

The Wherry was lively being composed of all that which kept Oulton Broad in existence, people, by dint of sitting together in the same place and the same relative positions, doing exactly the same things for a great many years mingled with virtually the same visitors who holidayed regularly in this part of the world.

Lukas sat alone in a corner snug looking impatiently at his watch. He twisted sideways when the main door swung open and in walked a couple of locals. It was so damn warm he loosened his tie and undid the button of his single breasted jacket, blood catching his margin of sight. Thinking very steadily of what he had just now observed, he buttoned up and Thomas sidled into view.

'He's definitely not here.'

'Did you look outside?'

'Yeah, course I did.'

'Well go look again.'

Before Thomas could respond, the main door opened again and in walked Oban stuffing his Ray-Bans in his top suit pocket. He leaned on the back rest of a chair. 'Let's sit outside.'

'Tom, get in another round.'

Pushing through slim and wide shoulders and dying for a smoke, Oban bent his head to a flame the moment he hit air. He viewed the different patio levels, slatted tables and benches, choosing the quietest spot with river views.

'Never knew you smoked.'

'I don't. This is my reward for being a good boy.'

'Do we get to meet the top bod?'

Oban ignored the question. 'I'm married, Giddy, do you know that…course you don't, why would you. Anyway, my wife and her mother look like sisters…sixty-eight and she's still got her teeth. Every time I see her, she says the same thing, you should've married me. And every time I say the same thing back, I would've done if you hadn't told me your age.' The meaning of which implied he would never get to meet the top bod.

Their conversation paused when Thomas emerged with three pints of beer. After a spot of general banter and cheers, Oban was down to business, keeping his voice trimmed. 'We're after the hackers stealing our secrets, a new generation of whiz-kids holding us up for ransom. The Secretary of State wants these bastards wiped out, quietly and efficiently. We can't get a lock on them, so before we go any further, can you do it?'

'Absolutely,' they voiced in unison.

'You just saved your arses.' No doubt Oban was in a good mood. He passed over a disc. 'That's what we got so far. We've identified a couple of cogs in the wheel of something much larger. Last year we finalized an audit trail and discovered three million was taken out of the Works & Pensions' fund…in pennies…a bit here, a bit there…nothing to draw attention until some guy down in Crawley starts writing letters asking why his monthly pay is always twenty pence short. That's just one side of it. The other is selling our secrets to the highest bidder.'

Lukas spoke. 'You think they're one of the same?'

'That's for you to find out.' Then Oban referred to Thomas. 'Never took much notice of quantum mechanics, not my field. Our bods reckon these hackers are way ahead of us. Now I asked myself if you're using the same tool to steer the *Abracadabra*, how they got to be as clever as you.'

'They're not, never will be.'

'Care to tell me why?'

Lukas intervened. 'All you have to concern yourself is that we can do the job. You want these guys then we can wipe them out.'

'Giddy, you get a bigger gun not a licence to wipe them all out. We need to interrogate the main users so leave that end to us. Now what else do you get. Two million plus expenses to close their operation, thereafter you get a basic million to keep your finger on the buzzer.'

'Then you're talking to yourself.' Thomas said. 'We made two million last year, anything less we starve research and development.'

'We'll fund your research and development.'

And get to swipe the cream off the milk, Lukas considered. 'Tell you what. Four million to close their operation, thereafter three to keep our finger on the buzzer and you get to keep your nose out of our toys.'

Oban fished a fat gold watch from his pocket and held it to his ear, his eyes directing their challenge straight at Lukas. 'My wife gave me this watch…keeps great time and that's about all.'

'Tom, let Oban have one of our watches.'

'You got yourself a deal. And Giddy, keep your dick out of whores, no ambulance chasing or freebees.'

'Do we pay into a graduated pension scheme?' They enjoyed his joke but Thomas was not joking. 'Seriously, guys, we have to think of our future. Dad gets a jolly good pension.'

'I understand you just had a son.' Oban said and Lukas knew something good was going to come out. 'Does he keep you up at night?'

'Oh, he's a great little fellow, hardly any trouble.'

'Then take good care of him because he's your pension.'

Lukas doubled up laughing, popping a stitch in the process. Nothing was taken seriously from that point on.

'You know why I was late?' Oban continued. 'Two cops pulled me over for doing eighty. I told them, that can't be right. Why's that, one of them said to which I replied, it's a bloody disgrace doing eighty in a Merc, you sure it wasn't a hundred.' They laughed again. 'Giddy, you're rear tyres must get very hot on that bike.'

'I can't go any slower. As soon as I kick in at ninety my number plates switch to DR NO.' More laughter, more stitches popped, Lukas answered his mobile in a frivolous mood. 'Double O7 at your service.'

'Miss Moneypenny here.'

Taking him by surprise, Lukas wended his way down the steps beyond the car park and stood at the waters' edge being cool as a cucumber in a microwave. 'Why didn't you tell me you were a Metellus?'

'Oh, I couldn't, Luke. Utmost secrecy had to be maintained to keep Marcus in the dark. You could have involuntarily let slip a word, a clue to put him on the qui vive. After all, you two slept on the same pillow.'

'I thought we covered that subject?'

'With a sheet not a coffin lid. Is Midnight doing well?'

'How did you know about Midnight?'

'Because I gave her to you, just as we agreed which means you owe me the fee.'

Lukas blinked a few times, his voice going deeper. 'I don't know if it's escaped your attention but I made the kill.'

'No, I made the kill.'

'Excuse me?'

'Who do you think was up a tree, Santa Clause?'

This irritated him further. 'You tried to bloody kill me!'

'Rubbish, you just moved too quickly.'

'Let me get this straight,' he said, his voice going deeper still. 'You took a shot at Marcus and then what? I would have been dead too.'

'Nonsense, you're alive, aren't you?'

'I made the kill, that's why I'm standing here talking to a brainless idiot who thinks I'm dumb enough to hand over the fee!'

'I would remind you we had a bargain,' her voice climbing an octave higher. 'You asked me to save Midnight, I agreed, that was the terms.'

'Is this why you telephoned, to ask for the fee?'

'I said I would be in contact if you were still alive.'

'I made the kill!'

'No! I made the kill! Midnight proves it or am I talking to a brainless idiot who thinks I'm dumb enough to give up the fee!'

'Okay, clever clogs, what's your take?'

'It was simple really. I just looked upon you two like countries at war so if a third came in on the equation without giving notice, then what you have is an altered outcome, ergo you were not penalized. And were you penalized in any way?'

Bollocks! 'Where do I send the money?'

'Why not keep it to wipe your arrogant arse.'

Oops! He looked back at Oban in conversation with Thomas, then back at his mobile, pressing redial, haunted by an unobtainable number. Instead of smelling a sweet future with Daphne, he was inhaling the cold river born kisses and petrol fumes from a motor nearby. Even the concrete beneath his feet seemed to leak blood. Misery for Lukas, he just stood there and watched the tail end of Oban disappear into the lights of The Wherry while Thomas was making his way toward him.

'Are you alright, my man?'

'I think I need sewing up again.'

Almost anything that caught his wandering eye, Thomas gathered the circumstance and bundled Lukas in the motor launch moored close by. From there they took the wide and winding river that was partly lit by dreamy homes on the north bank.

'Dad,' Thomas spoke into his mobile, 'Luke's coming apart. Can you ask Mum to get out her needle?' There was a pause before he spoke again. 'Okay, will do.'

With Lukas now having told Thomas of recent events, they docked at an aging jutting pontoon, crossed the massive lawns and in spite of his condition, there was no doubt now in his mind that he had something to worry about.

As the back door flew open and Benjamin filled the gap, Lukas abandoned this unsettling train of thought and took in the sober activities of Kate, wholly absorbed as she prepared and bound his injury in the kitchen.

'You were told to rest,' she reprimanded.

'I was resting.'

'Dear, you are like an ocean liner, once you get going it takes considerable effort to stop you.'

'How bad is it?' Thomas asked.

'Oh, he will live to die another day.'

'Dad, I need a word in your ear.'

When Benjamin and Thomas left the kitchen, Lukas said, 'Kate, remember when you said the bond of love is greater than any manufacturer's glue, and I thought you were referring to Midnight?'

'Young people nowadays use the word love like a lollipop…put down your arm, dear…they lick at it, suck on it and then throw away the stick…arm up again.'

'Then I was her lollipop.'

'Why, dear?'

'She made the kill.'

Quietly, Kate was having hysterics at the bin as she dumped the bloodied spoils and ran a cold tap at the same time. 'Did she give a reason why?'

'She telephoned to say she completed our part of the bargain. She knew Midnight would be saved, even knew I still had my power.'

'No mention was made you still had your power, dear.'

'I felt it return this afternoon, wasn't sure at first so I practiced on Marmite which upset Midnight.'

'Ah, that would explain why they hide in my knitting basket. Have you told your father?'

Lukas shook his head and said nothing.

'I am sure there is a rational explanation to all this. She must regard you with some innocent regret, with some blameless thoughts of what might have been. And you must do the same. You need to get some rest.'

But Lukas was still resonating with what Daphne had said and raked his hands through his hair, glancing at the dusty moth circumnavigating the ceiling light in misty recollection. He neither knew her name nor where she lived. Teacher, historian or doctor though she did know the physical make-up of a dormouse. Her clothes, he considered, were bought to play a specific role which was performed with surpassing brilliancy that he had never truly felt she belonged to anyone else but him.

Kate kissed him fondly on the head. 'Be a good boy and get some rest. I'll make you a hot chocolate.'

'I like hot chocolate.'

'I know, dear, that's why I am making you one.'

Pondering on his lot, he withdrew to his room and laid out on the bed listening for a long time, expecting every moment to hear creaking footsteps on the stairs, to be greeted by Kate with a cup of hot chocolate. But neither voice nor footstep came and though some distant echoes as of closing doors from time to time, no nearer sound disturbed his place of retreat.

It was an hour later or thereabouts when Thomas walked in with a cup of hot chocolate, Benjamin not far behind.

'Luke, Dad has something important to say.'

Benjamin moved the legs over to sit on the bed, his face as grave as his voice. 'We can say at the equinox you both stood equal and vulnerable to the vicissitudes of fate. So, from her point of view, war was declared between two countries. You took the hand as if placing your mark on his territory thus your power and mascot, namely Midnight remained. By a third country poking its nose into the affairs of others, it altered the outcome. Hence, you were not penalized by death or sacrifice. But-'

'Oh, I hate the conjunctions.'

'The curse has not been broken for she took his life, not you. Must we assume Andate will penalize her? Did she give any indication of this?'

'The opposite, she was full of herself, told me to wipe my arrogant arse with the money.'

'This makes no sense. She must be mistaken, there again can we assume the curse will be broken by default.'

'Default?'

'She is the last of her line, her blood will continue the curse unless she is resolved to stay motherless.' Benjamin touched the arm and stood. 'We must err on the side of caution and add this to the library walls.'

'If you can find some space,' Thomas added.

'My son, if needs must there is space on the ceiling.'

Thomas nodded and looked back at Lukas. 'You have to admit she's a clever sod.'

'Excuse me?'

'Aw, come on, Luke. You're down, okay? Look, there's no more Marcus to affect you. Everything went your way. Everything went her way. Remember what she said when you two were at the Castle Museum, she said she would take you on?'

'And that's exactly what she was doing, taking me on and I'm the stupid bastard that fell for it. Have you told Woo?'

'Oh, she's on your side, my man. Daphne's name is mud…of course we mustn't be too discriminatory.'

'That's a long word.'

'The biggest one I got. The way I see it, Luke, you and her had something going, eh? Perhaps we should make an effort to trace her and-'

'Nope, end of story.'

'Okay, on another note, something Woo brought up, how do you feel about swapping quarters so Eddy can have a cabin next to us?'

'Is it possible to put an elevated deck in your quarters?'

'Time and money, anything is possible.'

'Not so easy then.'

'Look, she submerges, right? If we cut through the main bulkhead, we'll have to fit new plates and hydraulics. How about taking the stateroom then we cut a hole in the floor to pinch the cabin below, bedroom and en-suite, done deal, fireman's pole, Bob's your uncle.'

'Why do I need a fireman's pole?'

'Yeah, it'll be great for my little man.'

'So, my quarters are to be invaded?'

'What are uncles for?'

'I'll take your quarters.'

Oh, the machinations of men and mice. Midnight, followed by Marmite, scrambled up the covers and took a position on Lukas's outstretched lap, her black eyes staring back at him. '*We want a garden.*'

THE DENOUEMENT

26

Muffled up to the eyeballs, Oban wended his way toward Westminster Bridge thinking of a great many things, and most of all in which to relate his advice and so account satisfactorily to Lukas.

The *Abracadabra*, which lay outstretched before him like a silver shadow on the water, visible in the darkness by its own faint light had travelled a zillion miles in three long years. And in those three long years the counter-attack against treasonable hackers had made its mark. Targeting them was Thomas's most important priority and built around a core function specifically designed to infiltrate, his program merged effortlessly with the sophisticated databases that were operated world-wide. Even in the brains of Exit, it was a different aspect. Justice was not so far removed, or hard to find, and although there were busy trades in Europe, and beyond, Britain was a safer place than many would readily believe.

In the sweeping stateroom, Lukas was pouring a drink at the mirrored bar, gone were the customary things that once fed his soul. The snakeskin boots were highly polished, the suit black, its long jacket bore initialled solid gold buttons. To the side of his brow, the trace wound told of the battle at Friars Wash. With his hair tied back and a goatee beard, he regarded himself as a diplomatic pirate. Though he quite understood the purpose of this statement was to rid the image of his old self, he had every distinct memory of the woman he once loved.

Oban walked in rubbing his hands against the damp chill. 'Make mine a whisky.'

'Took you long enough to get back to me?'

'Who do you think we are? A drop-in centre to conjure up man-power for private vendettas?'

Lukas ignored the remark and passed over the whisky to a smug face. 'Okay, what have you got for me?'

'The only one whose wife buggered off was Bradshaw.'

'Got me a picture?'

'It's him alright.'

'Yes!' Lukas punched the air. 'Yes! I've finally got the bastard.' Three years he waited for this, three years for Hodge to surface.

'What made you lock on to him?'

'Now there is a story.' Lukas took a seat at the table and propped up his feet while Oban shrugged out of his overcoat revealing a dark suit with a hint of conflict to his paisley tie. 'Since Hodge dealt in stolen identities it seemed a good move to check out passports, nine months on we never got anywhere. Tom believed Hodge was laying low with a woman, his usual MO. Then it occurred, why keep to the usual MO? Why not find a bloke his size, weight, etcetera, no family as such, knock him off, bury him deep and hey presto, a valid identity. Now we come to the hardest part. We had no photograph of Hodge, so all we could do is feed in what details we had against passports and driving licences. Ten hit the bottom pile because they had a wife, no kids. Too dodgy for Hodge to kill off the wife then Tom suggested Hodge may have done her in, made it look like she packed her bags, and that's where you came in.'

'We want the assets.'

'I want a pay rise.'

'Your pay is non-negotiable.'

'You need another toy.'

'That pen in your breast pocket looks interesting.'

'Can you write?'

Oban smiled. 'Make the kill quiet, Giddy.'

Lukas shot to his legs and walked slowly up to the deck doors, flattened his nose against the cold glass. The evening was pouring sleet in the twilight of November. At length a gloomy derision came upon his features. 'I need to know his movements.'

Oban came to his side, sharing the looming view of Westminster, its forest of towers, turrets and spires rising from a vast honeycomb of courts, corridors and chambers. 'He went into the bookies, placed a two grand bet, popped into his local and came out with some beers. Probably watching tonight's game.'

'I have a dinner date.'

'So do it between courses, keep the desert until last.'

'Are we done with the jokes?'

'I do have one more.' Oban slipped his hand inside his suit pocket and pulled out a packet of Viagra. 'The last time I took one of these, her mother called round and I was left with a stonker for three hours, couldn't even take a piss. Moral of the story, get in while the going is good.'

They both smiled. It was part of the ritual. With a six figure income guaranteed for life, this tough as nails negotiator could enjoy the thousand pound tailored suits that hung so comfortably from his well-built frame. He strolled nonchalantly across the room, placed his empty glass on the bar, picked up his overcoat and left.

'*Bossy boots*,' Midnight squeaked from a jungle of greenery sprouting from an enamelled sink lodged on the floor. '*We were looking forward to crispy duck.*'

'Want to come with me?'

Her large rounded eyes viewed the weather and then glanced back at Marmite scratching his ear. No contest. To be out in the cold was one thing, to be eliminating Hodge, was another.

With his knife tucked up his sleeve nice and sharp, it could bury itself vertically, driving up through the rib cage as the limbs shook. That would be pleasing but not to Oban. He looked at his gold signet ring, a practical piece of gadgetry, part of the concept which came from a time when viewing ancient jewellery behind a glass cabinet at the Castle Museum. That would be pleasing to Oban.

At which point Thomas walked in. 'What did Oban have to say?'

'Hodge and Bradshaw are one of the same.'

'Yeah!' Now it was Thomas who punched the air. 'Great stuff. When are you taking him out?'

'Tonight.'

'So, you're cancelling your dinner date?'

The thought barely troubled him. 'Give Oban a pen.'

'Ah, see, that's exactly what I mean. Give him a watch, now he wants a pen. Next, he'll be asking for a ring.'

'The brain, currently the only device known to be capable of generating a sense of consciousness, makes use of many modes of activity, yup? Most of these modes are in your computer so what if we gave it a level of consciousness.'

'It has a level of consciousness.'

'Remind me where we got this from?'

'Okay, one pen and no more.'

'I'll not take the bike.' Lukas slugged down his drink, wormed into his trench coat then grabbed his mobile, punching in numbers. 'I'll take the train instead.' When the line picked up, he said, 'It's me. Can we make it tomorrow?'

'No can do, I'm off to the Canaries on a shoot.'

Lukas knew nothing of her prior commitment, at least none he was involved with. 'Give me a call when you return, yup?' He logged off and glanced back at Thomas. 'Ask Woo if she can rustle up some crispy duck for the love birds.'

'No problem.'

The sleet had turned to snow, tiny icicles forming on his hair as it came down heavy. He took the circle line to Notting Hill Gate, swapped lines for West Ruislip. It was here Hodge lived, in a character detached property situated in a premier location with delightful views over the Golf Course and set within easy walking distance to the underground station.

Now Hodge was treading on glass. The only cloud on the horizon was the happy thought of paying off his gambling debts, which was in effect a highly explosive umbrella. At the same time of acting as Bradshaw, he would play golf with the big-wigs but it only lasted as long as he could get away with it.

Lukas cracked his knuckles, flipped the tip to his poisonous ring and gazed around before pressing the bell. His resolve was unshaken. There would be no tactics, no finesse, no quarter given. The moment the lock turned, his foot to the door propelled Hodge to the floor.

'What makes you think you can hide from me?'

'Oh shit!' Any dispatch was likely to be grim.

With a back-handed blow to the face, the sentence passed on a screech of pain. The poison would work quickly, would consume him, setting his heart afire, his breath fast and shallow, his limbs restrained. At best he would live one minute. At worst he would suffer three and recount his sins.

Lukas did not stay to find out. He opened the door, glanced about then made his way to the station thinking the lives of all were in his hands. He looked up to the full embrace of snow, the sky pouring white with a strange quietness.

Someone brushed by, said oops, sorry and carried on. He glanced back. True love is a curious thing. Twisting on his heels, he followed the cream coat and bobble hat picking its way to the ticket machines. Turn, damn you, turn and let me see your face. Three others crowded round, one moved off, she moved next with her head in her shoulder bag. It had been mostly like this. Seated in a restaurant, standing on a platform, taking a walk in the park, wherever, he would look around and wonder if by now he had truly forgotten what she looked like.

Fastening the catch of her bag, head bent, taking a few steps away, she looked up. Their eyes locked onto to each other and both stood still. For Lukas, a layer of sweat broke across his forehead, his mouth was dry and he could not swallow. The times he sat blank at a photograph that had been folded and unfolded so many times that the ragged creases had almost obliterated her face.

'Lukas?' She mouthed and met him half way, her face almost white with shock. 'My goodness, you're hardly recognizable.'

'Sometimes I hardly recognize myself.'

'Are you keeping well? You look well.'

'You look like you need a cup of coffee.'

'Actually, I can't stop.' Then she quickly changed her mind. 'Yes, why not, I could do with a coffee.' They fell into step. 'Do you know this area?'

'I was visiting a friend. And you?'

'Oh, I just got on the wrong train.'

'Lost your brains?'

Their conversation boarded on the rim of polite emptiness as they weaved a slushy street and crossed the road into a corner pub that had dark hole-in-the-wall seats. Lukas ordered two coffees and leaned hard on the bar looking at the wine menu.

'Not for me.' Her head tilted to one side. 'Have you forgotten or just being crafty?'

'Quite right, two coffees coming up.'

He carried the cups to a vacant table, the world and everything in it could blow up for all he cared. Fifteen minutes or two hours, he had her all to himself.

'Daphne,' she said, unbuttoning her coat. 'In case you ask, please register my name as Daphne but you can call me Dap if you prefer.' Then she removed the bobble hat and her rich brown hair fell in torrents. She looked ravishing in a yellow jumpsuit, wearing a tan belt to show off her slim waist, accessorized with a gold choker and bracelet. 'Do you still work for you know who?'

'It's Casino Royale stuff now.'

'Wow, how impressive, that definitely calls for brass buttons and a pony tail.'

'Gold,' he corrected her.

'Wow, even better. Gold buttons in case you get short of money.' At thirty years of age, the past three years had thoroughly consumed her and she no longer cared. Now she was looking at Lukas, a rare event and one she treasured. 'How is Tom and Woo? Did she have a boy?'

'Eddy, Edward Giddy born on the *Abracadabra*. You know, I never thought much about names…all things considered *Abracadabra* fits the bill. People come and go, you disappeared, not a trace, nothing and then here you are, gee, I can hardly believe it.' He ran his fingertips over his eyebrows, then dropped his hands to his lap in fear she would see them shake. 'At what point did you know Midnight would survive?'

'In between calls. It just seemed logical if you base the equations on war because that is what it was. Everything to do with Boudicca is about war.'

'After you took the shot, were you affected in anyway?'

'Affected?' she said an octave higher.

'Yes, affected, sick, half a limb lost or whatever because I'm surprised Andate never penalized you for interfering.'

'Well, as you can see, all limbs intact, fully mobile.'

'Are you with anyone?'

She dipped her eyes. 'Um, that's a hard question to answer. Yes, figuratively speaking and no, realistically speaking…probably at this point in time I might be able to look at my future. And what about you, do you still-'

'Nope, I don't have to pay for it anymore.'

'I was going to ask if you still had Marmite.'

'Glad we got that sorted.'

'Are you happy, Luke?'

He was almost afraid to say no, a sad bastard jerking off some nights thinking of her. Every thought took him back to the first time, those virgin breasts which came long after school. If anything, he was only happy with one thing and said, 'Yes, Marmite is still around and Midnight is still crunchy nut crazy. I bought one of those big sink stands for tall plants, yup? She loves it…well, they both do.'

'Nothing better than giving them a home in natural surrounds. Is she with you?'

'It was too cold.' He leaned forward, kept his voice down to a whisper. 'I found Hodge.'

Dramatically, she responded likewise. 'I thought he was dead.'

'He could swim with one arm.'

'Wow, quite the Olympian. Are you positive you got him this time?'

'Do you want to check?' He closed his eyes for a moment like a boy expecting to get slapped by an angry mother. 'Sorry, that wasn't called for. Truth, when you telephoned asking for the fee, the cause never occurred to me. Later, Ben highlighted a probability the curse is still active. Had you considered this?'

'Oh, but Marcus is gone, Luke. You are free of the pain and Midnight was saved. Was Ben very upset?'

He shrugged. 'He knew you had your reasons to do what you did and I had mine, like Philippe once said, we all have our ghosts. You hunt your way. I hunt mine. How is your father keeping?'

'Very well, he's keeping well. Of course, he was so relieved to know that vile creature was dead, gone, pulverised, despicable, contemptible, loathsome, and two times again.'

'How do you spell that?'

'Correctly.'

He chuckled, more relaxed now. 'We travel a lot. Eddy likes living on the water and Woo still cooks flied rice. Never saw Philippe again, went back to see him and discovered his ruins had been flattened and so ended the ghostly era of the wizard. Did you ever get to see him?'

'No, unfortunately. My father did. I'm sure he's very happy now.'

'Are you happy?'

'I have my own vegetable patch and grow cabbages for rabbits to eat.' It seemed she avoided the question too. 'Not all were lies. I did study to become a vet but truthfully, I never got round to owning my own practice, things to do, people to see.'

'Do I get a surname?'

'Frisk, Daphne Frisk.'

'Not a common name, not easy to find.'

'Perhaps your search was not so enthusiastic.' She waved it away. 'Best we leave explanations for another time.'

'Will there be another time?'

She reached over and took his pen. 'I will give you my number but on no account must you ring before seven.'

Lukas smiled. He watched her unscrew the cap and place it aside just as Thomas had predicted for such a simple act and began to write on the back of a beer mat. It would only be a matter of moments. One, two, and he moved her coffee cup aside, three, four, and the pen went limp in her hand, five, six seconds later her eyes finally closed and the head met the table.

Close by, a burly stranger in a thick woollen jumper called out. 'Is she alright, Mate?'

'I need to get her home. Do you have a car?'

'Yes, but-'

'Two hundred notes to take us to Westminster.'

'It's just round the corner.'

There were undercurrents in their conversation, Lukas could feel them and given the way she volunteered her number made it all the more intriguing. He stuck her knitted hat in his pocket, fed her bag round his shoulder and then picked her up in his arms, breathing in the smell of her. It was wonderful, that familiar aroma of Nivea cream.

'Norman's the name.'

'Is that your vehicle?'

Norman opened the back doors to his van, his bald patch gathering white flakes. 'It's all cosy like, use it to sleep off the job. Where's about in Westminster do I drop you?'

'The bridge will do.' The rear doors shut and Lukas pulled her tight into him, kissed and stroked her damp hair. Those beautiful eyes could tell him everything. 'No more broken dreams,' he whispered.

Three years and it had seemed like a lifetime of wining and dining the opposite sex, women with ambition and vanity, those whose slender and perfect form seemed to tread on air, while their tender animation of their sparkling eyes expressed a cold and calculating heart.

'They say we're in for a week of this.' Norman broke into his train of thought. 'I don't go a bundle on snow.'

'Do you have any children?'

'No, Mate. My wife buggered off with another woman so I share my house with granny…she's got her head screwed on right.'

Always on the look-out for contacts, Lukas considered Norman a good bet, wide in the shoulders, a prominent forehead and ever ready on the balls of his feet. 'What kind of work where you sleep off the job?'

'Anything going, petrol's expensive, so I use the van to sleep over until the job is done, plumbing, painting, if you need a handy man, I'm your bloke.'

'Do you have a business card?'

Norman scrambled around in the glove box and passed a dirty one over. 'I'm a bricklayer by trade, not much work in that direction now the housing market is in a slump.'

'What's your take on British justice?'

'There's none, Mate. What do you do?'

'I play the stock market.'

'Core, got any tips?'

'Stay out of shares.'

Norman took the hint and led a stream of amusing anecdotes, witty observations and encyclopaedic knowledge, so much so that in talking he was rather above than below the ordinary man. An hour later, he was opening the doors to the back of his van. 'I could have dropped you off at your door.'

'No, this is fine.' Lukas pulled out a wad of notes. 'Thanks a lot…you've been a life saver.'

'Never got your name.'

'Your mate will do.'

Taking her into his arms again, he watched Norman get into the van and take off before proceeding over the snow covered steps that led down to the snow-covered *Abracadabra*.

Thomas, always in tune, was there. 'See, I told you the pen would come in handy.'

'Take us out, anywhere will do.'

Ducking under cover, they proceeded along the carpeted walk way and up the polished oak treads where they veered in different directions. Thomas went forward to the bridge house, and Lukas turned back on himself and went into the captain's quarters which now preached his suite of rooms with a fireman's pole to the snooker room one deck below.

Placing Daphne on the double bed, he shrugged out of his trench coat, flung it over a chair and then removed her ankle length boots and coat, rolled her to one side, tempted to unzip her yellow jump suit. Covering her over with the patchwork quilt made by Kate for his thirty-third birthday, he grabbed her handbag and left the room, tipping the contents on the coffee table. There was a small unopened packet of tissues, lip balm, loose change, six twenty pound notes and pain killers.

Thomas came to his side. 'Anything?'

'Nothing, no driver's licence, no address, no mobile, it's almost as if she doesn't want to be found.'

'I thought we already established that.' Thomas picked out the tablets. 'These are strong pain killers.'

Lukas walked back into the bedroom and grabbed her coat, digging into the pockets. There was a half opened packet of polo mints, and a train ticket. Closing the door behind him, he said, 'Now why would she have a one way ticket to Liverpool Street station?'

'Maybe she lives at Ruislip.'

'Then where is her return ticket?'

'You think she was waiting for you?'

'Come to think about it, she tallied at the machines and before that she swept passed me muttering apologies, and the way she lifted my pen.' Lukas shook his head. 'She set me up.'

'No, Oban set you up. He took a long while to get back to you, eh? And he wanted Hodge done tonight.'

'And that guy, Norman, he was quick to give us lift. I knew there was something above average about that guy.'

'This is not good, Luke. Our number one rule, yeah? Never take on passengers.'

'Woo's a passenger.'

'She's my wife.' The same old rhetoric, same old argument and a little face appeared in a dressing gown, wide eyes swimming. 'Hey, my little man, you should be in bed.'

'You said Uncle Luke would finish his storwee.' His three and a bit year old eyes locked onto the tablets.

Thomas batted his hand away. 'They belong to Goldie Locks and the three bears.'

The boy scanned the room so Lukas lodged him in one arm and quietly opened the door. 'She's sleeping off Midnight's crunchy nut cornflakes.'

'Where's the bears?'

'Hiding in the wardrobe.'

Woo emerged as Edward wriggled out of his uncle's arms. 'Eddy, wha' did I tell you. Uncle Luke can finish his story tomorrow. Come to bed and be a good boy.'

'No!' He ducked under the coffee table.

'I hope you know wha' you're doing,' Woo told Lukas. 'No good come of this, no good at all. Why she no tell her name?'

'She did.'

'I would not name baby after a rock plant.'

'Sweetheart,' Thomas stepped in. 'You got it all wrong. Daphne is not a rock plant.' Then he made a glance at the coffee table. 'Who's got the tablets?'

Edward had slid off like an eel through the grass with them, making his sly get-away as usual. Woo gave a frantic shout and ran after him.

'Kids,' Thomas said with a wan smile. 'You have to watch them every minute until they get some brains.'

27

Lukas stood in the shadows, places bypassed, landing sites ignored. In the snow laden dawn, the shapes were vague that unless one was clued to the *Abracadabra's* position on the River Thames it would be difficult to pin-point an exact location. Occasionally an object splashed soundless in the water and lent definition to the distance.

With Midnight on his right shoulder, Marmite on his left it was only slowly he became aware of a presence, that she had taken a position beside him.

'Where are we?'

'I do believe we are passing Woolwich.'

She turned under his steady gaze, sat herself down on the sofa and felt a cold coffee pot. 'It was no mere coincidence we bumped into each other.'

'Tell me something I don't know.'

'At what point of our life is in our control, Luke?'

He walked up to her and looked down into her upturned face. His rich, deep voice played to his mood. 'I had no choice in my life the moment you stepped on board. You manipulated events, conspired with Oban, and here you are conspiring again. Has there ever been a moment in your entire life when you know who the hell you are because I sure don't.'

'Do you know how ridiculous that sounds? You abducted me. Nobody asked you to do that. Why did you do that?'

'I'm the one asking the questions.'

'And I'm the one listening to your crap, again.'

Lukas knew from past experience a curved course rather than a straight one was the only way to get information from Daphne Frisk. So, informing her to go straight to the galley he travelled a level down to his old quarters where Thomas was wrapped up in dreams. What those dreams were, Lukas could only hazard a guess because Thomas never loved him for that.

Moving on from there, Lukas followed the smell of Nivea cream which seemed to have lost its bearings.

'Luke, you've altered the accommodation.'

'Tom took my old quarters, gives him more room so Eddy has his own cabin on the same level. I moved into his.'

'Is there a reason why you have a fireman's pole in the snooker room?'

'Now that is easy to explain. I wanted an open deck. It was too complicated to build one off the lounge so I took the room below.'

'So why not have stairs?'

'That would mean we'd have nowhere to put the snooker table.'

Midnight stuck her head into an empty packet of crunchy nut cornflakes. *'Ohh, Goldie Locks ate my breakfast.'*

'Don't be silly.' Lukas switched on the kettle and brought out a new packet. 'Where is Marmite?'

'In the bread bin.'

'Luke, sorry to be a pain in derriere but wouldn't that snooker table fit into the stateroom?'

'Yes, but then where do you eat when we have company?'

'Well, I would have thought you could eat off the snooker table.'

'Give up,' Midnight suggested. *'Chuck her over the side before she disintegrates you.'*

He watched the gleam come to Daphne's eyes as she lightly deployed a few bowls on the table and then Thomas waltzed in, followed by Woo and little Edward, all feathered with sleep. There were the customary hellos and the courteous how are you and of course the mandatory question by Lukas as to whom set him up.

'My father, who else.' So over crunchy nut cornflakes and in a dream-telling voice that set Daphne apart, she began to unwind a mystery that had slipped from ordinary life. 'I wish to take you back to a time when you were six years old. Ben had disposed of your father and a mark appeared on the left hand of Marcus, which of course gave validation to the curse.'

'In Japan, they shun cursed babies.' Woo tapped Edward's roving hand. 'Stop poking your finger in Daffannee's milk.'

'Come here, Eddy.' Lukas sat the boy on his knee. 'Misbehave again and your daddy will put you in the brig.' He pointed with his spoon. 'There is one who served her time under his whip. Do you want to come out looking like a girl?' The boy shook his head like a windmill. 'Carry on, Dap.'

'It was at this juncture Philippe distanced himself from his brother, Francois who had a child of his own, three years old and that was me. I never remembered much of my early years only that we moved to another location, England as it so happened. My father had a good job in London, I went to university, then my Mother died of cancer and only when the diary popped up was I made aware of our history. My father took great pains to give us a new identity so my mother and I could live like normal, decent human beings. Well, anyway, by passing that, I was then told what my father did for a living.' She paused for the bombshell. 'He's the one who runs Exit.'

A deathly silence fell in the room, not a sound was created, not a cough or a gasp, everything tipped into the centre of this moment. If nobody spoke the story would never continue.

Lukas obliged. 'Eddy, go play with Midnight on the floor, Uncle Luke is having a fit.'

And Thomas was none too pleased either, growling behind his whiskered face. 'You better tell us exactly what he's done to our family before I put you back in the brig and throw away the key.'

'Nothing detrimental, I assure you.'

'I beg to differ, by your intervention, you stopped Luke from breaking the curse.'

'That's true in a way but there were jolly good reasons.'

'Give me one!' Lukas irritated. 'One good reason why you failed to tell me who you were then none of this would've happened. And don't you dare throw

Midnight in my face. You and your father came on board to manipulate events. I was perfectly happy with the way things were.'

'But my father wasn't, Luke.' She pushed her bowl of untouched cereal aside. 'I know this is hard to believe but my Father is a good man.'

'Not only is your father a walking branch of the Metellus tree, he's the damn head of Exit so how good is that. Pray tell, did he enjoy pulling the strings of the Giddy line?'

'You know sarcasm is the lowest form of wit.'

'I don't care if it's the lowest form of shit.' He waved angrily. 'Please, carry on, give me more bad news.'

'I can't speak to you when you're like this. I'm trying to explain and all you want to do is pre-empt my motives.' She sent a meaningful look at Thomas. 'It was my decision to pull that trigger, Tom. My Father was angry when he discovered what I did. He's a great admirer of your work. Why he regards you both as his prized operatives, proud of what has been achieved. With increased use of the internet and clever hackers, our country was under attack. Who better to sort the problem? But how do you get rid of the blighted Marcus without penalizing Luke?'

'Luke can handle anything, with or without his power.'

'That was never in dispute.' She looked back at Lukas steaming from the ears. 'What was in dispute, your life determined by your counterpart and that counterpart had to go because he took everything away from Philippe including his life. I was one hundred per cent behind my Father when that diary popped into my shopping basket. Philippe was reaching out to us. And yes, we were apprehensive at first. We wondered if Marcus had sent the diary, had discovered who we were. But we had to grab the bull by the horns to get rid of that pestilence. It may have seemed as though we were pulling your strings but, in the end, you gained so much.'

'So why are you here if everything is hunky dory?'

'What a silly question. You bought me here.'

'You were tailing my arse.'

'No, that's untrue. One of my Father's men dropped me off at Ruislip station and told me to wait for Oban. But Oban never turned up. Instead, I bumped into you.'

'Where's your driving licence, credit card?'

'I don't have a driving licence or credit card.' She unzipped the top of her jump suit and pulled out a tag. 'This has my name and address in case I have an accident.' She batted his hand away. 'You're not entitled to look.' Concealing her tag again, she went on. 'My Father has this ridiculous notion we can all play happy families due to our entanglement with a curse.'

'Because you were dim witted enough to kill Marcus.'

'I gave you Midnight.'

'You gave me a blinding headache.'

'Like you give me.' Her hand swept across her brow as she gave a big sigh. 'I wish I never met you. But here I am, supposedly on an errand, let bygones be bygones, no more assertions or aspersions. I will apologise for my misdemeanours and you can apologise for yours.'

'What the hell do I have to apologise for? Everyone knows I'm arrogant and rude. Your father should do, he employed me to babysit his daughter, had the bloody cheek to ask if I would take you off his hands. That shows how desperate he is to get rid of you.'

'If you must know, you would be the last man on earth I would marry. Not only are you arrogant and rude, you have a deep propensity for self-destruction. And you definitely have no brains. I tried so many times to drop clues in your lap but oh no, never once did you pick up on them, more interested in your ego. Now, we can walk away in animosity or we can accept each other's apology and part amicably.'

Lukas was overlapping his lips, considering her chosen vocabulary. She certainly looked apologetic, perhaps a little too desperate, or perhaps a misguided soul who worked in her father's best interests. But why had it taken so long? He looked at Thomas whose face was eagerly awaiting a positive outcome with a frying pan in his hand, then at Woo holding her breath at the toaster, and then back at Daphne. Those eyes, those beautiful brown eyes, they were simply irresistible but not today.

'Why did it take three years to work up an apology?'

'Oh, gosh,' she said so matter of fact and went to the sink, 'the grammar, geography and geometry of my family delayed the process.'

Oops, wrong answer. 'No.'

'No?'

'Do you have a problem in hearing?'

She walked up to him. 'You want me to beg?'

'Gee, let me think, that's a difficult one.'

'I shall not supplicate to your whims.'

'I was on bended knee begging you! In fact, I was on bended knee the moment you walked in and out of my life like a damn yoyo, turning everything on its head, one continual drama act, and now you want my forgiveness when you can't even spell the word liar.'

'Oh that's not true or fair. I forgave when you took a pillow dive with Angel.'

'It was my job.'

'Huh, a good get out clause.'

'Which you manufacture by the dozen.'

'Why should it be so difficult for you to see the good side of people?'

'Three reasons why!' He held up four fingers. 'Look, one, two, three years and not a word, not even a note. Four, you told me to go wipe my arse with the fee. And you have the damn cheek to set up this meeting and talk about forgiveness.'

'Then dry up your own dishes!' She threw the tea towel in his face and stormed out, Marmite trailing behind.

'Christ! She's bloody infuriating. I mean, am I making any sense here or what?'

'So we don't get to kiss and make up?'

Lukas turned his head slowly round and looked back at Thomas. 'Tell me why you never thought to put the snooker table in the stateroom?'

'Don't you like the fireman's pole? Ed likes it, don't you, my little man?'

Edward nodded like a donkey, not entirely insensible and Woo was the colour of stone beneath her cheeks, tightening the cord of her silk dressing gown. 'She not right in the head. In Japan we say, take honourable way out and kill self.'

'Ah, so we know where you stand.' Thomas picked up the boy. 'We speak about this in private and leave Luke to make up his own mind.'

It was a fairly bland effort but it did convey warmth and intelligence. Lukas grabbed a bacon sandwich and picked up his feet to find Daphne. He had witness the weight return to Woo's shoulders, what damage it might wreak upon Thomas and his son. But underneath, he was finding it difficult not to yield to a lowness of spirit.

Searching took time and the bacon sandwich was tossed over the side. With the white noise of the Thames behind her, Daphne was on the bow, open to the cold cutting winds as if she was wishing herself pneumonia. She turned back briefly when she heard her name being called, the rest of his words stolen by the wind. So he came up from behind using a different approach, wrapping his arms protectively about her, viewing a pod of Dolphins taking the lead from the *Abracadabra*. He had never seen that before in these waters.

'They say Dolphins are quite intelligent.'

'I don't disagree.'

She turned into him shivering like a dying last leaf on a tree. 'Oh, Luke, I'm so sorry about all this. I really do mean it from the bottom of my heart. All I ask is that you give it some consideration, do not condemn me or my motives for keeping away.'

'Will I know why you kept away?'

'Can we go inside?'

She was shiveringly cold, teeth chattering as he ran a hot bath. How her body had changed, the nipples were riper, her breasts fuller, the belly softer and round. Gone was the tight bud of a rose, in its place a blooming flower that still had a number of petals to pluck.

'Do you wish me to leave you to it?'

'No, I wish you to stay.' She passed over a sponge as he rolled up his sleeves. 'The last time anyone washed my back was my Mother.'

'Did your father know you took the shot?'

She shook her head vigorously. 'I told no one. If he knew he would have stopped me, of that I am certain. It became a terrible mess afterwards. I left home, Dad eventually found me and oh dear does it really matter.'

'It matters to me.'

'I know, Luke. I really am sorry but you see my history was never divulged until that diary popped up then I became totally obsessed with Boudicca, a bit like Edward, I suppose. I was so into it that I convinced Dad I would make a wonderful operative, even helped with the planning. I never made such a mess in all my life. You were the most frustrating man I had ever encountered, totally unpredictable. I honestly believed you would have jumped at the chance to go searching for a cure but you just set the thought aside.'

'So, whose bright idea was it to nail me to the ground?'

'Mine. Dad had virtually given up so I convinced him to send Oban with a heart rendering tale. Poor Oban, he only found out our connection to Marcus long after I took the shot…well, actually, he started to have deep suspicions a little before then. And I was so glad it worked, so glad you came to the banquet, our protectorate. You looked so handsome in your dinner jacket. I can tell you this much. I never prayed as hard as I did that night. It would have been a major catastrophe had Marcus twigged who we were.'

Lukas remembered now, how she sat in the corner like a cloudy bubble. A little forgiveness was coming forward. 'Where did you learn to shoot like that?'

'The moment I worked it out, you know, how to save Midnight, I took a crash course on a shooting range. Dad thought I was with friends in Chelsea. I would never have pulled that trigger unless I was absolutely certain…pity, you moved so quick…sorry about that.' She chuckled. 'I have to admit I did get a kick out of your challenges and to see the look on your face when Midnight came out of the wall with a postcard of the Needle. It was priceless.'

Yes, it was her pleasure all the way and his agony in transit. Wrapping a towel around her, he lifted her out of the bath, lusting for her body, a hunger grown so deep it was difficult to put it at the back of his mind. 'I suggest you keep warm. Watch some films, dinner at five.'

Where man and wife once graced the captain's quarters injecting new life on board the *Abracadabra*, it was possible in the swell of giddy love to conjure the same inexorable magic. For Lukas, he never stayed for that possibility.

28

He stepped from his private elevator, ignored his mail, dismissed the nanny, went directly into the privacy of his lounge, poured a single whisky and stepped out onto the terrace overlooking the rich shores of France. He had always secretly loathed the French who shut up shop for three hours and thought their wine the best in the world. He also hated their coffee. But it was his hotel and he made the rules.

The air was raw and windy. Oban had cautioned him about Lukas Giddy and his capacity to do the most unexpected things. Fate can go begging, he said with a long pull on the malt. Destiny has to be won.

Like clockwork, Oban emerged in a fine dark suit with a hint of conflict to his paisley tie. He found a cigar, rolled to his ear and stepped up beside Frisk. 'What do you want first, the Giddy news or the good news?'

'Just because you gave up cigarettes does not entitle you to smoke my cigars.' In the murky world of undercover work, where loyalties shift overnight and a friend can become an enemy by noon, men like Oban were known to be trustworthy. 'Give me the Giddy news.'

'He took out Hodge.'

'Excellent. And the good news?'

'He got her on board.' Oban went inside, followed by Frisk and struck up a match, lit the cigar feeling pretty apprehensive about the whole thing. 'He used the pen trick, damn if I don't want one of them. Then our guy stepped in, took them back to the *Abracadabra*. Let's hope you have a daughter after all this.'

Frisk smiled. It took planning. It took nerve. It took him three years to get Daphne there. 'I have waited a long, long time for this, Oban.'

'You're not there yet. She might sing God Save the Queen and he'll dump her in the river.'

'Giddy is not stupid. He will figure it out.' Frisk poured himself another drink and sat heavy in his favourite armchair. 'Do you know what fascinates me the most about him…his capacity to take on the world without a blink of an eye, no thought of failure, amazing, truly amazing.'

'Marcus made him wet his pants.'

'Giddy was concerned for his family. I like that in a man. Would you risk life and limb for your wife?'

'I don't have a wife.'

'The very reason why you crack terrible jokes…no, he will see the light, he just needs a little time to accept I work in his interests.'

'I hope your bloody right.' Oban lost interest in the cigar and stubbed it out. 'If this goes tits up, he will hold you to ransom, already he's asked for a raise.'

'Have you told him our budget was cut by 20%?'

'A pen is on its way.'

'Does it write?'

'Only if you want to gas yourself…I suggest you wait until he makes contact.'

'He has a right to see his daughter.'

'Well, aren't you a smart son of a bitch,' Oban fired back. 'Kids don't make happy families when they're not planned.'

'Stuff away your pessimism. When he sees her, all the bad memories will fade and good ones returned.'

'Grandpa, is Daddy in trouble?'

Frisk looked round at the door, at the curly shine warming up the handle as if stuck to it. 'Come here, my little poppet, I have something to tell you.'

She was tall for her age, fluent and strong, stomping up like a marching guardsman in her daisy white pyjamas.

'We are going to see him.'

'Yeah!' She left no room for doubt about her excitement, jumped up and down, and kicked Oban in the shins for she had a distinct dislike to his attitude. 'When,' was her next and most obvious question?

'Why, we make our way soon. Go choose a pretty dress to wear.' He assumed the *Abracadabra* would make its way to France, and so he had a few moments to think about its passage. 'Has Giddy got anything lined up?'

'Not that I'm aware. He might take the ocean road if they kiss and make up or he might dump her at Westminster and take off for Lowestoft.'

'Oban, you have a serious negative attitude.'

'It's my job to be negative.' He picked up his feet. 'Do you want the helicopter?'

'I think a nice leisurely time on the road will serve equally well.'

With his cheeks almost meeting his eyebrows, Frisk moved through the motions of getting his granddaughter ready for the trip, the lifting of arms, the wriggling of a cotton vest over a reluctant head, the rolling of socks and the put your feet in here now. From wardrobe to bedside and back again, he was a grandfather without a wife dressing a nearly three year old child. He crouched at her feet, pushing her shoes on, fastening the Velcro straps. When she learns to tie shoelaces it will not be from him.

29

'Where're we going with this, my man?'

Lukas gulped his gin neat without taking his eyes off Thomas. 'I told her dinner at five.'

'Are you going to accept her apology?'

'Sure, why not. Just so long she doesn't expect me to do the same.' As usual, he conjured up a reefer, stuck it between his lips and lit up, again keeping his eyes on Thomas. 'You know what I find hard to stomach is her talent for making me feel like a prat.'

'Luke, has it ever occurred that she's in love with you?'

'That's the best joke you've cracked all year.'

'No, I'm serious, Luke. I heard you two talking, what she said about you. It was a big deal, eh? She put you in the clouds, my man and couldn't handle you. I don't think it was her idea to come on board as Miss Congeniality. I think she was telling the truth for a change. Her father wangled the set-up.'

'Then why wait three years?'

'Look, I'm not saying she's right or wrong. I'm saying we're wrong and Dad was right. She's got a good heart but she can't handle you no more than you can handle her. Maybe she stayed away because she sees no future with you but her father does.' Thomas looked around. The port-holed doors to the stateroom were shut, no one was listening. To ease discomforting thoughts away, he decided to inject a semi-intelligent question. 'What do you think would happen if you two forged an alliance, better still, had a kid?'

Predictably, Lukas gave this some thought, scratched his head, nibbled the rough edges of his bearded lip and then searched into the far reaches of his mind. 'Well,' he finally said, 'it would certainly cause a problem for Andate.'

'I know a great place to get a ring.'

'Hang on a minute. I'd much rather marry a letter box than a nutcase.'

'Look, you can't keep posting your sperm in a vacant gap. Think of the advantages. The curse is squashed by default, right? Frisk is well heeled, can't get any better than that. She's got brains in a decent body, loved yours when you were old and grey, has taste, forget the Kaftan and pyjamas, and, this is the best bit. You get to play with your toys.'

Lukas was warming to the prospect, nodding gently while the journey from the South of France was taking Frisk and his granddaughter closer to Agde.

'And,' Thomas continued, whetting his appetite further, 'she's seen every one of the James Bond films.'

'How do you know that?'

'She told Mum. In fact, she tried to get her to knit you some socks with the title Octopussy. Tell me if you don't miss wearing the gear. You have to get rid of the goatee beard, it's not double O7.'

'I get to keep my knife.'

'And your gun.'

'Any chance of making one in gold?'

'Done deal, my man.' But Lukas was not convinced yet so Thomas laid it out flat. 'You got to swallow your pride and apologize, Luke. I know it sticks in your throat but you gave as good as you got, don't forget that. All you have to do is float up casually, drop a nice word, watch the smile and let suggestion roll off your lips, say something like, we've all made mistakes or let's put the past behind us, make it appear you're willing to forgive by not actually saying the word sorry, eh?' Suddenly Thomas disappeared under the bar and popped into view with a jumper. 'This would be a great ice breaker, instead of from Russia with love, put from Giddy with love, yeah?'

This was met with approval. A felt tip pen was found, a plain napkin cut down to size and four safety pins with enough devious grins from Thomas. For the first time, he understood it was Daphne or a lonely road ahead for his brother.

Having done this much, Lukas picked his way to his quarters and walked into the lounge where she was sat on the sofa in her coat, wrapped in her own cloudy bubble of thought. Without word, he slipped off her coat, placed her arms high and wriggled her into the jumper.

Now swamped in wool, she tucked her chin into her chest and read the upside-down words. 'You did this for me?'

'It was Tom's idea.'

'I get the feeling he would like to kiss and make up.'

'I can't kiss you, Dap. Once I go down that road, I would be strapping you to the bed until my balls dropped off.' He watched the smile but that apology was sticking in his throat. 'Got an idea…how about giving Woo a hand with dinner? I have to get back and help Tom tinker with my bike.'

'What's wrong with your bike?'

'Do you like my goatee beard?'

'I think you grew so fast your brain hit the top of a doorway. Mine hit the underside of a wall unit.' They chuckled and moved on. 'One of the things that puzzled us is where Marcus kept his money.'

'Surely your father has enough pull to find that out.'

'Oh we've covered every possible avenue, names, addresses, past contacts, banks, home and abroad, blah, blah. We know he took money off wrinkly widows, had this knack of getting virtually every asset out of them. They would mortgage their house or houses, nothing left to distribute upon death, if anything only debts.'

This provoked a new train of thought. Staying their journey at mid-ships, he said, 'Your father inherited Philippe's land, yup? Once I got rid of Marcus, he flattened the land, probably built a new home and that's where you live.'

'Yes. Philippe had named my father as beneficiary in the will so he laid claim to it when he died. I never knew, not until you told me you saw Philippe. Of course, he couldn't develop the land, not while Marcus was alive.'

'Surely Marcus looked through the records.'

'You forget my Father holds a great deal of weight.'

'And before that, where did you live?'

'Originally, two doors away then when the mark appeared on Marcus we moved to England and adopted the surname Frisk. When Mum died, he bought the Claris Hotel and we had the whole of the top floor, still do.'

'Very clever, yes very clever…Marcus could check Frisk out while my attempts were being blocked.'

'I suppose this has not endeared you to my Father?'

'On the contrary, if I was in your father's position I would do exactly the same.' He moved a step closer. 'Dap, I'm going to give it straight here. I don't feel I have anything to apologize. I am what I am, arrogant, rude and sometimes completely off my rocker when you're about.'

'Likewise, I'm sure.' She held out her hand. 'Let's agree that whatever transpires between us it should not affect others.'

He took the proffered hand. 'I agree.'

Deep inside them there was still that empty aching place which they had filled for a few fleeting moments more than three years ago, but it was buttressed and fortified, both impregnable once again.

Lukas moved on to the hold where Thomas had his head stuck in a bucket. 'Tom, take us to Agde.'

'Eh? Say that again?'

'Frisk inherited Philippe's land, built a place and that's where Daphne lives.'

'Ah, so that's what she was hiding.' Thomas grabbed an oily rag and wiped his hands. 'Come on, my man. Let's get this tub to Agde.'

'Frisk owns the Claris. Hell, I feel such a damn prat, all the clues they kept dropping and it never twigged.'

'Have you two kissed and made up?'

'We have agreed to let whatever develops between us not to affect the rest of our families.'

'That's good, try to develop the positive. Did she like the jumper?'

'She's wearing it. To tell me or anyone would have alerted Marcus. I remember the last time I saw Philippe when he was in limbo. He told me his son visits a desolate habitation which he cannot have, angry with himself for yielding to the impulse so soon.' They swung into the bridge house. 'He also showed me his will and testament made the day after Marcus slaughtered his wife and unborn child. I think he knew a day would come when this would happen.'

As the *Abracadabra* swung her bows into the English Channel, Thomas kissed the computer screen. 'You little beauty.'

'I thought I was the only sad bastard on this vessel?'

'Luke, you have no idea how sad I can be.' He went to the peculator. 'Now, as I see it, Daphne will invite you in for a few bevvies and-'

'I love her.'

'Well of course you do.'

'No, I'm serious, Tom, joking aside, I really do want to merge, keep her all to myself until death do us part.'

'Luke, she was the only woman who ruffled your feathers and the only non-family member you opened up to. I just never knew how deep it went until it twigged.'

Lukas took the proffered mug. 'What twigged?'

'That your dick has stayed in your trousers for the last three years. Oh come on, my man, don't give me that what-a-load-of-bollocks look. I saw the tatty photograph sticking out of your back pocket. You must have been wanking on that for three years.' Thomas paused in the laughter he had generated. 'So this is what we do. I'll pull the plug on the lights so Woo brings out the candles, you put on the music, we talk and eat, no bringing up the past then when we take Eddy to bed, the stateroom is yours for half an hour before we come back with coffee just in case we need to break up an argument.'

'Gee, thanks, Tom.'

'Hey, don't mention it.'

It was a mixed hot spread of curry, rice and vegetables laid out in the stateroom with a view of the ocean that was as grim as the sky. The boy was sat on a cushion at the table with a clean bowl over his head, Woo and Daphne pottering back and forth, Thomas and Lukas grabbing their chairs.

'What's with the plate, my little man?'

'My fault,' Daphne owned up, placing Marmite in the fruit dish. 'When the lights went out, I told him atmospheric pressure affects the brain.'

'Daddy, can I have a jumper like that?'

'Sure, we can get grandma to knit you one.'

'Where's Midnight?' Lukas asked.

The boy giggled, cupping his hand to his mouth, pointing to a dish full of rice. Midnight popped into view, claiming it to be hers. So Lukas, in an attempt to create more giggles, grabbed his empty bowl and placed it on his head. There was probably no one more capable of bringing laughter to the table than him.

After that, the conversation ebbed and flowed in a light-hearted fashion which sometimes grew into a spell of witty confusions. Then Daphne would watch Lukas as if in a trance of romantic memories, clinging on to every breathless word of his story told to Edward.

'So, this sword shone brighter than the moon, yup? In fact, it was so bright the dragon had to wear sunglasses.'

'Dwagons don't wear sunglasses.'

'How do you know? Have you met a dragon?'

The boy shook his head with his mouth half open, his eyes half shut. Here, Woo precipitately interrupted with a hand gesture to quieten the room where they focused on the boy who slumped against the chair then suddenly shook himself awake, fighting the almost irresistible languor of sleep. It was clearly then, in the twilit tenderness the table candles created, that he was ready for bed.

Thomas enfolded his son and went to the door opened by Woo, carefully and without noise, leaving Lukas and Daphne with their eyes fixed upon each other, she hunched over the table supporting her chin on her clenched fist.

'What are you thinking?' he asked.

'That you're a natural father.'

'Me? No, I'm a natural uncle.'

'Do you want children, Luke?'

'Are you proposing?'

She smiled. 'Can you meet my shopping list?'

He smiled. 'Can you meet mine?'

'Tell me what's on it.'

'A woman I can trust.' When her cheeks flushed, he knew then he had her cornered. 'Are you going to tell me why you're really here?'

'Truthfully, I was against it. It just hurt so much being in love with a man who could pop his broomstick in any old cupboard.'

'Dap, I-'

'It's alright, Luke, you don't have to explain. A man cannot be expected to live like a eunuch. Do you have a girlfriend?'

'I think you know the answer to that.'

'You looked happy in her company.'

'Then the dragon should pass his glasses to you. I loved a woman I thought I could never have and Penny loved a man who was a closet queer. And you?'

'I was far luckier,' she said, watching his face, choosing her words carefully. 'I had someone to love for nearly all my time away from you. Her name is Elizabeth and perhaps her father might like to tell her bedtime stories.'

A nerve tugged beside his eye. He had made love to Daphne twice, first when the weather came in like a lion and went out like a lamb, and the second when she threw up over the side. What would she be, three years old or less? Those first steps missed, those first words missed, the list was growing in his war drawer.

'Speak to me, Luke.'

'What do you wish me to say?'

'Be angry if you must. Just say something.'

He shook his head and said nothing.

'Am I to assume, you don't want to see your daughter?'

'Fuck you, Dap! It was my right to know! I don't care what defence you put forward, you had no right to keep me from her, no right at all! There's something screwy in your head. You say you love me yet you could have killed me, that I can probably understand but to keep away for three years, tailing my arse, not a damn word, not a damn note and suddenly you pop up because it suits your father?'

'You had Penny!'

'I never had Penny! I never had anyone! My dick was limp for most of the time!' He pushed back his chair and stood, paused as if thinking things through then sat back down with a wallop. 'Who's got her now?' He watched her eyes dip, not the signal he desired to see. 'Well, that's just great!'

Tentatively, she reached to touch his hand, instinctively knowing he would withdraw it. The gesture was barely worthy of his interest, sulking seemed to be his promised route. 'Luke, not in all the time we were together did you once tell me you loved me. In fact, you regarded me as a passing fancy.'

'I held you with these hands, loved your body, told you my secrets, and asked if we had a future together. What is that if not a statement of love?' He stood again, another potty notion popped into his head. 'Ah, now I understand why you wanted a pact. She hasn't got a clue who's her father.'

She waved his nonsensical notion away, the culmination of her secrets about to be revealed. 'There is a video diary for every day you missed. Her birth, her first smile, her first steps, her first word and it was not mummy or grandpa. She has a picture of you at her bedside to kiss you goodnight. It was put there the first day I came back from the hospital. And every week I speak of your travels, how you ride the ocean waves, how the wind blows free in your hair, how tall and handsome her daddy, how he catches all the horrible monsters to make it a safer world for us to live in. She draws pictures for you, of the flowers that surround her, of the bedroom in which she sleeps, of the mummy who bakes fairy cakes, of the friends she has made. She draws so many, I bought a large chest, and in the evening, she sits on the chest and looks out of her window, up at the moon, calling for you to come home.'

Even fat bellied Midnight was crying into her empty bowl. With such knowledge of it ready-made, all the sensitive feelings, all the happiness it kept alive became more poignant.

'I'm so sorry, Luke. I really am. It was never meant to be this way. I fell pregnant second time round, was scared, angry and hurt.' She wiped her eyes with the ball of her hand, tears streaming wet down her cheeks. 'Elizabeth was born on the spring equinox and I couldn't face what you would say, not once you found out I was a Metellus so I just disappeared after I shot Marcus, up a tree like a dumpling. Dad found me, wanted to contact you but I threatened to run away again so he built me a home at Lamalou.'

He crouched to face her, wiping her coursing tears with his thumbs. 'I'd rather fight with you than make love to anyone else.'

'Really?'

'Oh yes, really. Now tell me, what were you hoping to achieve? Feed me a lifetime of tapes when I'm old and grey?'

'I was trying, Luke, really trying. I did follow you at times in this latter year but there was always Penny on your arm and then I thought I could send the tapes, explain in a letter but would you want a child with my blood?'

'Then it's my turn to beg forgiveness.' He pressed his lips to hers, to her ear, her cheek, her neck, smoothing her hair, touching her skin. 'It never occurred you were without precaution, so used was I to the uncomplicated models of whores. Elizabeth, you say?'

'Her birth was registered as Elizabeth Giddy.'

'Elizabeth Giddy,' he rolled off his tongue. 'I named Edward, did I tell you? Yes, honestly, Woo asked me to, she wouldn't have it any other way.'

'Fate, Luke. Fate it should be Edward and Elizabeth.'

'What about them?' Thomas came into the room.

'I'm a father.'

'Hell! That was quick.'

'Dap was pregnant when she left me.'

'I knew tha!' Woo appeared with the coffee. 'I knew tha! I said she was sick and no one listen.'

'Sweetheart, your English was not really up to par in those days. You said she was sick in the head.'

An angry scowl might confirm the suspicion she was a bit off her rocker. So Woo settled on a simple blank face, with just a hint of amusement. 'She also sick in the head.'

'Dap, who does she take after?'

'Oh Luke, she's beautiful. Her hair is bright auburn. In the summer it goes terribly red and she has freckles on her cheeks. She has your eyes, deep bluish eyes that go very dark when she gets in a paddy. She weighed 8lbs and 4ozs and put me in labour for five hours but worth every drop of pain.'

Woo's turn for comparison. 'Eddy weighed 8lbs and 7ozs, popped out like a cork. He was a good baby, never cry only for food. Did you breast feed?'

'I had considerable trouble getting Elizabeth to suck on my nipples.'

"Nipples" and Lukas was crossing his legs. 'Is she with your father at the Claris?'

'Yes.'

'It's very fortunate we are heading for France.'

'We are? I thought we were still in London?'

'No, Dap. We're not in London.' Then he plunged headlong into an issue before Daphne could respond. 'I want you to contact your father and tell him you're on your way home.'

Here was an opportunity not to be missed. Lukas proffered his mobile, waited for her to get through and then snatched it away. 'Frisk,' he said, 'quake in your shoes because you won't have them for much longer.'

'Are you marrying my daughter?'

'Well, the thought had crossed my mind.'

'Good man and God help you.' They laughed. 'What's your position?'

'Coming round the Bay of Biscay. What's yours?'

'Just arrived at Lamalou.'

'Can you put my daughter-'

'Daddy!' she shrieked down the line. 'Where are yoo?'

'Elizabeth, listen very carefully.'

'I can hear yoo.'

'Good, that's good. I can hear you too.'

'Mummy said you were deaf.'

'Did she now? Remind me to smack her bottom.'

'I never get my bottom smacked.'

'Listen, Elizabeth, I shall be with you in two days.'

'Aww.'

'I promise, cross my heart, I will be there quicker than you can spell magic.'

'M, a, g, i, c.'

'How about irrestibubble?'

'Eurrh…dunno. Can I see Midnight?'

'Yes, you can see Midnight.'

'Yeah!' She shrieked down the line again. 'I hab to go now and get grapes…see yoo on the moon.'

Without further word, he passed over the mobile and walked out of the room with cartloads of rising emotions. Laughter and tears, they poured in armfuls as he struck into his quarters. He was entirely possessed by Elizabeth. She had been conceived in July to be born the following year on the spring equinox, forgotten in the wider scheme, delivering him and Daphne safe, giving physical form to his conviction that Andate had heard his prayers.

30

The Giddy Lodge was still standing thirty years on, a loan woman with flowing red hair to her waist scribing the library walls. In stature, she was very tall and her voice harsh, the glance of her eye most fierce. She had already written that her mother had died on the spring equinox. Now she was writing the epitaph of her father, gone in that same year on the 23rd September at midnight. He requested to be dressed in a black jumper *never say never again* embossed in white, a stiffened Midnight tucked in his breast pocket.

BOUDICCA

48AD

Ostorius Scapula, the Roman Governor of Britain, directed to forcibly remove the personal weapons of the men of Southern Britain. Although the Iceni (present day East Anglia) were allies of Rome, they were included in this repressive measure. Their weapons were of great significance to them and they were outraged. The Iceni were a proud and independent people and became the first to rise up in open revolt against Rome.

The Iceni had not been defeated in battle by the Romans. They led an alliance of neighbouring tribes against the imperial armies. The Roman historian Tacitus tells us that the Iceni chose a battlefield at a stronghold, defended by earth banks. The Roman army stormed the embankments from all sides. The Iceni were imprisoned by their own defences and were overwhelmed. Tacitus says that the Iceni fought for their lives with great courage. The Iceni were humiliated by their defeat and tried to live peacefully with the Romans during the following 12 years.

After the revolt, the Roman armies marched west and left behind the Iceni tribe ruled by a king named Prasutagus who was husband of Boudicca.

60/61AD - The introduction of Suetonius

During the consulship of Lucius Caesennius Paetus and Publius Petronius Turpilianus, a dreadful calamity befell the Roman army in Britain. The current Governor made few incursions into Britain, content with maintaining the conquests already made. However, Paulinus Suetonius succeeded to the command, an officer of distinguished merit. His military talents gave him pretensions, and the voice of the people, who never leave exalted merit without a rival, raised him to the highest eminence. By subduing the mutinous spirit of the Britons, he hoped to equal the brilliant success of Corbulo in Armenia. With this view, he resolved to subdue the isle of Mona (Anglesey), a place inhabited by a warlike people, and a common refuge for all the discontented Britons. In order to facilitate his approach to a difficult and deceitful shore, he ordered a number of flat-bottomed boats to be constructed.

In these he wafted over the infantry, while the cavalry, partly by fording over the shallows, and partly by swimming their horses, advanced to gain a footing on Mona.

On the opposite shore stood the Britons, close embodied, and prepared for action. Women were seen running through the ranks in wild disorder, their apparel funeral, their hair loose to the wind, in their hands flaming torches, and their whole appearance resembling the frantic rage of the Furies. The Druids on Mona were ranged in order, with hands uplifted, invoking the gods, and pouring forth horrible imprecations. The novelty of the fight struck the Romans with awe and terror. They stood in stupid amazement, as if their limbs were benumbed, riveted to one spot, a mark for the enemy. The exhortations of the General diffused new vigour through the ranks, and the men, by mutual reproaches, inflamed each other to deeds of valour. They felt the disgrace of yielding to a troop of women, and a band of fanatic priests and advanced their standards and rushed on to the attack with impetuous fury.

The Britons perished in the flames, which they themselves had kindled. Mona fell, and a garrison was established to retain it in subjection. The religious groves, dedicated to superstition and barbarous rites, were levelled to the ground. In those recesses, the natives stained their altars with the blood of their prisoners, and in the entrails of men explored the will of the gods. However…while Suetonius was employed in making his arrangements to secure the island of Mona, he had received intelligence that Britain had revolted, and that the whole province was up in arms.

Three causes for the revolt

An excuse for the war was found the confiscation of the sums of money that Claudius had given to the foremost Britons; for these sums, as Decianus Catus, the procurator of the island, maintained, were to be paid back. This was one reason for the uprising.

Another was found in the fact that Seneca, in the hope of receiving a good rate of interest, had lent to the islanders 40,000,000 sesterces that they did not want, and had afterwards called in this loan all at once and had resorted to severe measures in exacting it.

But the person who was chiefly instrumental in rousing the natives and persuading them to fight the Romans, the person who was thought worthy to be their leader and who directed the conduct of the entire war, was Boudicca, a Briton woman of the royal family and possessed of greater intelligence than often belongs to women. Prasutagus, the late king of the Icenians, in the course of a long reign had amassed considerable wealth. By his will he left the whole to his two daughters and the Emperor Nero in equal shares, conceiving, by that stroke of policy, he should provide at once for the tranquillity of his kingdom and his family. The event was otherwise. His dominions were ravaged by the centurions, the slaves pillaged his house, and his effects were seized as lawful plunder. His wife, Boudicca, was disgraced with cruel stripes and her daughters ravaged, and the most illustrious of the Icenians were, by force, deprived of the positions which had been transmitted to them by their ancestors.

The whole country was considered as a legacy bequeathed to the plunderers. The relations of the deceased king were reduced to slavery. Exasperated by their acts of violence, and dreading worse calamities, the Icenians had recourse to arms. The Trinobantians joined in the revolt. The neighbouring states, not as yet taught to crouch in bondage, pledged themselves, in secret councils, to stand forth in the cause of liberty. What chiefly fired their indignation was the conduct of the veterans, lately planted as a colony at Camulodunum (Colchester). These men treated the Britons with cruelty and oppression. They drove the natives from their habitations and calling them by the shameful names of slaves and captives, added insult to their tyranny. In these acts of oppression, the veterans were supported by the common soldiers – a set of men, by their habits of life, trained to licentiousness, and, in their turn, expecting to reap the same advantages. The temple built in honour of Claudius was another cause of discontent. In the eye of the Britons, it seemed the citadel of eternal slavery. The priests, appointed to officiate at the altars, with a pretended zeal for religion, devoured the whole substance of the country. To over-run a colony, which lay quite naked and exposed, without a single fortification to defend it, did not appear to the incensed and angry Britons an enterprise that threatened either danger or difficulty. The fact was that the Roman generals attended to improvements to taste and elegance but neglected the useful. They embellished the province and took no care to defend it.

Boudicca assembled her army

So, this woman, Boudicca, assembled her army to the number of some 120,000, and then ascended a tribunal which had been constructed of earth in the Roman fashion. In stature she was very tall, in appearance most terrifying, in the glance of her eye most fierce, and her voice was harsh. A great mass of the tawniest hair fell to her hips, around her neck was a large golden necklace, and she wore a tunic of many colours over which a thick mantle was fastened with a brooch. This was her invariable attire. She now grasped a spear to aid her in terrifying all beholders and spoke as follows:

'You have learned by actual experience how different freedom is from slavery. Hence, although some among you may previously, through ignorance of which was better, have been deceived by the alluring promises of the Romans, yet now that you have tried both, you have learned how great a mistake you made in preferring an imported despotism to your ancestral mode of life, and you have come to realize how much better is poverty with no master than wealth with slavery. For what treatment is there of the most shameful or grievous sort that we have not suffered ever since these men made their appearance in Britain? Have we not been robbed entirely of most of our possessions, and those greatest, while for those that remain, we pay taxes? Besides pasturing and tilling for them all our other possessions do we pay a yearly tribute for our very bodies? How much better it would be to have been sold to masters once for all than, possessing empty titles of freedom, to have been slain than to go about with a tax upon our heads. Yet why do I mention death? For even dying is not free of cost with them. Nay, you know what fees we deposit even for our dead. Among the rest of mankind death frees even those who are in slavery to others; only in the case of the Romans do the very dead remain alive for their profit. Why is it that, though none of us has any money, we are stripped and despoiled like a murderer's victims? And why should the Romans be expected to display moderation as times goes on, when they have behaved toward us in this fashion at the very outset, when all men show consideration even for the beasts they have newly captured?

'But to speak the plain truth, it is we who have made ourselves responsible for all these evils, in that we allowed them to set foot on our island in the first place instead of expelling them at once as we did their famous Julius Caesar. Yes, and in that we did not deal with them while they were still far away as we dealt with Augustus and with Gaius Caligula and make even the attempt to sail hither a formidable thing. As a consequence, although we inhabit so large an island, or rather a continent, one might say, that is encircled by the sea, and although we possess a veritable world of our own and are so separated by the ocean from all the rest of mankind that we have been believed to dwell on a different earth and under a different sky, and that some of the outside world, yes, even their wisest men, have not hitherto known for a certainty even by what names we are called, we have, notwithstanding all this, been despised and trampled underfoot by men who nothing else than how to secure gain. However, even at this late day, though we have not done so before, let us, my countrymen and friends and kinsmen – for I consider you all kinsmen, seeing that you inhabit a single island and are called by one common name – let us, I say, do our duty while we still remember what freedom is, that we may leave to our children not only its appellation but also its reality. For, if we utterly forget the happy state in which we were born and bred, what, pray, will they do, reared in bondage?

'All this I say, not with the purpose of inspiring you with hatred of present conditions – that hatred you already have – nor with fear for the future – that fear you already have – but of commending you because you now of our own accord choose the requisite course of action, and of thanking you for so readily co-operating with me and with each other. Have no fear whatever of the Romans for they are superior to us neither in number nor in bravery. And here is the proof. They have protected themselves with helmets and breastplates and greaves and yet further provided themselves with palisades and walls and trenches to make sure of suffering no harm by an incursion of their enemies. For they are influenced by their fears when they adopt this kind of fighting in preference to the plan we follow of rough and ready action. Indeed, we enjoy such a surplus of bravery, that we regard our tents as safer than their walls and our shields as affording greater protection than their whole suits of mail. As a consequence, we when victorious capture them, and when overpowered elude them, and if we ever choose to retreat anywhere, we conceal ourselves in swamps and mountains so inaccessible that we can be neither discovered nor taken.

Our opponents, however, can neither pursue anybody, by reason of their armour, nor yet flee, and if they ever do slip away from us, they take refuge in certain appointed spots, where they shut themselves up as in a trap. But these are not the only respects in which they are vastly inferior to us. There is also the fact that they cannot bear up under hunger, thirst, cold, or heat, as we can. They require shade and covering, they require kneaded bread and wine and oil, and if any of these things fail them, they perish. For us, any grass or root serves as bread, the juice of any plant as oil, any water as wine, and any tree as a house. Furthermore, this region is familiar to us and is our ally, but to them it is unknown and hostile. As for the rivers, we swim them naked, whereas they do not across them easily even with boats. Let us, therefore, go against them trusting boldly to good fortune. Let us show them that they are hares and foxes trying to rule over dogs and wolves.'

The first two battles

Having finished an appeal to her people of this general tenor, Boudicca led her army against the romans, for these chanced to be without a leader, inasmuch as Suetonius, their commander, had gone on an expedition to Mona (Anglesey). This enabled her to sack and plunder two Roman cities, (Colchester and London) and to wreak indescribable slaughter. Those who were taken captive were subjected to every known form of outrage. The worst and most bestial atrocity committed by the Britons was the following. They hung up naked the noblest and most distinguished women and then cut off their breasts and sewed them to their mouths, in order to make the victims appear to be eating them. Afterwards, they impaled the women on sharp skewers run lengthwise through the entire body. All this they did to the accompaniment of sacrifices, banquets, and wanton behaviour, not only in all their other sacred places, but particularly in the grove of Andate, Dark of the moon and Cutter of threads. This was their name for Victory, and they regarded her with most exceptional reverence.

Suetonius abandoned London

Suetonius, undismayed by the disaster at Colchester, marched through the heart of the country as far as London, a place not dignified with the name of a colony, but the chief residence of merchants, and the great mart of trade and commerce. At that place he meant to fix the feat of war but reflecting on the scanty numbers of his little army, and the fatal rashness of Cerealis at Colchester, he resolved to quite the station, and, by giving up one post, secured the rest of the province. Neither supplications, nor the tears of the inhabitants could induce him to change his plan. The signal for the march was given. All who chose to follow his banners were taken under his protection. Of all whom, on account of their advanced age, the weakness of their sex, of the attractions of the situations, thought proper to remain behind – not one escaped the rage of Boudicca and her army. The inhabitants of Verulamium (St. Albans), a municipal town, were in like manner put to the sword. The genius of a savage people leads them all places of strength. Wherever they expected feeble resistance, and considerable booty, they were sure to attack with the fiercest rage. Military skill was not the talent of Boudicca and her army. The number massacred in the places which have been mentioned, amounted to no less than seventy thousand, all citizens or allies of Rome. To make prisoners, and reserve them for slavery, or to exchange them, was not in the idea of a people, who despised all the laws of war. The halter and the gibbet, slaughter and defoliation, fire and sword, were the marks of savage valour. Aware that vengeance would overtake them, they were resolved to make sure of their revenge and glut themselves with the blood of their enemies.

Suetonius prepares to counter-attack

The fourteenth legion, with the veterans of the twentieth, and the auxiliaries from the adjacent stations, having joined Suetonius, his army amounted to little less than ten thousand men. Thus reinforced, he resolved, without loss of time, to bring on a decisive action. For this purpose, he chose a spot encircled with woods, narrow at the entrance, and sheltered in the rear by a thick forest. In that situation he had no fear of an ambush. The enemy, he knew, had no approach but in front. An open plain lay before him. He drew up his men in the following order: the legions in close array formed the centre. The light armed troops were stationed at hand to serve as occasion might require. The cavalry took post in the wings.

The Britons brought into the field an incredible multitude. They formed no regular line of battle. Detached parties and loose battalions displayed their numbers, in frantic transport bounding with exultation, and so sure of victory, that they placed their wives in wagons at the extremity of the plain, where they might survey the scene of action, and behold the wonders of British valour.

Boudicca addresses her army

Boudicca, in a chariot with her two daughters before her, drove through the ranks. She harangued the different nations in their turn. 'This,' she said, 'is not the first time that the Britons have been led to battle by a woman. But now she did not come to boast the pride of a long line of ancestry, nor even to recover her kingdom and the plundered wealth of her family. She took the field, like the meanest among them, to assert the cause of public liberty, and to seek revenge for her body seamed with ignominious stripes, and her two daughters infamously ravished. From the pride and arrogance of the Romans nothing is scared; all are subject to violation; the old endure the scourge, and the virgins are deflowered. But the vindictive gods are now at hand. A Roman legion dared to face the warlike Britons. With their lives they paid for their rashness. Those who survived the carnage of that day, lie poorly hid behind their entrenchments, meditating nothing but how to save themselves by an ignominious flight. From the din of preparation, and the shout of the British army, the Romans, even now, shrink back with terror. What will be their case when the assault begins? Look round and view your number. Behold the proud display of warlike spirits and consider the motives for which we draw the avenging sword. On this spot we must either conquer or die with glory. There is no alternative. Though a woman, my resolution is fixed: the men, if they please, may survive with infamy, and live in bondage.'

Suetonius addresses his army

Suetonius, in a moment of such importance, did not remain silent He expected everything from the valour of his men, and yet urged every topic that could inspire and animate them to the attack. 'Despise,' he said, 'the savage uproar, the yells and shouts of undisciplined barbarians. In that mixed multitude, the women out-number the men. Void of spirit, unprovided with arms, they are not soldiers who come to offer battle. They are bastards, runaways, the refuse of your swords, who have often fled before you, and will again betake themselves to flight when they see the conqueror flaming in the ranks of war. In all engagements it is the valour of a few that turns the fortune of the day. It will be your immortal glory, that with a scanty number you can equal the exploits of a great and powerful army. Keep your ranks, discharge your javelins, rush forward to a close attack, bear down all with your bucklers, and hew a passage with your swords. Pursue the vanquished and never think of spoil and plunder. Conquer, and victory gives you everything.'

This speech was received with warlike acclamations. The soldiers burned with impatience for the onset, the veterans brandished their javelins, and the ranks displayed such an intrepid countenance, that Suetonius, anticipating the victory, gave the signal for the charge.

The decisive battle

The engagement began. The Roman legion presented a close embodied line. The narrow defile gave them the shelter of a rampart. In that instant, the Romans rushed forward in the form of a wedge. The auxiliaries followed with equal ardour. The cavalry, at the same time, bore down upon the enemy, and, with their pikes, overpowered all who dared to make a stand. The Britons betook themselves to flight, but their wagons in the rear obstructed their passage. A dreadful slaughter followed. Neither sex nor age was spared. The cattle, falling in a promiscuous carnage added to the heaps of slain. The glory of the day was equal to the most splendid victory of ancient times. According to some writers, not less than eighty thousand Britons were put to the sword.

The Romans lost about four hundred men, and the wounded did not exceed that number.

There are differing opinions as to Boudicca. Tacitus wrote she died by a dose of poison, another claimed she fell sick and died (unlikely). Nevertheless, her grave has never been found to this day, nor can it be said with any conviction the exact spot of the last battle.

News of Suetonius' brutality reached Rome and an excuse was found of remove him from his post as Governor of Britain. His career was not harmed too much. He became a consul in 66AD. In 69AD, during the year of civil war that followed the death of Nero, he found himself on the losing side but was granted a pardon. What became of him after that is unknown.

A visit to the Castle Museum in Norwich is worthwhile, therein containing a separate section on Boudicca.

ALSO BY LEVITY BROWN

GALLOWS HUMOUR

IT'S A MATTER OF LIFE & DEATH

Solomon Monday is ready to jump off the media rungs and accept his bizarre legacy, a converted mid 18th century courthouse tucked in the folds of Norfolk...and so begins an extraordinary mystery which has its roots in the eccentric staff, six poor souls innocently hung at the gallows. It takes the appearance of Izabo Tuesday to force Monday to confront his demons and find their ancestor's book, Week's Work, the element to clar Gallows Humour of its hauntings.

In a place where love and membership comes at a very high price, Gallows Humour is simply irrsistible.

PHANTOM JIGSAW

Strident Cutter, owned by third generation Tony Black, is on the brink of bankruptcy. His twin, Jason, an eminent chemist arrives from America to help with the sale, unwittingly walking into a nightmare. What first appears to be a blank jigsaw puzzle found in the store room, the phantom riddles catapult the twins into the realms of the paranormal.

This mystery is of a soul who needs Jason's expertise to alter the course of history. There is rivalry, revenge and forbidden love; an unforgettable impact of human relationships.

BOOK OF HORTUS

Sat naked in a puddle of mud, all that he knows of himself is his name - Quercus Coccinea. Befriended by Nina, a librarian, this legendary hero will never yield - one hundred years does not make a man forgive or forget. In a world of breathtaking beauty, Quercus gathers his thousand strong army to defeat an unbeatable enemy, gain immortality and find the lost halves to the Book of Hortus.

Suspenseful and endlessly exciting,

this mystery is sure to thrill anyone who enjoys action,

mysticism and nature on an epic scale.

COMEBACK

THE LADY IN GREY

The Chief Executive

Godfrey Shilling of Fair Life Assurance is limiting the liabilities against his company. Shortly issuing a million pound life policy, the client drops dead of natural causes. Coincidence? With no proof, he calls upon the woman in Grey.

The woman in Grey

Enigmatic, expensive to hire, Miss Grey walks into a Norfolk Town as Godfrey Shilling's Trojan horse. With a 100% success rate as a ruthless private investigator, she is about to turn a carpenter's world upside down.

The Carpenter

Ruben Stone, hiding more than a secret or two, lives above a shop selling beautiful dollhouses and related items. No profit, no loss, no gain, no shame.

**The Black Panther writes again in this stylish mystery
murder is on the menu for those who want to die and live again.**

www.ingramcontent.com/pod-product-compliance
Lightning Source LLC
Chambersburg PA
CBHW061017120726

47910CB00006B/1980